DEATH AT DAWN

CARO PEACOCK

Death at Dawn

HARPER

This novel is entirely a work of fiction. The names, characters and incidents portrayed in it are the work of the author's imagination. Any resemblance to actual persons, living or dead, events or localities is entirely coincidental.

Harper
HarperCollins*Publishers*
77–85 Fulham Palace Road, London W6 8JB

www.harpercollins.co.uk

Published by HarperCollins*Publishers* 2007

1

A catalogue record for this book
is available from the British Library

ISBN 978 0 00 724417 1

Typeset in Sabon by Palimpsest Book Production Ltd,
Grangemouth, Stirlingshire

Printed and bound in Great Britain by
Clays Ltd, St Ives plc

To Caroline Compton

CHAPTER ONE

'Would you be kind enough to tell me where they keep people's bodies,' I said.

The porter blinked. The edges of his eyelids were pink in a brown face, lashes sparse and painful-looking like the bristles on a gooseberry. Odd the things you notice when your mind's trying to shy away from a large thing. When he saw me coming towards him over the cobbles among the crowds leaving the evening steam packet, he must have expected another kind of question altogether. Something along the lines of 'How much do you charge to bring a trunk up from the hold?' or 'Where can I find a clean, respectable hotel?' Those kinds of questions were filling the air all round us, mostly in the loud but uneasy tones of the English newly landed at Calais. I'd asked in French, but he obviously thought he'd misheard.

'You mean where people stay, at the hotels?'

1

'Not hotels, no. People who've been killed. A gentleman who was killed on Saturday.'

Another blink and a frown. He looked over my shoulder at his colleagues carrying bags and boxes down the gangplank, regretting his own bad luck in encountering me.

'Would he not be in his own house, mademoiselle?'

'He has no house here.'

Nor anywhere else, come to that. He would have had one soon, the tall thin house he was going to rent for us, near the unfashionable end of Oxford Street when we . . . Don't think about that.

'In church then, perhaps.'

I thought, but didn't say, that he was never a great frequenter of churches.

'If an English gentleman were killed in . . . in an accident and had no family here, where might he be taken?'

The porter's face went hard. He'd noticed my hesitation.

'The morgue is over there, mam'selle.'

He nodded towards a group of buildings a little back from the seafront then turned, with obvious relief, to a plump man who was pulling at his sleeve and burbling about cases of books.

I walked in the direction he'd pointed out but had to ask again before I found my way to a low building, built of bricks covered over with black tarry paint. A man who looked as thin and faded as driftwood was sitting on a chair at the door, smoking a clay pipe. The smell of his tobacco couldn't quite mask another smell coming from inside the building. When he heard me approaching he turned his head without shifting the rest of his body, like a clockwork automaton, and gave me a considering look.

'It's possible that you have my father here,' I said.

He took a long draw on his pipe and spoke with it still in his mouth.

'Would he be the gentleman who got shot?'

'Possibly, yes.'

'English?'

'Yes.'

'She said his clothes had an English cut.'

'Who said?'

Without answering, he got up and walked over to a narrow house with a front door opening on to the cobbles only a few steps away from the morgue. He thumped on the door a couple of times and a fat woman came out in a black dress and off-white apron, straggly grey hair hanging down under her cap. They whispered, heads together, then he gave her a nudge towards me.

'Your father, oh, you poor little thing. Poor little thing.'

Her deep voice was a grieving purr in my ear, her hand moist and warm on my shoulder. Her breath smelled of brandy.

'May I see him, please?'

3

She led the way inside, still purring '*Pauvre petite, oh pauvre petite*.' Her husband in his cloud of pipe smoke fell in behind us. There were flies buzzing around the low ceiling and a smell of vinegar. The evening sun came in through the slats of the shutters, making bars of red on the whitewashed wall. Three rough pinewood tables took up most of the space in the room but only one of them was occupied by a shape covered in a yellowish sheet. The woman put her arm round me and signed to the man to pull the sheet back. I knew almost before I saw his face. I suppose I made some noise or movement because the man started pulling the sheet back over again. I signed to him to leave it where it was.

'Your father?'

'Yes. Please . . .'

He hesitated, then, when I nodded, reluctantly pulled the sheet further down. They'd put my father in a white cotton shroud with his hands crossed on his chest. I took a step forward and untied the strings at the neck of the shroud. The woman pulled at my arm and tried to stop me. *Trust your own eyes and ears*, he'd said. *Never let anybody persuade you against them*. He'd been talking at the time about the question dividing some of his naturalist friends as to whether squirrels were completely hibernatory, standing in some beechwoods with Tom and me on a bright January day. I tried to keep the sound of his voice in my head as I lifted up his right hand, cold and heavy in mine. I pulled the shroud aside with my other hand and looked at the

4

round hole the pistol ball had made in his chest, right over the heart, and the livid scorch-marks on his skin surrounding it. No blood. They'd have sponged his body before they put it in the shroud. That probably accounted for the vinegar smell. It would have been done by the same plump, liver-spotted hand that was now pulling at my arm, trying to make me come away. The thought of that hand moving over him made me feel sick. I pulled the shroud up, crossed his right hand back over his left and watched while they covered him up again.

'His clothes?' I asked.

She looked annoyed and left us, wooden clogs clacking over the cobbles. The flies buzzed and circled. After a minute or two she was back with an armful of white linen, streaked with rusty stains. Breeches, stockings, a shirt. On the left breast of the shirt was a small round hole. I bent over it and smelled, through the iron tang of blood, a whiff of scorched linen and black powder. I think the woman imagined I was kissing it, holding it so close, because her arm came round me, sympathetic again. The man was repeating some question insistently.

'You will need an English priest?'

'I don't think . . . Oh, I see. For the burial. Yes.'

He produced a dog-eared calling card from his pocket. I heaped the linen back into the woman's arms and took the card. She'd tried to be kind to me so as I left I slid some coins from my bag into the pocket of her apron. It struck me as I walked away that they were English coins and of no use to her, but then in Calais she could find somebody to change them. It came to me too that she hadn't shown me his outer clothes, shoes, hat or jacket. One of the perquisites of her job, probably. Some lumpish son or cousin of hers might be wearing them even now. There should have been rings as well. I made myself picture the crossed hands against the shroud. They'd let him keep the narrow silver ring on his left hand that he wore in memory of my mother. He usually wore a gold one with a curious design on his right, but I was certain that the hand I'd held had been bare. The thought of somebody else wearing his ring made me so angry that I almost turned back. But that was not sensible, and I must at all costs be sensible. I walked by the sea for a long time, watching the sun go down. Then I found a pile of fishing nets heaped in a shed, curled myself up in them and alternately slept and shivered through the few hours of a June night. In the shivering intervals, every word of the note that had jolted my world out of its orbit came back to me.

Miss Lane,
    You do not know me, but I take the liberty of addressing you with distressing news. Your father, Thomas Jacques Lane, was killed this Saturday, seventeenth June, in a duel at Calais . . .

CHAPTER TWO

Everybody knows the place in Calais where gentlemen go to fight duels, the long stretch of beach with the sand-hills behind. People point it out to each other from the deck of the steam packet. By the time the first grey light came in through the doorway of the fisherman's hut I knew that the one thing I wanted to do was follow the route my father would have taken three days before, at much this time of the morning. I unwrapped myself from the nets, brushed dry fish scales from my dress and walked along the harbour front, past shuttered houses and rows of tied-up fishing boats. Eventually the cobbled road runs out in a litter of nets and crab pots, just above the fringe of bladder wrack and driftwood that marks high tide line. They would have left their carriage there.

No carriage this morning, nothing but a fisherman's cart made of old planks, bleached silver by the wind and sea, with shafts just wide enough for a donkey. No pony, even the most ill-used one, could be so thin. The owner of the cart probably lived in one of the little row of hovels built of rocks and ships' timbers, so tilted and ramshackle they looked as if some especially high tide had dropped them. The windows were closed with warped wooden shutters. There was nobody looking out of them so early in the morning, not even a fisherman's wife watching for her husband. In any case, a fisherman's wife would know there was no use looking out for boats with the tide so very low, almost at its lowest, the silver strip of sea hardly visible across the wide sands. Would it have been so low at first light three days ago? I thought I must buy or borrow an almanack when I go back into the town. It might be of some importance to know. Anything might be of some importance, it was simply a matter of knowing what.

Later, I'd come back and try to talk to the fishermen's wives. It's easier, usually, to talk to women than to men.

'I am sorry for disturbing you, madame, but can you recall a carriage drawing up there where the road runs out, three mornings ago? Just as it was getting light, it would have been, or even while it was still dark.'

They might quite easily have arrived in the dark, perhaps waited in the carriage until that first strange, flat light that comes before sunrise, when they could see to walk along the beach. I'm sure if he had met a fisherman's wife that morning, he'd have raised his hat and wished her good day. But almost certainly he did not meet her, the morning being so early. And even if she had met him or seen the carriage standing there, I don't suppose for one moment she'd tell me. The men and women who live in that ruckle of cottages must be used to seeing carriages drive up in the early morning, dark silhouettes of gentlemen against the pale dawn sky walking across the sands, but I'm sure they don't talk about them to strangers. These gentlemen and their purposes have nothing to do with the fishermen's world, any more than if they'd come down from the moon, and the fishermen will know there is no good in what's happening, nothing but harm and blame. So I should ask, but nobody would tell me. It was simply one of those things which must be done.

Now that I considered, there should have been two carriages, not one. But then, he might not have come by carriage. It was only a short walk out here from the town and he was never one for taking a carriage when he could go on foot. He might have slipped out of the side door of an inn while it was still dark, the horses asleep in their stalls, only the dull glow of a fire through the kitchen window, where some poor skivvy was starting to poke up the fire for coffee. I dare say he'd have liked a cup of coffee, only he couldn't wait. So he might have walked here and seen the other carriage drawn up already and gone on without pausing over the sand.

Alone? He shouldn't have been alone. There should have been a friend with him – or at least somebody he called a friend. In that case, they would have stayed the night together in an inn. If I asked around the town somebody surely would have seen the two of them together and be able to describe the other man. I'd do that later, when I come back from my walk.

The sand was firm underfoot, only I wished I'd brought stouter footwear. But then my escape from Chalke Bissett had been so hurried I'd had no time to go to the bootroom and find the pair I keep for country walking. Besides, when I escaped I had no notion in my head of walking over French beaches. A day or two on English pavements was the very worst I'd thought to expect. Still, the shoes were carrying me well enough. The ramshackle cottages were already a mile behind me, the sand dunes and the point at the far end of the beach in sight. Nearer the tideline, there was a gloss of salt water over the sand. My foot pressed down, making a margin of lighter sand, then the footprint filled up with dark water behind me. Salt water and sand were splashing up to the hem of my skirts, making them drag damply round my ankles. From here, if there were figures on the point you'd be sure to see them. He would have seen them – three of them – with the sun rising behind them. They would have to pay attention to that sun, be quite sure it didn't get in their eyes. The figures would be waiting there, just where the gull has landed, and my father and the man he called his friend would have walked over to them, not slowly but not too fast either, like rational people who have business together. They'd have shaken hands when they met, I know that, and serious words would be spoken, a question put, heads shaken.

'Since your principal refuses to offer an apology, then things must proceed to their conclusion. Would you care to choose, sir?'

And the black, velvet-lined case would be snapped open. As the man challenged, my father would have first choice. So he'd take a pistol, weigh it in his hand and nod, and the other man would take the other. How do I know? The way that anybody who reads novels knows. I confess with shame that ten years or so ago, around the age of twelve when much silliness is imagined, the etiquette of the duel had a morbid fascination for me. I revelled in wronged, dark-haired heroes, their fine features admitting not the faintest trace of anxiety as they removed their jackets to expose faultless white linen shirt-fronts over their noble and so vulnerable breasts, shook hands with their seconds (who – not being heroes – were permitted a slight tremor of the fingers) then strode unconcernedly to the fatal line, as if . . . Oh, and any other nonsense you care to add. Write it for yourselves and thank the gods that no girl stays a twelve-year-old for ever. But that's why I knew enough to imagine how it would have happened three days before, at very much this time in the morning. The two pistol shots, almost simultaneous. Then the frightened seabirds wheeling and crying – unless the seagulls on the Calais sands are so blasé by now that they are not in the least alarmed by duellists' shots. A figure flat on the sand, the two seconds bending over him, the doctor opening his bag. A little further off, the survivor with his left arm over his eyes to shield out the dreadful sight, pistol pointed to the sand, anger drained out of him; 'Oh my God, what have I done?'

'It really is the most appalling nonsense,' my father said. 'I wish you would not read these things.'

Back to being twelve, and my father – who was so rarely angry with anything or anybody – much annoyed with me. I had just twirled into the room in my new satin shoes and a fantasy of being a princess carelessly mislaid at birth – trilling that I hoped one day men might fight a duel for love of me. He'd caught me in mid-twirl, plumped me down in a chair and talked to me seriously.

'Some day another man besides myself and your brother will love you. But hear this, daughter, if he proves to be the kind of fool who thinks he can demonstrate that love by violently stealing the life of another human being, then he's not the man for my Liberty.'

'But if he were defending my honour, Papa . . .'

'Honour's important, yes. But there's wise honour and foolish honour. I wish to say something serious to you now, and I know if your mother were alive she'd be in utter agreement with me. Are you listening?'

I nodded, looking down through gathering tears at my new satin shoes and knowing the gloss had gone from them forever. He seldom mentioned our mother, who'd died when I was six years old and Tom four, but when he did, it was always in connection with something that mattered very much.

'If you ever – may the gods forbid – get yourself into the kind of scrape where your honour can be defended only by a man being killed for you, then you must live without honour. Do you understand?'

I said 'yes', as firmly as I could, hoping the tears would not fall. He crouched beside the chair and put two fingers under my chin, raising it so that my eyes were on a level with his.

'Don't cry, my darling. Only, duelling is wasteful, irrational nonsense and I'm sure when you think more deeply about it, you will be of the same opinion. Lecture over. Now, shall we go out and feed the goldfish in the fountain?'

So that's how I knew, you see – knew for sure that I'd been told a black lie. It was there in my mind as I looked down at his body, although it didn't take clear shape until I walked across the beach. The duel never happened. My father was dead, that was true enough, even though not a fibre of my mind or body believed it yet. But it was impossible that he died that way, no matter what the note said or what the couple at the morgue believed. I was as sure of that as the sun rising behind the point, turning the rim of sea to bright copper. That rim was closer now and the tide seemed to be on its way in. I followed my own footsteps back over the sand, making a slow curve to the line of fishermen's cottages. It looked as if the people in them must have started their day's work, because there was a figure in front of the cottages looking out to sea. It would be a fine day for him, I thought. The sky was clear blue, with only a little breeze ruffling my bonnet ribbons. When I got to the town I'd drink some coffee and plan what questions to ask and where to ask them. Who saw him? Who were his friends in Calais? Who brought his body to the morgue? Above all, who wrote that lying and anonymous note to me at Dover? Insolent as well as lying, because the unknown writer had added a command:

> *Remain where you are for the present and talk about it to nobody. People who are concerned on your behalf will come to you within two or three days.*

As if I could read that and wait tamely like a dog told to stay.

The man I'd noticed was still standing by the cottages. Closer to, he didn't look like a fisherman. His clothes were black, like a lawyer's or doctor's, and he was wearing a high-crowned hat. He was thin and standing very upright, not looking out to sea now but back along the sands towards the point. Almost, you might think, looking at me. But of course he had no reason to look at me. He was simply a gentleman admiring the sunrise. Something about the stiff way he was standing made me think he might be an invalid who slept badly and walked in the sea air for the sake of his health. Perhaps he came there every morning, in which case he might have been standing just there three days ago, watching whatever happened or did not happen. I raised my hand to him. Of course, that was over-familiar behaviour to a man I'd never met, but the rules of normal life didn't apply any more. Either he didn't see my gesture, or he did and was shocked by it, because he turned and walked away in the direction of the town, quite quickly for a supposed invalid. Strange that he should be in such a hurry after standing there so long, but then everything was strange now.

CHAPTER THREE

Two mornings before I'd woken up on a fine Sunday in the inn at Dover, with nothing in the world to cause me a moment's anxiety. Nothing, that is, beyond whether my aunt might have sent one of her servants or even a tame curate to recapture me. It was a small side room, the cheapest they had, looking out over the stableyard of the larger hotel next door. I remember standing barefoot at the window with my woollen mantle round my shoulders, looking down at the sunlit yard and the grooms harnessing two glossy bays to a phaeton, feeling well satisfied with myself and the world in general. My escape from the dim, sour-faced house at Chalke Bissett had gone entirely to plan. Even before the servants were up I was on my way across the field footpath to the village, knowing the area well enough by then to guess that there'd be a farm cart

16

taking fruit and vegetables into Salisbury. The driver said he'd take me there for a kiss, but I bargained him down to one shilling and insisted on sitting in the back, along with withy baskets full of strawberries and bunches of watercress.

From Salisbury, I took a succession of stage and mail coaches, much as I'd planned from the road book giving coach routes and times in my aunt's small library. Her road book was out of date, like everything else in the house, so some of the times were wrong and I had to wait for hours in the street outside various inns, trying hard to be inconspicuous in my mantle that was too heavy for a warm June day and the battered leather travelling bag that I would not allow anybody else to carry because I was unsure how much to tip. Salisbury to Winchester took four hours and two changes of horses. At Winchester I managed to secure the last outside place in another coach that took me all the way across Hampshire.

It was a glorious evening, flying along on the top of the coach behind four fast horses with the scent of hay and honeysuckle in the air, haymakers out late with their scythes and rakes and the sun sinking in the west behind us, throwing their long shadows out over the shorn fields. I felt like singing, only it would have drawn the attention of the other outside passengers, a clerical-looking man with a cough and a farmer and his wife, loaded with packages that included a live duck in a basket with its head sticking out complacently, as if it too were

17

enjoying the sweet air. We arrived at the changing point of Hartfordbridge in the early hours of the morning, when it was already getting light, so that spared me the worry and expense of a room in the inn. I simply sat on the edge of a horse trough, wrapped my mantle round me and ate the last slice of bread and butter I'd taken from my aunt's kitchen.

From Hartfordbridge it was a long and expensive day's journey into Kent and Tunbridge Wells. In this fashionable place, spending the night on the edge of a horse trough was out of the question, but luckily I'd made friends with a lady on the journey, travelling to meet her husband from a boat at Chatham. We shared a room and a large but lumpy double bed at a modest inn. Over a supper of cold beef pie and two pots of tea – we were thirsty because the roads were dusty from the dry weather – she glowed with happiness at the idea of seeing her husband again.

'And I'll soon be seeing my father,' I said.

Now I'd put two good days' travelling between myself and my aunt, it seemed safe to talk about myself.

'Has he been away long?'

'Only since September.'

It seemed longer. I remember that my companion asked the waiter if he had any news of the king. He shook his head gravely, implying that it was not good. King William was elderly and ill, probably dying, but that was not causing any great outbreak of grief among his subjects. I thought he was probably one of the dullest men ever to sit on the throne of England and in any case our family's sympathies were far from royalist. But I said nothing for fear of offending my companion, who was a kind woman.

Next morning we breakfasted together on good bread and bad coffee, then she took the coach for Chatham while I passed some time looking round the town, admiring the fashions and waiting for the coach that would take me on the last stage of my journey to Dover.

I reached the port in the evening. I knew it quite well, from the occasions when I'd crossed to the Continent with my father and Tom, but I'd never been there on my own before. I stood at the inn where the coach had put me down feeling for the first time scared at what I'd done. Then, determined that my father should not come back to find a feeble young woman, I adjusted my bonnet, slung my mantle over my arm and picked up my bag. I was wearing my second-best dress in plain lavender colour, with tight-fitting sleeves and a little lace at the neck. My bonnet had suffered from travelling outside and my hair felt plastered with dust, but I hoped I looked respectable, though travel-worn. The inns and hotels along the seafront and near the harbour were too expensive and conspicuous. If my aunt sent somebody after me, those were the first places he'd try. I walked along a dimly remembered side street, at right angles to the sea, and hit on an old inn called the Heart of Oak that looked as if it catered for the better class of trades-person rather than the gentry. The dark panelled hall smelled of beer and saddle leather. A brass bell stood on a counter. I rang and after some time a plump bald-headed man arrived, wearing a brown apron stained with metal polish.

'I should like to engage a room,' I told him, as confidently as I could. 'Not one of your most expensive ones.'

'Just for yourself, ma'am?'

His voice was polite enough, but his boot-button eyes were weighing me up.

'Just for myself.' Then, losing my nerve a little, I added, 'I'm here to meet my father. He's coming across from Calais.'

Which was the perfect truth, even though the look in those eyes made it feel like a lie.

'How many nights, ma'am?'

'He may be arriving as early as tomorrow . . .'

'Tomorrow's Sunday.'

'. . . or I might have to wait a day or two. I am not entirely sure of his plans.'

That was true as well, although one thing I was entirely sure of was that my father's plans did not include having his daughter there to meet him at Dover. His latest letter – in my bag and marking my place in the volume of Shelley, which was the only book I'd brought with me – made it quite clear that I was to wait at Chalke Bissett until called for. The innkeeper grudgingly admitted there was a room on the second floor he could let me have.

'I'll take supper in my room,' I told him. 'Mutton chop, some bread and cheese, and a jug of barley water.'

He nodded gloomily and called the bootboy to carry my bag upstairs to a small but reasonably clean room, furnished with bed, chair and wash-stand. I tipped the boy sixpence and, as the door closed behind him, spread out my arms and opened my mouth in a silent but most unladylike yell of triumph. When supper arrived I ate it to the last crumb then slept in the deep featherbed as comfortably as any dormouse.

I idled Sunday away pleasurably enough, tipping the little maid a shilling to bring cans of warm water upstairs so that I could wash my hair. When it was dry I strolled along the front in the sunshine, watching families driving in their carriages or walking back from church, and sailors arm in arm with women friends, bonnet and bodice ribbons fluttering in the breeze from the sea. The white cliffs gleamed and the old grey castle on top of them seemed from a distance to have broken out in patches of pink-, green- and lilac-coloured mushrooms, from the parasols of the ladies sight-seeing. In such a busy place, nobody was in the least disturbed by a young woman walking unescorted. I revelled in being alone and the mistress of my own time for once.

But on Monday morning I woke at first light with a little demon of anxiety in my mind. Now that I might be meeting my father within hours, it occurred to me that he would perhaps be annoyed because I had disobeyed instructions. I took his letter out of my bag and read it by the window as the horses stamped and the ostlers swore down in the yard. It had been written from a hotel in Paris, posted express, and arrived at Chalke Bissett just the evening before I left, too late to change my plan of escape.

My dearest Daughter,

I am glad to report that I have said farewell to my two noble but tedious charges and am now at my liberty and soon to be on the way home to my Liberty. I have faithfully conducted His Lordship and cousin around Paris, Bordeaux, Madrid, Venice, Rome, Naples. All wasted, of course, like feeding peaches to donkeys. They pined for their playing fields, their hunters, their rowing boats at home. The stones Virgil and Cicero trod were no more than ill-kept pavement in their eyes, the music of Vivaldi in his own city inferior to a bawled catch in a London tavern.

But enough. I have justly earned my fee and we may now set about spending it as we planned. If I had travelled home with my charges I should have rescued you from Aunt Basilisk sooner, but I'm afraid my princess must fret in her Wiltshire captivity a week longer. I had business here in Paris, also friends to meet. To be candid, I valued the chance of some intelligent conversation with like-minded fellows

*after these months of asses braying. Already I
have heard one most capital story which I
promise will set you roaring with laughter and
even perhaps a little indignation. You know 'the
dregs of their dull race . . .' But more of that
when we meet. Also, I have just met an
unfortunate woman who may need our help and
charity when we return to London. I know I
may depend on your kind heart.*

*I plan to be at Chalke Bissett about a week
from now. Since even five minutes of my
company is precisely three hundred seconds too
many for dear Beatrice/Basilisk I'm sure she will
not detain us. So have your bags packed and we
shall whisk away. Until then, believe me your
loving father.*

Then, after his signature, a scrawled postscript.

*If you'd care to write to me before then, address
your letter to poste restante at Dover. I shall
infallibly check there on my arrival, in the hope
of finding pleasant reading for the last stage of
my journey.*

As I re-read it, I was seized with a panic that he might
at that very moment be stepping off a boat and posting
to Chalke Bissett, not knowing I was waiting for him
less than a mile away. I ran downstairs, secured paper,

pen and ink from the landlord and – lacking a writing desk – stood at the cracked marble wash-stand in my room to scrawl a hasty note.

Dearest Father,

I am here in Dover at an inn called the Heart of Oak. Anybody will direct you to it. I could not tolerate the company of La Basilisk one hour longer. So you need not brave her petrifying eye and we may travel straight to London. Please forgive your disobedient but loving daughter.

I didn't tell him in the note, and never intended to tell him, that the real reason I'd fled the house of my mother's elder sister was that I couldn't tolerate her criticisms of him. She'd never forgiven his elopement with my mother and used every opportunity to spray poisonous slime, like a camel spitting.

'Your father the fortune hunter . . .'

'He is not. He had not a penny from my mother.'

'Your father the Republican . . .'

'He's always said it was wrong to cut off the head of Marie Antoinette.'

'Your father the gambler . . .'

'Do not all gentlemen play games of hazard occasionally?'

She called me argumentative and said I should never get a husband with my sharp tongue.

*

I sealed my scrawled note and was waiting on the steps of the poste restante office as it opened. When I handed it over the counter I asked if there were any more letters waiting for Mr Thomas Lane. Three, the clerk told me, so I knew I hadn't missed him. I strolled by the harbour for a while, watching the steam packet coming in and passengers disembarking. The novelty of my escape was wearing off now and I was beginning to feel a little lonely. But that was no great matter because soon my father would be with me and a whole new part of my life would be starting. My father had talked about it back in September, nine months before, as he was packing.

'I'm quite resolved that if I have to leave you again it will be in the care of a husband.'

I was folding his shirts at the time.

'Indeed. And have you any one in mind?'

'As yet, no. Have you, Libby?'

'Indeed I have not.'

'Sure?'

'Sure.'

'Then we can look at the question like two rational beings. You agree it is time you were married?'

'So people tell me.'

'You mean the match-making matrons? Don't pay any heed to them, Libby. They'd have any poor girl married by the time she's off toddlers' leading strings. People should be old enough to know their own minds before they marry. Thirty for a man, say, and around twenty-two for a woman.'

25

I was twenty-one and six months at the time.

'So I have six months to find a husband?' I said.

He smiled. 'Hardly that. In fact, I am proposing that we should leave the whole question on the shelf . . .'

'And me on the shelf too?'

'Exactly that, until I return next summer and we can set about the business in a sensible fashion.'

He must have seen the hurt in my face.

'Libby, I'm not talking about the marriage market. I'm not proposing you trade your youth and beauty for some fat heir to a discredited peerage.'

'I don't think they'd rate higher than the second son of a baronet,' I said, still defensive.

He came and took my hand.

'You know me better than that. I'm not a young man any more.' (He was forty-six years old.) 'I must think of providing for you in the future. I shan't die a rich man and Tom has his own way to make.'

'I'd never be a burden on Tom, you know that.'

'I've not been as much of a father to you as I should. But I have tried to give you the important things in life. Your education has been better than most young women's. You speak French and German adequately and your musical taste is excellent.'

'That reminds me, I've broken another guitar string.' I was uneasy at hearing myself praised.

'And we've travelled together. You've seen the glaciers of Mont Blanc at sunrise and the Roman Forum by moonlight.'

26

I was wonderfully fortunate, I knew that. When I was back with my father it was easy to forget the other times, lonely and homesick in a cold French convent, or boarded out with a series of more or less resentful aunts or cousins. It was almost possible, though nowhere near as easy, to forget the glint of my brother's handkerchief waving from the rail of the ship as it left Gravesend to carry him away to India, and the widening gap of dark water.

'Couldn't we just go on as we are?' I asked. 'Tom will come back one day and I can keep house for him and you. Do I really need a husband?'

He became serious again. 'The wish of my heart is to see you married to a man you can love and respect who values and cares for you.'

I watched the steam packet go out again, arching sparks from its funnel and trailing a smell of coal dust. In three hours or so it would be in Calais, then perhaps bringing my father back with it. Around noon I felt weary from my early start and went back to my room. I took off my dress and shoes, loosened my stays and laid down on the bed. I must have dozed because I woke with a start, hearing the landlord's voice at the bottom of the stairs, saying my name.

'Miss Liberty Lane? Don't know about the Liberty, but she called herself Miss Lane, at any rate. Give it me and I'll take it in to her.'

As his heavy footsteps came upstairs I pulled my dress on and did up some essential buttons, heart

27

thumping because either this was a message from my father or my aunt had tracked me after all. But as soon as the landlord handed me the note – adding his own greasy thumb-print – I knew it had nothing to do with Chalke Bissett. The handwriting was strong and sprawling, a man's hand. The folded paper was sealed with a plain blob of red wax, and a wedge-shaped impression that might have been made with the end of a penknife, entirely anonymous. I broke the seal and read: . . . *take the liberty of addressing you with distressing* . . .

'Bad news, miss?'

The landlord was still in the room, his eyes hot and greedy. I gripped the edge of the wash-stand, shaking my head. I think I was acting on instinct only, the way a hurt deer runs.

'I must go to Calais. When's the next boat?'

CHAPTER FOUR

'Was your father a confirmed and communicant member of the Church of England?'

The clergyman was plump and faded, wisps of feathery brown-grey hair trailing from a bald pate, deep creases of skin round his forehead and jaw giving him a weary look. I'd traced the address on the card I'd been given at the morgue to a terraced house in a side street, with a tarnished brass plate by the door: *Rev. Adolphus Bateman, MA (Oxon).* This representative of the Anglican Church in the port of Calais was at least living in Christian poverty, if not charity. His skin creases had drawn into a scowl when I'd stood on his doorstep and explained my need. The scowl was still there as we talked in his uncomfortable parlour under framed engravings of Christ Church College and *Christ and the Woman Taken in Adultery.* He smelled of wet woollen clothes and old mouse droppings, familiar to me from enforced evensongs in country churches with various aunts. It was a late autumn English smell and quite how he'd contrived to keep it with him on a fine June morning in Calais was a mystery.

'Yes, he was.'

I supposed that, back in his schooldays, my father would have gone through the usual rituals. There was no need to tell this clergyman about his frequently expressed view that the poets talked more sense about heaven and hell than the preachers ever did.

'Half past three,' he said.

'What?'

'I shall arrange the interment for half past three. The Protestant chapel is at the far side of the burial ground. The total cost will be five pounds, sixteen shillings and four pence.' Apparently mistaking my expression, he added impatiently, 'That is the standard charge. There are the bearers and the gravediggers to be paid, as well as my own small emolument. I assume you would wish me to make all the arrangements?'

'Yes, please.'

I took my purse out of my reticule and counted the money on to the faded crochet mat in the middle of the table: five bright sovereigns, sixteen shillings, four penny pieces. It left the little purse as floppy as the udder of a newly milked goat. I'd had to sell a gold locket belonging to my mother and my grandmother's silver watch to pay for my journey. It had been a nightmare within a nightmare, going round the streets of Dover trying to find a jeweller to give anything like a fair price for them, with the steam packet whistling from the harbour for last passengers. In normal times I'd have cried bitterly at parting with them but, turned hard by grief and need, I'd bargained like an old dame at market. As I stowed the purse away the clergyman asked, with just a touch of sympathy in his voice, 'Have you no male relatives?'

'A younger brother. He is in Bombay with the East India Company.'

I had a suspicion he intended to pray over me, so moved hastily on to the other thing I needed.

'You must know the English community in Calais well.' (He did not look as if he knew anything well, but a little flattery never hurts.) 'Can you tell me if there are any particular places where they gather.'

'The better sort come to the Protestant Church on Sunday mornings. For the ladies, the Misses Besswell run a charity knitting circle on Wednesday afternoons and there are also a series of evening subscription concerts organised by . . .'

I let him run on. I could not imagine my father or his friends at any event known to the Reverend Bateman.

I left the house, filling my lungs with the better smells outside – seaweed and fish, fresh baked bread and coffee. This reminded me that I had eaten and drunk nothing since the message had arrived, back in Dover.

I was almost scared of doing either. That message had divided my life into before and after, like a guillotine blade coming down. Everything I did now – eating, drinking, sleeping – was taking me further away from the time when my father had been living. I still couldn't think of eating, not even a crumb, but the smell of coffee was seductive. I followed it round the corner and on to a small quay. It wasn't part of the larger harbour where the channel packet came and went, more of a local affair for the fishermen. There were nets spread out on the pebbles, an old man sitting on a boulder and mending one of them, his bent bare toes twined in the net to keep it stretched, needle flashing through the meshes like a tiny agile fish. The coffee shop was no more than a booth with a counter made of driftwood planks, a stove behind it and a small skinny woman with a coffee pot. She poured, watched me drink, poured again, making no attempt to hide her curiosity.

'Madame is thirsty?'

Very thirsty, I told her. It was a pleasure to be speaking French again.

'Madame has arrived from England?'

'Yesterday.'

'A pleasant crossing?'

'Not so bad, thank you.'

The sea had been calm at least. I'd stood at the rail all the way, willing the packet faster towards Calais but dreading to arrive.

'Is madame staying in Calais for long?'

'Not long, I think. But my plans are uncertain. Tell me, where do the English mostly stay these days?'

She named a few hotels: Quillac's, Dessin's, the Lion d'Argent, the London. I thanked her and walked around the town for a while, trying to get my courage up, past the open-fronted shops with their gleaming piles of mackerel, sole, whiting, white and orange scallops arranged in fans, stalls piled high with plump white asparagus from the inland farms, bunches of bright red radishes. At last I adjusted my bonnet using a dark window pane as my mirror, took a deep breath and tried the first hotel.

'Excuse me for troubling you, monsieur, but I am looking for my father. He may have arrived in Calais some time ago, but I am not sure where he intended to stay.'

After the first few attempts I was able to give a description of my father without any trembling in my voice.

'His name is Thomas Jacques Lane. In France he probably uses Jacques. Forty-six years old, speaks excellent French. Tall, with dark curling hair, a profile of some distinction and good teeth.'

But the answers from the hotels, whether given kindly or off-handedly, were all the same. No, madame, no English gentleman of that description.

It was midday before I came to the last of the big hotels. It was the largest one, newly built, close to the pier and the landing stage for the steam packet, with a busy stableyard. Carriages were coming and going all the time, some of them with coats of arms on the doors and footmen in livery riding behind. It was so far from being a place where my father might have stayed that I almost decided not to try, but in the end I went up the steps into a foyer that was all false marble columns and velvet curtains, like a theatrical set, crowded with fashionably dressed people arriving or leaving.

I queued at the desk behind an English gentleman disputing his account. Clearly he was the kind of person who, if he arrived at heaven's gateway, would expect to find St Peter speaking English and minding his manners. He was working his way through a bill several pages long, bullying the poor clerk and treating matters of a few francs as if there were thousands at stake. I had plenty of time to study him from the back. He was tall and strongly made, his shoulders broad, the neck above his white linen cravat red and wide as a farm labourer's. His hair was so black that I suspected it might owe something to the bottles of potions kept by Parisian barbers. He spoke and carried himself like a man accustomed to having an audience and I imagined him as some rural chairman of the bench, sentencing poachers or trade unionists to transportation.

After a while my attention wandered to a young man and woman standing by a pillar and arguing. She was about my age, and beautiful. Her red-gold hair was piled up, with a few curled ringlets hanging down, and a little hat that could only have come from Paris perched on top of it. She wore a rose-pink satin mantle with a square collar edged in darker pink velvet, pale pink silk stockings and pink suede shoes, also Parisian. The man with her was several years older, elegantly but not foppishly dressed in grey and black. He was tall and dark haired with a handsome face and a confident, rather cynical air. They might have been taken for husband and wife, except for the strong family resemblance in their fine dark eyes and broad brows. Except, too, for the way they were carrying on their argument. When a husband and wife disagree in public they do it in a stiff and secretive way, whispers, glances and half-turned shoulders. Brothers and sisters are different. They have been arguing from the nursery onwards and are not embarrassed about it. Although I loved Tom more than anybody in the world except my father, it was the arguments I missed almost as much as all the more gentle things. So it went to my heart to see the way the beautiful young woman frowned at her brother and how he smiled, stretched out a grey-gloved hand and pulled none too gently at one of her ringlets. She batted the hand away. He laughed, said something that was no doubt patronising and elder-brotherly.

'Stephen, come here.'

The man disputing his bill turned and called across the foyer. I'd been wrong to think his black hair might be dyed because his eyebrows, which joined in a single bar over dark and angry eyes, were just as black. His head could have modelled in outline for one of the Roman emperors with its great wedge of a nose and square jaw, but his lips were thin and drawn inward like a man sucking on something sour. He was looking at the brother and sister. As he turned back to the desk I saw them give each other that rueful grimace children exchange when in trouble with parents, their argument instantly forgotten in the face of a shared opponent. It had been a father's command, although there was no obvious likeness between the two men. I watched as Stephen crossed the foyer, obediently but none too quickly.

'Did you really order two bottles of claret on Sunday?'

I heard the older man's impatient question, saw the younger one bending over the bill, but nothing after that because, shamingly, my eyes had blurred with tears. That look between brother and sister had caused it. I felt suddenly and desperately how I needed Tom and how far away he was. I ran behind one of the pillars to hide myself and bent over gasping as if somebody had punched me in the stomach, hands to my face, rocking backwards and forwards to try to ease the pain.

'Is . . . is there anything wrong?'

A soft English voice, with the hint of a lisp. Through my fingers I saw pink satin, smelled perfume of roses. A gentle hand came down on my shoulder.

'Are you ill? Perhaps if you sat down . . .'

I stammered that I was all right really. Just a . . . a sudden headache. She was so soft and kind that I had to fight the temptation to lean on her and cry all over her rose mantle.

'Oh, you poor darling. I suffer such headaches too. I have some powders in my room, if you'd let me . . .'

I straightened up, found my handkerchief and mopped my face.

'No, it's quite all right, thank you. I have . . . I have friends waiting outside. I am grateful for . . .'

And I simply fled, through the foyer, down the steps and out to the street. I couldn't risk her kindness. It would break me down entirely.

I walked around until I'd composed myself, then began inquiring at the lodging houses and smaller, less expensive hostelries in the side streets. There was a different spirit to this part of the town, away from where the rich foreigners stayed. The narrow streets were shadowed, shutters closed, eyes looking out at me through doors that opened just a slit and then shut in my face. People here did not care for questions because Calais had so many secrets. Forty years ago those streets would have sheltered cloaked and hooded aristocrats, trying to escape from the guillotine, paying with their last jewels for the secrecy of the same brown-faced men who now looked at me with wary old eyes. Not much more than twenty years ago, in the late wars with Napoleon, spies from both sides would have come and gone there, buying more secrecy from the men of middle years who now leered from behind counters. Their many-times-great grandfathers had probably taken money from spies watching King Henry's army before Agincourt. Whatever had happened to my father was only the latest in a long line of things that were never to be mentioned. A few people opened their doors and were polite, but always the answer was the same. They regretted, madame, that they had knowledge of no such man.

And yet my father must have stayed somewhere, or at the very least drunk wine or coffee somewhere. In his last letter, written from Paris, he'd said he expected to be collecting me from Chalke Bissett in a week. Allow two days for travelling from Paris to Calais, one day for crossing the Channel, the next to travel on to Chalke Bissett, that meant three days spare. Had he spent the time in Paris with his friends, or at Calais? Was it even true that he'd died on the Saturday, as I'd been told? How long had his body been lying in that terrible room? I was angry with myself for all the questions I had not asked and resolved to do better in future.

A clock struck two. There were roads straggling out of town with more lodging places along them, but they'd have to wait until later. I tried one more hostelry with the sign of a bottle over the door, was given the usual answer, and added another question: could they kindly give me directions to the burial ground? It was on the far side of the town. The sky was blue and the sun warm, seagulls crying, white sails in the Channel, all sizes from small scudding lighters to a great English man-o'-war. My lavender dress and bonnet were hardly funeral wear but my other clothes were on the far side of the Channel. My father wouldn't mind. Too little care for one's appearance is an incivility to others: too much is an offence to one's intelligence.

Reverend Bateman's expression as he waited for me by the grey chapel in its grove of wind-bent tamarisks showed that my appearance was an offence to him.

'Are there no other mourners?'

'None,' I said.

An ancient carriage stopped at the gates, rectangular and tar-painted like a box for carrying fish, drawn by two raw-boned bays. They had nodding black plumes between the ears, as was fitting, but the plumes must have done service for many funerals in the sea breeze because most of the feathers had worn away and they were stick-like, converting the bays into sad unicorns. Two men in black slid off the box and another two unfolded from inside. The coffin came towards us on their shoulders. The black cloth covering it was so thin and worn that even the slight breeze threatened to blow it away and the bearers had to fight to hold it down.

I refuse even to remember the next half hour. It had nothing to do with my living father. He would have laughed at it. We had our five-pounds-sixteen-and-four-pence-worth of English funeral rites and that is all that can be said. Afterwards the four bearers and two men in gardener's clothes whom I took to be gravediggers, stood around fidgeting. It seemed that I was required to tip them. As I handed over some coins, and Reverend Bateman studiously looked the other way, I realised that the thinnest of the bearers was the man from the mortuary. I'd been trying to work up the resolution to go back there with some of the questions I'd been too shocked to ask on the first visit. At least this spared me the journey.

'Were you there when my father's body was brought in?'

He gave a reluctant nod.

'I was as well,' said one of the others, a fat man in a black tricorne hat with a nose like a fistful of crushed mulberries.

'Who brought him in?'

They looked at each other.

'Friends,' said the thin one.

'Did they leave their names?'

A double headshake.

'How many?'

'Two,' said the fat one.

'Or three,' said the thin one.

'What did they look like?'

An exchange of glances over my head.

'English gentlemen,' said the fat one.

'Young, old, fair, dark?'

'Not so very young,' said the fat one.

'Not old,' said the thin one. 'Not particularly dark or fair that we noticed.'

'Did they say anything?'

'They said they'd be back soon to make the funeral arrangements.'

'And did they come back?'

Another double headshake.

'What day was it that they brought him in?'

'Three days ago. Saturday,' the fat one said.

'Saturday, early in the morning,' the thin one confirmed.

Behind them, the gravediggers were shovelling the earth over my father's coffin. It was sandy and slid off their spades with a hissing sound. Reverend Bateman was looking at his watch, annoyed that I should be talking to the men, all the more so because he clearly didn't understand more than a word or two of French.

'I have an appointment back in town. I don't wish to hurry you, but we should be going.'

He clearly expected to escort me back. It was a courtesy of a kind, I suppose, but an unwanted one.

'Thank you, but I shall stay here for a while. I am grateful to you.'

I offered him my hand. He shook it coldly and walked off. The four bearers nodded to me and followed him. The raw-boned unicorns lumbered their box-like carriage away. Reverend Bateman assumed, of course, that I wanted to be alone at my father's grave, but I was discovering that grief does not necessarily show itself in the way people expect. I did indeed want to be on my own, but that was because I needed to think about what the bearers had said. Most of it supported the black lie. Two

41

or three nameless gentlemen arriving with a shot corpse – that might be how things were done after a duel. Either it had happened that way, or the two of them had been well paid to say it did. But wasn't it odd – even by the standards of duellists – that the supposed friends who brought his body to the morgue didn't return as promised to make his funeral arrangements?

I began walking to the graveyard gates as I thought about it. I suppose I had my eyes on the ground because when I looked up the figure was quite close, walking towards me. At first I took him for one of the bearers, because he was dressed entirely in black. But no, this man was elderly and a gentleman, although not a wealthy one. His jacket was frayed at the cuffs, his stock clean and neatly folded but of old and threadbare cotton, not stiff linen, and his tall black hat was in need of brushing. A mourner, I thought; probably come to visit his wife's grave. Indeed, his thin and clean-shaven face was severe, his complexion greyish and ill looking. He might have been sixty or more, but it was hard to tell because grief and illness age people. When he saw me looking at him he hesitated, then raised his hat.

'Bonjour, madam.'

The accent was so obviously English that I answered, 'Good afternoon, sir.'

He blinked, came forward a few steps and glanced towards the gravediggers.

'Do you happen to know whom they are burying over there?' he said.

It was not a bad voice in itself, low and educated. But there was something about the way he said it that made me sure I'd seen him before, and I went cold.

'Thomas Jacques Lane.' I tried to say it calmly, just as a piece of information, but saw a change in his eyes. So I added, 'My father.'

'Do I then have the honour of addressing Miss Liberty Lane?'

'You were watching me,' I said. 'This morning on the sands, it was you watching me.'

He didn't deny it, just asked another question.

'What are you doing here?'

'As you see, arranging my father's burial.'

He said nothing. I sensed I'd caught him off balance, and he wasn't accustomed to that.

'You knew him, didn't you?' I said. 'It was you who sent me that note.'

I'd guessed right about his watching me, so this was only a step further.

'What note?'

He sounded genuinely puzzled.

'That lying note, telling me he'd been killed in a duel, ordering me to wait at Dover.'

'I sent you no such note. But if you were at Dover, you should never have left there. Go back. I tell you that as your father's friend.'

All my misery and shock centred on this black stick of a man.

'There was only one person in the world who had

43

the right to give orders to me, and he's lying over there. And you, sir, are lying too – only far less honourably.'

I was glad to see a twitch of the tight skin over his cheekbones that might have been anger, but he mastered it.

'How have I lied to you?'

'Did you not write me that note? My father would never in his life have fought a duel, and anybody who knew him must know that.'

He looked at me, frowning as if I were some problem in arithmetic proving more difficult than expected.

'There has clearly been some misunderstanding. I wrote you no note.'

'Who are you? What do you know about my father's death?'

He stared at me, still frowning. I was aware of somebody shouting a little way off, but did not give it much attention.

'I think it would be best,' he said at last, 'if you permitted me to escort you back to Dover. You surely have relatives who –'

'Why don't you answer my questions?'

'They will be answered. Only for the while I must appeal to you to have patience. In times of danger, patience and steadfastness are the best counsel.'

'How dare you sermonise me. I have a right to know –'

Two men were coming towards us along the path

from the cemetery gates. A four-horse coach was waiting there, but it didn't look like a funeral coach and neither of them had the air of mourners. One was dressed in what looked like a military uniform – buff breeches and highly polished boots, jacket in royal blue, frogged with gold braid – although it was no uniform I recognised. The other appeared to be a coachman and had brought his driving whip with him. The man in black seemed too absorbed in the problem I presented to hear their heavy footsteps on the gravel path.

'Is this man bothering you, missy?'

The hail from the man in the blue jacket was loud and cheerful, with tones of hunting fields in the shires. I thought he was probably some English traveller who had happened to be driving past. His hearty chivalry was an annoying interruption and I was preparing, as politely as could be managed, to tell him not to interfere, but there was no time. The man in black spun round.

'You!'

'Introduce me to the lady.'

'I'll see you in hell first.'

Both the words and the cold fury were so unexpected from the man in black that I just stood there, blinking and staring. Unfortunately, that gave the hearty man his chance.

'Such language before a lady. Don't worry, missy, you come with us and we'll see you safe.'

He stepped forward and actually put a hand on my sleeve.

'On no account go with him,' the man in black shouted.

I shook off the hand. It came back instantly, more heavily.

'Oh, but we really must insist.'

Laughter as well as hunting-field heartiness in the voice. I tried to grab my arm back, but the fingers tightened painfully.

'Let her go at once,' said the man in black.

He advanced towards us, apparently intent on attacking the hearty man, who must have been around thirty years younger and three or four stone heavier. It would be an unequal contest, but at least it should give me a chance to pull away and run. But the hearty man didn't slacken his hold on my arm. He jerked his chin towards the coachman, who immediately grabbed the man in black, left arm round his windpipe like a fairground wrestler, and lifted his feet off the ground. The man fought back more effectively than I'd expected, driving the heel of his shoe hard into the coachman's knee. The coachman howled and dropped him and the whip. The man in black got up and took a step towards us, seemingly still intent on tearing me free from the hearty man. But the coachman didn't give him a second chance. He grabbed the man by his jacket and twirled him round. As he spun, the coachman landed a punch like a kick from a carthorse on the side of his bony temple. The man in black fell straight as a plank. He must have been unconscious before he hit the gravel path because he just lay there, eyes closed, face several shades more grey.

'I hope you haven't gone and killed him,' the hearty man said to the coachman, still keeping a tight hold on my arm.

'Let me go at once,' I said.

I'm sure there were many more appropriate emotions I should have been feeling, but the main one was annoyance that my man should have been silenced before I extracted any answers from him. At this point, I still regarded the hearty man as a rough but well-intentioned meddler and simply wanted him to go away.

'Oh, we can't leave a young English lady at the mercy of ruffians in a foreign country. We'll see you safely back to your friends.'

He assumed, I supposed, that I had a party waiting for me back in town. More to make him release his grip on my arm than anything, I accepted.

'Well, you may take me back to the centre of town if you insist. My friends are at Quillac's.'

I named the first hotel that came into my head.

'Are they now? Well, let's escort you back to them.'

He let go of my arm and bowed politely for me to go first. The coachman picked up his whip.

'What about him?' I said, looking down at the man in black. His eyes were still closed but the white shirt over his narrow chest was stirred by shallow breaths.

'He'll live. Or if he doesn't, at least he's in the right place.'

We walked along the path to the carriage at the gates, the hearty man almost treading on my heels, the coachman's heavy steps close behind him. It was an expensive travelling carriage, newly lacquered, the kind of thing that a gentleman might order for a long journey on the Continent. Perhaps they'd left in a hurry because there was an oval frame with gold leaves round it painted on the door, ready for a coat of arms to go inside, but it had been left blank. The team were four powerful dark bays, finely matched. There was a boy standing at the horses' heads dressed in gaiters and corduroy jacket, not livery. The coachman climbed up on the box at the front and the boy pulled down the steps to let us in. The hearty man gave an over-elaborate bow, suggesting I should go first.

'You might at least introduce yourself,' I said. In truth, I was still reluctant and wanted to gain time.

'I apologise. Harry Trumper, at your service.'

I didn't quite believe him. It was said like a man in a play.

'My name is Liberty Lane.'

'We knew that, didn't we?'

He was talking to somebody inside the coach.

'How?'

'We knew your father.'

It seemed unlikely that my clever, unconventional

father would have wasted time with this young squire. As for the man inside, I could only make him out in profile. It was curiosity that took me up the three steps to the inside of the coach. The man who called himself Harry Trumper followed. The boy folded up the steps, closed the door and – judging by the jolt – took up his place outside on the back. The harness clinked, the coachman said 'hoy hoy' to the horses, and we were away.

CHAPTER FIVE

There was a smell about the man inside the carriage. An elderly smell of stale port wine, snuff and candlewax. My nose took exception to it even as my eyes were still trying to adapt themselves to the half-darkness. The man who called himself Harry Trumper had arranged things so that he and I were sitting side by side with our backs to the horses, the other man facing us with a whole seat to himself. As my sight cleared, I could see that he needed it. It was not so much that he was corpulent – though indeed he was that – more that his unwieldy body spread out like a great toad's, with not enough in the way of bone or sinew to control its bulk. His face was like a suet pudding, pale and shiny, with two mean raisins for eyes, topped with a knitted grey travelling cap. The eyes were staring at me over a tight little mouth. He seemed not to like what he saw.

'Miss Lane, may I introduce . . .'

Before Trumper could finish, the fat man held up a hand to stop him. The hand bulged in its white silk glove like a small pudding in a cloth.

'Were you not told to stay at Dover?'

He rumbled the words at me as if they'd been hauled from the depths of his stomach.

'The note,' I said. 'Did you write it, then?'

'I wrote you no note.'

'I don't believe you.'

By my side, Trumper burbled something about not accusing a gentleman of lying. I turned on him.

'You said you knew my father. What happened to him?'

'He took something that didn't belong to him,' Trumper said.

I think I'd have hit him, only another rumble from the fat man distracted me.

'I said I wrote you no note. That is true, but if it matters to you, the note was written on my instructions. As soon as I knew of your father's misfortune, I sent a man back to England with the sole purpose of finding you and saving you unnecessary distress.'

But there was no concern for anybody's distress in the eyes that watched my face unblinkingly.

'He hated duels,' I said. 'He'd never in his life have fought a duel.'

'Sometimes a man has no choice,' Trumper said.

The fat man paid no attention to him, his eyes still on me.

'That is beside the point. Tell me, did your father communicate with you at all when he was in Paris or Dover?'

Why I answered his question instead of asking my own, I don't know, unless those eyes and that voice had a kind of mesmeric force.

'He wrote me a letter from Paris to say he was coming home.'

There was no reason not to tell him. Even talking about my father seemed a way of fighting them. Trumper sat up, feet to the floor, face turned greedily to mine. The fat man leaned forward.

'What did your father say in this letter?'

I was more cautious now.

'He said he'd enjoyed meeting some friends in Paris, but was looking forward to being back in England.'

'Gentlemen friends or women friends?' said Trumper, eager as a terrier at a rat hole.

The fat man looked at him with some contempt, but let him take over the questioning.

'Gentlemen friends,' I said.

'Did he mention any women?'

The eagerness of Trumper's question, practically panting with his tongue hanging out, made me feel that my father's memory was being dirtied. In defence of him, I told the truth.

'He mentioned that he'd met an unfortunate woman who needed his charity.'

And realised, from the look on Trumper's face and a

shifting in the fat man's weight that made the carriage tilt sidewards, that I'd made a mistake.

'Did he mention a name?' Trumper said.

'No.'

'You're sure of that?'

'I'm sure.'

'Or any more about her?'

'Nothing.'

'What did he propose to do about her?'

His letter had implied quite clearly that he was bringing her back to London with him.

'I really don't know,' I said. 'It was only a casual mention of her.'

'She's lying.' The fat man growled it without particular enmity, as if he expected people to lie. 'He was bringing her back to England with him, wasn't he, miss?'

'It seems you know more than I do, so why do you ask me?'

'He abducted her from Paris. We know that, so you need not trouble yourself to lie about it.'

'My father would not take away any woman against her will.'

'Did he write to you from Calais?'

'No. That letter from Paris was his last.'

'Are you carrying it with you?'

'No!'

From the fat man's stare, I expected him to order Trumper to search me there and then, and shrank back in the corner of the seat.

'Did he tell you to meet the woman at Dover?'

'No, of course not. I was waiting to meet him, only he didn't even know it.'

'Do you know where he lodged in Calais?'

It heartened me that their inquiries round Calais must have been as fruitless as mine.

'No. Not at any of the big hotels, I know that much.'

'So do we,' Trumper said, rather wearily.

The horses were moving at a fast trot now, the well-sprung carriage almost floating along. There was something I hadn't noticed until then, with the shock and the questioning.

'This isn't the way back to Calais.'

'It's a better road,' Trumper said.

I didn't know enough about the area to contradict him, but I edged forward in my seat, trying to see out of the window. We were stirring up such clouds of dust that I couldn't make out much more than the outlines of bushes. A look passed between the two men. Trumper pulled down the window and shouted something to the coachman that I couldn't hear above the sound of wheels and hooves. The whip cracked and the rhythm of our journey changed as four powerful horses stretched out in a canter. I'd never travelled so fast before. Trumper hastily shut the window as a cloud of white dust blew up round us. I reached for the door handle. I don't know whether I'd have been capable of flinging myself out at such a speed, but there was no chance to tell, because Trumper's heavy hand clamped mine and forced it down on my lap.

'Sit still. We're not doing you any harm.'

'Please take me back to Calais at once.'

'You must understand . . .' Trumper said. He had both of my hands now and was trying so hard to keep them held down that he was pressing them between my thighs. When I struggled it made things worse. The sweat was running down his forehead. He kept glancing over at the fat man, as if for approval, but the suety face watched impassively.

'We are only trying to protect you,' Trumper pleaded. 'You saw what happened back in the graveyard. You wouldn't stay in Dover as you were told, so all we intend is to take you somewhere safe until the trouble your father's stirred up settles down again.'

'Take me where?'

'There's a nice little house by a lake, very friendly and ladylike, good healthy air. It will set you up nicely.'

He sounded like some wheedling hotelier. I laughed at him.

'The truth is, you're kidnapping me.'

'No. Concern for your safety, that's all. I'm sure your father would have wanted it.'

'My family will miss me. My brother will come after you.'

'Your brother's in India. You have no close family.'

This growl from the fat man froze me, both from the bleak truth of it and the fact that this creature knew so much about me. For a while I could do nothing but try to keep back the tears. I suppose Trumper must have

55

felt me relax because he let go of my hands and sat back, though keeping so close to me that I was practically wedged in the corner of the carriage. The horses flew on, sixteen hooves thudding like war drums on the dry road, harness chains jingling crazed carillons. Several times the whip cracked and the coachman shouted, I supposed to warn slower conveyances out of our way. Dust stung my eyes, at least giving me an excuse for tears. Trumper started coughing but the other man seemed unaffected. Then –

'What the hell . . .?'

We'd stopped so abruptly that Trumper and I were propelled off our seats and on to the fat man. It was like being flung into a loathsome bolster. Above the unclean smell of it, and Trumper's curses from floor level, I was aware of things going on outside – loud whinnying, whip cracks and the coachman's voice, high with alarm, yelling at the horses. The carriage started bouncing and jerked forward several times. Trumper had been trying to claw his way up by hanging on to my skirt. This sent him back to the floor again, but since he still had a handful of skirt, it dragged me down with him. My face was level with the fat man's belly, a vast bulge of pale breeches, like a sail with the wind behind it.

There are better uses for your head than employing it as a bludgeon.

My father's voice from fifteen years back, on the occasion of a schoolroom quarrel when I'd butted my brother and caused his nose to bleed. I thought, Well, I'm sorry, Father, but even you are not always right, closed my eyes, drew my head back, and used all my strength to propel it like a cannonball towards the bulging belly.

There is no arrangement of letters that will reproduce the sound that resulted, as if an elephant had trodden on a gargantuan and ill-tuned set of bagpipes. The smell of foul air expelled was worse. The combination must have disconcerted Trumper because he made no attempt to stop me as I stood up and grasped the door handle. From the squawk he made, I may have trampled his hand in the process. As the door began to open I let my weight fall on it and tumbled out into the road. A pain in my elbow, dust in clouds round me, then the front wheel of the carriage travelling backwards, so close that it almost ran over my hand. I rolled sideways. Something in the dust cloud. Legs. A whole mobile grove of short pink legs. Much shouting all round me and other sounds, grunting sounds. A questing pink snout touched my cheek, quite gently, and a familiar farmyard smell filled the air, pleasanter than the one inside the coach. A herd of pigs. By some dispensation of Providence, the flying carriage had met with the one obstacle that couldn't be whipped or bullied aside. Many horses fear pigs and, judging by the way the lead horse was rearing and whinnying, he was of that persuasion.

I pushed the snout aside and stood up. The coachman was standing on the ground, trying to pull the horse down with one hand, threshing the butt of his whip at a milling mass of pigs and French peasantry, shouting obscenities. I took one look, turned and ran into the bushes beside the road. More shouting behind me, Trumper's voice from the direction of the coach, yelling to me to come back. I ran, following animal tracks through the bushes, with no sense of direction except getting as far away as I could. After some time I stopped, heart beating, expecting to hear the bushes rustling behind me and Trumper bursting through.

'Miss Lane. Come back, Miss Lane.'

His voice, but sounding breathless and mercifully coming from a long way off. I judged he must still be on the road, so I struck off as far as the tracks would let me at right angles to it. It was hard going in my heeled shoes so I took them off and went stocking-footed. After a while I came on to a wider track, probably one used by farm carts, with a ditch and bank on either side. I scrambled up the bank and saw, not far away, the sun glinting on blue sea. From there, it was a matter of two or three miles to the shore, with Calais a little way in the distance.

I thought a lot as I walked along the shore towards the town, none of it much to the purpose, and chiefly about how strange it was when pieces of time refused to join together any more to make a past or future. I realise that is not expressed with philosophic elegance, in the way of my father's friends, but then I'm no philosopher.

A few days ago I had a future which might have been vague in some of its details but flowed in quite an orderly way from my life up to then. I also possessed twenty-two years of a past which – although not entirely orderly – accounted for how I had come to be at a particular place and time. But since that message had arrived at the inn at Dover, I'd been as far removed from my past as if it existed in a half-forgotten dream. As for my future, I simply did not possess one. Futures are made up of small expectations – tonight I shall sleep in my own bed, tomorrow we shall have cold beef for supper and I'll sew new ribbons on my bonnet, on Friday the cat will probably have her kittens. I had no expectations, not the smallest. I didn't know where or when I would sleep or eat or what I would do, not then or for the rest of my life.

I walked along, noticing how large the feet of gulls look when they wheel overhead, how far the fishermen have to walk over the sand to dig for worms when the tide goes out, how the white bladder campion flowers earlier on the French side of the Channel than on the cliffs back home. It was only when I came to the first of the houses that I remembered I was supposed to be a rational being and that, if a future was necessary, I had better set about stringing one together. Small things first. I sat down on the grass at the edge of the shingle and examined the state of my feet. Stocking soles were worn away, several toes sticking through. I put my shoes back on, twisting what was left of the stocking feet round so that the holes were more or less hidden. The bottom of my skirt was draggled with bits of straw and dried seaweed, but a good brushing with my hand dealt with that. My hair, from the feel of it, had reverted to its primitive state of tangled curls, but since there was no remedy for that until I regained comb and mirror, all I could do was push as much of it as possible under my bonnet.

All the time I was tidying myself up, my mind was running over the events in the carriage and coming back to one question. Who was this woman they wanted so much? In my father's letter, she'd been not much more than a passing reference, an object of charity. If she was so important, or so beautiful, that she could be the cause of all this, why hadn't he given me some notion of it? But I had to tear my mind away from her and decide what I was going to do with myself. I reasoned it out this way. My father, without meaning to, had bequeathed me two sets of enemies, one represented by the thin man in black, the other by so-called Trumper and the fat man. The second set hated the first set so much that they were prepared to commit murder – since for all I knew the man in black might have died from the blow to his head. Both sides had wanted me to stay at Dover. Now the man in black wanted me to go back there, while Trumper and the fat man were planning to carry me off to some unknown destination by a lake. Geneva? Como? Or perhaps they had in mind the mythical waters of Acheron, from which travellers do not return. Stay in France or return to England? I feared the fat man and Trumper more than the man in black, though I hated all of them equally. If I stayed in France, they might capture me again. Quite probably they were looking for me already. So Dover seemed the safer option, and as quickly and inconspicuously as possible.

Footsore and hungry, I started towards the harbour to inquire among the fishing boats, thinking my enemies would be less likely to find me there than in the crowds coming and going around the steam packet landing place. Then, when I'd gone halfway, I told myself I was being a fool. Among the fishing boats and obviously not a fisherman's wife or daughter I might as well carry a banner marked *Foreigner*. If Trumper came looking for me, he'd find me in minutes. If there was any safety for me, it was in numbers. I turned back for the centre of town, queued at a kiosk and milked my small purse almost to its limits to buy a ticket to Dover on the steam packet.

The quay was already reassuringly crowded with fellow passengers, most of them English. There was a wine merchant with a retinue of porters, clucking over his boxes and barrels, several families with children and screaming babies, even a troupe of Gypsy dancers and jugglers who were collecting a few francs by entertaining the crowd. There was no sign of Trumper or the fat man. I bought a tartine and a cup of strong coffee from a man who'd set up a stall near the gangplank and found a refuge on the edge of the harbour wall, behind packing cases that looked as if they hadn't been moved for some time.

I sat with my back to a bollard until puffs of steam came out of the funnel of the packet and a shrill whistle blew. That was the signal for the carriages with the richer passengers to set out from the hotels. I watched from the shelter of the packing cases as three of them arrived in a line, with liveried footmen at the back and hotel carts with piles of trunks and boxes following. Still no sign of Trumper's coach. The gentry from the carriages went on board, fashionably dressed and obviously proud of themselves for surviving their tours of Europe. Their servants followed, arms full of blankets, sunshades, shawls, umbrellas and large china bowls in case the sea turned impolite in mid-Channel.

I was on the point of leaving my hiding place when another carriage came rattling up in a hurry, drawn by two greys, with a hotel's initials on the door. A tall, dark-haired young man was first out. I recognised him as the brother of the girl who'd been kind to me at the hotel. She followed him out, in a different Parisian hat and a travelling cloak of sky-blue merino, the sun glinting on her bright hair, and they crossed the wharf towards the gangplank. I dodged back out of sight, not wanting her to notice me again after my weakness in the hotel. The man I took to be their father had stopped to say something to the coachman – nothing grateful, judging by the expression on his face as he followed them over the cobbles. I waited until the three of them had disappeared on board, then, as the steam whistle blew a last long blast, pushed into the middle of a final rush of people – one of the families with a crying baby, a porter with a trunk on his back, a juggler with his sack of clubs over his shoulder.

Most of the fashionable passengers had gone below. I made my way to the stern and stood by the rail, watching sandy water churning between us and the quay. Ashore, the carriages that had brought passengers were manoeuvring round each other to go back to the hotels. The little crowd that had watched the steam packet depart was drifting away. A man in a royal-blue jacket was walking slowly towards the town, head bent and hands in his pockets. My heart pounded like a steam engine. There was no mistaking, in that air of a person who'd be more at home with a pack of hounds at his feet, the man who called himself Harry Trumper. I got myself as quickly as I could to the far rail. When the first shock had passed, I marvelled at my luck. Trumper had got there in time after all and only my embarrassed wish not to be seen by the girl had saved me. Without meaning to, she'd done me another kindness.

I stayed on a bench at the stern for most of the crossing. The smoke from the funnel blew back over it, dropping a rain of ash and smuts, but it was worth the smuts to know that none of the fashionable passengers would walk there. Strangely, though, one came quite close. It was towards the end of the crossing, dark by then, with some travellers standing at the rails to watch as the lamplit windows round Dover harbour came closer. A woman in a travelling cloak walked slowly in my direction, though not seeing me. Her head was bent and she seemed thoughtful or dejected. Then a shower of red sparks came out of the funnel and a man called from behind her.

'Be careful, Celia.'

'I'm quite all right, Stephen. Why can't you leave me alone?'

A voice with an attractive lisp. In spite of her protest to her brother, she turned obediently, still without seeing me. When she was safely gone I whispered into the darkness, 'Thank you, Celia.'

CHAPTER SIX

We'd slowed down for some reason towards the end of the journey, so the packet didn't tie up at Dover until the dark hours of the morning. Tired passengers filed down the gangplank into a circle of light cast by oil lamps round the landing stage. A two-horse carriage was waiting for Celia and her family. It whirled away as soon as they were inside, so they must have left servants to bring on the luggage.

With no reason to hurry, I disembarked with the last group of passengers, ordinary people with no carriages to meet them. Beyond the circle of light was a shadowed area of piled-up packing cases and huge casks. I felt as wary as a cat in a strange yard, half expecting Trumper or the fat man to step out and accost me, not quite believing I'd managed to leave them on the far side of the Channel. I walked along the dark seafront, listening for footsteps behind me but hearing nothing. There were very few people about, even the taverns were closed. When I turned into a side street, a few sailors were lying senseless on the doorsteps and my shoe soles slipped in the pools of last night's indulgence. An old woman, so bent that her chin almost touched the pavement, scavenged for rags in the gutter, disturbing a great rat that ran across the pavement in front of me into a patch of lamplight from a window. It was holding a piece of black crepe in its teeth. The old woman made a grab for it but missed and the rat darted on, trailing its prize, a mourning band from a hat or sleeve. The lamplight fell on the arm of one of the horizontal sailors, and I saw that he too was wearing a mourning band.

'Has somebody died?' I asked the rag woman.

I had to stoop down to hear her reply, from toothless gums, 'The king.'

She was adding something else, hard to make out. Itty icky? I made sense of it at the third try.

'Oh yes, so it's Little Vicky.'

William's niece, Victoria Alexandrina, a round-faced girl of eighteen, now Queen of Great Britain, Ireland and a large part of the globe besides. So a reign had ended and another begun while I'd been in Calais. It seemed less important than the coldness of my toes through the stocking holes.

I walked, sat on the sea wall then walked again, until

it was around six in the morning and I could show myself at the Heart of Oak. It had a new black bow on the door knocker.

'You again,' the landlord said, bleary eyed.

I collected my bag that I'd left in his keeping, secured my cheap side room again and requested a pot of tea, carried up by the same maid who'd brought me water to wash my hair on that Sunday morning, when I'd been so pleased with myself, not quite three days ago, but another lifetime. I slept for a couple of hours then put my head out of the room as another maid was hurrying past and asked for more tea, also writing materials. The pen she brought me was the same crossed nibbed one with its ink-stained holder that I'd used to write that foolish, light-hearted note to my father. It now served to write a very different letter to my brother Tom. I wrote on the top of the wash-stand, with my travelling mantle wrapped round me for a dressing gown.

Dear Tom,

I am sorrier than anything in the world to be sending such grief to you. I have to tell you that our beloved father is no more. He was killed in an accident in Calais, on his way home from escorting his charges on their Grand Tour of Europe. I was present at his burial. I know that when you read this, the first impulse of your kind heart will be to come home to me,

whatever the cost to your career. I am certain
that I speak with the authority of our father in
saying that you must do no such thing. I am as
well as may be expected in the face of such
news, and as you know we have relatives who
– while they may not be over-brimming with
the milk of human kindness towards our
father's children – are much aware of the
demands of Family Duty.

May God bless you, my dear, dear brother
and help you to bear your grief. I am at present
at Dover, and shall write again as soon as I am
more settled, with an address.

Your loving sister
Libby

Are you blaming me? If so, read it again and admit
that there is not one lie in it. Accident? Well, murder
is an accident to the victim, is it not? And suppose I
had written *Dear Tom, Our father has been murdered*
. . . would he have waited tamely in Bombay? No, he
would have been home on the next ship and all our
sacrifice in parting with him for the sake of his future
would have been wasted. Surely there had been enough
waste already. And the relatives? That was no lie either.
Three or four aunts would have indeed taken me in
from cold Duty. I was not bound to write in my letter
what I felt – that I should sooner put on pink tights
and dance in the opera or ride horses bareback in a

circus than accept the wintery charity of any of them. I should have had to pay dearly for it in endless days of criticism of my father. They'd be all too eager to believe the lie that he had been killed in a duel, hugging it to their hearts under their yellowed flannel chemises. Over the years, I'd dwindle to the grey and dusty poor relative in the corner of the room furthest from the fire, doling out physic in careful teaspoons, combing fleas from the lapdog. Besides, if I went to any of the aunts I'd have no freedom, hardly allowed to walk in the garden without asking permission. They would certainly not permit me to do the only thing in my life that made sense – discover who killed my father and why.

I addressed my letter by his full name, Thomas Fraternity Lane, care of the Company's offices in London. They should send it on by the first available boat, but it would still be weeks or months before it came into Tom's hands. I drew the curtains across the window and started to dress myself to take it to the post. The stockings I'd walked in were beyond mending and had to be thrown away. This reminded me that most of my clothes and possessions were in a trunk at Chalke Bissett. When I left them there I had assumed it would be only a matter of days before we'd be sending for it from our new lodgings in London. I unpacked my bag, picked up the pen again and made a list:

1 *merino travelling mantle with wide sleeves*
1 *straw bonnet with lavender ribbon*

1 *pair of brown leather shoes for day (scuffed and soles worn thin)*
1 *day dress (lavender cotton)*
1 *day dress (blue-and-white cotton print)*
1 *white muslin tucker embroidered with lilies of the valley*
1 *silk fichu pelerine trimmed with Valencienne lace*
1 *cotton petticoat*
1 *pair stays, blue satin covered*
1 *pair garters*
1 *pair white silk stockings*
1 *pair blue worsted stockings*
1 *pair white cotton gloves (soiled with smuts from the steam packet)*
2 *ribbons (blue, white)*

At that point, the maid came in for the tray. She looked so tired and was so shy that I couldn't refrain from tipping her sixpence, which reminded me of the thinness of my purse. I shook the coins out on the bed and counted those too:

1 *sovereign*
7 *shillings*
3 *pennies*
2 *halfpennies*
Total: £1 7s 4d.

This was not inspiriting. I'd have to make my rounds of the jewellers again, this time selling the last thing I had, a gold-mounted cameo ring my father had bought for me at Naples. I put on the lavender dress, packed the rest of the clothes into my bag and went out to take my letter to the post. The streets were crowded, full of carts and carriages coming and going from the harbour, an Italian playing a barrel organ with a monkey collecting coins in its hat. The tunes were jaunty, but the monkey had a black bow round its neck in concession to our supposed national grief. I kept glancing round, wary of anybody who seemed interested in me.

It was worse when I reached the office and had to stand in a queue behind several others. The fat man's agent had come looking for me in this place. The only way he could have known to deliver the note to the Heart of Oak was by intercepting the letter to my father I'd left there. I looked at the old clerk, sitting on his high stool with his pen behind his ear and ledger open on the counter in front of him, wondering, 'Are you in their pay?' When it came to my turn he blinked at me short-sightedly through his glasses, with no sign of recognition, and accepted my letter.

'Is there anything poste restante for Mr Thomas Jacques Lane?' I said, trying to make my voice sound casual. There had been three letters when I first inquired. The clerk blinked again and went over to a bank of pigeonholes. My heart thumped when he took out just one sheet of folded paper. Who'd taken the others?

'You have his authority to collect this?'

'Yes. I am his daughter.'

He gave me a doubtful look, asked me to sign the ledger, then handed it over. I hurried out with my prize, looking for a quiet place to read, already puzzled by the feel of it in my hand. It was thick, coarse paper with a smell about it, oddly familiar and comforting. I touched a gloved fingertip to my nose. Hoof oil, memories of stables and warm, well-tended horses. I took refuge in the doorway of a pawnbroker's shop with boarded-up windows and unfolded it.

With Ruspect Sir, We be here safly awayting yr convenunce if you will kindly let know where you be staying.

This in big, disorderly writing and a signature like duck tracks in mud: *Amos Legge.* I couldn't help laughing because it was so far from what I'd been expecting. Certainly not from one of my father's friends, yet hardly from an enemy either. Neither the man in black nor the one who called himself Trumper would write like that. I went back to the office, paid tuppence for the use of inkwell, pen and paper, and left a note for Mr Amos Legge, saying that I was Mr Lane's daughter and I'd be grateful if he would call on me at the Heart of Oak. I strolled back to the inn taking a round-about route by way of the seafront. As I passed a baker's shop, the smell of fresh bread reminded me that I was hungry and had eaten nothing since the tartine on the other side of the Channel. I stood in the queue behind a line of messenger boys and kitchen maids and paid a penny for a small white loaf, then, with a sudden craving for sweet things, four pence more for two almond tartlets topped with crisp brown sugar. I carried them back to the Heart of Oak, intending to picnic on them in my room and spare the expense of having a meal sent up.

As bad luck would have it, the landlord was in the hall. His little eyes went straight to my paper parcel, calculating profit lost.

'How long are you planning to stay here – madam?'

The moment's pause before 'madam' just stopped short of being insulting.

'Tonight at least, possibly longer.'

'We like payment on account from ladies and gentlemen without proper luggage.'

In other words, I was not respectable and he expected me to bilk him. Biting back my anger, telling myself that I couldn't afford to make more enemies, I parted with a sovereign, salving my pride by demanding a receipt. As he went away, grumbling, to write it, the door from the street opened.

''Scuse me for troubling you, ma'am, but be there a Miss Lane staying 'ere?'

I stared. The door-frame of the Heart of Oak was high and wide, but he filled it, six and a half feet tall at least with shoulders in proportion. His hair was the shiny light-brown colour of good hay, topped with a felt hat which looked as if it might have doubled as a polisher, his eyes blue as speedwells. The clean tarry smell of hoof oil wafted off him.

'You must be Amos Legge,' I said, marvelling. Then, 'I am Mr Lane's daughter.'

He grinned, good white teeth against the brown of his face.

'I thought you was when I see'd you back there, only I didn't like to make myself familiar, look. You do resemble 'im. 'E be here then?'

For an instant, seeing and feeling the cheerfulness of him, I was back in a safer world and I think I smiled back at him. Then it hit me that the world had changed and he didn't know it.

'I think we had better go in here,' I said, indicating the snug.

His grin faded but he followed me, stuffing the felt hat into his pocket, dipping his head to get through the lower doorway of the snug. I left the door open to the hall, otherwise the landlord would have put the worst interpretation on it.

'Had you known my father long?' I asked him.

His speech might be slow but his mind wasn't. He'd already caught a whiff of something wrong.

'Nobbut ten days or so, miss, when he helped me out of a bit of a ruckus in Paris. We was to go on to Dover and wait for 'im 'ere. Yesterday morning we got in.'

'We?'

I'd put my parcel of bread and cakes down on the table and the wrapping had fallen open. Unconsciously, his big brown hands went to the loaf and tore it in half. It would have been unforgivably impolite, except he did it naturally as a bird eats seed. He chewed, swallowed.

'Rancie and me.'

'Rancie?'

'That's right. Is 'e not here yet, then?'

He ate another piece of loaf.

'He's dead,' I said.

His eyes went blank with shock, as if somebody had hit him. He shook his head from side to side, like an ox troubled by flies.

'When 'e said goodbye to me and Rancie, he was as healthy as any man you'd ever see. Was it the fever, miss?'

'He was shot,' I said.

He blinked. Amazingly, his blue eyes were awash with tears.

'Oh, the poor gentleman. Those damned thieving frogs . . . Excuse me, ma'am, but you can't trust them, whatever they say. He should've come back with Rancie and me. I'd 'ave seen 'im safe.'

'I don't know that he was shot by a Frenchman.' I'd decided to trust him. I had to trust somebody, and he was as unlike Trumper or the man in black as any person could be. 'The fact is, there's some mystery

75

about it, and I need to find out everything I can about what happened to my father over the past week or ten days.'

I told him about the black lie and what had happened in Calais. As he listened, he engulfed first one then the other of the almond tarts, not taking his eyes from my face.

'How did you and my father meet?' I said. 'You mentioned something about a . . . a ruckus.'

He wiped crumbs from his mouth with his sleeve.

'I got in a bit of disaccord with a frog on account 'e was driving a horse that was as lame as a three-legged dog, only 'e didn't speak English and so there was no reasoning with 'im, look. So the frog took a polt at me, only I fetched 'im one first, and 'arder. No great mishtiff done to 'im, but 'is friends were creating about it and I reckon they'd've 'ad me in prison except Mr Lane saw what 'appened and made them see sense.'

Of course my father would side with the defender of a lame horse. I imagined that he must have slipped some money to the Frenchman to save Amos Legge from having to explain himself to a Parisian judge.

'So you see, when Mr Lane mentioned 'e was puzzled 'ow to get Rancie back to England, I was glad to be of use.'

'So you brought her back for him?' I said.

It amazed me that while the fat man and his agents were scouring Paris and Calais for this mysterious and fatal woman, this well-meaning giant should have escorted her across the Channel, apparently without fuss. But my heart was heavy and resentful because she – whoever she was – had survived and my father had not.

'Is she here in Dover?'

He nodded. 'I've got 'er here safe, yes.'

'Then I suppose I'd better come and see her.'

'Just what I was going to suggest myself, miss.'

The landlord was lurking in the hall, probably listening.

'Your receipt – madam.'

I tore it out of his hand. He looked up at Amos Legge then down at me with a greasy gleam in his eyes that made me want to kick him. I wanted to kick the entire world. I stalked out of the door, Legge behind me. I more than half resented him for bringing this female and when he came up alongside me, walking respectfully on the outside of the pavement, I kept as much space between us as I could. He must have sensed my mood because he uttered no more than 'Left, miss,' or 'Across 'ere, miss,' taking us towards the landward side of the town, away from the crowded streets.

Who was this Rancie person? Badly treated servant girl? Wronged wife? Betrayed sweetheart? Any of those could have appealed to my father's chivalrous and romantic instincts. He'd eloped with my mother and they lived ten years blissfully together until fever took her. He grieved all his life, but there is no denying that his nature inclined to women. He loved their company, their beauty, their wit. In our wandering life together there'd been Susannas, Rosinas, Conchitas, Helenas . . . I do not mean that my father was a Don Juan, a ruthless seducer. If anything, quite the reverse. Far from being ruthless, he'd do almost anything to help a woman in distress. His purse, his house, his heart would be open to her, sometimes for months at a time. Undeniable, too, that some of the Susannas, Conchitas and Rosinas took advantage of his chivalrous nature.

'There's no great 'urry, miss. She won't run away,' Amos Legge protested.

I suppose I was walking fast. We were clear of the town now, only a farm and barns on one side of the road, a broken-down livery stable on the other.

Well, if it had happened like that, it wouldn't have been the first time. But it had been the last. Violent husband or bullying father had resented it, caught up with him. For the first time, my unbelief in the black lie wavered. Suppose, against his will, that he had been forced into a duel after all.

'Nearly there, miss,' Amos Legge said.

We were level with the farm. I expected him to turn in at the gateway. Perhaps my father had instructed him to lodge this Rancie hussy out of town, for her protection. But we walked past the farm gateway and turned in under the archway of the livery stable with its faded signboard, *Hunters and Hacks for Hire*. There was a groom sweeping the yard. Amos Legge nodded at him and took my arm to keep me from treading in a trail of horse droppings. I drew the arm away. Seeming unoffended, he walked over to a loose-box in the corner, letting out a piercing whistle. A horse's head came over the door, nostrils flared in curiosity, eyes bold and questioning.

'What . . .?'

I was caught off balance, assuming that our journey was not yet over and we would have to ride. Amos Legge stroked the horse's nose, whispered something then turned to me, the grin back on his face.

'Well, miss, 'ere's Rancie for you.' Then to me, alarmed, 'My poor little maid, what be you crying for?'

CHAPTER SEVEN

I had the story of Rancie from Amos Legge, sitting in a broken-down chair in the tack room, saddles and harness all round us and flakes of chaff floating in the sunbeams that pierced the curtain of cobwebs over the window. He stayed respectfully standing at first.

'You see, miss, it all starts with a Hereford bull, look. Red Sultan of Shortwood 'is name was in the 'erd book, only we called 'im Reddy.'

He was clearly one of those storytellers who liked to take his time. I suggested he should sit down. He settled for a compromise, hitching a haunch on to a vacant saddle tree. I'll abandon my attempt to record his accent because in truth the broad Hereford he talked is the hardest thing in the world to pin down. Those dropped 'h's, for instance, are nowhere near the care-lessness of the Cockney, more like the murmur of a summer breeze through willow leaves over a slow-flowing river.

'Reddy belonged to this farmer I used to work for, name of Priest. Well, there was this Frenchman at a place called Sancloo, just outside Paris, decided he was going to build up a herd of Herefords. They do well anywhere, only you can't get the same shine on their coats away from the red soil at home, no matter how –'

'But Rancie and my father?'

'I'm getting to them, miss. Anyways, this Frenchman got to hear about Reddy and nothing would content him except he should have him. He offered old Priest a thousand guineas and all the expenses of the journey met, so we made Reddy a covered travelling cart fit for the sultan he was, and off to Sancloo we went, old Priest and Reddy and me. It took us four days and ten changes of horses to get to the sea, then another six days once we got to the French side, but we got Reddy safely to the gentleman, Old Priest pocketed his thousand guineas, and what do you think happened then?'

'You met my father?'

'Not yet, I'm coming to that. What happened was the old dev—, excuse me . . . He just took off for home and left me. He said all that travelling had brought on his arthritics, so he was going home the quickest way by coach. I was to follow him with the travelling cart and he'd give me my pay when I fetched it safely back to Hereford. So there I was in a foreign country, not knowing a blessed soul. So I took myself into Paris, thinking I'd have a look at it after coming all this way, and that's when I met your father. After he'd settled my bit of trouble, he mentioned he had a mare he wanted to bring back, and it came to me that if the cart had been good enough for Reddy, it would do for the mare, as long as I washed it down well to take the smell away.'

'Did he tell you how he came by the horse?'

Amos swatted a fly away from his face.

'Won her at cards, from some French fellow.'

'Did he say if the French fellow was angry about it?'

'No. From the way he told it, the mare had already changed hands three times on a turn of the cards. Your father was thinking of selling her in Paris, only he looked at her papers and decided to keep her.'

'Papers?'

'Oh yes, she's got her papers. And he wanted you to see her.'

'He said so?'

'He said he'd got a daughter at home with an eye for a horse as good as any man's, and it would be a surprise for her.'

I had to blink hard to stop myself crying again. My father loved a good horse as much as he loved music or wine or poetry, and I suppose I caught it from him.

'Was my father to travel with you?'

'No. He had things he wanted to do before he left Paris, he said. Me and the horse were to start right away and he'd probably go past us on the road, because we'd be travelling slowly. But if we didn't happen to meet in France, I was to wait for him at Dover and leave a message, which I did.'

'How was he, when you saw him?'

'How do you mean, miss?'

'Well or ill? Harassed or anxious at all?'

'Blithe as a blackbird, miss.'

'Did you talk much?'

'I told him I didn't think much to France, and he laughed and said it was the best place in the world, apart from England. He'd missed England, and you, and he was glad to be going home and settling with a bit of money in his pocket. Quite open about that, he was, and paid me expenses for the journey.'

'Did you meet any of his friends?'

'Yes, I did. When he'd finished sorting out my bit of business it was late so I had to stay the night in the same hotel where he was. He had friends there and they were up all hours talking and playing music. I looked into the room at midnight to say did he want me any more or could I go to bed? He said to sit down and take a glass of punch to help me sleep, which I did.'

'These friends, how many would you say?'

He thought, rubbing his head. 'Half a dozen at least, maybe more.'

'English or French?'

'Mostly English, but a couple of Frenchmen. Your

father was jabbering away to them in their lingo, easy as I'm talking to you.'

'Did they seem angry?'

'Not in the world. They were as comfortable a crew as you'd see anywhere; bowl of punch, pipes going, some books open on the tables – quite a few books, I remember – and fiddles and flutes and so on all over the place.'

It rang true. My father had a knack of finding friends wherever he happened to be. As children, many's the time Tom and I had crept out of our beds and looked through keyholes at exactly the scene Amos was describing.

'Were there any women there?'

'Not one. All gentlemen.'

'Do you remember what any of the men looked like?'

'Not to describe, no. Truth was, I was dog-tired by then.'

'Was one of them a thin, elderly man with a greyish face, dressed all in black?'

'I don't recall any elderly men there. They were mostly about your father's age.'

'Or a very fat man?'

'A couple of them stoutish, I wouldn't say very fat.'

'Or a young fair-haired Englishman in a blue jacket?'

'I don't recall a blue jacket, no.'

A blank. If my father's convivial party had included a snake in the grass, I was no nearer to him.

'Can you describe anybody there at all?'

Amos thought hard.

'There was this little black-haired gentleman, played the fiddle like he was possessed by Old Nick.'

'Not much taller than I am?'

He nodded.

'In his mid-thirties, and very thin?'

'Thin as a peeled withy.'

'With his hair coming to a point like this?'

I sketched a widow's peak on my forehead with my finger.

'Yes, that's the gentleman. You know him, miss?'

'Daniel Suter.'

I felt myself smiling as I said the name, it brought back so many good memories. Daniel Suter was one of my father's dearest friends, although around ten years younger than he was. He had ambitions as a composer but had to earn his living as a musician, playing everything from a piccolo to a cello. It was not surprising that he should be in Paris or that, being there, he and my father should have found their way to each other. It was my first step forward, that at least I knew the name of someone who'd shared part of my father's last week on earth. Daniel was witty, observant. If anything had happened in Paris, he'd know about it. The only drawback was that he was presumably still in Paris.

'Did you see any of them again?'

'No. Next morning your father met me downstairs at the hotel and took me round the corner to where the horse was kept. It was just daylight. He was wearing the same clothes he'd had on the night before, so likely he hadn't gone to bed.'

It was indeed quite likely.

'And there seemed nothing strange about him?'

'Nothing at all. Happy as a lad on a day's holiday, and pleased with himself on account of the horse. So we went to the stables and I took her off to where the cart was waiting.'

'And that was the last you saw of him?'

'Waving us on our way, yes.'

He asked if I wanted a proper look at the mare. My tearful reaction had clearly disappointed him, and indeed it was poor recompense for having brought her so far. We crossed the yard to the corner loosebox and he put a headcollar on her and walked her into the sun.

'Well, miss?'

No tears this time, but precious little breath to answer him. You know sometimes when you see a special picture or hear a few bars of music you feel a shock to the heart, as if you'd just breathed in frosty air, a delight so intense that it feels like fear? Well, that was the way I felt seeing the mare. She was a bright bay, not tall, no more than fifteen and a half hands at most, clean legs and a long build suggesting speed, broad chest for a good heart. Her eye was remarkably large and intelligent, ears well shaped and forward pricked,

86

small white blaze shaped like a comma. Above all, from the way she was standing and looking at me, she was used to admiration and knew she deserved it. *Ton*, the French call it, the highest praise for a fashionable lady or a dandy. The mare had *ton* enough for ten. She moved a step towards me, took the fabric of my sleeve very gently between flexible lips as if testing it, seemed to approve. I took off my glove and ran a hand down her neck, over her firmly muscled shoulder.

'Who is she?'

It seemed fitting to ask it that way, as if she were a person.

'The papers are here, if you want to see.'

When Amos had gone for the headcollar he'd also fetched an old leather saddlebag. There were two papers inside. One, dated the day before my father's last letter to me and written on a leaf torn from a pocket book, made over the mare, Esperance, to T. J. Lane Esq, in quittance of all debts incurred. The other was her pedigree. Now, as far as human lineage was concerned, my father was the least respectful person in the world and would sooner take off his hat to a crossing sweeper than a royal duke. Horses were a different matter. His friends joked that he could recite the breeding of any racehorse that ever ran, right back to the two that Noah took into the Ark. I unfolded the paper and . . .

'Oh Lord.'

'Something the matter, miss?'

'She's a great-great-granddaughter of Eclipse. And

there's the Regulus Mare in there, and she's half sister to Touchstone that won the Ascot Gold Cup last year and . . . oh Lord.'

The more I read, the more my head reeled. I looked at the mare, half expecting a pair of silver wings to sprout from her withers. She looked back at me, gracious and affable.

'He reckoned she was a good horse,' Amos said.

The flies were gathering and he said he'd better take her back inside. I followed slowly, trying to get back some composure. We were standing in the shadowy box, watching her nosing at the hay in the manger, when a dark shape came hurtling out of nowhere so fast I felt the wind of it ruffling my hair, making straight as a lance for the mare. I shouted, moved to protect her, but the thing was too fast and landed on her back. Amos laughed.

'Don't worry, miss. It's nowt but her cat.'

A cat like a miniature panther, sleek black fur, golden eyes staring at me as she stretched full-length along the horse's back. Rancie hadn't moved a muscle when she landed. Now she simply turned her head as if to make sure that the cat was comfortable and went back to her hay. The cat set up a purring, surprisingly loud for a small animal, that made the inside of the loosebox vibrate like a violin.

'Won't go anywhere without that cat,' Amos said. 'We tried chasing her out of the cart when we left Paris, but they made such a plunging and a caterwauling, the two of them, we had to bring her into the bargain.'

I ran a hand along the cat's velvet back.

'What's she called?'

'Lucy, I calls her.'

We watched horse and cat for a while, then went out into the sunshine. A man with white hair and a red face was standing outside the tack room, pretending to saddle-soap a pair of long reins on a hook, but looking our way.

'The owner,' Amos said, with a jerk of the head and a grimace.

I'd been thinking hard.

'That money my father gave you to bring her over – I suppose it's spent by now?'

He looked unhappy.

'I can account for every farthing of it, if it hadn't been most of it foreign, that is. But it was all spent on her.'

'I'm sure it was. But it's gone?'

He nodded.

'And the owner's watching us in case we flit with the mare?'

Another unhappy nod, along with a look of surprise. Amos didn't know it, but it wasn't the first time in my life I'd seen that look – halfway between obsequious and hostile – of a man doubting whether he'll be paid. My father always did pay, though, as soon as the cards came right.

'So we owe him for her keep. How much?'

'Two pounds three shillings, he says. He reckons it would have been more, only I've been helping him out a bit.'

I slid the cameo ring from my finger and put it into Amos's large palm.

'Would you please sell that in the town for me and pay him what's owed. If there's any over, keep it for your trouble.'

He looked at me doubtfully.

'Please,' I said. 'I should be most greatly obliged if you would.'

His reluctant fingers closed over it.

'What do you want me to do with Rancie, then?'

I said I'd let him know as soon as I'd decided, as if there were a world of possibilities open to me. He insisted on seeing me back to the door of the Heart of Oak, touched his hat and walked away.

I went straight up to my room, took off shoes, dress and stays, and lay down on the bed. 'Well,' I said to myself, 'so what are you going to do with her?'

Instead of answering that very reasonable question I fell into a day-dream, thinking of the way she'd looked at me and soft-lipped my sleeve, murmuring the syllables of her lovely French name, Esperance. I thought of what Amos had said about my father wanting me to see her. He hadn't mentioned her in his letter, so as not to spoil the surprise. Then she'd turned out to be the last of his many presents to me. Esperance, meaning

Hope. And then a hard little bit of my mind, not day-dreaming at all, said, 'At least a thousand guineas at Tattersalls.' There was no ignoring it. I was quite sure that my father – having nothing in the way of property – would have left no will. Therefore all his possessions would go to his only son, Thomas Fraternity Lane. Only Tom was many thousands of miles away, not yet twenty-one, so I was, in effect, his agent. (A lawyer would probably have told me otherwise, but I did not intend to consult one.) Therefore I could solve some of my problems at a stroke by instructing Amos to take the mare for sale at Tattersalls, along with her papers and the note transferring ownership. Once sold, I could give Amos something handsome for his trouble and he could return to his county of red cattle, hops and apples. Most of the money would go into the bank. (Would it be enough for Tom to come home? No, don't even think about that, yet.) But some of it – fifty pounds, say – I'd keep to find out the truth about my father.

Having decided that, my mind felt clearer. The thing to do was talk to Daniel Suter, the last friend I knew of to see him alive. I'd return to Paris and, if necessary, inquire at every opera house or theatre until I found him. I took my father's letter out of my bag to re-read.

My dearest Daughter,
I am glad to report that I have just said

farewell to my two noble but tedious charges . . .
I had business here in Paris . . .

That was not surprising. One of the ways in which my
father earned enough money to keep us was by acting
as a go-between for objects of art. His excellent taste,
wide travels and many friends meant that he was often
in a position to know who needed to sell and who was
aching to buy. Some classical statue or portrait of a
Versailles beauty was probably his additional business
in Paris.

> *. . . also friends to meet. To be candid, I value*
> *the chance of some intelligent conversation with*
> *like-minded fellows after these months of asses*
> *braying.*

He'd been long enough in Paris to pick up some gossip:

> *. . . I have heard one most capital story which*
> *I promise will set you roaring with laughter and*
> *even perhaps a little indignation. You know 'the*
> *dregs of their dull race . . .'*

It had puzzled me when I first read it, and still did.
Why indignation as well as laughter? As for the quota-
tion from Shelley, I knew it, of course. It came from
the poet's tirade of justified indignation against His
Majesty George III and his unpopular brood of royal

duke sons: *Old, mad, blind despis'd and dying King, Princes, the dregs of their dull race . . . mud from a muddy spring.* A fine insult, but King George was seventeen years dead. I might never hear the story, unless Daniel knew it. Still, I was making some progress. The mare to Tattersalls and I to Paris. I should have to set about it carefully though, sail from somewhere other than Dover and avoid Calais. I had no wish to see ever again the gentleman in black, or the toad-like monster, or the person who called himself Trumper. (Unless, I thought, side by side on the gallows for killing my father.)

Soon after that, I fell asleep. The decision had been made and I was mortally tired. For the first time since hearing that my father was dead I slept deeply and dreamlessly. When I opened my eyes, the jug and ewer were making a long shadow up a wall that had turned copper-coloured in the light from the setting sun. The buzz and clinking of people at dinner and drinking came up from the floor below. The strange thing was that – although I woke unhappy – there was a little island of warmth in my mind, where before there had only been cold greyness. I saw, as vividly as if they had been in the room with me, the generous eye of Esperance, Amos Legge's kind but puzzled look, even the golden stare of Lucy the cat. I had family of a kind after all, three beings who in some fashion depended on me.

And I was going to sell them. I'd decided that quite

clearly before going to sleep. Now, quite as clearly, the thing was impossible. Sell my father's last gift to me, for a hatful of greasy guineas? Use as my agent in this betrayal the good giant who'd brought her to me so faithfully (and so far at no profit to himself)? Even the cat had shown more loyalty than that.

I jumped out of bed and opened my purse. My small store was now seven shillings and four pence, not even enough to pay the rest of my score at the Heart of Oak. And yet here was I, proposing to make a trip to Paris and pay board and lodging indefinitely for an equine aristocrat. I heard myself laughing out loud.

Somebody else heard too. I froze, aware of a board creaking just outside the door. But there had been no footsteps since I woke up, so whoever it was must have been there while I was sleeping, quite probably looking in at me through the keyhole. I seized my travelling mantle and wrapped it round me. There was a knock at the door, knuckle against wood; quite polite sounding, if I hadn't guessed. The landlord, I thought, come to make sure of his money and, in addition, spying on me in my chemise and stockings.

'You'll have to wait,' I said.

I moved to be out of sight of the keyhole and dressed, taking my time, then put back the money in my purse. No need to let the fellow spy out the nakedness of the land in every sense. Then I went to the door and opened it, expecting to be looking into boot-button eyes and a pudgy face above a stained apron. Instead there was the gentleman in black, as straight and severe as when I'd last seen him at the Calais burial ground, although this time he was vertical, not horizontal. You might have taken him for his own spectre, except that he spoke like a living man, though not a happy one.

'Good evening, Miss Lane. I have a proposition to put to you . . .'

CHAPTER EIGHT

His high white cravat was the brightest thing in the shadowy passageway, the face above it grey as moonlight on slate. He held his hat in hand, as if making a social call.

'I thought you might be dead,' I said.

Admittedly it was hardly a cordial greeting, but when I'd last seen him he was barely breathing. In the half light, I could see no sign on his temple of the blow that had felled him, so perhaps there was not enough flesh and blood in him to bruise.

'It might be best if you would permit me to come in,' he said.

I came close to slamming the door in his face. My reputation was low enough with the landlord, without entertaining gentlemen in my room. But something told me that my virtue was in no danger, though everything else might be. The man had as much carnality as a frozen dish-clout. Even though he had been spying on me through the keyhole, it was for something colder than my charms *en chemise*. I opened the door wider. He walked in, looking round. I might have invited him to sit down, but with only one chair in the room, that meant I should have to perch on the bed. We stayed on our feet. He put his hat on the wash-stand.

'Our last conversation was interrupted,' I said. 'I was asking you what you knew about my father's death.'

'And I believe I counselled you to have patience.'

As before, his voice was low and level.

'An over-rated virtue. Were you present when he died?'

'No.'

'But you know what happened?'

He raised a narrow black-gloved hand in protest.

'Miss Lane, that is not what I have come to speak to you about.'

'Do you know what happened?'

He looked straight at me, as if he wanted to stare me down. Anybody with a brother has practice in that trick. I held his look. He sighed and walked towards the window, sliding a hand into his coat pocket.

'Miss Lane, do you recognise this?'

He was holding something small in the palm of his hand. I walked over to him and picked it up. When I saw it close, I felt as if somebody had caught me a blow.

'It's his ring.'

A signet with a curious design of an eye and a pyramid.

The one that should have been on his hand in the morgue.

'Yes,' he said.

'You robbed it from his body.'

'It was taken from his body. Not by me.'

'Who, then?'

'By persons at the morgue in Calais.'

'The fat drunken woman and her husband?'

The slightest of nods from him.

'I thought so,' I said. 'But what concern was it of yours?'

He must have been at the morgue before me, touched my father's hands as I'd done, and he had no right.

'I bought it from them,' he said. 'It should have stayed on his hand and been buried with him, but they'd only have stolen it again.'

'So you've come to return it to me?'

I was trying to bring myself to thank him, but could have saved myself the effort.

'No. I show it to you only to convince you that I knew your father. That in some measure I speak with your father's authority.'

He pulled off his right glove and stretched out his hand to me. On his middle finger was a ring identical to my father's, only the design was worn flat by time. Then he turned the hand over, palm up.

'If you please.'

He expected me to give him my father's ring back. Instead I dropped it down the front of my stays. It was cold against my hot and angry skin. The shock in his eyes was the first human reaction I'd had from him. We stared at each other and he drew another long sigh.

'I had heard that you possess an excellent understanding, Miss Lane. I fear you are not using it rationally.'

'The only understanding I care about is how my father died. Who is this woman he was trying to bring back to England?'

For a second, he couldn't hide the surprise in his eyes.

'Who told you about a woman?'

'The man who kidnapped me in the graveyard and a fat man in the carriage. You know who they are, don't you?'

'You did well to escape from them.'

'The fat man said my father had abducted a woman from Paris. They thought I'd know where she was. I don't. I know nothing about her.'

'That's good. You must continue to know nothing.'

'No! She's the reason my father was killed, isn't she? Don't I at least have the right to know who she is?'

'I'm not sure myself who she is.'

'But there is a woman, you admit that?'

'I have reason to believe that your father left Paris in company with a woman, yes.'

'He wouldn't have taken her away against her will.'

'Very well. I accept that.'

'So, whoever she is, she went with him of her own accord. But Trumper and the fat man found out about that and wanted her back.'

A reluctant nod from him.

'So they chased him from Paris to Calais?'

'Not chased, exactly. I understand that it took them some days to connect your father with the woman's disappearance.'

'Were you in Paris at the time?'

'No.'

'So how do you know about this?'

'I have no obligation to tell you how I know about anything. You must accept that I have been doing my best to observe these people for several months.'

There was a hint of weariness in his voice.

'The day they tried to kidnap me, they were still looking for this woman,' I said. 'Did they find her?'

'I don't know. As you may remember, I was indisposed for a while.'

'You mean knocked senseless by the fat man's coachman. Who are these people? Why are they doing this?'

He didn't answer for some time. We stared at each other. There were chalky rings round his grey pupils, a sign of bad health. He sighed.

'Miss Lane, your father became involved in something that was nothing to do with him. You are probably right in thinking that it cost him his life. When I met you in Calais, my wish was to protect you.'

'By ordering me to go back to England and forget about it?'

'I never said "forget". But it's true that I wanted to keep you away from them.'

'And now?'

'Since then, I have discovered two things about you. One is that you are, unfortunately, not on good terms with those whose natural duty it should be to shelter you. In fact, you are alone in the world and without means of income.'

Yes, I thought. You watched me counting every last penny.

'The other is that you are a young lady of some resource. Those two men in the carriage did not wish you well. I have heard some of the story of how you contrived to escape from them . . .'

How? From the toad-like man, the peasant with the pigs . . .?

'. . . and it suggests resolution and quick-wittedness. If it were not for these two discoveries, I should have had no hesitation in restoring you to some relative and counselling you to mourn your father and ask no more questions.'

'You have no rights over me. All I want from you is to know what happened to him.'

'In due course, you shall know everything. Only you must have –'

'Patience? What's to stop me opening this window and shouting to people to fetch a magistrate, that my father's murderer is in this room with me?'

He didn't move a muscle.

'Two reasons: one, that it would be untrue; the other, that it would be ineffective.'

I had my hand on the window latch. If he had moved to stop me I should have opened it. He stayed where he was and went on talking in that same level voice.

'I did not kill your father. If I could have prevented his death by any means, I should have done so. As for the magistrates, I should be able within a few minutes to convince them that your accusation was untrue. And you, Miss Lane, would appear a young lady driven out of her senses by grief. Is that a desirable outcome?'

I let go of the latch. If he'd knocked me to the floor he couldn't have defeated me more thoroughly, because what he said was true. I could imagine the cold, official looks and what would follow: my aunt sent for and my return to Chalke Bissett as a captive. Or, worse than that, strait-jacketed to a common asylum, fighting and screaming, spending the rest of my life among squalid gibberers. In this new world I'd fallen into, it could happen. He must have seen from my face that he'd won the round, because his voice became just a shade more soft.

'Miss Lane, I did not come here to threaten you. I came, as far as I may, to assist.'

I kept my back turned to him, looking out of the window. A drab in a doorway was beckoning to two sailors. They were taunting her, pretending to push each other in her direction.

'I give you my promise that, when it is possible, I shall tell you more about what happened to your father. But the time is not yet right, and there are more things bound up in this than the fate of any single man or woman. Your father was a good man on the whole . . .'

'On the whole!'

'. . . but of an impulsive temperament, as you clearly are. That, above all, was what led to his death.'

The two sailors were walking away, the drab shouting something after them. When she came out of her doorway you could see she was no more than a girl, perhaps fourteen or so. I turned back into the room.

'You said you had a proposition to put to me.'

He made it, standing there with his hand on the edge of the wash-stand. I sat down after all, because my legs were trembling from shock and anger, and I did not wish him to know it. I let him talk without a word of interruption and tried not to show what I thought.

'There is a small part which you may play in a great cause which I believe your father would approve. It may even in some measure help to put right the harm to that cause which your father unintentionally has done.'

How can I defend him, when I don't even understand what you're accusing him of? I hate you, as much as I've hated anybody in my life, but you possess something I want, so I must listen.

'So here is the proposal which I ask you to consider. It has the merit that it would meet, for a short time, your need for sustenance, a roof over your head, while permitting you to be of some service to a greater cause.'

Am I intended to assassinate somebody, like Charlotte

Corday and Marat? I suppose I'd have a roof over my head until they hanged me. Or does he wish me to put on a man's uniform and go for a soldier?

'I am proposing that you apply for the post of governess.'

'What?' That ended my silence, all this secrecy and drama leading to the most commonplace of conclusions. 'You invade my lodgings, spy on me, insult my father – to tell me that? I could have come to that conclusion myself, without your valuable . . . counsel.'

I threw his own word at him, bitterly. The fact was, for a woman like myself with some education but no means of support, becoming a governess was the only respectable alternative to the workhouse, and only slightly less miserable: an underpaid drudge, ignored by gentry and servants alike, neither the one nor the other, condemned to a lifelong diet of chalk dust and humble pie. Yes, it was probably my only prospect, but I hated him all the more for hurrying me towards it.

'Not just any governess,' he said. 'There is a particular family . . .'

'Friends of yours, I suppose.'

'No, anything but friends of mine.'

'Enemies, then?'

'Opponents.'

'So am I expected to put ground glass in their stew and saw through the brakes on their carriage?'

'Nothing so deleterious. You have merely to observe certain things and inform me, by means which shall be arranged for you.'

'In other words, to spy?'

'Yes.'

Honest, at least. My father's ring was now warm against my chest and I kept my hand on it through my stays to help me think.

'This family – are they something to do with why my father was killed?'

'We think so, yes.'

'How long should I have to stay there?'

'A few weeks, probably. Months at most.'

'And what are you in all this – a Government spy?'

'Far from it. The reverse, rather.'

'The reverse?'

'No government has any reason to love me.'

I waited for him to enlarge on that, but he just stood there looking at me in that arithmetical way I'd noticed in the churchyard. He was a miser with information, giving out as little as possible.

'You must tell me more about this family,' I said.

'Their name is Mandeville. They claim descent from one of William the Conqueror's knights and hold a baronetcy, conferred on them by Charles II. The present holder, the ninth baronet, Sir Herbert, is a very wealthy man and until recently was a Conservative MP.'

'Until recently? Do you mean he was one of those who lost their seats through the Great Reform?'

They'd been a huge joke to my father's circle, those lost Members of Parliament. They were mostly country squires and their friends who thought they had something like hereditary rights to seats in the House of Commons. For centuries they'd owned pocket boroughs, consisting of a mere half-dozen easily bribed or bullied electors. The Reform Act of five years before had swept them away, and not before time. I was laughing at the thought of it, but the man in black didn't smile.

'Great Reform, you call it. I should have thought it a singularly small reform. Did it give a vote to every working man?'

'No, but –'

'Did it do anything to help the tens of thousands toiling in the workshops and factories of our great cities?'

'No.'

'Did it take away a single shilling from the rich to give to children hungry for bread?'

'Sadly, no.'

His eyes were glittering, his thin body swaying to the rhythm of his words. So, I thought, the man is an orator. That explained his sparing way with words, like an opera singer guarding his voice. Perhaps he realised the effect he was having, because he smiled a thin smile.

'I am sorry to become warm, Miss Lane. You suppose, correctly, that Sir Herbert lost his seat because of the Reform Act. Until then, there had been Mandevilles in the House of Commons for four hundred years. But you would be mistaken to see him as simply a buffoon from the shires. He is a man of ability and ambition. In fact, he has held ministerial office under both Whig and Tory governments.'

'A turncoat, then.'

'Certainly a man of hasty and arrogant temperament.'

'Since he's rich, couldn't he simply buy himself another constituency?'

'For the present he prefers sulking in his tent, so to speak. Sir Herbert has become something of a focus for other men who think the country is going to the dogs.'

'But what does that have to do with how my father died? This baronet can hardly go round shooting everybody who favoured the Reform Bill. Even old King William had to support it in the end. Besides, how did they know each other? My father did not cultivate the friendship of rich Tories.'

'I doubt if your father and Sir Herbert Mandeville ever met. There is no reason to think so.'

'I repeat the question: what does he have to do with how my father died?'

'Quite probably nothing personally. Your father, unfortunately, blundered into something mortally serious that touches many people.'

'You keep criticising him and not telling me why.'

He said nothing. I could feel him willing me into doing what he wanted and tried to play for time.

'They are very rich, then, these Mandevilles?'

'They own substantial estates in the West Indies. The seventh baronet had profitable dealings in slaves.'

'I shall hate them.'

'Governesses can't afford hate.'

'Nor spies?'

'No.'

'Do they live in London?'

'They have a house there, but their main estate is at Ascot in Berkshire, not far from Windsor. If successful in your application, you would probably spend most of your time there.'

Ascot. A picture came to my mind of heathland, horses galloping across it. An idea began to form.

'I may not be successful. If they are opponents, you can hardly recommend me.'

'That will be attended to. They are advertising for a governess, so an application would not be unexpected.'

The sun was down, the room almost dark. I stood up to light the candle on the wash-stand. My legs had stopped trembling and the idea was growing.

'Very well,' I said. 'I shall apply for the post . . .'

'I am glad of that, Miss Lane.'

'But on two conditions. One, you must tell me what I am looking for. I can't be expected to guess. Is it this woman again?'

'No. Put the woman out of your mind. The main thing required of you will be to communicate to me news of any guests or new arrivals at Mandeville Hall. In particular, I have reason to believe that they will be holding a reception or ball in the next few weeks, and it would be very useful to us to know the guest list in advance. You will also inform me of the comings and goings of Sir Herbert himself and his family.'

'How am I to inform you?'

'Wait here for two days. Either I shall come and see you again, or instructions will be sent to you.'

As the candle flame steadied, I saw satisfaction on his face – and was pleased to be able to erase it instantly.

'I said there were two conditions.'

'What else?'

'I have inherited a mare from my father. If you can arrange and pay for her stabling at some place convenient to Ascot, I shall do as you suggest. If not, then I refuse your proposition.'

'A governess with a horse?'

He almost lost his self-possession. You could see him grabbing at the tail of it like some small animal bolting, and wrestling it back under his black jacket.

'A *spy* with a horse,' I said. 'That's different.'

He thought about it for half a minute or so.

'Very well, I accept your condition. If you will let me know where the mare is, I shall arrange . . .'

'No. Find a stables and I'll make the arrangements.'

We glared at each other. Then he said, 'Three days, in that case. Do not move from here. For necessary expenses . . .'

He picked up his hat from the wash-stand, clinked something down in its place, and went. As the door closed behind him I saw a handful of coins glinting in the candlelight. Ten sovereigns. I sorely needed them, but it was some time before I could bring myself to pick them up.

*

Three days passed. When he'd ordered me not to move, I don't know whether he meant the town of Dover or my room at the inn. It didn't matter in any case, since I had no intention of staying imprisoned. I slept, ate, walked by the sea, slept and ate again. The landlord had become polite now that I'd paid my reckoning to date and let him see the flash of sovereigns in my purse. Chops and cutlets, eggs, ham and claret were all at my disposal, so I made the best of them. I was like somebody cast up on a sandbank, with stormy seas in front and behind; it may have been only a short and precarious rest, but it was precious for all that. In my wandering round the town I kept an eye open for Trumper but saw no sign of him and hoped he was still on the far side of the Channel. Several times I was tempted to take the road out of town and visit Esperance and Amos Legge, but made myself defer that pleasure until I had news for them. It came on Saturday evening. A knock at my door and the landlord's voice.

'Letter for you, miss, just come.'

I opened the door only wide enough to receive it and took it over to the window. The paper and the writing were stiff and formal, like the man who'd sent it, the message very much to the point.

Miss Lane,
    The mare may be sent to the Silver Horseshoe livery stables on the western side of Ascot Heath. The manager of the stables, Coleman, has agreed

to pass on your letters to me, which should be addressed to Mr Blackstone, care of 3 Paper Buildings, Inner Temple. You will present yourself at 16 Store Street, near the new British Museum, on Monday. Ask for Miss Bodenham and act according to her instructions.

Early on Sunday morning I walked to the stables in sweet air between hay fields, with choirs of skylarks carolling overhead. Amos Legge was looking in at Esperance, leaning over the half door. He turned when he heard my step and gave a great open smile that did my heart good because it was so different from the man in black.

'Just given Rancie her breakfast, I have.'

She was munching from a bucket of oats and soaked bran, the black cat looking down at her from the hay manger.

'I've found a place for her,' I said.

I'd expected him to be pleased, but his face fell.

'Where's that then, miss?'

'The Silver Horseshoe, on the west side of Ascot Heath. You can take her there in the bull's cart, then you're on the right side of London for getting home to Herefordshire.'

He still looked unhappy, and I supposed he was calculating how little profit his long journey would have brought him.

'You won't go home quite empty-handed,' I said. 'This

is for the expenses of the journey, and what's left over you are to keep for yourself.'

I put five sovereigns into his hand. He deserved them, and being reckless with Blackstone's money was some consolation for having to take it. He looked down at the coins and up at me.

'I'm sorry it isn't more,' I said. 'I am very grateful to you and hope I may see you again some day.'

The sovereigns went slowly into his pocket, but his hand came out holding something else.

'My cameo ring? But you were to sell it.'

'We managed after all, miss. She do resemble you somehow, the lady on it.'

Tears came to my eyes. That was what my father had said when he bought it for me. I drew out the ribbon I wore round my neck with my father's ring that the black one had so reluctantly given me and knotted the cameo beside it. I thought my good giant might have gone hungry. His cheeks looked hollow.

'Thank you, Mr Legge. That was a great kindness.'

He murmured something, then ducked into the box to pick up the empty feed bucket and went away across the yard. I spent some time with Esperance, stroking her soft muzzle, watching the way her lower lip drooped and twitched, sure sign of contentment in a horse.

'I shall come and see you at Ascot when I can,' I told her.

It occurred to me that, by sending her ahead, I'd committed myself to winning the governess post. Until then, I'd been priding myself on my cleverness, but now I was beginning to see how thoroughly I'd got myself enmeshed.

'And I suppose you'd better go too,' I said to the cat Lucy.

She gave a little mipping sound in answer and jumped lightly down to her place on the mare's back. I left them there. In the yard, Amos was filling buckets at the pump. I held out my hand and wished him goodbye, but again he insisted on escorting me back to town. We didn't speak much on the way and he seemed cast down, but perhaps that just reflected my own sadness at having to part from him.

The London Flyer drew out on Monday, prompt to the minute. I'd arrived early and secured a seat by the window and when I looked out there was Amos Legge, taller by a head and a faded felt hat than the crowd of grooms, ostlers, boys and travellers' relatives come to see our departure. I waved to him as we clattered away, but if he waved back I didn't see it for the cloud of dust we were raising.

CHAPTER NINE

Store Street is not in a fashionable part of London. It lies, as Blackstone had said, near the British Museum, off the east side of Tottenham Court Road. They'd been building the new museum for almost my entire life and were still nowhere near to finishing it, so the streets around it were dusty in summer and muddy in winter from the coming and going of builders' wagons. It was an area I knew quite well because, being cheap, it provided rooms for exactly the kind of musicians, writers, actors and wandering scholars who tended to be my father's friends. So when I got down from the Flyer on Monday afternoon, I had no need to ask directions.

In other circumstances it would have delighted me to be back among the London crowds, on this sunny day with the season at its height, the barouches whirling their bright cargoes of ladies to afternoon appointments,

114

the shouts of the hawkers and snatches of songs from ballad sellers, the smell compounded of soot and hothouse bouquets, whiffs of sewage from the river and crushed grass from the parks, baked potatoes and horse dung, that would tell you what city of the world you'd arrived in if some genie dropped you down blindfold. Even now, my heart kept giving little flutters of delight, like a caged bird that wanted to be let out, only the bars of the cage were the memory that this was not how I was meant to come back to London. I should have been walking at my father's side, laughing and talking about the people we'd soon be meeting again, the operas and new plays we were planning to see. Another reason for sadness was that there seemed to be more beggars in London than when I was last there: not just the usual drunkards or boys holding out hands for halfpennies, but men who looked as if they might have been respectable once, in workmen's clothes with hungry faces.

My progress was slow because of the heavy bag and I had to keep stopping to change arms. I suppose I should have paid a boy a shilling to carry it – certainly there were enough of them around – but the slowness suited me. It was evening by the time I got to Store Street. Many different families or solitary individuals found living space in the terraces of houses, like sand martins nesting in a river bank. The sound of a guitar and a man singing in a good tenor voice drifted from an open window. From another window on a first floor, a woman's laughter rang out over a green-painted balcony with pots of geraniums and a parrot in a cage. I couldn't help smiling to myself. According to one of my aunts, the combination of green balcony, geraniums and parrot were unmistakeable signs of what she called a 'fie-fie' – a fallen woman. Well, that woman sounded happy enough and even her parrot looked more cheerful than my aunt's. Number 16 was blank and drab by comparison. I knocked and the door was opened by a thin, frizzy-haired maid, chewing on her interrupted supper. I gave her my name and said Miss Bodenham was expecting me.

'Second floor left.'

The bag and I had to bump and stumble up the two flights, so it was hardly surprising that Miss Bodenham heard us coming.

'Miss Lane? Come in.'

An educated voice, but weary and rasping, as if her throat were sore. She held the door open for me. It was hard to tell her age. No more than thirty-five or so, I'd have guessed from her face and the way she moved, but her dark hair already had wide streaks of grey, and her complexion was yellowish, her forehead creased. She was thin and dressed entirely in grey: dark grey dress with a kind of cotton tunic over it in a lighter grey, much ink-stained, and grey list slippers sticking out under her skirt. The room was almost as colourless, dominated by a large wooden table piled with sheets of paper covered in small, regular script, with stones for paperweights. A small, cold fire grate overflowed with more paper, screwed up into balls. Apart from that, the furniture consisted of two upright chairs without cushions and a shelf of well-used books. The floor was of bare boards and even the rag rug, which is usually the excuse for a little outbreak of colour in even the dreariest homes, was in shades of brown and grey. The place smelled of ink and cheap pie.

'Please sit down, Miss Lane. Have you eaten?'

I hadn't. The smell came from half a mutton pie, wrapped in yet another sheet of paper and left down by the grate, as if she hoped that even its fireless state could give a memory of warmth. If so, the hope failed. The pie was as cold as poverty and mostly gristle.

'There is tea, if you like.'

The tea suited the rest of the room, being cold and grey.

'I have your letter of application,' she said. 'You will need to copy it out in your own hand.'

She went to her bookcase, moved some volumes aside and brought out more written sheets of paper. By then I was so tired from the long day that I could have put my head down on the table and slept, but tea and pie seemed to be Miss Bodenham's only concession to human weakness. She cleared a space for me among the papers, put written sheets, blank sheets, a pen and an inkwell down in front of me. I looked at the letter I was to copy and recognised the severe and upright hand from the note he'd sent me.

'Is this by Mr Blackstone?' I said.

She had already sat down on the other side of the table and started writing something herself. She looked up, annoyed.

117

'Who?'

'The gentleman who sent me to you.'

'It is not necessary for you to know that.'

'Why not? Do you know?'

She bent back to her writing. She was copying something too, although the hand was different.

'Is Mr Blackstone his real name?'

Only the scratching of her pen for an answer.

'What did he tell you about me?' I said.

'That I was to lodge you, assist you in applying for this post, and instruct you in your duties.'

'As a governess?'

I meant '. . . or spy?', wondering how much she knew. The expression of mild irritation didn't change.

'As a governess, what else? I understand you have no experience of the work.'

'No.'

'Then we should not waste time. Copy it carefully, in your best hand.'

The address was given as 16 Store Street, the date the present: 26th June.

Dear Lady Mandeville,

I am writing to make application for the post of governess in your household. I have recently returned to London after being employed for three years with an English family resident in Geneva and am now seeking a position in this country.

The reason for leaving my former position, in which I believe I gave perfect satisfaction, is that the gentlemen who is head of the family has recently been posted to Constantinople and it was considered best that the three children who were my charges should be sent back to school in England. I enclose with this a character reference which my previous employer was kind enough to furnish.

As well as the normal accomplishments of reading, writing, arithmetic, history, geography, use of globes and Biblical knowledge, I am competent to teach music, both keyboard and vocal . . .

'Should I mention that I could also teach them guitar and flute?' I said.

She didn't look up from her writing.

'The flute is not considered a ladylike instrument. Keep strictly to what is written there.'

. . . plain sewing and embroidery. If I were to be fortunate enough to be offered the position, I should be able to commence my duties as soon as required.

Yours respectfully,
Elizabeth Lock

'Must I use a false name?' I said.

'Apparently.'

So even my poor father's name was denied to me. With so much else gone, I should have liked to keep one scrap of identity.

'Could I not still be Liberty at least?'

'Who in the world would employ a governess named Liberty?'

Miss Bodenham stood up, flexing her fingers, and lit candles on the table and mantelpiece. Outside a summer dusk had settled on Store Street. 'Have you finished? Put it in the envelope with the character reference. You'll find the address on the back of the letter.'

I thought it was as well to read the reference before I sealed it. It seemed that I had given perfect satisfaction to my previous employer for three years, that my manners were ladylike and my three young charges had become perfect paragons under my instruction. They had parted from me with great regret and could most warmly recommend me to any gentleman's household. The phrasing had all Blackstone's stiffness, but it was copied in a flowing and feminine hand. The thoroughness of his preparations scared me and I tried one last attempt.

'Does Mr Blackstone often perform this kind of service?'

'Please don't plague me with questions. I've neither the knowledge nor the time to answer them. Seal it up and I'll deliver it first thing tomorrow.'

She opened a drawer in the table with her left hand and threw me a stubby piece of sealing wax, her right hand still writing. It was all brutally clear. My poor father was judged to be an impulsive blunderer so his daughter was to be used but not trusted. The address was St James's Square, so presumably Lady Mandeville was at her town house. I lodged the application on the mantelpiece and, with nothing else to do, sat and watched Miss Bodenham copying. She was amazingly sure and quick, like a weaver at his loom. I noticed the pages she was copying from were a horrid mess of scratching out and over-writing, some lines travelling at right angles down the margins, others diagonally into corners. When, around midnight, she paused to mix some more ink, I risked a question.

'Is it a novel?'

'Not this time. Political economy. After a while it doesn't matter much whether it's one or t'other. Words, words, words.'

For the first time she risked a smile, a little roguish twist to her lips that made her look younger and friendlier.

'You are copying it for a friend?'

'I am copying it for money. Printers are very clever on the whole at deciphering an author's intentions, but there are some writers whose hands are so vile the printers won't take them. The publishers send them to me to make sense of them.'

The fingers of her right hand seemed permanently bent, as if fixed for ever in the act of holding a pen. Once she'd mixed the ink she yawned and said the rest would wait for tomorrow after all. Nearly unconscious with tiredness by now, I expected to be shown into a bedroom, but she bent down and pulled out from under the table two straw-stuffed pallets with rough ticking covers and a bundle of thin blankets.

'You can put yours by the fireplace. I'll go nearer the door because I'll be up earlier in the morning.'

Quite true. Around four o'clock in the morning, just as light was coming in through the thin curtains, she was up and out, taking with her my letter from the mantelpiece and the cold teapot from the grate. I rose soon afterwards, tidied our pallets and blankets back under the table, and found a kind of cubbyhole on the first landing with a privy, a jug of water for washing and a piece of cracked mirror. With nothing else to do, I looked round her room trying to find some clue to her connection with the man in black, but it was as barren in that respect as the stones she used for paperweights. Her bookshelves were interesting though, old and well-used books, mostly from reformers and radicals of previous generations: Tom Paine, William Godwin, Mary Wollstonecraft, even Rousseau himself in the original French. If they were her choice, then Miss Bodenham and I had views in common. It might even account for her caution, since reforming views were no more popular at present than when Tom Paine was threatened with hanging as a traitor.

Before six o'clock she was back with the teapot, a small loaf and a slice of ham.

'Your books . . .' I said.

'Are my own business.'

She pushed papers aside and we had our breakfast at the table: fresh white bread, half the ham each and cups of blessedly hot tea. She ate delicately in small bites, relishing every mouthful, so perhaps my arrival had brought a little luxury for her. But as soon as we'd finished, that was an end of softness.

'I've delivered your application. She will probably want to see you tomorrow, Wednesday. We have a lot of work to do.'

All that long summer day, with the scent of lime trees and coos of courting pigeons drifting in through the window, Miss Bodenham coached me in my part.

'The family lived in Geneva, down by the lake. You know Geneva?'

'Yes. We stopped a week there on our way back from the Alps.'

'Keep to yes and no whenever possible. She will not be interested in you and the Alps. Your charges were two girls and a boy: Sylvia who is now twelve, Fitzgeorge, nine and Margaret, five. Repeat.'

'Sylvia, twelve, Fitzgeorge, nine, Margaret, five. Was I fond of them?'

'It is unwise for a governess to express fondness. The mother may be jealous. You found them charming and well-behaved.'

'Were you ever a governess?'

'Yes. But you must cure yourself of asking questions. Governesses don't, except in the schoolroom.'

'Is it very miserable?'

'How old is Fitzgeorge?'

She seemed pleased, in her gruff way, with my speed in getting this fictional family into my head. Less pleased, though, when it came to my accomplishments.

'She will probably ask you to show her a sample of your needlework.'

'I don't possess one.'

'Not even a handkerchief?'

I eventually found in my reticule a ten-year-old handkerchief which the nuns had made me hem. She looked at it critically.

'The stitches are too large.'

'That's what Sister Immaculata said. She made me unpick it nine times.'

'It will have to do, but you must wash and iron it.'

She issued me with a wafer of hard yellow soap. I washed the handkerchief in the basin on the landing, hung it from the window sill to dry, went downstairs to beg the loan of a flat iron from the frizzy-haired maid and the favour of heating it on the kitchen range. I was ironing it in the scullery when somebody knocked at the door. The maid had gone upstairs, so I went to answer it and found a footman outside in black-and-gold livery, powdered wig and hurt pride from having to stand on a doorstep in Store Street.

'I have a letter for a Miss Lock.'

Scented paper, address written in violet ink, seal a coat of arms with three perched birds. Inside, a short note hoping that Miss Lock would find it convenient to call at eleven o'clock on Wednesday, the following day, signed Lucasta Mandeville. I told the footman that Miss Lock would keep the appointment, then fled to the scullery from which a smell of burned linen was rising. Handkerchief totally ruined with a flat-iron shaped hole in the middle. Miss Bodenham sighed as if she hadn't expected anything better and found me one of her own. It was more neatly stitched, but I had to go through the whole laundering and ironing process again.

In the evening, Miss Bodenham put on her bonnet, bundled together a great sheaf of papers, and said she must go and deliver it to the printers in Clerkenwell.

'I'll come with you.'

My head felt muzzy from a long day of study.

'No, you stay here. I'll bring back something for a supper.'

I watched from the window as her straw bonnet with its surprisingly frivolous green ribbon turned the corner, then caught up my own bonnet and hurried down the stairs. I was tired of being obedient. Blackstone and Miss Bodenham might think they'd taken control of my life, but I had my own trail to follow. It took me southwards down Tottenham Court Road towards St Giles. It was the busiest time of the evening with the streets full of traffic; at the point where Tottenham Court Road met Oxford Street there was such a jam of carriages that I could hardly find a way through. Wheels were grinding against wheels, drivers swearing, gentry leaning out of carriage windows wanting to know what was going on, horses whinnying. It seemed worse than the usual evening crush so I asked a crossing sweeper who was leaning on his broom, watching, the cause of the commotion. He spat into the gutter.

'Layabouts from the country making trouble as usual.'

From further along Oxford Street, above the grinding wheels and the swearing, came the funereal beat of a drum and voices chanting, 'Bread. Give us bread. Bread. Give us bread.'

I went towards the sound and saw a procession of working men in brown and black jackets and caps, mufflers round their necks in spite of the warmth of the day. They were walking and chanting in perfect unison, keeping time to the beat of the drum. Some of them carried placards: *No Corn Laws*, *Work Not Workhouse*. Their faces were pinched, their boots falling apart, as if they'd come a long way. Some of the spectators looked quite sympathetic to them, but the London boys as usual were taking the opportunity to shy stones or bits of vegetable at anything that moved. Then, above the chanting, a shrill cry from one of the lads: 'The Peelers are coming.' A line of about a dozen Metropolitan Police came pushing past me at a run in their top hats and tail coats with double rows of gleaming brass buttons. They carried stout sticks and their treatment of political demonstrations over recent years had shown they weren't slow to use them. Ordinarily, I'd have stayed to see what happened, but now I couldn't afford to be caught up in a riot, so I pushed my way back through the crowd, dodged among carriage wheels and got safely into St Giles High Street. From there it was an easy journey to Covent Garden.

I reached the theatre, as I'd hoped, just before the interval. Carriages were waiting at the front of the house for fashionable people who'd decided that one act of an opera was quite enough. I went round to the stage door, confident that it would only be a matter of minutes before I met somebody I knew by sight. There was not a theatre orchestra in London without a friend of my father in it, and on such a warm night some of them would surely come out to take the air. The first were three men I didn't recognise, making at some speed for an inn across the road, brass players, by their hot red faces. Long minutes passed and more musicians came out, but none I knew. I worried that the interval would soon be over and wondered if I dared go inside on my own. Then a group of men came out slowly, talking together. I recognised one of them and stepped in front of him, trying to drag a name up from my mind.

'Good evening, Mr . . . Kennedy.'

He stopped, obviously racking his brains, then said,

in a soft Irish accent, 'Well, it's Jacques Lane's daughter. How are you and how is he?'

Foolishly, it hadn't occurred to me that I should have to break the news. Because it filled my heart, I was sure the whole world knew it.

'I'm afraid he's dead,' I said.

His face went blank with shock. He asked how and I told him that my father was supposed to have been shot in a duel, only I didn't believe it. There were a lot more questions he wanted to ask, but already sounds of instruments re-tuning were coming from inside.

'I'm hoping to send a message to Daniel Suter,' I said. 'He was in Paris, and I think he's still there.'

'I knew he was going to Paris,' Kennedy said. 'He disagreed with the conductor here about the tempo of the overture to *The Barber* and took himself off in a huff. He should be back soon though.'

'Yes, Daniel never huffs for long, and then only about music.'

'Will you ever come in and wait, if I find you a seat? We can talk afterwards.'

'I'm sorry, I must go. When you see Daniel, or anybody who knows him, could you please ask him to write to me urgently at . . . at Mandeville Hall, near Ascot, Berkshire.'

The other men were going inside. The brass players came back, wiping their mouths.

'You must go too,' I said. 'But you will ask him, if you can, won't you?'

Kennedy's hand went to his pocket.

'Are you all right for . . .?'

'Yes, thank you.'

'Friends of yours, these people at Ascot?'

I nodded. The truth was too complicated, and some-body was calling from inside for the damned fiddles to hurry up. He squeezed my hand and departed, still looking shocked. I headed back at a fast walk, calculating how long it would take Miss Bodenham to get back from Clerkenwell. Luckily, Oxford Street was clear. All that remained of the unemployed men's procession was a broken drum, trampled placards and two men squatting beside a country lad in the gutter, binding up a leg that looked as if it might be broken. Back at Store Street, I just had time to take off my bonnet and wipe the dust from my shoes before I heard Miss Bodenham's footsteps coming wearily up the stairs.

Although my interview with Lady Mandeville was not until eleven o'clock on Wednesday morning, we were up at dawn for more coaching.

'Where were you educated?'

'Nearly everywhere. We kept moving quite frequently, you see, so . . .'

'Lady Mandeville will not wish to know that. You should say you were educated at home by your father, a country clergyman.'

'Another lie, then.'

'That's for your conscience. Do you want this position or not?'

Several times, bored and rebellious, I came close to shouting, No, I did not! and walking out. If it had been simply a matter of my bread and butter I should have done just that, but I was not so rich in clues that I could afford to throw this chance away.

'Where did you learn French?'

'In Geneva, with the family who employed me. Some German, too. Should I mention Spanish?'

'Only if asked, and I don't suppose you will be. And don't speak so loudly. You're a governess, not an actress. Also, you should look down more, at your hands or at the floor. If you try to stare out Lady Mandeville like that, you'll seem impudent and opinionated.'

'These Mandevilles – have you ever met them?'

'No, of course not.'

'But you know something about them?'

'A little, yes.'

'How?'

She hesitated, then seemed to come to a decision.

'I am acquainted with a young woman who was formerly a governess with them.'

'You mean I am taking the place of a friend of yours?'

I wondered if she had been my predecessor as Mr Blackstone's spy.

'She was dismissed last year. I believe there has been another since then.'

'Two in a year. Are they ogres who eat governesses?'

Another fleeting twist of her lips.

'Sir Herbert Mandeville has a black temper, and his mother-in-law, Mrs Beedle, has strict standards.'

Just as well, I thought, that Mr Blackstone only expected me to stay for a few weeks.

'I might be wrong in telling you this,' she said, 'but you do not seem to me a person easily dismayed.'

I guessed that she was going beyond the limits set for her by Mr Blackstone and even offering me a kind of wary friendship.

'How many children shall I be teaching?'

'He has three from this marriage, two boys and a girl. The elder boy, the heir, is twelve.'

'So there were other marriages?'

'One. Sir Herbert's first wife had several miscarriages and died in childbirth. He married his present wife, Lucasta, thirteen years ago. She was then a young widow with two children of her own, a boy and a girl. They are now both of age, live in the Mandeville household, and have taken his name.'

'And this Lucasta, Lady Mandeville, she will be the one who decides whether to hire me?'

'It's possible that Mrs Beedle will decide. Her daughter relies heavily on her opinion.'

'Why? Surely as the mistress of the house she may engage a governess for herself?'

'You'll see.'

'Was she rich when Sir Herbert married her?'

'No, but she was regarded as a great beauty in her time. He needed to father a son to inherit the property and title.'

'And she'd proved she could bear a son. How like an aristocrat, to choose a wife by the same principles as a brood mare.'

'That is a most inappropriate sentiment for a governess.'

Later, we turned our attention to my appearance, which caused her more anxiety. She discovered my particular curse, that my hair is naturally crinkly and no amount of water or brushing will make it lie smoothly or stop it popping out of pins. In the end, we managed to trap it under my bonnet with the strings tied so tightly under my chin that I could hardly speak.

'Good,' Miss Bodenham said. 'It will keep you quiet.'

We had decided that my lavender dress, worn with the white muslin tucker at the neck, was the more suitable one, though she insisted I must remove the bunch of silk flowers from the waist. My shoes were scratched from scrambling around at Calais, but would have to do, so I must tuck them away under my skirt as far as possible.

'You can't wear those stockings.'

'Why not?'

I was pulling them on carefully. They were my only good pair.

'Governesses don't wear silk stockings.'

'Very well. I'll wear my blue thread ones.'

'Blue stockings are even worse. They suggest

132

unorthodox opinions. You'll have to borrow a pair of mine.'

White cotton gone yellowish from much washing, darned knubbily around toes and heels. I had to garter them tightly to take out the wrinkles and what with that and the bonnet strings felt as thoroughly trussed as a Christmas goose. Miss Bodenham looked at me critically.

'It will have to do. Be careful of stepping in gutters on the way and make sure you arrive ten minutes early.' Then she added, unexpectedly, 'Good luck.'

The house in St James's Square had the elegant proportions of old King George's time, an iron arch over the bottom of the steps with a candle-snuffer beside it, stone pots of blue hydrangeas with a thin maid watering them. She couldn't have been much more than twelve years old and stepped aside to let me up the steps as if she expected to be kicked. As instructed, I was precisely ten minutes early. A footman – the same one who had resented the doorstep in Store Street – opened the door to me and led me to a small drawing room overlooking the square, where I was to wait until summoned. If I had been, as I pretended, a timid applicant for a much-needed post, it would have unnerved me thoroughly. In truth, it almost did. I got back some of my self-possession by reminding myself that I was a spy and that this family, this very house perhaps, could tell me something about my father's death. I must keep my mouth shut, my eyes and ears more wide open than they'd ever been.

The drawing room told me nothing that I didn't know already – that the Mandevilles were rich and proud of their ancestry. For evidence of wealth, the room bulged and writhed with marquetry, carving, inlaid work and gilding as if the sight of a plain piece of wood were an offence against society. Swags of golden flowers and fruit, probably the work of Chippendale, surrounded a great oval mirror over the fireplace. Golden, goat-footed satyrs gambolled up the edges of two matching cabinets in oyster veneer with veined red marble tops supporting a pair of large porcelain parrots in purple and green. The chairs, gilt-framed and needlepoint embroidered, looked as comfortable as thorn hedges for sitting on, so I stood and stared back at the Mandeville family portraits that encrusted the silk-covered walls. Hatchet-like noses and smug pursed mouths seemed to be the distinguishing features of the men. There was the first baronet, with his full wig and little soft hands, and his lady who, from her expanse of white bosom and complaisant expression, was probably the reason King Charles gave the family their title. An eighteenth-century baronet stared at the world from between white marble pillars with palm trees to the side, presumably the Mandeville West Indian plantations. One portrait near the door clearly belonged to the present century and seemed more amiable than the rest. It showed the head and shoulders of a beautiful golden-haired woman in a blue muslin dress, hair twined with blue ribbons and ropes of pearls. She was young and smiling, eyes on something just out of the picture. The lightness of her dress suggested the fashion of twenty years or so ago. Puzzlingly, she seemed familiar, but I couldn't think why. I was still staring at her when the door opened and the footman told me to follow him.

CHAPTER TEN

Two women sat facing me, side by side in gilt-framed armchairs, their backs to a window draped with heavy curtains in peacock-blue brocade. The older woman, in her late sixties, wore a ruffled black silk dress and a white lace cap with lappets framing a sharp little face. The other was the girl from the portrait, twenty years older. The realisation of that, and the feeling that I'd seen her before, made me forget Miss Bodenham's tuition and stare at her. She was handsome still, but the twenty years had not been good to her. Even with her back to the light, her complexion was sallow, with unmistakeable circles of rouge on the cheekbones. Her eyes met mine and looked away.

'Please sit down, Miss Lock,' the older woman said.

A plain chair had been placed facing them. I took a few steps across the Turkey carpet and sat down, aware that every move I made was reflected in large mirrors on the walls to left and right. Behind me as well, for all I knew. It made me feel like a specimen in a scientist's bell jar. The younger woman – Lady Mandeville, presumably – had a dainty pie-crust table at her elbow with my letter of application and character reference on it.

'I see you have worked abroad.'

Her voice sounded tired. She picked up the character reference and stared at it, as if having trouble in focusing. It trembled in her hand.

'It all seems . . . satisfactory enough, I should say.'

The older woman, whom I assumed to be Mrs Beedle, fired a question at me.

'What's nine times thirteen?'

'One hundred and seventeen, ma'am.'

She nodded. It was Lady Mandeville's turn, but she seemed to find it difficult to gather her thoughts.

'You are accustomed to teaching boys?'

An edge of uneasiness in her voice, as if playing a part she had not learned entirely. But why should she be uneasy, mistress in her own grand house?

'Yes, ma'am. I had charge of Master Fitzgeorge from six to nine years old.'

'What is the Fifth Commandment?' Mrs Beedle again.

'Honour thy father and thy mother, ma'am.'

We went on like that for some time; Lady Mandeville, with that same distracted air, asking questions about my past that I found it easy enough to deal with after

Miss Bodenham's coaching. Her mother was another matter. It wasn't so much the questions themselves, although they covered everything from the Old Testament prophets to the rivers of America. Her eyes were what made me uneasy. They were dark and shrewd and took in every detail of my appearance from bonnet ribbon to scuffed shoes. When I was answering Lady Mandeville's questions, I was aware of those eyes on me, as if Mrs Beedle saw through me for the impostor I was.

'Did your previous employer expect you to darn the children's stockings?'

Something amiss there. The harmless domestic question came from Mrs Beedle, when I'd expected something more scholastic. With those eyes on me, I faltered for the first time in the interview. Miss Bodenham hadn't foreseen this and I didn't know what the answer should be.

'I . . . I always tried to do whatever . . .'

'Did Mrs McAlison expect you to darn their stockings?'

She'd even remembered the name of my fictitious employer. I felt my face turning red.

'No, ma'am.'

Mrs Beedle nodded, though whether in approval or because her suspicions had been confirmed, I had no notion. Lady Mandeville murmured something about Betty always seeing to that sort of thing. The two women looked at each other.

'Well?' said Lady Mandeville, fingers pressed to either side of her forehead, as if for an aching head.

'Wait outside, please,' Mrs Beedle said to me.

I went into the corridor leading to the front door, staying just far enough away to prove I wasn't eavesdropping. A door opened at the far end of the corridor. It must have led to the servants' quarters because the footman appeared and held it open for a maid with an armful of dust covers. The two of them were whispering and giggling together, obviously good friends. I caught what the maid was saying.

'Just wish they'd make up their blooming minds, that's all. Get it all uncovered, then have to cover it up again. When are they off back down there?'

'First thing tomorrow she is, and the old lady. Supposed to be the day after, only a letter came from over the water this morning and her ladyship was running around like a hen with its head cut off. New curtains, complete set of new silverware, six dozen of champagne, all to go down in the old coach after them.'

They noticed me in the corridor and went quiet, casting curious looks at me as they passed by on their way to the front drawing room. Soon after that a bell tinkled from Lady Mandeville's room, which I took as my signal to go back inside. My legs were shaking. I was half-expecting to be denounced as a fraud and handed over to the constabulary. This time they didn't invite me to sit down. Lady Mandeville was making a visible effort to be businesslike.

'I understand from your letter that you are free to take up your duties immediately. We are living in the country at present.'

'Yes, ma'am.'

'Your wages will be forty pounds a year . . .'

'Payable six monthly in arrears,' Mrs Beedle added sharply.

'Yes, ma'am.'

'You will please make your own way to Windsor. You will be met at the White Hart, near the Castle, at two o'clock tomorrow. Have you any questions, Miss Lock?'

'No, ma'am.'

So I found myself going down the steps, engaged as a governess, within half an hour of entering the house. I'd known women take longer to choose a pair of gloves. And what, if anything, had I discovered in that half-hour? One, that Lady Mandeville was unhappy. Two, that her mother, Mrs Beedle, was a woman to be treated warily. Three, the household was confused and on edge because of changes of plan. Four, and probably most important, her footman attributed the latest change of plan to a letter from over the water. When people said 'over the water' they usually meant the Channel. Therefore it was possible at least that the letter had come from France and . . . Yes, you see where I am headed and are no doubt saying to yourself that hundreds of letters come to England from France every day and there is no logical connection at all with the fact that my father died there. Bear in mind, though, that Blackstone had said that my post as spy in the household was somehow connected with his death. Still no logical connection? Very well, I admit it. But then, logic is a plodding horse and now and then you need one which will take a leap.

As I turned the corner into Store Street I added a fifth fact to my list: judging by the silverware and the champagne, the Mandevilles were preparing their country home for entertainment on a grand scale. Presumably this was the ball or reception that interested the black one. How had he known? Perhaps I was only the latest filament in a whole web of spies, but if so, what made Sir Herbert Mandeville and his household so interesting to Blackstone? No point in asking Miss Bodenham. She'd made it clear that I'd get no information from her. Indeed, she hardly looked up from her copying when I climbed the stairs and told her I'd gained the position.

I spent the afternoon booking a seat on the first stage-coach I could find leaving for Windsor next morning and shopping for necessities. Of the money that Blackstone had given me, I had three pounds, two shillings and a few odd pence left after paying my coach fare. By the end of the day my purse contained only two shillings, three pennies, a halfpenny and a farthing.

My battered bag was plumper by a plain green cotton dress, a pair of black shoes that were serviceable but unlovely, two white collars, a white muslin chemise, two pairs each of cotton pantaloons and white thread stockings. It went to my heart to spend the last of my money on clothes so dull.

My farewells to Miss Bodenham early on Thursday morning did not take long. I shook her hand and thanked her and she said, 'You have nothing to thank me for.' By the time I'd pushed my bag through the door, she'd gone back to her copying.

I hired a loitering boy to carry the bag and arrived in plenty of time to take up the seat I'd reserved on the Windsor coach, only to find the vehicle surrounded by a crowd of people pushing, trampling on each other's toes, waving pieces of paper.

'. . . sent my man to reserve seats three days ago . . .'

'Quite imperative that I arrive in Windsor by three o'clock or . . .'

'. . . travel outside if need be, but I must get to Windsor . . .'

A couple of harassed ostlers were trying to hold them back, while the coach guard slowly spelled out names on a list. For some reason, half London seemed possessed of a desire to travel the twenty miles or so to Windsor. It was only when I'd claimed my place, after some unlady-like elbowing and shoving, and we were going past Hyde Park Corner that I recalled the reason for this migration of people. They all hoped for a chance to see the new queen. As far as anybody knew, she was still in London, but was expected any day to travel to her castle at Windsor. I was wedged in between a lawyer-like man with an umbrella and an Italian confectioner with – of all things – a large cake on his lap. In spite of the crush, with two extra passengers crammed inside the coach, he couldn't resist unwrapping it to show us all. It was marzipan-striped in red, white and blue, with gilt anchors, bells, and a tiny sugar replica of Westminster Abbey.

'For Her Majesty.'

'Has Her Majesty asked for it?' the lawyer-like man said.

'Poor little Vicky,' said a man in the corner, who seemed at least three parts drunk. 'Such a weight on such young shoulders.'

From the murmur of approval round the carriage, he did not mean the cake. Their voices mingled like pigeons in a loyal cooing: so young, so beautiful, so alone, so dignified. All the men in the coach were wearing black cloth bands on their sleeves in mourning for the king and the lawyer had a black streamer round his hat, but grief for William seemed lost in excitement over little Vicky. I said nothing. Even if my own world had not fallen apart, I could have raised no great enthusiasm about a grand-daughter of mad King George succeeding to a thoroughly discredited crown. Of course, that was the kind of thing said by my father's friends, but even to hint at it in this patriotic coachload would bring down on my head accusations of republicanism, atheism, treason and revolution. 'Well, that explains the six dozen of champagne, at any rate,' I thought. Lady Mandeville's haste and anxiety, the disruption of her household, were no more than symptoms of royalty fever. Any person of consequence living within an easy drive of Windsor Castle would be expected to entertain housefuls of guests drawn by the mere chance of seeing Her Majesty riding in Windsor Great Park. The advantage was that, in the middle of such a stir, nobody was likely to pay attention to a new governess. The disadvantage, from a spy's point of view, was that one of the puzzles had such a simple explanation.

We reached Windsor half an hour late because of the amount of traffic on the outskirts and unpacked ourselves from the carriage. The confectioner strode away through the crowds carrying his preposterous cake like the Holy Grail. I hoped the flunkey who received it would treat him politely at least.

There is no getting away from the castle at Windsor. Its old grey walls tower above the little town like the slopes of the Alps. The narrow streets were crowded with people in their best clothes, most of the respectable sort looking hot and uncomfortable in black, but with a carnival sprinkling of parasols and brightly coloured frocks. I stood outside the inn where the coach had put us down, wondering how I was to recognise the vehicle from Mandeville Hall in the confusion of broughams, barouches, fourgons, calèches, landaus and every other type of conveyance that clogged the centre of town.

'You Miss Lock, the governess?'

A phaeton drew up beside me, drawn by a bay cob with a grey-haired coachman in the driving seat. It was crowded with packages and parcels, a large fish kettle, crates of bottles.

'Where you got to?' the driver grumbled. 'I been looking for you an hour or more. Now we'll be back late and they'll say it's my fault as usual.'

It was no use pointing out that it wasn't my fault either. I managed, without his help, to find a gap for myself and my bag between a box of wax candles and a large ham, and settled back for a ride through the Berkshire countryside. For much of the journey we went through Windsor Great Park, with cattle grazing under oak trees old and gnarled enough to have seen Queen Elizabeth out hunting. Every time I looked back, there was the castle, silver in the sun, dwindling gradually into a child's toy castle as we trotted in a cloud of our own white dust between hedges twined with honeysuckle and banks of frothy white cow parsley, though in that royal county it probably goes by its country name of Queen Anne's lace. The smell of strong tobacco from the driver's clay pipe mingled with the chalky dust, flowers and ham. I'd thought that once we got clear of the town he might turn and speak to me and I could ask him about the family, but he never once looked back.

We came out of the parkland alongside an area of common land that I guessed must be Ascot Heath. The horse races had been run earlier in the month, while the old king was still alive, but a string was at exercise in the distance, stretching out at an easy canter. I thought of Esperance and longed to see her. The racing, and the nearness of Windsor, had clearly attracted the gentry, because there were some grand houses close to the heath. I thought any of them might be Mandeville Hall, but we trotted on past various walls and gatehouses until we came alongside a park railing. The uprights of it flickered into a blur in the sunshine and it was a while before my eyes cleared. They focused first on the railings themselves, newly painted, topped with gilt spearheads. Three men were at work with pots and brushes, re-gilding the spearheads. As we went past, one of them shouted at the driver and looked angry, probably because our dust was spoiling their work. He took no notice. Behind the railing an expanse of parkland sloped upwards, with oaks like Windsor Castle's but much younger. At the top of the slope was . . .

'Good heavens, another castle.'

I said it aloud, to the ham and the fish kettle. At second glance it wasn't quite a castle, only a very grand notion of an Englishman's country house. It had enough towers and turrets for a whole chorus of fairy-tale princesses and was bristling with battlements and perforated with arrowslits as if ready to take on an army. In reality, an army of boys armed with catapults could have done it mortal damage because the front was more glass than stone. Three storeys of windows dazzled in the sun, most unmedieval. The whole thing was a perfection of the modern Gothic style, as much antiquity as an ingenious architect could pile on without sacrificing the comfort of the family who were paying his fee. We slowed to a walk, approaching two open gates. They were wrought iron, twenty feet high, freshly painted and gilded like the railings. Cast-iron shields, as tall as a man, with the device of three perched birds were attached to each gate. A small lodge stood beside the right-hand gate, built like a miniature Gothic chapel to match the house.

'Is this Mandeville Hall?' I asked the driver, appalled at this magnificence. He nodded, without turning round.

'Built on slavery,' I whispered to the ham, desperately trying to keep up my spirits. I knew the Mandevilles lived in some style, but had expected nothing as bad as this. The memory of my father's body in the morgue came into my mind and I felt a black depression. I was wasting my time. How could his life or death be connected with all this pomp?

A man in a brown coat and leggings came out of the lodge, through an arched gateway between two haughty stone saints. He glanced at me, simply registering my presence, and then away. The driver leaned down from his seat and gave him something in a twist of paper, probably a roll of tobacco. They seemed like old friends as they filled their pipes and started muttering together. I caught the words 'new governess' and a moan about the traffic in Windsor. The driver jerked his head towards the house and asked, 'They back, then?'

'She is. He isn't.'

'When's he expected?'

'No telling. I haven't slept these two nights past, listening for him. You know what he's like if he has to wait while the gates are opened.'

The driver nodded and tapped out his pipe on his seat.

'Seeing as they're open, might as well go up the straight way.'

'Better not. What if her ladyship sees you?'

'See two of me, if she does.'

The driver made a tilting motion with his elbow and they both laughed. He jerked the reins and the cob, tiring now, went trotting slowly up the steep drive towards the castle. We hadn't gone more than a few hundred yards when a shout came from the gate lodge behind us. I turned round and there was the gatekeeper, waving his arms and pointing back the way we'd come. The driver turned too and his face went slack.

'That's done it.'

A great cloud of white dust was coming along the

road from Windsor, a much larger one than we'd made. At the centre of it was a travelling carriage drawn by four horses, coming at a fast canter. At that point they must have been a half mile away, but we could already hear the harness jingling, the thudding of their hooves and a whip cracking. My driver seemed frozen, irresolute. Then he swore and jerked at the cob's head, as if intending to go back down to the gate lodge. But it was too late. The carriage was thundering between the gates, at a trot now but still fast. The gatekeeper had to jump aside. There were two men on the box, one in a plain caped coat, the other in a burgundy-coloured jacket, with whip and reins in hand. My driver tried to pull our phaeton off the drive and on to the grass. The wheel must have stuck in a rut because it lurched and wouldn't go. He struck at the cob with his whip, swearing. By now the carriage was so close the air was full of the sweat of the four labouring horses. The face of the man driving it was red and sweating, his black eyebrows set in a bar.

'Oh God.'

It was the gentleman who'd disputed his bill in the hotel at Calais. He must have seen that the phaeton was stuck in his path, but he was still whipping up the horses. I don't know why I didn't jump out. Perhaps I believed that the driver of the carriage must swerve at the last minute. But he didn't. The phaeton lurched and juddered as the cob, writhing under the driver's lash, tried to drag us clear. Then the world came apart in a confusion of whinnying, swearing and splintering wood, and I was in the air with a great downpour of wax candles falling alongside, making splintering sounds round me as I landed with my face on the gravel of the drive and my knee on the fish kettle.

When I managed to get to my feet I found that the cob had saved us at the last second by managing to drag the phaeton out of its rut and far enough on to the grass for the carriage to give us no more than a glancing blow. But the blow had been enough to tear the nearside wheel from its axle and throw the phaeton sideways. The cob, trapped in the shafts, had gone with it and was threshing on his side. The driver was slashing at the harness with a knife, trying to release him, letting out a torrent of obscenities. I limped over to them.

'Sit on his head, for gawd's sake,' he yelled at me.

As instructed, I sat on the cob's head. That kept him still enough for the driver to release him. When he told me I could get up, the cob scrambled to his feet. His face and neck were grazed, his eyes terrified.

'He'll live,' said the driver, after running his hands down his legs.

'He could have killed him. He could have killed all of us.'

I was boiling with the anger that follows terror. The driver felt in his pocket for his pipe, found it broken, threw it down on the grass.

'Shouldn't have been coming up that way, should we. Only it's another mile round by the back way.'

At least our danger had made him more conversational, though depressed.

'But he must have seen us,' I said.

'Oh yes, he saw us all right.'

'Is he a guest here? Surely Sir Herbert will be angry that . . .'

He was staring at me as if I'd said something stupid.

'What are you talking about, girl? That was Sir Herbert.'

CHAPTER ELEVEN

My hot anger turned to something colder and harder. Until then, I'd had misgivings about entering any man's house as a spy. Now I knew that if there was any way I could find to repay Sir Herbert for treating my life (and the horse's and coachman's lives) so lightly, I would find it. I looked for my bag and found it in the wreckage.

'Where are you going, then?' the driver said.

'To the house. I'm allowed to walk on their sacred drive, I suppose.'

'In that case, you can go through to the stableyard and tell them to send a man down.'

The bag was heavy and my knee hurt, though I hoped it was nothing worse than bruising. I walked slowly up the drive, my eyes taking in the place like any sight-seer while my mind was otherwise occupied. A broad terrace stretched from the row of windows on the ground floor dotted with marble statues – Apollo, Aphrodite, Hercules, Minerva – looking out at the grazing cattle in the park. Gleaming white steps ran down from it to a formal garden with yew bushes clipped into pyramids and box hedges in geometric shapes. It did not match the Gothic architecture of the house, but it must have cost a lot of money, so perhaps that was the point. A ha-ha divided the formal garden from the pasture, and a bridge large enough to span a good-sized river carried the drive across it, decorated with more marble mythology: Leda and her swan at one end, Europa and the bull at the other.

I felt very conspicuous, as if the hundreds of window panes were eyes watching me. 'They're not the spies though,' I said to myself. 'I am.' I gloried in the word now because I thought that I'd found my enemy at the very start. A man who could deliberately run down his own groom driving one of his own vehicles was surely capable of anything, murder included. Blackstone had only told me part of the truth when he said the Mandeville household had something to do with my father's death. He surely meant Sir Herbert himself. I'd seen for myself that he'd been in Calais three days after my father died and might well have been there for some time. What my father had done to earn the hatred of this money-swollen bully I didn't know, but I'd find it out and tell the world. He could do what he liked to me after that, I didn't greatly care.

*

On the far side of the bridge the drive divided itself into two unequal parts. The broader, left-hand one passed through a triumphal stone arch to the inner courtyard of the house. I glanced inside and there was the carriage Sir Herbert had driven. Evidently this was the entrance for the Mandevilles and guests, not limping governesses. I stopped at the point where the drive divided and put my bag down to change arms. Before I could pick it up again, the carriage wheeled round and came towards me, this time at a slow walk, with only the coachman on the box. When I moved out of the way to let it pass, he didn't even glance down at me, but the footman standing at the back of it gave me a look. The poor man was so plastered with dust from the road that he could have taken his place among the statues on the terrace without attracting notice, apart from a few glimpses of his gold-and-black livery jacket. His wig must have come off somewhere on the journey because he was clutching it in his hand and his muscular stockinged calves were trembling.

I let them go past, then picked up my bag and followed. The side of the house was on my left, with fewer and smaller windows than the front. To the right, a high brick wall probably enclosed the vegetable garden. There was a brick wall on the other side as well and a warm smell of baking bread. We had come out of grandeur, into the domestic regions. I followed as the carriage turned left and left again, through a high brick archway with a clock over the top of it, into the stableyard. A dozen or so horses looked out over loosebox doors as their tired colleagues were unharnessed from the carriage, flanks and necks gleaming wet as herrings with sweat. A team of boys with mops and buckets had already started cleaning the carriage. The footman was walking stiffly away through an inner arch and the coachman was having a dejected conversation with a sharp-faced man in gaiters, black jacket and high-crowned hat who looked like the head stableman. I put my bag down by the mounting block, picked my way towards them over the slippery cobbles and waited for a chance to speak to the man in gaiters.

'The driver of the phaeton asks will somebody please come down and help him.'

'And who may you be?'

'I'm the new governess, but that doesn't matter. The phaeton is quite smashed and the cob . . .'

He clicked his fingers. Two grooms immediately appeared beside him.

'Bring in the cob and phaeton,' he told them. Then, to me: 'Beggs – can he walk?'

I was pleased by this evidence of humanity.

'The driver? Yes, he's not badly hurt, he –'

Cutting me short, he turned back to the men.

'So you needn't waste time bringing Beggs back. Tell him from me he's dismissed and to take himself off. If there's any wages owing, they'll go towards repairing the phaeton.'

'But it wasn't his fault,' I said. 'Sir Herbert . . .'

He walked away. I went and sat on the mounting block with my bag at my feet. After a while an older groom with a kindly face came over to me.

'Anything wrong, miss?'

'I'm . . . I'm the new governess and I don't know where to go.'

He pointed to the archway where the footman had gone.

'Through there, miss, and get somebody to take you to Mrs Quivering.'

He even carried my bag as far as the archway, though he didn't set foot into the inner courtyard on the far side of it.

'The driver,' I said, 'it isn't at all just . . .'

'There's a lot that's not just, miss.'

The courtyard I walked into was sandwiched between the stableyard and the back of the house. A low building on the left was the dairy. Through a half-open door I could see a woman shaping pats of butter on a marble slab. The smell of bread was coming from a matching building on the right, its chimney sending up a long column of sweet-smelling woodsmoke. The back of the house itself towered over it all, with a line of doors opening on to the courtyard, one with baskets of fruit and vegetables stacked outside. The dust-covered footman was standing by another door, talking to a woman in a blue dress and white mob-cap. When he went inside, I followed him into a high dark corridor.

'Excuse me,' I said to his back. 'Can you please tell me who Mrs Quivering is and where I can find her?'

He turned wearily.

'Housekeeper. Straight on and last on the left.'

He disappeared through a doorway. The passage was a long one and the door at the far end was green baize, marking the boundary between servants' quarters and the house proper. At right angles to it, another door marked *Housekeeper*. I knocked, and a voice sounding harassed, but pleasant enough, told me to come in.

Mrs Quivering reminded me of the nuns. She looked to be in her thirties, young for somebody holding such a responsible position, and handsome, in a plain black dress with a bundle of keys at her belt and smooth dark hair tucked under her white linen cap. But her eyes were shrewd, twenty years older than the rest of her. She looked carefully at me as I explained my business.

'Yes, you are expected, Miss Lock. I understand there was an accident on the drive.'

'I'd hardly call it an accident. What happened –'

'You are unhurt?'

'Yes, but –'

'I'm sorry that I can't allocate you the room used by your predecessor. We are expecting a large number of house guests shortly and I am having to set rooms aside for their servants. You might share with Mrs Sims, or there is a small room two floors from the schoolroom that you might have to yourself.'

I had no notion who Mrs Sims, might be. I said I'd take the small room two floors up, please, and she made a note on a paper on the desk beside her.

'I'm sure Lady Mandeville will want to talk to you about your duties, but she's occupied at the moment. I shall let her know you've arrived.'

She rang a bell on her desk and a footman appeared, not the one from the carriage. His wig was perfectly in place, the gold braid on his jacket gleaming.

'Patrick, this is Miss Lock, the children's new governess. Please show her to the schoolroom.'

He bent silently to pick up my bag. We'd gone no more than halfway along the corridor before he dropped it like a terrier discarding a dead rat and gave a low but carrying whistle. A boy appeared from nowhere. Patrick nudged the bag with his foot and the boy picked it up. It was clearly beneath the dignity of a footman to carry servants' bags. The boy looked so thin and exhausted that I'd have spared him the burden if I could, but he followed us through a doorway and up two flights of uncarpeted stairs. There was no lighting on the stairs, except for an occasional ray of sunshine through narrow windows on the landings. It reminded me of the times I'd been allowed backstage in theatres when calling on my father's actor or musician friends. Out front, palaces, moonlit mountains and magic forests; behind the scenes, bare boards, dim light and people scurrying quietly about their business.

I tried to keep note of where we were going, aware that much might depend on knowing my way round this backstage world. On the second landing, a maid with a chamber pot stood aside to let us past.

'How many servants are there?' I asked the footman.

'Fifty-seven.' He said it over his shoulder, adding, 'That's inside, not counting stables or gardens, of course.'

We went from the landing into a carpeted corridor with sunlight at last, streaming through a window at the end. The footman knocked on a door halfway along it.

'It's the governess, Mrs Sims.'

The door was opened from the inside, on to one of the most pleasant rooms I'd seen in a long time. It wasn't as grand as I'd feared, much more on a normal domestic scale. A square of well-worn Persian carpet softened the polished wood floor. The windows were open, letting in the mild air of a late summer afternoon. A doll with a smiling porcelain face lolled on the window-seat, alongside an old telescope. A dappled rocking horse stood on one side of the window and a battered globe on the other, next to a cabinet of birds' eggs. Three small desks were lined up along the wall, blotters, pens and inkwells all neatly ranged. Three children, two dark-haired boys and a yellow-haired girl, were sitting at a table with bowls of bread and milk in front of them, a vase of marigolds and love-in-a-mist in the middle of the white tablecloth.

Overseeing them was a grey-haired woman in a navy-blue dress and white cap and apron. She turned to me, smiling.

'You'll be Miss Lock. I'm right glad to see you. I'm Betty Sims, the children's nursemaid.' Her accent was Lancashire, her welcome seemed genuine. 'And these are Master Charles, Master James and Miss Henrietta. Now, stand up and say good afternoon to Miss Lock.'

The children did as she told them, obediently but with no great enthusiasm. The older boy, Charles, at twelve years old, already had his father's black bar of eyebrows and something of his arrogant look. His brother James was three or four years younger and more frail, glancing at me sidelong as if weighing me up. The girl, Henrietta, was between them in age, masses of fair ringlets framing a round face with plump babyish cheeks. Betty Sims told them they could sit down again, so they resumed spooning up the soft paps of bread, though not taking their eyes off me.

'Did anyone offer you a cup of tea?' Betty asked.

I shook my head. My throat was parched and I was so hungry that I even envied the children their bread and milk. She told me to take the weight off my feet and keep an eye on the children and went out. I sank into a chair by the window, upholstered in worn blue corduroy.

'That's my chair,' Henrietta said. 'But you can sit in it for now if you want to.'

'Thank you.'

160

'Do you know Latin?' Charles said.

'Yes.'

'I don't suppose you know as much of it as I do. Do you know about Julius Caesar?'

'Yes.'

'He was the greatest general who ever lived, apart from Wellington. Did you ever meet the Duke of Wellington?'

'No.'

'Papa met the Duke of Wellington.'

James dropped his spoon with a clatter and wailed, 'Where's Betty? I feel sick.'

'He doesn't really,' Henrietta said. 'He's a terrible liar. Did you know you've got dust all over your shoes? I have fifteen pairs of shoes.'

'You're a lucky girl.'

'A red leather pair, a green leather pair, pink satin with bows, pink satin without bows, white brocade . . .'

She was still reciting her wardrobe when Betty came back carrying a tray with tea things and half a seed cake.

'I feel sick,' James said. 'I want some cake.'

Unperturbed, Betty cut thick slices for herself and me, thin ones for the children. When they'd finished them, she said they should go to their bedrooms and be quiet. She'd come along in five minutes and help them change.

'Change for bed?' I asked her, when they'd filed out of the room. It wasn't yet six o'clock.

161

'No, changed in case their mother and father want them downstairs before dinner. They usually do, but they might not this evening because of Sir Herbert only just getting back.'

'Getting back from where?'

It felt mean, commencing my career as a spy on a person who'd been kind to me, but I had to begin somewhere.

'London, I expect. He's always up and down from London. Sir Herbert's an important man in the government.'

She said it with simple confidence, but if Blackstone and Miss Bodenham were right, any importance he might have had was in the past.

'So he has a lot of business to attend to?' I said, finishing my second cup of tea.

'Yes.' But her attention was on something else. She was staring at the draggled and dusty hem of my dress.

'If the children are sent for, their governess and I usually take them down together – when there is a governess, that is.'

She was hinting gently that I wasn't fit for company. My heart lurched at the thought that I might soon be standing in the same room as Sir Herbert Mandeville.

'But you do look tired out, Miss Lock. If you like, I could make your excuses for you . . .'

She sounded worried about that.

'Thank you, but of course I must come down with you. I'll go and change at once, only . . .'

'Did Mrs Quivering say you were to share with me?'

She was obviously relieved when I said I'd opted for the little room two floors up.

'I hope they've got it ready for you. It's through the door at the end and up past the maids' dormitory. Shall I ring for a boy to take your bag?'

I refused out of pity for the over-worked boys, so my bag and I made the final stage of our journey together, up two steep and narrow staircases. The room was small, no more than eight steps in either direction, with a tiny square of window at shoulder height looking on to the back courtyard. It was clean and simply furnished with a chair, a table, a wash-stand with a large white china bowl, and a bed made up with clean sheets. I had to go down to the maids' floor to find a cubicle with a privy and water to wash myself. Water pails stood in a line, but most of them were empty. I found one quarter-full, carried that upstairs, stripped off my dress and stockings and sponged myself as well as I could. The green cotton dress I'd bought in London would have to do, along with my lace-trimmed fichu pelerine for a modest touch of style, and the stockings and black shoes. There was no looking glass in the room, so I couldn't judge the effect, but it was good to feel clean again.

I went down to find the children changed into their best clothes – boys in breeches, waistcoats and short blue jackets with brass buttons, Henrietta in white-and-pink striped silk with frills and a ribbon in her ringlets.

She'd reclaimed her chair and was whispering in her doll's ear, the boys looking at a book. Betty Sims was on the window-seat, eyes on the little bell on its spring over the door. She seemed nervous.

'They usually ring about now if we're wanted.'

'Do the children always have to dress up, even if they're not wanted downstairs?'

'Oh yes.'

'So if they're not, they just have to get undressed again?'

'They're wanted more often than not.'

'When did the last governess leave?'

'Three weeks ago. I've been trying to teach them a bit on my own since then, but I can't keep all the tables in my head, and if I make a mistake Master James goes running to Mrs Beedle.'

'Mrs Beedle seems a holy terror,' I said.

I'd overstepped the mark, I could see that in her face.

'Mrs Beedle might have her funny ways, but she takes more notice of the children than anybody else does. Several times a week, she'll be up here hearing them recite their lessons.'

'They have regular times for their lessons, I suppose?'

'Yes. I get them up in the morning and washed at half past six, and they have a glass of milk, then an hour with their governess for prayers and reading. Then, if it's fine, we usually take them out for a walk in the flower garden or the orchard. Breakfast is sent up for all of us at nine o'clock, then it's studying from ten o'clock till two. Their dinner's at half past two, then Master Charles usually has his pony brought round. Master James hasn't cared for riding since his pony bit him, so he and Miss Henrietta play or work in their gardens. They're supposed to be in bed by half past eight, but it's not easy these light evenings.'

'And then we have the rest of the day to ourselves?'

I was secretly appalled at the amount of work demanded.

'I usually mend their stockings and things of an evening. Lady Mandeville sometimes calls the governess down to play cards if they need an extra hand. But she – There you are.'

The bell over the door had started ringing, bouncing up and down on its spring. Betty Sim's expression was precisely that of a nervous actor about to make an entrance, and perhaps mine was as well. The children stood up obediently at the sound of the bell, but I couldn't help thinking they didn't look overjoyed at the prospect of seeing their mother and father. No backstage this time. The Mandeville children belonged – for these occasions, at any rate – in the other world on the public's side of the backdrop. So the five of us went quickly along the corridor, through a proper varnished wood door instead of green baize, down a flight of carpeted stairs. We paused on the first-floor landing outside another grander door, painted white with gilt mouldings, while Betty checked the boys'

165

neckcloths and re-tied Henrietta's ribbon. When she was satisfied, she tapped quickly and nervously on the door and it opened inwards, apparently of its own accord.

It seemed at first like magic, but there was a footman on the other side of it – a different one, the fourth I'd seen so far – who must have been standing there waiting for the signal. Betty gave Charles a nudge on the shoulder and he walked through it, with his brother and sister following him, then Betty, then me. I was reciting in my mind, *A man's a man for a' that,* to remind myself that I was my father's daughter. In spite of that, I was dazzled and breathless. We were standing at the top of a double staircase, level with a chandelier that sparkled rainbows in the sunlight coming through a glass cupola several storeys above our heads. The staircase curved down in a horseshoe, left and right, to a circular hallway. The floor was white and blue mosaic, the family coat of arms with its three perched birds by the far door. A carved stone fountain played in the centre of the floor, surrounded by real hart's tongue ferns. Orange and lemon trees alternated in bays round the walls, their scent rising round us as we went down the left staircase, treading an aisle of soft carpet between expanses of white marble. We crossed the hall. James wanted to linger to watch the fountain splashing into its bowl, but Betty urged him on.

On the far side was another white-and-gilt door,

with yet another footman waiting to open it to us. It led into what they called the small drawing room, as I found out later, the one the family used when there were few or no guests in residence. Still, it was at least twice as large as any room I was accustomed to, at the front of the house overlooking the terrace and parkland. Plaster oak leaves and acorns flourished across the ceiling and grew down in gilded swags to frame the many mirrors round the walls, so that everything in the room was enclosed and reflected in a kind of frozen glade, beautiful in its way. The furniture looked mostly French of the previous century, not a straight line anywhere, all curves and gilding and ornate gold hinges.

Lady Mandeville was sitting on a sofa by the window, with her mother Mrs Beedle sewing on an upright chair beside her. Lady Mandeville smiled when she saw the children. James went running to her and buried his face in her chest. Charles followed at a slow march over the blue-and-red Turkey carpet. Henrietta stood just inside the doorway, very much aware of her own reflection in the mirrors.

'Good evening, Papa.'

She dropped a grand curtsey. Sir Herbert Mandeville had been standing by the fireplace, talking to a grey-haired man I hadn't seen before. He broke off what he was saying when he heard Henrietta's voice, smiled and kissed his fingers at her. I had to fight the impulse to go straight over to ask him if he knew he'd nearly killed me that afternoon and whether he made a habit of killing.

'Say good evening to your father, James,' Lady Mandeville said, gently pushing the boy upright. He glanced towards his father and mumbled, 'Good evening, sir.' Sir Herbert nodded but hardly looked at him.

'What about you, Charles?' he said. 'Cat got your tongue?'

'Good evening, sir.'

Charles stood stiff and straight, as if for inspection. His father looked him over and gave a more approving nod, as if he'd passed muster this time, and turned back to his conversation with the grey-haired man. I saw Lady Mandeville blow out her cheeks in a look of relief. There was only one other person in the room. She wore a pink and grey satin dress and was standing close to Mrs Beedle's chair but with her back to the company, looking out over the terrace, and hadn't turned when the children came in. Her red-gold hair was swept up and held with a pearl-studded comb. Would Celia recognise me from the hotel at Calais? Possibly not. Servants are invisible. Lady Mandeville was looking in my direction, signalling with a lift of the chin that I should come over and speak to her.

'Good evening, ma'am,' I said. 'Good evening Mrs Beedle.'

I could see Lady Mandeville struggling to remember my name.

'Good evening Miss . . . Lock. I hope you had a pleasant journey.'

'Yes, thank you.'

I was tempted to add that it had been well enough until I encountered her husband. From the way Mrs Beedle was looking at me, I guessed she'd heard the story of the phaeton, but perhaps she hadn't told her daughter. I was trying to look over her shoulder at Celia Mandeville. She still had her back turned, but she seemed tense, as if it took an effort of will not to turn round. Then, while I was looking at her, she did turn and our eyes met. There wasn't a shade of doubt about it. She'd recognised me, possibly had known from the time I opened my mouth. Mrs Beedle turned.

'Celia, this is Miss Lock, the new governess. Miss Lock, my grand-daughter, Celia.'

Celia murmured something, gracious enough, I think, and I suppose I replied in kind. I was looking at her eyes, seeing first puzzlement, then the dawning of a question. She opened her mouth to say something else, closed it again. If she had thought of saying, in front of the family, *But I met you at Calais*, the thought died in that second. Henrietta came bouncing across to her mother.

'Mama, may I have a pearl comb like Celia's?'

'When you're older, darling.' Her mother ruffled her ringlets with a hand that trembled slightly. 'Have you been a good girl today?'

For the next few minutes the children clustered round their mother's sofa, more relaxed now that their father's attention was not on them. Betty and I stood out of the way near the door. Mrs Beedle went on sewing something white and ruffled and Celia stood staring down at a book on a small pie-crust table, not turning the pages. Sir Herbert finished his conversation and announced that it was high time to go into dinner. Lady Mandeville gently put the children aside and stood up.

'You must go, darlings. Sleep well. See you tomorrow.'

Betty hurried forward to claim them and I followed more slowly. The family began filing through a door on the opposite side, presumably to the dining room, while we went towards the hall. I was almost through the doorway when I felt a hand gripping my arm.

'Miss Lock?'

Celia's voice, with its little lisp. I turned.

'I need very much to speak to you,' she whispered.

'Now?'

'No. Tomorrow. Will you meet me and not tell anybody?'

'When?'

'Early, very early. I hardly sleep. Six o'clock in the flower garden.'

'Celia?'

Mrs Beedle's voice, sharply, from the drawing room.

'You will, won't you? Please.'

I nodded. She put a finger to her lips and turned away. I followed Betty and the children back up the horseshoe staircase, still feeling the pressure of Celia's fingers on my arm.

CHAPTER TWELVE

Later, when the children were in bed and Betty Sims and I were sharing supper in the schoolroom, I asked her where the flower garden was.

'Right-hand side of the house looking out, behind the big beech hedge.'

She showed no curiosity about why I wanted to know, because by then I'd asked her a lot of other questions about the house and the Mandevilles – all perfectly reasonable for a new governess. She'd been there thirteen years, from a few months before the birth of Master Charles, but her time of service with Lady Mandeville went back longer than that.

'She wasn't Lady Mandeville then, of course, she was Mrs Pencombe. I came to her as nursemaid when her son Stephen was six years old and she was confined with what turned out to be her daughter Celia.'

'So you've known Celia from a baby?'

I wanted to know everything I could about Celia. It might help me decide how far to trust her.

'From the first breath that she drew.'

'What was she like as a child?'

'Pretty as a picture and sweet winning ways. But head-strong. She was always a child that liked her own way.'

'What happened to Mr Pencombe?'

'He died of congestion to the lungs when Celia was six years old. We thought we'd lose Mrs Pencombe too, from sheer grief. It was a love match, you see. With her looks, she could have married anybody in London.'

'And yet she must have married Sir Herbert quite soon afterwards.'

Betty put down her slice of buttered bread and gave me a warning look.

'Two years and three months, and I hope you're not taking it on yourself to criticise her for that.'

'Indeed not.'

'What would anyone have done in her place? Mr Pencombe hadn't been well advised in the investments he made and he left her with nothing but debts and two children to bring up. She was still a fine-looking woman, but looks don't last for ever.'

'Did she love Sir Herbert?'

'A woman's lucky if she marries for love once over. I don't suppose there's many manage it twice. May I trouble you to pass the mustard?'

That was her way of telling me I was on the edge of

173

trespassing. It might also have been a gentle hint that she'd made a comfortable little camp for herself and the children in this great house and that it was kind of her to let me into it. At first I took her achievement for granted and it was only when I began to learn more about the household that I appreciated her quiet cleverness. The fact was that we should not have been enjoying our ham, tea and good fresh bread in the schoolroom at all. For all her long service, Betty as nursery maid was only entitled to a place about halfway down the table in the servants' hall – well above kitchen maids but a notch below the ladies' maids. I as governess – stranded somewhere between servant and lady – would have been permitted the lonely indulgence of eating in my own room. Over the years, patient as a mouse making its nest, Betty had built up such a network of little privileges and alliances that the nursery area was hers to command. We had our own tiny kitchen with an oil burner for making warm drinks and a bathroom for the children's use, grandly equipped with a fixed bath, water closet, piped cold water and cans of hot water carried up twice a day by Tibby, the schoolroom maid. Betty was bosom friends with Sally the bread and pastry cook, so tidbits arrived almost daily from the kitchen, in exchange for Betty's sewing skills in maintaining Sally's wardrobe. All this I found out later and was ashamed of my readiness to take its comforts for granted. On that first evening, the tea and candlelight were so soothing I could scarcely keep my eyes open.

'You're for your bed,' Betty said. 'Take that candle up with you, but remember to blow it out last thing. You can sleep in tomorrow, if you like. I'll see to the children.'

In spite of my tiredness I must have slept lightly because I was aware of the rhythms of the house under me, like a ship at sea. Until midnight at least the sounds of plates and glasses clinking and the occasional angry voice or burst of laughter came up from the kitchens four floors below, as scullery staff washed up after family dinner. Later, boards creaked on the floor immediately below me as maids shuffled and whispered their way to bed in the dormitory. Then the smaller creakings of bedframes and the sharp smell of a blown-out candle wick. After that there was silence for a few hours, apart from owls hunting over the park and the stable clock striking the hours.

By four o'clock it was growing light. An hour after that the floorboards below creaked again as the earliest maids dragged themselves back downstairs. I got up too, folded back the bedclothes and put on my green dress and the muslin tucker. There was still nearly an hour to go before my meeting with Celia but I was too restless to stay inside. I tiptoed past the maids' dormitory so as not to wake the lucky ones who were still snoring and crept on down the dark back stairs, with only the faintest notion of where I was going. I had a dread of going through the wrong doorway and finding myself on the

175

family's side of the house, onstage and with my lines unlearned. But I need not have worried because it was mostly a matter of keeping bare boards underfoot and travelling on downwards by zigzagging staircases and narrow landings towards the sounds coming from the kitchen.

The last turn of the staircase brought me into the light, a smell of piss and a glare of white porcelain. Chamber pots, dozens of them, clustered together like the trumpets of convolvulus flowers. They must have been gathered from bedrooms and brought down for emptying. I picked my way carefully through them and out into the courtyard. A kitchen maid was carrying in potatoes, a man chopping kindling, but they took no notice of me. There was an archway with an open door on the far side of the courtyard. I walked through it and the parkland stretched out in front of me, glittering with thousands of miniature rainbows as the sun caught the dew. I bent down and bathed my face and eyes in it, breathing in the freshness.

On the other side of the ha-ha, cows were already up and grazing. Nearer to hand, a narrow flight of steps led up to the back of the terrace, with a stone nymph guarding them. At right angles, a freshly mown grass path stretched to an archway cut into a high beech hedge. I followed it and found myself in an old-fashioned kind of garden, not so grand and formal as the rest of the grounds and to my eye all the better for that. Four gnarled mulberry trees stood at the corners of the lawn, with an old sundial at the centre. Hollyhocks grew at the back of the borders, love-in-a-mist and mignonette at the front, with stocks, bellflowers and penstemons in between. The whole area, no more than half an acre or so, was enclosed by the beech hedges with a semi-circular paved area on the south side, a rustic bench and a summerhouse dripping with white roses.

I sat down on the bench and made myself think how to manage the conversation with Celia Mandeville when she arrived. I was reluctant to do it because, instinctively, I liked her. But she wanted something from me and – although she didn't know it – I badly wanted several things from her. The most important by far was confirmation that Sir Herbert had been in Calais the day my father died. I could hardly expect from her proof that Sir Herbert had killed him. Surely she couldn't know anything so terrible and be in the same room as the man?

It wasn't a great wrong I was doing her, after all. Her stepfather was an arrogant, cruel man and she surely could not love him. At the very least, she must be ready to go behind his back, or why should she want this meeting with me?

She was late. Ten minutes or so after the stable clock had struck six she came running through the archway in the beech hedge, face anxious and hair flying.

'Oh, here you are. Thank you, thank you.'

She was wearing a rose-pink muslin morning dress,

thrown on hastily with only the most necessary buttons done up and, I couldn't help noticing, no stays underneath. Her feet were stockingless in white satin pumps, grass-stained and wet from the dew. Perhaps I should have stood up, since she was my employer's daughter, but it never occurred to me. She sat down beside me and took my hand, panting from her run.

'Last night . . . I couldn't believe it. What are you doing here?'

'Your mother was kind enough to engage me as governess.'

'But when we met in Calais, I thought . . .'

I think she might have been on the point of saying that she'd taken me for a social equal. She glanced at me, then away.

'I suppose you've had some misfortune in life?'

'Yes,' I said.

Another glance at my face. She seemed nervous, poised to run away. But she, if anybody, should feel at home on this stage and sure of her part.

'I liked you, you know,' she said. 'Liked you at once.'

'And you were kind to me.'

Part of me wanted to reassure her, but a harder and colder part that had been born only in the last few days told me to wait and see.

'Your poor head. Is it better now?'

'Head? Yes, oh yes. Thank you.'

We stared at each other. Her eyes were a deep brown, not the periwinkle sparkle of her mother's in the portrait.

'Can I trust you?' she said. The question should have been offensive, but somehow it wasn't. She seemed to be asking herself rather than me. 'You see, I do very much need to trust somebody.'

Perhaps I should have leapt in there and assured her of my total trustworthiness, but I couldn't quite bear to do it. I watched her face as she came to a decision.

'I must trust you, I think. Goodness knows, there's nobody else.'

That in a household of – what was it – fifty-seven people, not counting the family.

'You have a mother and a brother,' I said.

She looked away from me. 'Stephen doesn't always do what I want, and my poor mother is . . . has other things to worry her. Then if he found out that I'd confided in her and she hadn't told him, he'd be so angry with her . . .'

'"He" being your stepfather?'

She looked away from me and nodded. A full-blown rose had dropped down from its own weight so that it was resting on the arm of the bench. She began plucking off its petals, methodically and automatically.

'Miss Lock, would you do something for me and keep it secret?'

'What?'

'Promise me to keep it secret, even if you won't do it?'

Rose petals snowed round her grass-stained pumps.

'I promise.'

'Oh, thank you.'

She let go of the despoiled rose and gripped my hand. I could feel her pulse beating in her wrist, like a panicking bird. I remembered what Betty had said – *sweet winning ways.*

'What is it that you want me to do?'

'Take a letter to the post for me.'

'Only that?'

I felt both relieved and disappointed.

'Only that, but nobody must know. I can't trust any of the servants, you see. They're nearly all his spies.'

'Spies?'

'I'm sure my maid Fanny is, for one. Or they're all so terrified of him, they'd tell him at the first black look. But he'd never guess it of you, being so newly come here.'

'This letter is to a friend?'

'Yes. A gentleman friend. Not a love letter, in case that's what you're thinking.'

She glanced sideways at me and must have caught my sceptical look.

'It's more important than that. It's . . .'

She hesitated.

'Yes?' I said, waiting.

'If . . . if a certain thing happens, my life may be in danger.'

There was a flatness about the way she said it, more convincing than any dramatics might have been.

'What certain thing?'

She let go of my hand.

'I mustn't tell you, and you mustn't ask any more questions. But you'll take the letter for me?'

'I've already said so. But how am I to get it to the post?'

Though Celia was not to know it, I'd been giving the question some thought on my own behalf. With the amount of work demanded from a governess, I couldn't see how I was to find the time to get to the Silver Horseshoe, let alone make regular reports to Mr Blackstone.

'There surely must be a way,' she said.

I let her see that I was thinking hard.

'There must be some livery stables near here, with carriages that meet the mail coaches,' I said. 'If I could take your letter to one of those . . .'

'Yes. Oh, Miss Lock, how very clever of you. Could you do that?'

Her eyes were shining. She took hold of my hand again.

'I think so, yes. I've heard somebody talking about a place called the Silver Horseshoe, on the west side of the heath.'

'Yes. We pass it in the carriage sometimes. I think they keep race horses there as well as livery.'

'Is it far away?'

'About two miles, I think.'

'If I were to walk there, in the very early morning, say, do you suppose anybody would notice me?'

'You must not be noticed. You simply must not be noticed.'

Which was hardly an answer to my question. She turned her head suddenly.

'What was that?'

A chesty cough came from the far side of the beech hedge. A bent old gardener in a smock limped through the arch into the garden, trug over his arm. He didn't glance in our direction and moved on slowly to a bed of delphiniums.

'I must go,' she said. 'We must not be seen alone together.'

'You surely don't take him for a spy?'

I kept a firm hold of her hand.

'It was strange, wasn't it, meeting in Calais like that?' I said.

She nodded, but her hand was tense and her eyes were on the old man.

'Yes.'

'What were you and your stepfather doing in Calais?'

With an effort, she brought her attention back to me.

'He had business in Paris. He wanted me to go with him.'

'Does he often travel abroad?'

'Not very often, no.'

'I suppose you stayed several days in Calais?'

'Not even a day. He'd worked himself into such a fume about getting home, we hardly had time to sleep. It was nearly two o'clock on Tuesday morning before we got to Calais and we were on the packet out by Tuesday afternoon.'

She said it so naturally, with half her mind still on the old gardener, that it sounded like the truth. My father's body was brought to the morgue in Calais early on Saturday morning. So if she was right, by the time the Mandevilles arrived there, he was nearly three days dead. And yet a memory came to me of the foyer of the Calais hotel, and her stepfather disputing a bill several pages long.

'You'd built up a very long hotel bill in a few hours,' I said.

She blinked, as if she didn't understand what I meant at first.

'Oh, that was mostly Stephen's. He was there waiting for us. My stepfather frets if he thinks Stephen's being extravagant.'

She let go of my hand and stood up. The stable clock was striking.

'What time is that?'

'Seven,' I said.

'Fanny will wonder what's become of me. I shall say I couldn't sleep. Lord knows, that's true enough. I'll make some excuse to come to the schoolroom and give you the letter.'

She took a step or two then turned round.

'I *can* trust you, can't I?'

'Yes.'

Then she was gone through the gap in the beech

hedge, a few white rose petals fluttering after her. The old gardener went on cutting delphiniums, not noticing anything.

I went through the back courtyard and the backstairs route to my room in the attic. From there, I hurried down to the schoolroom as if I'd just got up. Betty had the three children round the table, choosing pictures to paste into their scrapbooks.

'Say good morning to Miss Lock.'

They chorused it obediently.

'It's such a lovely morning, I thought we might all have a walk on the terrace before breakfast,' Betty said.

So we went on to the terrace through a side door and the children played hide and seek among the marble statues.

'I let them run wild when there's nobody about,' Betty said. 'They're not bad children, considering.'

After breakfast at the schoolroom table of boiled eggs and soft white rolls with good butter, it was time to start my governess duties. I realised that, with all my other concerns, I'd given no thought to the question of teaching, and with three freshly washed faces looking up at me and three pairs of small hands resting on either side of their slates I felt something like panic. Still, we managed. I devoted most of the morning to finding out how much they knew already, and the results were patchy. They were very well drilled in their tables and the Bible (I thought I detected Mrs Beedle's influence there), adequate in grammar and handwriting and able to speak a little French, though with very bad accents. Their geography and history seemed sketchy, with many gaps, although they could all recite the kings and queens of England from Canute to the late William. Charles's Latin was nowhere near as good as he believed and consisted mostly of recognising a few words in a passage then giving an over-free translation from memory. That possibly explained why he had not been sent away to school yet, although he was clearly old enough. I discovered early on that he had a passion for battles. Problems in addition and multiplication that otherwise brought only a blank stare were solved in seconds if I presented them in terms of so many men with muskets and so many rounds of ammunition. It was a principle of my father's, following the great Rousseau, that learning should be made a pleasure for a child. I decided that in what would probably be a very short time with the Mandevilles, I'd try to put it into practice. After all, whatever had happened was hardly the children's fault.

Around midday, we moved on to poetry. To my astonishment, they'd never even heard of Shelley so I went straight upstairs to get the treasured volume from my bag and read to them.

I met a traveller from an antique land,
Who said: Two vast and trunkless legs of stone
Stand in the desert. Near them, on –

The door opened suddenly and Mrs Beedle walked in. She was wearing her usual black silk and widow's cap and carrying an ebony walking cane. I stopped reading. She came over and looked at my book.

'I don't approve of Mr Shelley. If they must have poetry, Mr Pope is best. Mr Pope is sensible.'

'I'm sorry, ma'am.'

It was no part of my plan to be dismissed on my first morning. She turned to the children. At least they did not seem scared of her.

'Have they been good, then? Have they been quiet and obedient?'

Not the occasion either to discuss the educational theories of Jean Jacques Rousseau.

'Yes, ma'am.'

'You must keep them working hard. Henrietta, what's fourteen minus seven plus nineteen?'

She fired questions at them for several minutes and, from the nod she gave me, seemed reasonably satisfied. Yet, now and again, I caught her looking at me in a considering way. Perhaps it was only to do with my suspect taste in poetry, because at the end of it she simply wished me good morning and went with as little fuss as she'd arrived.

Our dinner at half past two was shepherd's pie and blancmange with bottled plums. In the afternoon I helped Henrietta and James cultivate their plots on the south side of the walled vegetable garden. Henrietta was wrapped in a brown cotton pinafore from neck to ankles to protect her dress. She said she hated gardening because it was dirty. Every time she saw a worm she screamed and one of the gardeners' boys had to come running over to take it away. I liked the kitchen garden because it felt warm and secure inside its four high walls of rosy brick, with the vegetables growing in lush but orderly rows and the gardeners hoeing in between them in a slow rhythm that was probably much the same when Adam was a gardener.

When the stable clock struck five it was time to take the children back to the schoolroom for their bread and milk and have them washed and changed for their summons downstairs. This time there was no sign of Sir Herbert. Lady Mandeville was on her sofa, Mrs Beedle and Celia sitting by the window sewing. A tall, dark-haired young man was standing looking out of the window with his back to the room and his hands in his pockets. From his manner of being at home and my memory of him in Calais, I knew he must be Celia's brother. I stopped a few steps inside the doorway and bent down to straighten James's collar, giving myself time to think. There was no reason to fear Stephen Mandeville would recognise me. As far as I remembered, he hadn't even glanced my way in the hotel foyer and it had been dark at our second near-meeting on the deck of the steam packet. The question was whether Celia had said anything to him about seeing me at Calais. I glanced towards her, hoping for some signal, but caught Lady Mandeville's eye instead. She nodded at me to come over to her.

'Miss Lock, may I introduce my son Stephen. Stephen, Miss Lock, our new governess.'

It was graceful in her, to introduce us properly. Her son's response was equally graceful, a touch of the hand, a slight movement of the upper body that was an indication of a bow, though not as pronounced as it would have been to a lady. The dark eyes that met mine gave no indication that he remembered seeing me before. Celia glanced up from her sewing.

'Miss Lock, do you sketch? Should you mind if I consulted you sometimes about my attempts?'

Her anxious eyes answered my question. She hadn't told her brother. I should be delighted, I said. Soon after that they went in to dinner and we were free to escape to the nursery quarters.

The next day, Saturday, followed much the same pattern in the schoolroom. On Sunday we all went to church, the children travelling with their parents in the family carriage a mile across the park to the little Gothic church by the back gates, the rest of us walking in the sunshine. The family sat in their own screened pew up by the altar, at right angles to the rest of the congregation, so I had only a glimpse of Celia, solemn and dutiful in an oyster-coloured bonnet, and Sir Herbert looking stern, as if he were only there to make sure that God and the clergyman did their duty.

After church, once the family had driven away in the

carriage, there was a rare chance for the servants to linger in the sun and gossip. I strolled among the gravestones and round the old yew trees, catching the occasional scrap of conversation. There were quite a few complaints about being worked too hard, not only the usual burden, but something more.

'. . . all the bedrooms opened and cleaned, even the ones they haven't used for years . . .'

'. . . bringing waiters in from London, just for the weekend. Where they're going to put them all . . .'

'So I said I didn't think it was very respectful having a ball, with the poor old king not even buried yet.'

'Well, he will be by then, won't he?'

'I think they're going to announce an engagement for Miss Celia.'

'They'd never go to all that trouble, would they?'

I tried to hear more, but the women who were talking saw me and lowered their voices. I wandered away to look more closely at some of the gravestones. The oldest of them went back two hundred years or more and although they looked higgledy-piggledy, leaning at angles among the long grass and moon daisies, there was an order about them. Ordinary folk were on the outside, nearest the old stone wall that divided the churchyard from the grazing cattle, then upper servants at Mandeville Hall, still defined even in death by their service to the family, forty years a keeper, thirty years a faithful steward. Nearest the church, protected by a grove of yew trees, were the big table tombs of the Mandeville family themselves. I was reading the florid description of the virtues of the fifth baronet, *as distinguished in his Piety and Familial Duty as in the high service of his Country,* when I heard footsteps on the dry ground behind me.

'He really was the worst villain of the lot of them,' a man's voice said over my shoulder. 'Made a fortune selling bad meat to the army.'

I turned round and saw Stephen Mandeville standing there smiling in grey cutaway jacket and white stock with a plain gold pin, tall hat in hand. I dare say my mouth dropped open. I'd assumed he'd gone back in the carriage with the rest of the family. He came and stood beside me.

'I'm sorry. Did I startle you?'

I tried to compose myself and answer him in the same light tone.

'Not in the least. I suppose he had some good qualities.'

'Not that I've heard of.'

The irreverence for the family surprised me, until I remembered that they weren't his ancestors. He strolled on to the next tomb and in politeness I had to follow him.

'The carving on this one is thought to be quite fine, if you have a taste for cherubim.'

To anyone watching – and I was quite sure that some of the servants would be watching – the son of the house was simply being polite and showing some of the family history to the new governess. I knew there was more to it than that.

'I am glad that you're here, Miss Lock. My sister needs a friend.'

He said it simply in a quiet voice, unlike his bantering tone when he'd been talking about the tombs. I glanced up at him.

'I'm sure Miss Mandeville has many friends.'

'Not as many as you might think. She leads a very quiet life here and we don't visit much in the neighbourhood, owing to my mother's health.'

'If there's anything I can do to help Miss Mandeville, naturally I will, but . . .'

'There've been other governesses, of course, but they wouldn't quite do. You seem to be around the same age as she is, if you'll permit me to be personal, and I think she's taken a liking to you already.'

'Has she said so?'

From the lift of his eyebrow I could see he hadn't expected a direct question, but I wanted very much to know if they'd talked about me.

'She doesn't have to say it. I can read my sister like a book. So, you'll be a friend to her?'

'If I can, of course I will.'

'Thank you. Now, if you'll excuse me, I must go and join them.'

He smiled, gave a little nod and strode away.

I walked back across the park with Betty and her friend

Sally, a cheerful and plump woman with flour from all that bread-making so deeply engrained in the creases of her knuckles that it had even survived a Sunday-best scrubbing. Naturally they wanted to know what Mr Stephen had been saying to me. Talking about the tombs, I said. Betty seemed worried.

'I don't blame you, Miss Lock, but he should be more careful.'

'Careful of what?'

'The governess and the son. It's not my place to say it, but people do talk so.'

'I assure you, it was nothing like that.'

I felt myself blushing and was on the verge of defending myself by telling them about his concern for his sister. Betty looked hurt by my sharpness and for some time the three of us walked in silence. I broke it by going back to the talk I'd overheard.

'There's to be a ball then?'

'Two weeks on,' Sally said. 'A hundred people invited and a dinner the day before.'

I have reason to believe they will be holding a reception or a ball in the next few weeks . . . So Blackstone had been right. But how did he know and what in the world did it matter to him? He did not seem the kind of man to take a close interest in the social calendar.

'Is it to celebrate anything in particular?'

'Not that I know of.'

'Don't worry, Miss Lock,' Betty said. 'We shan't have

much to do with it, except keeping the children looking nice when they're wanted.'

'Her ladyship looks worn out with worry about it already,' Sally said.

Betty gave her a look that said some things should not be discussed in front of new arrivals and turned the conversation to a bodice she was trimming for Sally. The rest of our walk back was taken up with details of cotton lace, tucks and smocking, leaving me with plenty of time to wonder why Miss Mandeville should be so much in need of a friend.

On Monday afternoon, Mrs Quivering intercepted me as I was bringing Henrietta and James in from the garden.

'Miss Lock, a word with you.'

She beckoned a maid to see the children back upstairs and led me into her office.

'A letter has arrived for you, Miss Lock.'

My heart leapt. The only person to whom I'd given my address was Daniel Suter.

'Oh, excellent.'

I held out my hand, expecting to be given the letter, and received a frown instead.

'Miss Lock, you should understand that if anybody has occasion to correspond with you, letters should be addressed care of the housekeeper and they will be passed on when the servants' post is distributed. Is that quite clear?'

Since childhood, I'd never felt so humiliated. When

she brought an envelope from under the ledger, I took it without looking at the writing on the envelope, thanked her and marched out.

At least dear Daniel had not failed me. It was sweet to have this link with my father so I carried it back upstairs to my attic room at last and turned the envelope over, expecting to see Daniel's fine Italic hand. It was like running into a thorn hedge where you'd expected lilacs – not Daniel's hand after all but the upright, spiky characters of Mr Blackstone.

Miss Lock,
Livery bills will be paid for the mare Esperance at the Silver Horseshoe until further notice. Please let me know of your safe arrival as soon as is convenient.

That was all; no greeting, no signature. When I read it a second time I saw that it contained a small threat. I had not told him the mare's name. He'd discovered that for himself and used it, I guessed, quite deliberately to show I could hide nothing from him. Well, I was being a good, obedient spy. In my first few days I'd found out something he wanted to know and had even seized a chance of getting it to him with the help of the daughter of the house.

As for Celia, I'd by no means made up my mind about her. Our talk kept coming back to my mind and sometimes I managed to convince myself that she was nothing more than a spoiled young lady with a lively sense of drama. Then I'd remember the tone of her voice saying she might be in danger and at least half believe it. In any event, we had her brother's approval of our friendship, though whether that would continue if he knew she wanted me to carry secret letters was another matter.

CHAPTER THIRTEEN

Celia paid a visit to the schoolroom just before the end of our morning session. The surprise on the faces of her half brothers and sister showed that this was not a usual event.

'Miss Lock, may I steal you, please?'

As it was so close to their dinner time I told the children they could put their books away and joined her in the corridor. She was wearing a morning gown of cream mousseline, with a pale apricot sash.

'It was so obliging of you to offer to help with my sketching. It's driving me quite distracted.'

I realised that she'd said it loudly for the benefit of Betty, who'd come hurrying out of her room to see who the intruder was.

'I can't claim to be an expert,' I said.

'You're being modest, I'm sure. I'm working on something that simply won't come right. Would you come and give me your opinion?'

'Now?'

'Why not? Betty can see to the children, can't you, Betty?'

I followed her along the corridor and down the stairs to the first floor, where the family had their rooms. The pale green carpet was soft as moss underfoot, the doors deeply recessed into carved and gilded frames. Celia opened a door into a sunny room with a blue canopied bed, blue velvet window curtains, two chairs and a sofa upholstered to match. It was pleasantly untidy, a white dress thrown over one of the chairs, a novel upside down on the sofa, and a canary singing in an ornate Turkish-style cage by the window, seed scattered all round it on the carpet. A half-open doorway showed a dressing room with a screen and a full-length mirror.

'Where's your sketch?' I said, humouring her.

'Don't worry, it's quite safe to talk. I've sent Fanny down to the laundry to find my pleated silk collar. It will take her a long time because it's at the bottom of my drawer in there. My letter's ready.'

She brought it over to me from her desk. It was plump and scented, addressed to Philip Medlar Esq at an address in Surrey. She dropped a smaller packet on to my lap.

'There's some money in there for you to give whoever takes it to the post. I've tried to think of everything, you see.'

She was anxious to please me. Perhaps she'd caught

the look on my face when she gave me the letter. The smell and feel of it had convinced me that it was nothing more than a love letter after all and she'd not been truthful with me. Still, it suited my plans and I wasn't being wholly truthful with her.

'How soon can you take it? Tomorrow?'

'Yes. If I leave at first light, I can be back by the time the children have to be got up.'

She knelt on the carpet and took my hand between both of hers.

'Oh, I am so very grateful. I do believe you've saved my life.'

'Not quite as dramatic as that, surely.'

'Oh, you can't know.'

I said, as gently as I could manage, 'Are you so very scared of your stepfather?'

'I am scared of him, yes, but that isn't the worst of it. Miss Lock . . . Oh, I can't go on "miss"-ing you. What's your name?'

'Lib—, Elizabeth.'

'Elizabeth, there are things I mustn't tell you. But do believe that I might be in the most terrible danger of being put in prison or . . . or killed even, for something that isn't my fault at all.'

I wanted to say that there was no need for this drama because I'd carry her letter in any case, but I bit my tongue and slipped my hand from hers.

'I'd better go back to the children.'

'How shall I know you've sent it?' she said.

'That bench we sat on, in the flower garden – if I'm back safely, I'll pick a flower and leave it there.'

'Yes. I mustn't be seen talking with you too much, specially now Stephen's back. He notices more than Mama.'

'Where has your brother been?'

'He stays in London, mostly. He's studying to be a lawyer.'

I wondered whether to tell her about my conversation with Stephen. It would have reassured her, of course, but I was still annoyed by her dramatics.

Or perhaps I was falling into the spy's habit of secrecy.

I got back to the schoolroom just in time for my share of minced mutton and green peas. In the afternoon, as a treat for the children, we were allowed the use of the pony phaeton to take them over to the keeper's cottage on the edge of the estate to see a litter of month-old puppies. Mrs Beedle had half-promised Charles he might have one for his own, if my reports on his progress in Latin and arithmetic were satisfactory. It was good to see them playing and laughing with the puppies, so much more at ease when they were away from the house.

'I shall tell her he's doing well, whether he does or not,' I whispered to Betty.

'Yes. Goodness knows, they don't have an easy life, poor mites.'

Betty was watching Henrietta clutching a wriggling puppy and not caring about her dress for once. It seemed an odd thing to say about three children who lived lives of such privilege, but that evening I had an illustration of what she meant. The bell rang as usual, and we escorted them downstairs. Only the immediate family were present, including Stephen. He was sitting on a chair beside his mother's sofa, showing her something in a book. Lady Mandeville was smiling, more animated than I'd ever seen her, as if he were a lover instead of a son. When James went running to her, she hugged the boy as she usually did and spoke to him, but still with half her attention on Stephen. Celia was sitting by the square piano painted with swathes of roses and forget-me-nots, but didn't look as if she'd been playing it. She said good evening, mostly to Betty rather than me. Mrs Beedle was by the window, sewing as usual, and Sir Herbert was standing by the fireplace, reading letters and paying no attention at all to the rest of his family. Henrietta, who hated to be ignored, went over and stood beside him.

'Papa, may I have a puppy too?'

She said it in a wheedling lisp, so at first I wasn't sorry when he ignored her and went on reading.

'Papa, may I . . .?'

He gestured to her to be quiet. Lady Mandeville called across from the couch.

'Henrietta, come here and stop bothering your father.'

Anybody could tell the letter was annoying him. His face was going red, his shoulders rigid. But the child wouldn't budge.

'Cowards. Miserable, temporising pack of damned cowards!'

He shouted it at the top of his voice, crumpled the letter and threw it into the empty fireplace. As he turned, his elbow caught Henrietta on the side of the face. He might not have intended it, but when she cried out and went sprawling on the carpet, he made no move to pick her up.

'Herbert, the children . . .' Lady Mandeville protested.

James had started to cry and was clinging to her, so she couldn't get up and go to her daughter.

'Damn you and damn the children.'

Betty and I ran to Henrietta. Sir Herbert cannoned into Betty and almost knocked her off her feet as he made for the door to the hall. As he went out, I heard him giving an order to the footman about hock and sandwiches in the library. By now Henrietta was howling and even Charles was biting his lip and looking scared. Mrs Beedle was the first of the family to recover.

'Henrietta, please stop that noise. Celia, see to James. Betty, have you arnica ointment in your room?'

She wanted the children out of the drawing room, back to the safety of the schoolroom and, in spite of James's reluctance to leave his mother, we managed it.

We calmed the children, fed them bread and milk and put them to bed. Henrietta had a bruise developing on her jaw where her father's elbow had struck. Betty and I didn't discuss what had happened until we were sitting at the schoolroom table over a pot of tea.

'Is he often as bad as that?' I said.

'He's always had a black temper, but it's been worse in the last few months. A lot worse.'

'How does Lady Mandeville stand for it?'

'What can she do?'

'She could leave, couldn't she? She must have family or friends.'

'And lose the children? Children are a father's property, remember. If she walks out of here, she'll never see them again. So what choice has she got?'

'Can't anybody do anything? What about the son? He seems fond of his mother.'

Betty gave me a look. I had the impression that what had happened downstairs had made a bond between her and me.

'Mr Stephen's part of the trouble. If it weren't for him, she might stand up for herself more than she does.'

'Why?'

Betty took her time deciding whether to answer, finishing her cup of tea and swirling the dregs round to look at the pattern the tea leaves made.

'After university, he took up with some bad company and got himself into debt.'

'Gambling debts?'

'Mostly. Other things as well. He doesn't have any money of his own, of course, not a shilling. So . . .' She hesitated, looking into her cup. 'He got put into debtors' prison.'

She whispered it, her eyes scared. I was perhaps not quite as shocked as she expected me to be. The fact was, some of my father's friends had been put into debtors' prison from time to time and seemed to regard it as no worse an inconvenience than an attack of fever or rheumatics.

'Not even the gentlemen's part of the prison,' Betty insisted. 'In there with the common criminals without even a blanket to cover himself and rats running over him. And Sir Herbert let him stay there for three whole weeks.'

I thought of Stephen's elegant manners and quizzical eyebrows failing to impress the rats and did feel rather sorry for him.

'Lady Mandeville was on her knees to Sir Herbert, literally down on her knees, begging him to have her son out,' Betty said. 'He could have settled the debts ten times over and hardly missed it, and everybody knew that. But he wouldn't do it, not until Stephen had learned his lesson, he said. Ever since then, she's been terrified. That was what started . . . you know.'

She tipped a hand towards her mouth, as if holding a glass. She might have said more, but Henrietta was crying out and we had to go to her. What with that and James wetting his bed, we had a hard night with them, and it was past one in the morning before they were all three sleeping. Betty said she'd listen out for them, so I could go upstairs.

I didn't sleep because I was too scared about the

journey I must make in the morning. At first light, before even the earliest maid could have begun her cleaning duties, I crept down the back stairs to the drawing room and retrieved from the fireplace the crumpled letter that Sir Herbert had flung there. It was the kind of thing that spies did, after all. I took it back to my room to read. It had the address of a gentleman's club at the top and was in small, cramped writing.

Dear Mandeville,

Yours of the 23rd ult. has only just come to my hand. I am writing in haste to urge you to desist from this most dangerous folly. You are aware of the extent to which I share all the concerns of yourself and others about the deplorable weakness of the present administration and the threat to our dignity, profits and rights of property which must inevitably result if they continue cravenly to appease the masses. But there are remedies which are more perilous than the disease and, if I understand your hints aright (which I am very much afraid I do, greatly though I should wish otherwise), your proposed cure is one such.

If in the past my too-great warmth on such subjects has led you to the erroneous conclusion that I might in any way support what you propose, I can only apologise for unwittingly misleading you. Bluntly, I want no part in this.

*If indeed a wrong was done, then it was done
twenty years ago. To attempt to right it in these
changed times would be no service to our
country or to him you wish to serve. Let him
not cross the Channel. If a pension must be
discussed, then – provided that stretch of water
remains for ever between him and England – I
might be prepared to say a word in certain ears.
Otherwise I must ask you not to correspond
with me on the subject again.*

Believe me, your most alarmed well-wisher,
Tobias

I added a postscript to the note I'd written to
Blackstone and sealed up the letter along with it. Then
I put the note and Celia's letter into my reticule and
went stocking-footed down the back stairs so as not to
wake the maids.

CHAPTER FOURTEEN

Even so early in the morning it was unthinkable to walk down the main drive, with all those windows watching me. The back road was reassuring by comparison. After passing a big, lightning-scarred tree it dipped between high banks crowded with cow parsley, wild geraniums and red campion, the air so sweet after a long time inside that it began to raise my spirits.

Once clear of being seen from the house, my mind was free to think about other things, like the letter I'd taken from the fireplace. *Let him not cross the Channel.* The man who had written that was scared, and the reason for his fear – as the reason surely for my father's death – came from France. So did the unknown, unfortunate woman that the fat man was hunting. And yet my last letter from my father, hinting at a secret, had not mentioned danger, rather the reverse: . . . *one most capital story which I promise will set you roaring with laughter and even perhaps a little indignation* . . . Blackstone could probably make sense of it all, but he wouldn't tell me. Well, I was being his good spy. After only a few days under the Mandeville roof, I was bringing him a fat packet of news.

The banks on either side flattened out and the back road joined the main road that I'd travelled on from Windsor. Half a mile in that direction were the great gates of Mandeville Hall. They were closed, but a trail of smoke rose from the chimney of the gate lodge into the blue sky. I turned in the opposite direction, making for what I hoped was the heath. For half a mile or so I had the road to myself, then four figures appeared, coming towards me. I fought against the impulse to jump into a ditch and went on walking. They were three haymakers, walking with their scythes over their shoulders, and a boy scuffling his boots in the dust behind them, trailing their long shadows as the sun came up. They nodded to me and the boy gave me a sideways look. If I'd had more confidence I might even have asked them the way, because I wasn't sure I was on the right track for the livery stables.

After a while a lane went off to the right, deeply marked with hoofprints, and a signboard with a horseshoe pointed to the stables. The heath opened out, with skylarks singing overhead and from far away a vibration of drumming hooves that seemed to come

207

up through my bootsoles and straight into my heart.
I envied what must surely be the uncomplicated happiness of the people riding those horses. Then the line
of them came into view, pulling up from a gallop to
a canter. I stood back from the path. They came
towards me, but the lads riding them didn't give me
a glance. They had their hands full, bringing the
excited horses back to a walk before they came to the
harder ground of the path. The air was full of the
smell of horse sweat and leather. There were five
horses, three of them bunched together, then a calmer,
cobby type with a big man aboard. Then a gap and
a bright bay mare a little smaller and more finely
made than the others. The lad riding her was having
trouble slowing her to a walk, but that was because
he was so heavy-handed. He'd pulled the reins in tight
and was trying to hold her by sheer force so that she
was dancing on the spot, fighting the bit. His face
was white and terrified. He looked no more than
twelve or so and I supposed they'd put him on the
mare because he was the lightest. A sideways jerk of
her head tugged the reins out of his hands. He grabbed
and got one rein, slewing the bit sideways in her mouth
at an angle that must have hurt. She reared up and,
as her head came round towards me, I recognised the
comma-shaped blaze and intelligent eye, now terrified.

'Rancie.'

The boy rocketed out of the saddle and landed on

his side on the path. Rancie came down to earth and galloped past the other horses. One of them wheeled round to get out of her way and barged into his neighbour, who kicked him. I think I'd said her name aloud, but with the shouting, whinnying and groans of the lad on the ground, nobody noticed me. I ran after her, scared that she'd catch a leg in the trailing reins and throw herself down. Some way along the path I caught up with her. She'd stopped and was snatching at grass, not like a happy horse eating but a desperate one looking for consolation in something familiar. Scraps of grass were falling uneaten from her trembling lip. She rolled her eye at me and flinched as if expecting punishment. I think a kindly horse feels guilt when it loses its rider.

'Rancie, girl, it's all right, Rancie . . .' I put a hand on her sweat-soaked shoulder. 'It's not your fault. Poor Rancie.'

With my other hand, I gathered up the trailing reins. By then, the other horses were coming past us. The man on the cob was leading one of them because its rider had dismounted and was looking after the lad who'd been thrown. They were coming slowly along the path together, the lad limping and holding an arm crooked across his chest. The man on the cob called out to me as he passed.

'Well done, miss. I'll take her.'

If an oak tree could have spoken, it would have been in that deep Hereford voice. Amos Legge, my fair-haired giant. He threw the reins of the horse he was leading to one of the lads and sprang off the cob's back, landing neatly beside Rancie and me.

'Thought it was you, miss. You be come to see Rancie, then?'

He didn't even sound surprised. As he ran his hand down Rancie's legs, checking for injuries, she bent her head and nuzzled his back with that deep sigh horses give when anxiety goes out of them.

'No great mishtiff done. Will you lead her in then, miss?'

We followed Amos and the cob along the lane and through a gateway into the yard, Rancie as quiet as a pet dog. The yard was busy, with the horses coming in from exercise and a pair of greys being harnessed to a phaeton. Amos seemed to sense that I didn't want to attract attention and led us to a box in the far corner.

'You two wait in there, while I go and see to this fellow.'

The straw in the box was deep, and good clean hay in the manger. At least Blackstone was keeping that part of our bargain, so perhaps he'd keep others. I stayed in a dark corner, talking to Rancie, until Amos came back. He untacked her, plaited a hay wisp and used it in long, sweeping strokes to dry off the sweat. When he put her rug on, he reached under her belly to hand me the surcingle strap, as if we'd been working together for months. As soon as the rug was on, the gold-eyed cat jumped down from the manger and settled in her usual place on Rancie's back.

'I thought you'd have gone home to Herefordshire by now,' I said.

'No hurry, miss. There's work for me here if I want it, so I thought I might stay for a bit, see her settled. And it was in my mind I might be seeing you again.'

A voice from the yard called, 'Amos. Where's Amos?'

'I have letters for the post,' I said. 'Could you see they go on the next mail coach?'

Blackstone had instructed me to send letters through the owner of the stables, but this was the chance of a little independence. Amos nodded, took both letters from me but gave back Celia's coins.

'I'm doing well enough, miss, but what about you?'

'I'm employed at Mandeville Hall, only they mustn't know about this.'

'Amos.'

The call was impatient. Amos picked up the saddle and bridle.

'You wait here till I come. You'll be safe enough.'

'I can't wait.'

I'd lost track of time, but Betty would surely be getting the children up soon and I'd be missed. Still, one thing was urgent.

'Rancie must be exercised properly. Isn't there anybody who can ride her?'

'I'm too heavy and the lads are feared of her, miss. That's the third she's had off.'

'It's because she's light-mouthed. They'll kill her spirit if they go on like this. Can you tell them you've had word from her owner that nobody should ride her until further instructions?'

He nodded, but looked worried.

'Needs a lady's hand, she does.'

I don't know if he was deliberately putting an idea into my mind.

'I'll think of something,' I said. 'I'll be back on . . .' I did a quick calculation. In four days there might be an answer to one or both of the letters '. . . on Saturday.'

He nodded and went out to the yard, taking his time. When I glanced out, everybody in the yard seemed to be occupied, so I slipped past them without anybody noticing and out of the gates.

'You look feverish,' Betty said. 'Did you sleep badly?'

She'd been kinder than I deserved, getting the children up and dressed, taking them for their walk before breakfast. I'd almost bumped into them on my way back from the flower garden where I'd put a clove carnation on the rustic seat for Celia to find. I'd had to hide behind the beech hedge then rush up the back stairs to wash and tidy myself. By the time they came back to the schoolroom, I was tolerably neat in my blue-and-white print dress and muslin tucker, reading from the *Gallic Wars*.

'She's wearing rose-water,' Henrietta said, sniffing.

Observant little beast. The maids had taken most of

the water as usual, and there had only been enough left for a superficial wash, not enough to abolish the lingering smell of stables.

'It smells just like my rose-water.'

It was. Desperate, I'd gone into her room and sprayed myself from the bottle on her white-and-gilt dressing table. What do nine-year-old girls need with rose-water in any case? It marked the start of a difficult day in the schoolroom. The children were short of sleep and sullen, still shaken by their father's anger the evening before. I could hardly keep my eyes open, let alone summon up any interest in Julius Caesar or multiplication in pounds, shillings and pence. Towards the end of the morning, when we'd moved on to French conversation, Mrs Beedle paid us a visit of inspection. She sat listening for a while, very stern and upright, but from the thoughtful way she looked at her grandchildren I guessed she was trying to tell if they were affected by what had happened. What was more alarming was that I caught her looking at me with a puzzled frown, nostrils flaring. She'd certainly noticed the rose-water and probably guessed where it came from, but had she caught a whiff of horse as well?

'Miss Lock, I am concerned . . .' she said, and paused.

'Concerned, ma'am?'

'. . . that you are teaching Henrietta the wrong kind of French.'

I tried not to show my relief.

'I hope not, ma'am. Her accent has improved quite remarkably in a few days.'

213

It was my one pedagogic achievement. The child had a good ear and I had coached her to utter some sentences of politeness in a way that would not have caused pain in Paris.

'Please do not contradict me. I couldn't understand a word she was gabbling. I shall examine her again next week and expect her to be speaking French like an English gentlewoman.'

The children slept in the afternoon and so did I, so deeply unconscious on my attic bed that I woke thinking I was back at my aunt's house, until the clash of saucepans from the kitchens below reminded me. I cried for a while, then dressed and tidied my hair and went down. Betty was laying out Henrietta's white muslin frock with the blue sash.

'We're surely not taking them down tonight,' I said. 'Not after what happened.'

'If they're sent for, they'll have to go.'

At first, James flatly refused to change into his best clothes. He wanted to see his mother but his fear of his father was greater.

'Your papa is a very important man,' Betty told him. 'He's angry sometimes because he works hard, that's all.'

But her eyes, meeting mine over his bowed head, told a different story. Henrietta was impatient with her brother.

'Don't be silly. Papa didn't mean to hurt me.'

I looked at the blue bruise on her jaw and thought

there was a kind of courage in her. James let himself be dressed at last, but began crying when the bell rang for us and clung tightly to my hand as we went down the staircase to the grand hall. There were servants at work, dusting and polishing. This was a surprise because normally cleaning was done early in the morning, before the family were up and about. The reason seemed to be a re-arrangement of the pictures. There were dozens of them round the hall, some of be-wigged Mandeville ancestors and their white-bosomed ladies, others of great moments from British history. Julius Caesar confronting the Druids had been one of the most prominent, next to the door to the larger of the two drawing rooms. Now it had been taken down and propped against the wall and a portrait was being put up in its place. Sir Herbert himself was supervising, with Mrs Beedle, the butler, Mrs Quivering and two footmen in attendance. Since all this was barring the way to the drawing room, we could only stand there with the children and wait. When they'd fixed it in place at last, and Sir Herbert had nodded his grudging approval, the painting seemed a poor substitute for noble Caesar. The portrait was a comparatively modern one of a pleasant though somewhat pop-eyed young woman, dressed simply in white silk with a blue sash, arms bare and hair piled in curls on top of her head, surrounded with a wreath of roses, all in the easy Empire style of our parents' time. To my surprise, I recognised her from other portraits I'd seen, and when

James tugged at my hand and whispered, 'Who is she?' I was able to whisper back.

'That's poor Princess Charlotte.'

My father had not encouraged concern about the doings of royalty, but even a republican's daughter may be interested in princesses, especially young ones who ended sadly. So although I was no more than a baby when Princess Charlotte died, I knew a little about her. She was a grand-daughter of mad King George III, the only legitimate child of his son George IV and his unruly and hated Queen, Caroline. Her lack of brothers and sisters was accounted for by the fact that her father, on first being introduced to his arranged bride, had turned pale and called for a glass of brandy. They spent just one night together in the royal matrimonial bed and Princess Charlotte was the result.

Charlotte showed signs of being one of the best of the Hanoverian bunch, which to be sure is not saying a great deal. She was, by most accounts, more amiable than her father and more sensible than her mother. They married her before she was twenty to one of those German princelings who are in such constant supply, and she became pregnant with a child who would have succeeded her and become king of England – only she died in childbirth and her baby boy died too. Which was why we were about to celebrate the coronation of a different grand-daughter of mad King George, Charlotte's cousin, little Vicky. In the circumstances, going to such trouble to commemorate Charlotte seemed another of Sir Herbert's eccentricities.

'Is she the new queen?' James whispered to me.

'No. I'm afraid she died.'

Sir Herbert stood staring at the picture. None of us could move before he did. James fidgeted and gripped my hand even more tightly. He probably needed to piss.

'What did she die of?'

An awkward question. I could hardly explain death in childbirth to the boy, especially in such public circumstances. I began, in a whisper, that she had caught a fever, but a higher voice came from my other side.

'She was poisoned.'

Henrietta, in that terribly carrying tone of hers, determined to be the centre of attention. There was a moment of shocked silence, then her father's head swung round, slow and heavy like a bull's, from the picture to where we were standing. After his violence the night before, I was terrified of what he might say or do to the child. I was scared for myself too, certain that I should be blamed for Henrietta's lapse both in manners and historical knowledge. The child's lurid imagination and over-dramatic nature would be no excuse. I forced myself to look Sir Herbert in the eye, determined on dignity at least, and the expression under his black brow so disconcerted me that I fear my mouth gaped open. The man was smiling – a phenomenon I'd never before witnessed. He took a few heavy steps towards us, then, amazingly, bent down until his eyes were level with Henrietta's, gently tweaked one of her ringlets and put a finger to his lips.

'Shhh,' he said to her.

I think everybody there was as amazed as I was, not believing him capable of such a kindly and humorous rebuke. Henrietta was wriggling and simpering, having achieved exactly what she wanted. He touched her hair again, straightened up and said a few more words, equally surprising.

'It is a pity you are not ten years older.'

They were said in an undertone, and I think I was the only one apart from Henrietta who caught them. Then he turned and walked into the drawing room and we followed him with the children. James had his half-hour with his mother, then we managed to get him back upstairs before he wet his breeches.

That evening, Betty went to her room soon after the children were in bed. I stayed on my own in the school-room with the window open and a lamp on the table, preparing notes on the geography of India for next day's lesson. I was dozing over the tributaries of the Ganges when the door opened quietly and somebody came into the room.

'Is one of the children awake?' I said, thinking it must be Betty.

'I hope not,' Celia said, coming over to the table.

She was in evening dress, peach-coloured muslin with darker stripes woven in silk, bodice trimmed with cream lace. Her face was pale in the candlelight, eyes scared.

'You were seen, Elizabeth.'

She took hold of the back of a chair and pivoted from side to side on the ball of one satin-shod foot, in a kind of nervous dance step.

'By whom?'

'One of the laundry maids has a sweetheart who works at the livery stables.'

'Why didn't you warn me?'

'Am I supposed to know every servant's sweetheart? I only heard about it from Fanny when she was doing my hair for dinner.'

'What did she tell you?'

'The stable boy was sent up here on some message. He told his laundry maid a tale of a woman appearing out of nowhere and catching a horse that was bolting.'

'She wasn't . . . I mean, how did he know it was me?'

'He didn't. Only he described you and what you were wearing and the laundry maid said it sounded a bit like the new governess.'

'They don't know for certain, then?'

'Not yet, no. I was shaking. Fanny must have felt it. Then I had to sit through dinner wondering if Sir Herbert had heard about it yet.'

'Did he give any sign?'

'No, but then he may just be waiting for his time to pounce.'

I put down my pencil and found my hand was shaking too.

'What are we going to do?' Celia said. 'I must have the reply to my letter.'

'Oh, there's certain to be a reply, is there?'

I was nettled at her refusal to consider any problem but her own.

'I'm sure Philip will reply by return of post. I told him to write care of the stables. It should be there by Friday or Saturday at the latest.'

'Is a love letter so important that I must risk dismissal for it?'

She sat down heavily on Henrietta's blue chair.

'It's more than that. I wish . . . oh, I must trust you. I've asked him something. I need his answer.' She looked down at the map of India, picked up my pencil and turned it over and over in her fingers. 'I've asked him to elope with me.'

'Doesn't the suggestion usually come from the gentleman?'

'I'm certain Philip would suggest it if he knew. But he can't know until he reads my letter. You see, somebody's coming soon and I want Philip to take me away and marry me before he arrives.'

'This other person, is he the one your stepfather wants you to marry?'

She nodded.

'When is he arriving?'

'I don't know. He's expected any day.'

'But your stepfather surely can't have you married against your wishes, the moment this person sets foot in the house.'

'It would be so much safer in every way if I weren't here.'

I supposed she was referring to Sir Herbert's violent temper. I felt sorry for her, but wished she hadn't planted her burden on my doorstep.

'Your stepfather said something surprising to Henrietta this evening,' I said.

'What?'

'He wished she were ten years older.'

'I wish to heaven she were.' It burst out of her, vehement and unguarded. 'When did he say it?'

I told her about Princess Charlotte's portrait and the rest. All the time she stared at me, as if every word mattered. I hoped at the end of it that she'd tell me why it concerned her so much, but she just heaved a sigh nearly as deep as Rancie's.

'So what are we to do about your letter?' I said.

Whatever happened, I must keep open a way of communicating with Blackstone.

'I was hoping you'd think of something,' she said.

'You know the ways of the household better than I do.'

She stared down at her silk-stockinged ankles, looking so lost that I pitied her in spite of my annoyance.

'If I can think of something, will you do it, Elizabeth?'

'If you can, yes.'

221

She got up slowly, and took a few steps to the door, as if reluctant to leave the sanctuary of the schoolroom. At the door she turned round.

'Don't fail me. You're my only hope.'

'I'm my only hope as well,' I said, but she was gone by then.

CHAPTER FIFTEEN

The next few days were almost calm, probably because Sir Herbert was away in London. I gathered that from Betty, who picked up most of the gossip from the other servants. I say 'almost calm' because even I was aware that the staff were having to work harder than ever. Whenever we left the snug little world of the nursery corridor, maids were flying in all directions, cleaning rooms, carrying armfuls of linen, washing the paint-work round doors and windows. Betty's friend Sally reported that the kitchens were worse than Bedlam. Whenever I saw Mrs Quivering she had a worried frown on her face and two or three lists in her hand. Even the gardens, usually a peaceful refuge, seemed to have caught the panic, with a dozen men trimming lawn edges and clipping box hedges so precisely that we could have used them for illustrations in geometry. Relays of boys trotted from vegetable gardens to the back door of the kitchens with baskets of carrots, white turnips, new potatoes, radishes, spring onions, salsify, artichokes, great swags of feathery fennel, sage, thyme. The appetite of the house seemed endless, but Betty said this was all just practising. They were making sure they had the new recipes right. As a result, the servants hall was eating better than it had for years, which was one blessing at any rate, if everybody hadn't been too harassed to enjoy it.

'But what are they celebrating?' I asked Betty.

She shrugged. Sir Herbert was a law unto himself. When we took the children down on Friday evening, he was still away. Stephen was there, talking to his sister by the window. They both looked serious. Celia glanced over her shoulder and soon afterwards came across to me.

'Miss Lock, my trees simply will not come right. Do look.'

She said it loudly enough for anybody in the room to hear and had brought her sketchbook with her. Stephen stayed where he was, but gave me a glance and a nod of approval. We bent over the sketch on one of the pie-crust tables, heads together. Her hair smelled of lily-of-the-valley and I was aware that mine was sticky and dusty.

'Will you be in the schoolroom later?' she said, under her breath.

'When?'

224

'Around midnight. Will Betty have gone to bed by then?'

'Yes, usually.'

'I've thought of a way, only . . . You see, they look like cabbages and I promise you I've tried so hard.'

This for the benefit of Mrs Beedle, who was coming over to look. The three of us pored over Celia's mediocre landscape until it was time for the family to go into dinner. Betty was tired and went to bed early. I waited in the schoolroom with *Gallic Wars* and a single candle, listening to the stable clock striking the hours. Celia arrived soon after midnight, dragging a blanket-wrapped bundle.

'What's that?' I said.

'Some things to make you invisible.'

'Are you setting up as an enchantress?'

'Not of that kind. Open it.'

When I undid the blanket a tangle of clothes flopped out: plain brown jacket, tweed cap, coarse cotton shirt, red neckcloth, corduroy breeches, gaiters and a pair of that hybrid form of footwear known as high-lows, too high for a shoe and too low for a boot. They were all clean but had obviously been worn before.

'Men's clothes?'

'Boy's. It's the next best thing to being invisible. Boys go everywhere and nobody gives them a second glance.'

'I can't wear these. It's not decent.'

'Why not? Women in Shakespeare are always dressing up as boys – Viola and what-was-her-name in the forest – and they all of them end up marrying dukes and things.'

'Then why don't you do it?'

For a moment, in my confusion, I'd forgotten I had my own risks to run.

'Of course I can't. Imagine if I were caught.'

'And what if I were caught?'

'You won't be. In any case, you'll make a much better boy than I should. I'd never fit into the unmentionables.'

I picked up the breeches carefully.

'They're clean,' she said. 'I saw to that.'

'Where did you get them?'

'My grandmother collects old clothes from the household for the vicar to give to the poor. She was pleased when I offered to help her. Do the high-lows fit?'

I slipped my feet into them. They did, more or less. Somehow the touch of the leather against my stockings made the idea more thinkable, as if the clothes brought a different identity.

'Very well,' I said. 'I'll try it.'

She put her arms round me and kissed me on the forehead.

'Oh, you brave darling. You're saving my life, you know that?'

I turned away and picked up the neckcloth, not wanting to encourage her dramatics.

'You'll go tomorrow morning, early?'

'Yes.'

'There'll be a reply for me, I know. Leave a flower on the bench again when you get back, and I'll find an occasion for you to give the letter to me. I must go now. Fanny will notice if I have bags under my eyes in the morning.'

Luckily there was nobody to notice my eyes when I got up at four in the morning because I hadn't slept at all. The boy's clothes were piled on the chair beside my bed and I puzzled my way into them by the first grey light of the day, not daring to light a candle in case the light or smell of it penetrated to the maids' rooms downstairs. It took time because my fingers were shaking, but I managed at last to work out the buttons and to pin my hair up under the cap so tightly that it dragged at my scalp. I slid my arms into the sleeves of the brown jacket and put my latest report to Blackstone into a pocket. The lack of a mirror to show me what I looked like was one mercy at least.

I went barefoot down the stairs carrying the high-lows and sat down on the edge of the pump trough in the back courtyard to put them on. Though the household would soon be stirring, I hoped the servants would be too bleary-eyed and weighed down with their own tiredness to worry about anything else. And yet, when I took my first steps across the courtyard, the feeling was so exposed and indecent that I felt as if the eyes of a whole outraged world were staring at me. I missed the gentle movement of skirt hems against my ankles, the soft folds of petticoats. The roughness of breeches against my thighs seemed an assault on my softest and most secret parts. The high-lows were a little too large and, since Celia had not thought to steal socks as well, my feet slid around in them like butter in a churn. I tried to work out a way of walking that suited them, kicking one foot ahead and planting it firmly before moving the other. By this method I got myself through the archway and to the point where the drive divided, one part heading towards the bridge over the ha-ha and the front of the house, the other down the back road.

I sat down on the bank, plucked handfuls of grass and used it to pad out the high-lows so that my feet didn't slip round so much. After that, walking became easier. I learned to bend my knees and swing my legs less stiffly, although it felt odd to look down and see brown breeches where there should have been lavender or green skirt. After a while, I was almost enjoying it and even pushed my fists into my pockets and tried whistling. When I passed the reapers and their boy on much the same part of the road as I'd met them before, the men hardly gave me a second glance, though the boy threw me a hard stare that might have been meant as a challenge. I dropped my eyes until they were well past.

It was full light when I arrived at the Silver Horseshoe. I waited by the gate until I saw Amos Legge coming out of one of the looseboxes and walked up behind him.

'Good morning, sir. Any horses to hold?'

I'd been practising my boy's voice as I walked along. A hoarse mumble seemed to work better than a boyish treble. He turned round.

'You'd best ask . . . Well, I'll be dankered. It issun May Day, is it?'

'May Day?'

'When the maids dress up for a lark. None of them made as good a lad as you, though.'

Rosalind in the Forest of Arden had poems written for her and stuck on trees. His compliment might not be Shakespearean, but it pleased me.

'I thought it was in your mind,' he said. 'Only I didn't know you'd do it. I'll go and get the tack on her.'

'Tack?'

All I'd intended was to give him my letter for Blackstone, collect Celia's reply and go. Before I could explain that a big red-faced man came up to us.

'Who's that, Legge?'

'Lad come to ride the new mare, Mr Coleman. Recommended especial by the owner.'

The man gave me a quick glance, then nodded and walked away.

'Ride Rancie?' I said.

'That's what you came here to do, isn't it?'

In a daze, I followed him to her loosebox and helped him tack up. When he led Rancie out to the yard with me following, some of the lads were already mounting.

I watched as they faced inwards to the horse and crooked a knee so that a groom could take them by the lower leg and throw them up into the saddle. When it was my turn, my legs were trembling so much that Amos must have felt it, but he gave no sign. He helped my toes into the stirrups and my hands to gather up the reins, and stood watching as the string of six of us walked out of the yard, Rancie and I at the rear. It felt oddly unsafe at first to be riding astride instead of side-saddle, but the mare's pace was so smooth that after a half-mile or so I wondered why anybody should ever ride any other way. The fear began to fall away and something like a prayer formed in my mind.

Your horse, Father. Your present to me. I know it was not meant to be this way. I'd have given my whole heart for it to be different, for you to be riding her on this fine morning and I watching you. But since it can't be different, I have this at least, perhaps for the first and last time. I haven't forgotten my promise to nail that great lie they told about you. But this is here and now, and for you too and . . .

Oh gods, we're cantering. Cantering, then galloping. She stretched out, hooves hardly seeming to touch the cushiony grassland, mane flying. I bent forward as the other boys were doing, the whole world a blur of green and blue and a pounding of hooves. It was the memorial to my father that the wretched ceremony by the grave in Calais had not been, this flying into the morning light, this certainty that in spite of everything it was worth going on living and breathing.

For a few minutes fear, confusion and even grief itself were swept away in the sunlight and the rush of cool morning air against my face. I hardly needed to touch the rein because Rancie seemed responsive to my very thoughts. When the others drew up panting at the end of the gallop, her breath was coming as lightly as at the beginning. I found myself grinning with delight at one of the other riders, a red-haired lad with a pale face and no front teeth. He grinned back, saying something about her being a winner. I just remembered in time not to reply, and to pull the cap well down over my hair. We turned back to the stables in a line, some of the horses jogging and fidgeting from excitement, but Rancie walking calmly like the lady she was, between hedges thick with honeysuckle and clamorous with blackbirds.

Amos was waiting outside the gate, looking down the lane for us. He walked alongside as we came back into the yard and caught me as I slid down from the saddle. My head only came up to his chest, and I was half smothered in the hay and fresh-sweat smell of him.

'Best get her inside her box quickly, with all this pother going on.'

The stableyard was in confusion. A large travelling carriage had arrived, dust covered and with candle-lamps still burning, as if it had driven all night. Four fine bay horses were being unharnessed from it and could hardly walk for weariness. The nearside front wheel was off and leaning against the drinking trough, its iron rim half torn away and several spokes broken.

'What happened?' I asked Amos, as we went across the yard.

'Hit a tree a mile up the road. Driving too fast, he was, and . . .'

He went on telling me, but I wasn't listening because I'd noticed something on the door of the coach. An empty oval shape, framed with a wreath of gold leaves, waiting for a coat of arms to go inside it.

'What's the trouble, lad?'

I suppose I must have stopped dead. Amos pushed me gently by the shoulder. Once the half-door of the loosebox had closed on us, he was all concern.

'You look right dazzed, miss. Are you not well?'

'Mr Legge, who does the carriage belong to?'

'Two gentlemen from London, wanting to get to the hall. The fat one's in a right miff because there's nobody to get the wheel fettled. The guvnor's sent a boy galloping for the wheelwright, but that's not fast enough for him.'

'Is he a very fat man, like a toad?'

'If a toad could wear breeches and swear the air blue, yes, he is. You know him, miss?'

'I think I might.' I was sure of it, cold and trembling at the thought of being so near him again. 'I don't want him to see me. Where is he?'

'In the guvnor's office, last I saw. He was trying to convince the guvnor to take a wheel off one of his own carriages to put on the travelling coach. The guvnor offered him the use of his best barouche and horses instead and said he'd send the coach up to the hall later, but that wouldn't answer. It's the travelling coach or nothing.'

'So he could be here for hours.'

And me trapped in the loosebox in my boy's clothes, with Betty and the rest wondering what had become of me, probably being found out and dismissed. All the time, Amos Legge was untacking and rugging up Rancie.

'I'll have a look for you, while I take this over. If he's still going on at the guvnor, you can slip out like an eel in mud and he won't notice.'

He left with the saddle and bridle and I cowered back into the dark corner by the manger. He'd mentioned two gentlemen and I assumed the other one was the man who called himself Trumper. I feared him too, but not a fraction as much as the fat man.

There was still a lot of noise and activity going on in the yard and a sound of hammering. Hurrying feet came and went on the cobbles by Rancie's door, but nobody had any reason to look in. Amos seemed to have been gone for a long time. I'd almost decided to make a run for it, when the square of sunlight above the half-door was obscured by a figure in silhouette.

'Mr Legge, thank good—'

Then I shut my mouth because the person looking over the loosebox door wasn't Amos Legge. He was shorter, not so broad in the shoulders, and must have approached very quietly because I hadn't heard him until he was there.

'Well, well, well,' he said. 'Why are you hiding in there, boy?'

Then he slid open the bolt on the half-door and walked a few steps inside the box.

The voice was a high drawl. As he turned and the sunlight came on him I knew that I'd never seen him before. There was no doubt, though, that he was one of the two gentlemen just arrived from London. He walked delicately into the rustling straw, like a nervous bather testing the temperature of the sea with his toes, looking as if he'd just stepped off the pavement of Regent Street. He wore a plum-coloured coat, a waist-coat in plum and silver stripes, a white ruffled shirt and a silver-grey cravat with a ruby and diamond pin, breeches of finest buckskin and beautiful boots of chestnut leather, with soft tops ornamented with plum-coloured tassels to match the coat. He was about my age, soft and plump, with a clean-shaven, pale face as if he spent most of his days indoors, hair clubbed back under a high-crowned grey beaver hat with a big silver buckle. His eyes were pale blue and protruding, his expression vacant, but amiable enough. As he waited for an answer from me, he hitched up a coat-tail, reached into the pocket of it and brought out a round gold box with a diamond on top that flashed when the sun caught it. He opened the box, drew off a glove, ran his little finger round the contents of the box and applied it delicately to his rather full lips, pursing them in and out. Lip salve. The box went back into his coat-tail pocket.

'What's the trouble, boy? Lost your voice, have you?'

Lucy the cat had jumped up to the manger as soon as he came in, but Rancie was unafraid and turned her head to see if he had a tidbit for her. He stroked her nose cautiously, but his eyes never left me.

'What are you hiding from? Have you been a naughty boy? Threatened you with a beating, have they? Threatened you with a birching on the seat of your little pants?'

His affected lisp made it 'thweatened'. There was such a gloating in his voice that I was sure he'd discovered my secret and knew I was no boy. In my shame and confusion, I clamped my hands over the front of my breeches. He sniggered, a horse-like sound.

'Pissed yourself, have you, boy? Is that what your trouble is? Oh naughty boy, naughty boy.'

I thought he was taunting me. There was a strange greed in the pale eyes. I turned away, trying to cram myself into the dark corner, but he stepped towards me. His hand slid over my haunches, then round towards my belly. I opened my mouth to scream and closed it again, unwillingly gulping in the smell of him: bay-leaf pomade, starched linen, peppermint breath. Then a warmer, earthier smell as Rancie caught my fear, lifted her tail and splatted steaming turds on to the straw. I wriggled away from him and dodged under Rancie's neck, putting her body between him and me. He came round behind her, still giggling.

'Don't be shy, boy. Don't stand on ceremony.'

He was between me and the door. I was too shamed to even think of screaming and had even taken hold of Rancie's mane, wondering if somehow I could manage to clamber up on her back, when a larger shape appeared at the half-door.

'You all right in there, boy?'

Amos Legge, a pitchfork in hand. The word 'boy' that had sounded a slithery thing in the fashion plate's voice was different and reassuring in his. I said 'no', trying to make it sound masculine and gruff, but the fashion plate's high drawl cut across me, speaking to Amos.

'He's been a naughty boy and I'm dealing with him. Go away.'

Amos took no notice. He slid back the bolt and walked in, giving the fashion plate a considering look. He said or did nothing threatening, but the size and assurance of him was enough. Fashion plate took a step away from me and his voice was less confident.

'Go away. You can come in and clear up later.'

'Best do it now, sir.'

Amos picked up Rancie's droppings with the pitch-fork. In the process he let some fall on the toe of fashion plate's highly polished boot. The man let out a howl.

'You clumsy oaf.'

236

'I'm sorry, sir. Mucky places, stables.'

Fashion plate opened his mouth then looked up at Amos and decided not to say anything. He pushed past us to the door and went, slamming it behind him.

'You all right, miss?' Amos said.

I nodded, not trusting my voice.

'You'd best be off, miss. You just walk along with me as far as the midden and no one will take any notice.'

We went side by side across the yard, Amos carrying the bundle of soiled straw on his pitchfork. Most of the people in the yard were fussing round the travelling coach and took no notice of us. There was no sign of the fat man. The fashion plate had his boot up on a step of the mounting block and a trim man in a black jacket was wiping it with a cloth, both of them looking as serious as if he were performing delicate surgery. The muck heap was right alongside the gate.

'Off you go then,' Amos said. 'If you're in any trouble, you get word to me, look. And here's your letters –'

He took a slim bundle out of his pocket and slid it into mine. Until then, I'd forgotten, in my fear and distress, the reason for being there.

'Here's another one for the post,' I said, almost dropping it in my haste to hand it over and be gone.

I covered the first half-mile or so at a pace between a stumbling run and a walk, fearful all the time of hearing shouts or horses' hooves behind me. Fashion plate, once his boot was out of danger, would surely tell the fat man about the woman in disguise, and if the fat man somehow guessed who she was . . .

I know the fear wasn't reasonable. Perhaps it should have occurred to me that fashion plate had hardly cut a noble picture in the loosebox so might not be eager to talk about it. The fact was, I credited the fat man with almost demonic powers and wanted to get as far away from him as I could. A stitch stabbed at my ribs and my breath came short, but I would not slow to an ordinary walk until I was on the main road again, within sight of Mandeville Hall. I went up the back road as usual, into the kitchen courtyard, through the room with the chamber pots and up the four flights of wooden stairs to my room. The letters crackled in the pockets as I took off my jacket. There was one addressed to me in Mr Blackstone's hand, another plumper one for Miss Mandeville. No time to do anything about them now. The stable clock was striking seven and I was already late for the children's prayers. I put the letters in my bag, changed, did my hair and ran downstairs.

The two boys were already dressed and sitting at the schoolroom table. Betty was brushing Henrietta's hair.

'There's straw on your dress,' Henrietta said.

I brushed it off. Betty looked a little disapproving, probably convinced I was a lazy lie-a-bed. Once prayers had been said, I made amends by volunteering to take the children for their before-breakfast walk on my own. The fact was, I wanted to go to the flower garden to leave my signal for Celia. As they ran around among the flower beds, I chose a spray of white sweet peas and wove it into the curlicues of the rustic bench.

'Why are you doing that?' Henrietta said.

The child was worse than a whole army of spies. I distracted her by making a crown of sweet peas for her hair. She was delighted and wore it at breakfast, but it didn't stop her noticing things.

'Miss Lock has eaten four slices of bread and butter.'

Betty told her a lady never made comment on what people were eating, but I was shame-faced, wondering if I'd developed a boy's appetite to go with the rest. After that, I yawned my way through the after-breakfast session in the schoolroom. Luckily, Saturdays were less formal than the rest of the week and the children were put into pinafores and allowed to do things involving paint or paste. Charles painted meticulous red jackets on to his lead soldiers, Henrietta attempted a watercolour and James re-arranged his formidable collection of empty snail shells. Seeing them so happily occupied, I was wondering whether I might sneak upstairs and read my letter from Mr Blackstone when there was a knock on the door. Patrick the footman stood outside.

'Mrs Quivering's compliments, and would Miss Lock kindly go down to the housekeeper's room.'

Betty gave me a look that said, Oh dear, what have

you done? and I followed Patrick's black-liveried back down the stairs, wondering which of my many sins had found me out, almost certain that in the next few minutes I faced dismissal. I could only hope it was nothing worse than that.

CHAPTER SIXTEEN

She was sitting at her desk with a pile of papers in front of her, cap tilted sideways as if she'd been running her hands through her hair. She looked tired and worried, but not especially hostile.

'Miss Lock, it's good of you to come down. I'm sorry to take you away from your pupils.'

Was it sarcasm? If so, there was no sign of it on her face.

'As you may have heard, Miss Lock, we are planning to entertain a large number of people next weekend, a dinner for forty people on Friday and a ball for more than a hundred on Saturday.'

I nodded, not sure if I was supposed to know even as much as that.

'Amongst other things, there is a deal of writing to be done: place cards, table plan, menus and the like.

Mrs Beedle has suggested that you might take on the duty.'

She must have mistaken my look of amazement for reluctance and went on, rather impatiently.

'I am sure you could accommodate it with your other duties. Mrs Sims could supervise some of the children's lessons, if necessary.'

Almost overcome by relief and my good luck, I assured her, truthfully, that nothing would give me more pleasure.

'Thank you, Miss Lock. I suggest you start this afternoon. I shall have a table brought into this room for you. The first thing I want you to do is make a complete and accurate copy of the guest lists here.' She picked up from her desk several pages pinned together. My eyes followed the lists like a dog craving a bone. 'Then you may use it to work from when you do the place cards. You understand?'

'Perfectly, Mrs Quivering. I'm delighted to have an opportunity to be of use.'

By mid-afternoon I was sitting by the window in the housekeeper's room, the precious lists on the table in front of me. There were three of them, the longest, some 120 names, consisted of those invited to the ball on the Saturday night. A shorter one listed the 40 guests who would also be at dinner the night before. An even more select group of 20 would be staying at Mandeville Hall for the weekend, the majority bringing valets or maids with them.

I read through the lists, looking for names I recognised. The house guests included one duke, two lords, four baronets and their ladies, and six Members of Parliament. (I refrain from giving their names here because most of them were nothing worse than foolish and easily flattered, and I am sure they would not now want the world to know that they had ever set foot in Mandeville Hall.) I racked my brains, trying to remember what I'd heard or read about any of them. The duke was eighty years old or so, and I remembered from accounts of Reform Bill debates in the Lords that he had been a bitter opponent of it. Given his host's views on the subject, it was not surprising to find him on the guest list. The same applied to two of the Members of Parliament, both to my knowledge die-hard Tories of the old school. I'd heard my father talk about them. It was a reasonable guess that the other four, of whom I'd never heard, shared their opinions.

'Have you everything you need, Miss Lock?'

Mrs Quivering came sweeping into the room, followed by her assistant, who was burdened with a bad cold and an armful of bedsheets.

'Yes, thank you, Mrs Quivering.'

I started mixing ink. The ink powder and pens were of fine quality, much better than in the schoolroom. Mrs Quivering took a bedsheet from the pile in her assistant's arms and spread it out on her table. They were on the far side of the room from me, so I couldn't hear all of their conversation but gathered that some wretch in the laundry room had ironed them with the creases in the wrong places. Then they started talking about other things. I caught 'wheel off' and 'didn't get here till nearly midday' and stopped stirring ink powder so that I could listen more carefully.

'. . . blue room all ready for him, then we have to change it because his man must sleep in the room next to him. So Mr Brighton offers to take the blue room, his valet goes upstairs with the others, and Lord Kilkeel has the oak room, which was . . .'

She unfolded another sheet, muffling the end of what she was saying. I looked at the papers I was to copy. A Mr H. Brighton was at the top of the list of guests who would be staying at Mandeville Hall, with Lord Kilkeel just below him. Which was the fat man and which was fashion plate?

'Take them back,' Mrs Quivering said, sighing. 'Tell her she's to do them again in her own time, and I don't care how long she has to stay.' She heaped the sheets back into her assistant's arms. 'Miss Lock, Mrs Beedle says when you do the place cards you must make your 's's the English way, not the French way.'

Soon afterwards she went out, leaving me alone with the lists. It was clear to me that I must make not one but two copies, one to stay in Mrs Quivering's office, the other for Mr Blackstone. It was an awkward business because my sleeve kept brushing the wet ink and making smudges, so I had to use quantities of blotting paper and the inkwell seemed as thirsty as a dog on a hot day, needing constant replenishing. I was never a tidy worker, not even in convent days, and got blots on my cuffs, smears on my face, the top two joints of my pen finger so soaked with ink I thought it must be black to the very bone. I had no time now to register the names I was copying: they were just words to be harvested. Mrs Quivering came back towards evening and seemed to approve of my industry, even showed some concern.

'You'll miss your supper, Miss Lock.'

'I think I should like to finish the lists today, Mrs Quivering.'

The true reason was that I wanted to have a reason not to be there if the children were sent for. The fat man and fashion plate were under Mandeville's roof now and would surely be in the drawing room before dinner. Fashion plate might not recognise the boy from the loosebox, but the fat man would surely remember the woman who'd butted him in the stomach. How I'd avoid him for a whole week, I didn't know.

Mrs Quivering was so pleased by my zeal that she had sandwiches and a pot of tea sent in, proper plump beef sandwiches on good white bread. I tried not to get ink on the sandwiches as I ate, then went back to copying. It was a fine evening outside, but the light inside was past its best and my eyes were tired.

I was near the end of the ball guest list when the door opened. It was Celia, in a flurry of pink silk and white ribbons.

'Betty said you were here. Have you got my letter?'

I'd brought it down with me and had it under the blotter. She went over to the window and read, her hand shaking so much I was surprised she could make out the writing.

'Oh, thank God.'

Her body sagged in a swish of silk and muslin. I think she'd have fallen to the floor if I had not jumped up and caught her. I put her down in my chair and she still clung to me.

'What's wrong?' I said.

'Nothing's wrong. Everything's right. Philip will come for me.'

'When?'

'He leaves that to me. He'll come to Ascot and be ready for a word from me. Oh, I can't think. You must help me think.'

I had no wish to be an accomplice in an elopement – my life was too tangled already – but I could hardly desert her.

'When will he get to Ascot?'

'Tuesday, he says. Wednesday at the latest. But how shall I get away? If I as much as walk in the garden, somebody notices. And now Mr Brighton's here . . .'

She said the name as if she'd bitten into something bad-tasting.

'Mr Brighton?'

'Didn't you see him? Oh, I forgot, you didn't come down with the children.'

She made a face, pushed out her lips and pretended to smear something on them with her little finger. It was exactly the gesture of fashion plate with his lip balm.

'So the fat one is Lord Kilkeel,' I said.

'Yes. Isn't he the most hideous person you've ever seen? He's a great friend of my stepfather's, though.'

I was on the point of telling her how essential it was that Kilkeel should not see me, but before I could get the words out, she was demanding my help as usual.

'Tell me, Elizabeth, you're clever, how do I get away without them noticing?'

'If there are a hundred and twenty people coming here for a ball, will anybody notice an elopement?' I said.

'But that means waiting until next weekend – a whole week.'

'Is that so bad?'

'A lot of things may happen in a week. But I'll think about it.' She stood up, rather shakily. 'Philip says I must write to him at Ascot poste restante. I'll decide tomorrow, so you must take the letter on Monday morning.'

I thought, Must I? but didn't argue because I knew I'd go to the stables in any case to send my copies of the lists to Mr Blackstone. Celia was on her way to the door.

'If anybody sees me and asks what I was doing here, say I brought you a message from my grandmother. I think she approves of you. She keeps asking me questions about you.'

'What sort of questions?'

But as before, she went without answering.

I finished copying the list and, in the last of the daylight, took the note from Mr Blackstone out from under the blotter and read it.

> *My dear Miss Lock,*
>
> *You have done well. Please do your best to communicate with me every day. In particular, be alert for the arrival of a person calling himself Mr Brighton and let me know at once.*

On Sunday afternoon I wrote my reply.

> *Dear Mr Blackstone,*
>
> *Mr Brighton arrived Saturday, in the company of Lord Kilkeel. He will be staying at least until the dinner and ball next weekend. They were in the family pew in church this morning, but I did not have a clear sight of him because I was sitting in the back pew so as not to be seen by him. I enclose lists of the guests at the dinner and ball, and also of the house guests. I hope you will consider that I have earned the right to ask why you wish to know about Mr Brighton and how it concerns my father's death. What is Lord Kilkeel's part in it?*

I wrapped it up with the lists and addressed it, wondering why I had not admitted to Blackstone that I had already been considerably closer to Mr Brighton than the length of a church away. One reason was that I distrusted the man and did not see why I should give him more than our bargain. The other and deeper one was that the memory of Mr Brighton's hands on me in the loosebox made me feel so dirtied that I could not face writing it down for another man to read.

On Sunday afternoon Celia came into the flower garden when Betty and I were there with the children. She'd brought scissors and a trug with her, to cut some sweet peas for her dressing table. When Betty wasn't looking, she slid a letter out of the trug and into my hands.

'I've taken your advice. I'm telling him to come for me on Saturday.'

When she'd gone, I watched the children and worried. It was wrong that Celia should depend on me for advice in something so important. Until then, the matter of the elopement had been useful to me, but now I felt guilty. Her position at Mandeville Hall might have its disadvantages, but at least she was provided with a permanent roof over her head, a life that connected one day with the next and the company of a mother and a brother who cared for her. Missing all of those, I valued them more than she did and wondered if this Philip were worth the loss and whether she really knew her own mind. I supposed I should have to speak seriously to her but did not look forward to it with any pleasure. Betty said she was happy to look after the children while I went back to my other work. Now that the lists were done, I turned to a stack of forty blank place cards that Mrs Quivering had set out for me. She'd suggested that I leave them till morning, but they gave me the excuse for missing the children's visit to the drawing room again and a close-quarters encounter with Kilkeel and Brighton. How I'd manage to spin out the excuses for the rest of the week, I couldn't imagine.

On Monday morning I woke with my eyes still tired from all that penmanship, body stiff and weary after an uneasy night. The thought of being under the same roof as the fat man had kept snatching me back from the edge of sleep. I fumbled in the half dark with the buttons and buckles of my boy's clothes, hating them for the memory of Mr Brighton's hands. No ride on Rancie this morning. The delight of that had been lost in what followed it and I had more serious things to do, although how poor Rancie was to be given her exercise was one of the thoughts that had nagged at my brain through the night. I hurried down the back stairs, through the room of the chamber pots and across the courtyard.

When I came to the drive and took the turning for the back road, the clouds in the east were red-rimmed, the sky overcast and rain threatening. About a hundred yards down, to the right of the road, was the big dead oak tree. On the other occasions I'd passed there had

250

been two or three crows sitting on it, but there were none that morning. I don't know why I noticed that. Perhaps I sensed something, as dogs and horses do. I passed the tree and had my back to it when a voice came from the other side of the trunk.

'Good morning, Miss Lock'.

A woman's voice. An elderly voice. Even before I turned round I knew who I'd see, though it was so wildly unlikely that she'd be there in the early hours of the morning. She'd come out from behind the tree and was standing there dressed exactly as she always was, in her black dress and black-and-white widow's cap, ebony walking cane in her hand. She stood where she was, clearly expecting me to walk towards her. I did.

'Well, aren't you going to take off your cap to me?'

Confused, I snatched off my boy's cap. My face, my whole body felt as red as hot lava while her cool old eyes took in everything about me, from rag-padded highlows to disorderly hair.

'I wondered where those clothes had got to,' she said. 'Where are you going so early, if I might ask?'

I didn't answer, conscious of the two letters padding out my pockets and sure she was aware of them too.

'It's going to rain,' she said. You are likely to get wet before you reach the Silver Horseshoe, Miss Lock.'

'Oh.'

'So I hope you have those papers well wrapped up. It would be a pity if they were spoilt, after all your careful copying.'

251

'Oh.'

I was numb, expecting instant dismissal or even arrest.

'So you had better hurry, hadn't you?' she said.

'Umm?'

She gave a sliver of a smile at my astonishment.

'May I ask for whom you are spying? Is it the Prime Minister? I wrote to him and to the Home Secretary. I was afraid that they'd taken no notice of me, but it seems one of them has after all.' Then, when I didn't answer. 'Well, it's no matter and I'm sure it is your duty not to tell me. I did not know that they used women. Very sensible of them.'

'You mean . . .?'

'Only I must impress on you, and you must pass this on to whoever is employing you, action must be taken at once. This nonsense has gone quite far enough, and it must stop before somebody dies.'

No smile now. Her hand had closed round the top of her cane, as if she were trying to squeeze sap out of the long-dead ebony.

'Somebody has already died,' I said.

'All the more reason to stop it then. What are you waiting for? Hurry.'

I went. When I looked back from a bend in the road there was only the oak tree, no sign of her.

There was a letter for Celia at the stables that Monday morning, but nothing from Mr Blackstone. On Tuesday, when Mrs Beedle came up to see the children at their lessons, she gave not the slightest sign that she regarded me as anything but the governess.

'I notice that you haven't been coming down with the children, Miss Lock.'

'I'm sorry, ma'am, but there is a great deal to do for Mrs Quivering.'

In fact, the place cards were all written and she probably knew that, but she gave me a nod and corrected a spelling mistake on James's slate that I'd missed.

'Sharp eyes, Miss Lock. Sharp brains are all very well, but there's nothing like sharp eyes.'

On Wednesday morning I made my usual journey to the livery stables, but the crows were sitting on the dead oak tree as usual and there was no sign of her. There were two letters that day, a thin one for Celia and a thinner one for me. I opened it on the journey back.

> *You have done well, Miss Lock, Your duties are*
> *at an end. You need not communicate with me*
> *any further. I shall see you again when this affair*
> *is over, or provide for you as best I can.*

I crumpled it in my hand, furious. So Blackstone thought I could be dismissed with a pat on the head, like an unwanted hound. He had a debt to me – everything he knew about my father's death. I intended to collect that debt, however long it took me.

Just one phrase of his note interested me: *when this affair is over* . . . It added to the sense I had of things moving towards a crisis. It increased all through the day as house guests began arriving in advance of the weekend. Every hour brought another grand carriage trotting up the drive and the children wouldn't settle and kept jumping up to look at them. It was a relief when Mrs Quivering summoned me downstairs again.

'Miss Lock, do you understand music?'

She had a new pile of papers on her desk and a more than usually worried expression.

'Understand?'

'There are musicians arriving tomorrow who, it seems, must have parts copied for them.'

'Will they not bring their own music?'

'It is something newly written. Sir Herbert ordered it from some great composer in London and is in a terrible passion . . . I mean, is seriously inconvenienced because the person delivered it late and with the individual parts not written out.'

'I'll do it gladly,' I said, meaning it.

It was just the excuse I needed for keeping behind the scenes on the servants' side of the house for the next two evenings. I'd often done the same service for my father's friends, so it was a link too with my old life.

She dumped the score on my desk and left me to look at it. A few minutes were enough to show that Sir Herbert's 'great' composer was a competent hack at best. The piece was headed *Welcome Home* and came in three parts: a long instrumental introduction, rather military in style, scored for woodwind, two trumpets and a side

254

drum. Then a vocal section for woodwind, strings, baritone and high tenor, with pinchbeck words about past glories and future triumphs, followed by an instrumental coda with so much work for the trumpets that I hoped they'd demand an extra fee.

I wondered if Mrs Beedle had proposed me for the copying work and, if so, what I was expected to gain from it. As the afternoon went on, I guessed that it had nothing to do with the music, but very much to do with keeping me in a convenient place for spying. Everything in a household, from kitchen maids with hysterics to guests mislaying their toothbrushes, came to the housekeeper's room.

There was one particular incident that afternoon. The assistant housekeeper came into the room and whispered something to Mrs Quivering, who followed her out to the corridor. She left the door half open and I saw one of the under footmen leaning against the wall, pale-faced, with tears running down his cheeks. I knew him slightly because he sometimes brought coal and lamp oil to the nursery kitchen. His name was Simon and he was fourteen years old, tall for his age but childish in his ways. I believe he owed his promotion from kitchen boy to under footman to the fact that his shoulders were broad enough to fill out the livery jacket. Mrs Quivering gave him a handkerchief to mop his eyes and listened with bent head to what he was saying. I couldn't hear him, but her voice carried better.

'It is not your fault, Simon, but you must not talk

about it. While he is here, you will go back to working in the kitchen, then we'll see. But if you talk about it, you will be in very serious trouble.'

Her assistant led the boy away and she came back into the room, heaving a sigh and not looking very pleased with herself. Soon after that, the butler came in, a sad-faced man named Mr Hall. They carried on a conversation in low voices, heads close together, with Mrs Quivering doing most of the talking.

'I will not tolerate it, Mr Hall. The servants are under our protection. A word must be said.'

'He won't take it well.'

'I am almost past caring how he takes it. I had Abigail in tears this morning too. She said Lord Kilkeel swore at her most vilely when he found her in his room. She'd gone in there to clean and make the bed, and he told her nobody was to set foot in there, for any reason, without his express permission. The poor girl was so terrified she's been quite useless since. And now the other one and Simon. If you won't speak to him about the two of them, then I shall. And if I lose my position through it, there are others.'

The butler said yes, he'd speak to him as soon as he had the opportunity. I could see Mrs Quivering didn't quite believe him, but they parted on civil terms and she went back to her lists.

Towards the end of the afternoon, I grew tired of having to draw musical staves with Mrs Quivering's knobble-edged ruler and went up to the school-room for a better one. I found Charles and James arguing, Henrietta sulking and Betty so worn out with having to cope with them on her own that it was the least I could do to give her an hour's relief by taking them for a walk in the grounds. We went out by a side entrance because they were in their plain school-room clothes and not fit for being seen by company. With that in mind, I guided them quickly towards the flower garden, for the protection of its high beech hedges.

'Celia? Celia, where are you?'

Stephen's voice came from the other side of the hedge. Henrietta stopped. I whispered to her to go on, but she put her eye to the hedge.

'He's with Mr Brighton,' she said in a loud whisper.

I caught Henrietta by the arm and fairly dragged her along a gravel path to the safety of a little ornamental orchard behind the flower garden, with the boys following. It was a pleasant acre of old apple and pear trees with a thatched wooden summerhouse in the middle, too far from the house to be much used by adults. Once we were safely there, I helped Henrietta tuck her skirts up to the knee and encouraged them to play hide and seek. Soon they were absorbed in their game and I sat on the bench in the summerhouse, still uneasy at having come so close to Mr Brighton, even more so in case Kilkeel came to join him.

'Elizabeth.'

Celia's whisper, from behind me. I spun round but couldn't see her until she hissed my name again. One alarmed eye and a swathe of red-gold hair showed in a gap between the planks that made up the back wall of the summerhouse.

'Miss Mandeville, what in the world are you doing there? Your brother's looking for you.'

'I know. Would you please keep the children here long enough for them to get tired of looking for me.'

'Why?'

'Because my stepfather wants me to be pleasant to Mr Brighton.'

She said the name with such scorn and anger that I half expected it to scorch the planks between us.

'But why should you be . . .?'

I was puzzled. She had no reason, as far as I knew, to share my abhorrence of the man.

'Haven't you understood anything? He's the reason why Philip must take me away.'

'You mean your stepfather wants you to marry that . . .'

'Shh. Yes.'

My voice must have risen in surprise. Luckily, it was masked by Henrietta's shriek of triumph as she discovered James hiding behind a pear tree.

'My turn to hide. My turn to hide.'

The boys closed their eyes. Charles started counting.

'One hundred, ninety-nine, ninety-eight . . .'

'I've been trying to keep away from him all afternoon,' Celia whispered. 'He must surely get tired soon.'

'Eighty-seven, seventy-nine . . .'

'You're not counting properly,' Henrietta protested.

She was plunging round among the trees, looking for a hiding place. Then she changed direction and came running towards the summerhouse.

'No, don't let her,' Celia hissed through the planks.

I stood up, but too late to intercept Henrietta as she ran behind the summerhouse.

'I've found Celia. I've found Celia.'

'Go away you little pest.'

But Henrietta's voice must have carried over the hedges. Stephen called from some way off in the flower garden, 'Celia?' Two pairs of footsteps sounded on the gravel path, one quick, one slow and heavy.

'Go to them,' Celia said to me. From her voice, she was near to tears. 'Tell them she's lying and I'm not here.'

By then I was in a fair panic myself.

'I can't.'

'Why not?'

'Mr Brighton saw me at the stables dressed as a boy. Supposing he guesses?'

A gasp from behind the planks, then silence apart from Henrietta's capering steps on the grass. Stephen appeared at the gap in the hedge. I sat down again, curling into the darkest corner of the summerhouse. As he came striding in our direction I stayed where I was, determined that Celia must solve her own problem for once.

'Celia, are you there?' he called.

Celia came out from behind the summerhouse looking far cooler than I'd expected, tucking a wisp of hair behind her ear.

'You're too hot, Henrietta. You'll make yourself ill.'

Her voice was cool too, but she threw me a glance of pure terror. As far as I could tell, Stephen hadn't noticed me in the summerhouse.

'Celia, where have you been? We've been looking for you everywhere.'

'Here, with the children,' Celia said. 'But Henrietta's made herself over-excited running about. I'm taking her back to the house to lie down.'

'Can't Betty or Miss Lock see to them?' Stephen protested.

But Celia took a firm grip of her half-sister's hand and began walking towards the hedge. She was almost there when Mr Brighton arrived, flushed of face but gorgeously dressed in pale green cut-away coat with green-and-pink striped waistcoat. He stood staring at Celia like an actor unsure of his cue. Anything less like an ardent suitor I'd never seen.

'Charles, James, come here,' Celia said, ignoring him entirely.

She collected the boys and shepherded the three children straight past Mr Brighton as if he were no more than another apple tree. When they'd disappeared, he prodded his walking cane into the grass a few times with a vacant look, then his hand went to the pocket in his coat-tail, the gold box came out and his little finger carefully applied pink balm to his full lower lip. He seemed lost. Stephen had to escort him away in the end, much as Celia had done with the children.

I stayed in the summerhouse, surprised by her resourcefulness and weak with relief at not having come face to face with Mr Brighton. Something about him was nagging at my mind – something apart from what had happened in the stables. When I saw the vacant expression on his face, a kind of half-recognition had come to me, as if I'd seen that look before a long time ago, though where and when I couldn't say. I remained there for some time. It was cool and restful and I was in no hurry to return to all the complications inside the house. I think I must have fallen into a half doze, because I didn't hear the footsteps coming back on the gravel path until they were almost at the hedge. They were male steps, but rather uncertain, as if the person didn't know what he'd find on the other side. I hoped it was simply a guest taking a stroll and started to stand up, intending to say a polite good afternoon and leave. But it wasn't a guest. Stephen Mandeville was standing in front of me.

'Miss Lock, I was hoping you'd still be here. No, please, sit down.'

So he'd seen me after all. He seemed weary, dark hair disordered, shadows under his eyes. There was nothing for it but to sit down again. He settled himself on the far side of the bench, with a respectable distance between us. I waited, heart thumping. It was in my mind that Mr Brighton might have told him about seeing me at the stables.

'I'm very glad to find you on good terms with my sister,' he said. 'I was right to think she'd find you sympathetic.'

His voice was low and gentle, no hint of accusation in it.

'Miss Mandeville is very kind. I fear I'm not as much help as I should like to be with her sketching.'

I looked down at our feet – his polished brown boots, my serviceable black – just as a governess should. In fact, I was feeling too guilty to meet his eyes. Here he was, showing concern for a sister, just as I'd hope Tom would do for me, and I was helping her deceive him.

'My sister knows no more about sketching than my spaniel does, and cares even less.'

'Oh.'

'I'm not blaming you in any way, Miss Lock. I suggested you should make a friend of Celia, after all. But we've always been close and I sense sometimes when things are not well with her. Have you a brother, Miss Lock?'

'Yes.'

I looked up at him and away again.

'You'll understand what I mean, then. I hope I'm wrong, but I sense Celia may be contemplating a step that might be very harmful for her.'

'Harmful?'

262

'A young woman's reputation is easily harmed. My sister is the most warm-hearted girl in the world but, to be frank, without much forethought.'

'Then I'll be frank as well,' I said. I looked him in the eyes now, not even trying to talk like a governess but doing my best for both of them. 'The most important decision a woman makes is who she'll marry. Shouldn't she follow her own wishes?'

'It's not always as simple as that, is it, Miss Lock? Especially when families of some note are involved.'

I was on the point of replying sharply that note or no note, it made no difference to the heart. What silenced me was the thought that he might be thinking of his own mother who had married once for love and once for money. He let the silence draw out for a while.

'I'm not asking you to betray a confidence, Miss Lock. I can only hope if you knew that Celia were on the point of doing something really unwise, you'd give a hint to me. In that case, I might be able to convince her to draw back before things went too far and came to other ears.'

The meaning was plain – Sir Herbert's ears.

'I understand.'

'You'll keep that in mind, Miss Lock?'

'Yes. Yes, I shall.'

He stood up, gave me a brief nod as if something important had been agreed and walked away through the gap in the hedge.

CHAPTER SEVENTEEN

I waited in the summerhouse until I thought family and guests would be dressing for dinner, then slipped in at the side entrance and returned to my copying. Near midnight, Mrs Quivering found me there and insisted I must go to bed. Crotchets and quavers danced behind my eyes all night and by six o'clock in the morning I was back at work. Mrs Quivering rewarded me with a cup of chocolate and warm sweet rolls for breakfast.

'Just like Lady Mandeville has. Shall we be ready in time? The musicians are supposed to be arriving by midday.'

Soon after midday, she put her head round the door.

'They've arrived and they're eating. Then they want to start rehearsing in the damask drawing room.'

'I'm just finishing. I'll take them in.'

There was still a page of the second trumpet part to

do, but in my experience, musicians were not readily torn away from free food. I finished the page, blotted it and carried the whole pile of parts to the damask drawing room. It was one of the largest and most pleasant rooms in the house, with wide windows looking on to the terrace, white-painted wall panels, blue damask curtains and upholstery and a beautiful plaster ceiling with a design of musical instruments and swags of olive leaves against a pale blue background. When I arrived servants were putting out rows of chairs on the blue-and-gold carpet and the musicians were trickling in with music stands and cases. I asked a flautist where I might find their director.

'Just coming in, ma'am.'

A dapper little figure came through the doorway, dark hair shining in the sun like a cap of patent leather.

'Mr Suter,' the flautist started saying, 'there's a lady –'

But he got no further because Daniel Suter and I were embracing like long-lost sister and brother and my carefully copied parts had gone flying all over the carpet. Indecorous, certainly, and goodness knows what Mrs Quivering would have said, but he had been part of my life as long as I could remember and dearer to me than almost all of my relatives by blood.

'What a miracle,' I said, when I got my breath back. 'What a coincidence.'

'Miraculous I may be, child, but I disdain mere co-incidence. Kennedy gave me your message two days ago. I'd been in France until then.'

'But how did you manage to be here with the orchestra?'

'An acquaintance of mine had accepted, but was more than happy to pass on the honour when I helped him to three days of more congenial work.' Then his smile faded. 'Forgive me child, running on like this. Your father . . .'

'I want so much to talk to you.'

'And I to you, child. But what are you doing here?'

I knelt down and began gathering the scattered parts.

'I'm the governess.'

'Why in the world?'

'I can't tell you now. May we meet later?'

'Later, when I've come all this way to find you? Not at all.'

'But your rehearsal . . .'

I handed him the score. He looked through the first few pages, eyebrows raised. They were fine, expressive eyebrows. Some people joked that he could direct an orchestra with them alone. They came together as his forehead pinched in artistic pain, rose again in amusement as he flipped to the last few pages.

'Ah, child, the sacrifice I have made for you.' He called out a name and tossed the score across the room to one of the other musicians, who caught it neatly. 'Take them through it,' he said. 'I don't suppose you'll encounter anything you haven't met a hundred times before. Sir Herbert informs me that he has no liking for pianissimo – or indeed any other fancy foreign issimo – so kindly keep that in mind.'

266

The other musician smiled, clearly used to Daniel. He took the rest of the parts from me and dumped them on the pianoforte.

'Now, my dear lady, let us wander in the garden.'

'People might see us.'

'Am I such a disgrace?'

'Guests, I mean. Governesses do not mix with them.'

'Judging from what I've seen and heard of Sir Herbert, you may be wise in scorning his guests.'

'Please be serious. I should be dismissed if I were seen walking with you.'

'Where is the spirit of Figaro? But very well, we shall hide ourselves among the vegetables.'

'Vegetables?'

'There must surely be an honest vegetable garden where guests don't go.'

Half a dozen gardeners were at work behind the warm brick walls when we got there, but they hardly looked up from their hoeing. We walked along gravel paths between borders of parsley, oregano and marjoram, alive with butterflies. Daniel Suter offered me his arm in a kind of courtly parody of a lady and gentleman strolling, but it was a good firm arm, and I was glad to keep hold of it.

'My dear, why did you run away? All of your father's friends will help you. There was no need for this servitude.'

'I want to know who killed my father.'

'What have they told you?'

'They? Nobody's told me anything, except one man, and I don't know how far to believe him.'

'Who?'

'A man who calls himself Mr Blackstone.'

I felt his arm go tense under mine. We'd come to the end of our path, facing the wall, and had to choose right or left. There were beans growing on strings up the wall, their red and white flowers just opening and fat furry bees blundering round them. Daniel stood, apparently staring at the bees, but I guessed he was not seeing them.

'So what do you know?' I asked him.

'Child, please leave it be. I'd give my own life, if I could, to bring your father back to you. But since I can't . . .'

'Since you can't, at least do this for him. You know very well he wasn't killed in a duel, don't you?'

He gave the faintest of nods, slight as the movement of a bean leaf under the weight of a bee.

'What else do you know?' I said.

'Very little. I'm sorry to say he'd been dead two weeks before I even heard about it. A few days after he left Paris, I went to Lyon. Somebody wrote to me there . . .'

'Who?'

'A friend.' He mentioned a name that meant nothing to me. 'He said he'd been shot, no more.'

We started walking again, turning left between beds of lettuces and chicory. I told him everything that had happened to me, from the time I left my aunt's house.

When I came to how I was almost carried off by Lord Kilkeel and Mr Trumper, he said, 'Damn them!' so loudly that a couple of gardeners raised their heads from weeding.

'You know them?'

'The man Trumper, I think, yes. But go on.'

It took us three complete tours of the garden. Several times he stopped and looked at me as if he couldn't believe what I was saying, then shook his head and walked on. I stopped before I came to Mr Brighton's arrival and the incident in the loosebox. I couldn't quite bring myself to talk about that.

'So Blackstone sent you here?' he said at the end.

'Yes.'

'He had no right.'

'He had my father's ring.'

I brought it out, untied the ribbon and put it into his hand. He held it for a while, then gave it back to me.

'Blackstone gave you this? How did he get it?'

'He said he bought it from the people in the morgue. He wanted to keep it, but I took it from him. He wears a ring like it. Who is he? Did he have some kind of power over my father?'

'No.' He sounded angry, then, more gently, 'He had no kind of power over your father. But Blackstone is a man involved in many wild schemes, always has been. I think your father may unwittingly have been caught up in one of them.'

'What?'

'I don't know.' He shook his head. 'What you've told me is so new to me, I can't make sense of it.'

'What about this woman who needed help? How does she come into it? Blackstone says he doesn't know who she is, but I think he has some idea.'

'She's as mysterious to me as she is to you. Your father and I were in Paris together and he said nothing about a . . .'

He stopped suddenly.

'You've remembered something?'

'No. Nothing to the purpose.'

We were near a stone water trough. He let go of my arm, sat down on the edge of it, and put his head in his hands.

'Child, if I had the slightest idea, I'd have dragged your father back to England, bound hand and foot if necessary. But how could any of us tell? It seemed no more than a joke.'

'He talked about a joke in his letter, then the quote from Shelley about princes. I couldn't understand it, for a long time. Only I think I do now. There was somebody in Paris, wasn't there? Somebody you were laughing at?'

'Yes.' He said it reluctantly, head bowed.

'That person, I think he's here now, in this house.'

'What?' His head came up.

'He's the reason Mr Blackstone wants me to spy. I think I know now why my father was killed. I knew yesterday.'

When I'd seen Mr Brighton in the orchard, the look on his face, his whole posture, had gathered so many threads together. Daniel's large dark eyes were fixed on mine. There was so much sadness in them that it scared me. He took my right hand between both of his.

'Child, you are coming with me now.'

'Where?'

'Back to London. Don't even go in to collect your bonnet. We shall go to the stables and steal a horse if necessary.'

'I already have a horse and I am not going anywhere.'

'Then I shall carry you.'

He shifted as if he intended to make good his threat. The thought of neat, ironic Daniel carrying a struggling woman over his shoulder was too much for me and I laughed out loud.

'Oh my dear, I have already been carried off by my father's enemies. Spare me the same treatment from his friends.'

He didn't laugh. 'So I failed to protect your father and I'm to fail again with his daughter?'

'If you owe him anything, isn't it justice at least?'

'I owe it to him to keep you alive.'

'I don't believe I'm in danger. Another person may be.'

'Why did you want to find me, if you won't let me care for you?'

'I wanted to know what happened when you were

with my father in Paris. But I believe I've guessed most of it now. There are two other things I need you to do for me.'

'What?'

'Look at a picture and look at a person.'

His eyebrows went up to his hair-line.

'The picture is to the left of the big drawing-room door,' I said. 'The person is an honoured guest and will probably be sitting close to Sir Herbert at dinner. If I am right, you'll have seen him at least once before.'

'We are to play quartets to them after dinner. If I do this, will you come back to London with me?'

'After the weekend, yes.'

'Tonight.'

'No. Carry out your engagement, play their *Welcome Home* nonsense, then we'll go.'

Whatever happened, I could not desert Celia until either I'd talked her out of elopement or she was safely in the arms of her Philip.

'I'd rather play his funeral march,' he said.

I knew then that I'd won my point and gave his hand a squeeze.

'I'll leave first. We should not be seen together any more. Will you meet me here tonight, after you've played your quartets?'

For reply, he hummed a few bars from Figaro about meeting in the garden, but his dark eyes were miserable. I left him sitting on the water trough.

*

Back in the schoolroom, Betty was mending a pinafore.

'Where did you get to? Miss Mandeville came looking for you. She wants some more help with her sketching. She said to tell you she'd be on the terrace.'

I found her sitting alone on a bench by a statue of Diana the Huntress, sketchpad on her lap, face shaded by a lavender parasol wedged between the slats of the bench. The sketch consisted of a few vague lines that might have been ploughland or seashore.

'Where's Mr Brighton?' I said.

'Playing billiards with Stephen.' She stuck out her lower lip, moistened her finger on it and dabbed at an imaginary billiard cue. 'How could anybody think I'd marry such a ragdoll of a man? I shouldn't do it if he were Czar of all the Russias.'

She scored a line across her sketch, so savagely that the point of her pencil broke.

'Your brother spoke to me about you,' I said.

She gripped my arm.

'What did he say?'

'He thinks you might be on the point of doing something unwise.'

'You didn't tell him? Surely you didn't.'

Her fingers dug into my arm.

'No, I didn't.'

She let go of my arm.

'He said you were close,' I said.

'We were. Until this.'

It was no more than a murmur. I thought of Tom and

how he'd feel if I were to elope without telling him.

'I do believe he cares about you,' I said. 'Perhaps if you were to make him understand how totally opposed you are to Mr Brighton . . .'

'No.'

'Why not?'

'Stephen does care for me, but he doesn't understand. And I think he's scared of my stepfather.'

'He did not strike me as a person easily scared.'

'Sir Herbert bought off his IOUs to get him out of prison. He could use them to put him back, if he wanted.'

'How do you know?'

'Stephen told me that himself. You mustn't tell him, Elizabeth. I forbid you to even think about telling him.'

She scored another line across the page, splintering wood from the broken pencil.

'Why did you want to see me?' I asked.

'Philip is coming for me on Saturday night, at nine o'clock. He'll have a carriage waiting on the back road. I want you to come with me.'

'Elope with you?'

'Of course not. Just as far as the carriage. I don't know my way down the back road and I'll have things to carry. And we must be so much more careful now, if Stephen suspects.'

Her fingers picked nervously at the pencil.

'It's a serious decision to make, leaving your family,' I said.

'Do you think I don't know that? I'll probably never see my mother again, or Stephen, or Betty.'

Tears ran down her cheeks.

'Perhaps if you were to speak to your mother . . .'

'What good would that do? She's terrified of my step-father too, surely you've seen that. I dread to think what he'll do to her after I've gone.'

'He could hardly blame her.'

'He will. I suppose you think badly of me, leaving my mother in danger.'

'I hope she will not be in danger.'

'I hope so too, with all my heart. But she chose to marry him and she'll always be unhappy now, whatever happens. Does that mean I must waste my life too?'

'So you won't speak to either of them?'

'No. If I spoke to anybody it might be my grand-mother, but . . .'

'Perhaps you should.'

I was on the edge of telling her about Mrs Beedle's behaviour but stopped myself. It wasn't my secret.

'No, I've made my choice and I choose Philip, and that's all there is to it.'

'This Philip, do you know him well?'

I cared enough for her to hope she wasn't throwing herself away on some worthless man just to escape.

'Of course I do. A year ago, we were practically engaged to be married.'

'But your stepfather disapproved?'

'No, that's the cruel part of it.'

'What happened?'

'Philip and I met at Weymouth last summer. Sir Herbert was prescribed sea bathing for pain in his joints, so of course we all had to pack up and go. Philip's father was there for the bathing too. I think my stepfather approved, as far as he cared at all. It would get me off his hands without having to pay a settlement because Philip's family are very comfortably situated. They have an estate in Buckinghamshire and Philip will inherit a baronetcy if his uncle dies before he has any children, and the uncle's sixty-three and a bachelor, so . . .'

She paused for breath.

'So altogether a most suitable match,' I said.

She looked sharply at me.

'I wonder why you have such a low opinion of me. The fact is, I love Philip, he adores me and I'd marry him even if he were a pauper.'

'I'm sorry.'

'Only I'm glad he isn't, of course.'

I believed her, both about that and loving him, which was a relief in its way.

'When did your stepfather change his mind?'

'Only in the last month or so.'

'When Mr Brighton came on the scene?'

She nodded.

'It would be treason, wouldn't it?'

She asked the question very softly, looking down at the sketchpad. The paper was damp from her tears.

'I think so, yes.'

'And my stepfather's trying to drag me into it, for his own ambition. So I've no choice, you see, no choice at all.'

'Yes, I see.'

She dried her eyes with her handkerchief and took a deep breath.

'So now there are just two days and seven hours to live through and I'll be away with Philip and it will be all over. Only there's that terrible dinner to get through first. I know they'll make me sit next to him. I'm glad you'll be there, at least. I shall be able to look down the table at you and know somebody understands what I'm suffering.'

'I? At the dinner?'

'Didn't Mrs Quivering tell you? You're to fill a gap in the table. Lady Arlen is *enceinte* again so has cried off the dinner, and that put out the whole table plan because they were a woman short. So my grandmother said you were perfectly ladylike and they could move somebody else up and put you down at the far end. Why are you looking so scared?'

'He'll recognise me. He can't fail to if we're sitting at the same dinner table.'

My panic was about Lord Kilkeel, but she naturally thought it applied to Mr Brighton.

'How can he? There are forty people, remember, and you'll be at the very far end of the table, and by candle-light. The people at the other end won't even see you.'

I hoped she was right. Mrs Beedle had been clever, seizing the chance to provide her spy with a seat at the dinner. I might have tried again to persuade Celia to confide in her, but two of the house guests, a gentleman and a lady with a little dog, were approaching from the far side of the terrace.

'Botheration,' Celia said. 'I suppose they're coming to talk to me.'

She crumpled her damp apology for a sketch and rose from the bench to face them while I slipped away, down the side steps of the terrace and into the back entrance.

Mrs Quivering's assistant was in the housekeeper's room, drinking sage tea for her sore throat.

'There's a letter come for you, Miss Lock.'

She handed over a coarse grey envelope.

'When did it arrive?'

'I don't know. Somebody delivered it to the stables and a boy brought it over.'

The writing was Amos Legge's. I went into the corridor and opened the envelope.

> Miss Lane,
>   Ther is a thing I heard about the two gentlemen in the travling coach. I will come when I can and ask for you at the back door.
>   Yours ruspectfully,
>   A. Legge

If I could, I'd have gone straight to the livery stables to find him, but I was needed back in the schoolroom to superintend the children's dinner and afternoon walk

278

in the grounds. With so many visitors in residence, ladies and gentlemen kept stopping us, talking to the children and petting them. It made them over-excited and above themselves, but at least we were spared the ceremony of taking them down before dinner.

'Lady Mandeville has one of her headaches,' Betty said.

That saved me from having to invent a headache of my own as an excuse. We took off their best clothes, supervised their washing and tooth brushing and got them into their beds by half past eight. When we'd set the schoolroom straight, I said I needed a walk to clear my head. It was time to keep the appointment with Daniel. The light was fading, the brick walls of the vegetable garden radiating back the heat of the day. The gardeners had gone by then, but they must have watered the plants last thing because warm, damp earth scented the dusk, along with lingering whiffs of carrot, spring onions, bruised tarragon. Pale moths wafted around the bean flowers like flakes of ash blown up from a bonfire and a hedgehog rooted and grunted under the rhubarb leaves. I sat on the edge of the water trough and waited.

'Liberty.'

Daniel Suter's voice, from the door in the wall.

'I'm here.'

He came over to me, practically running, tripping on the gravel path.

'Well?' I said.

'You were right, child. Ye gods, what a situation.'

He sat down beside me, breathing hard. I'd known him all my life, but had never seen him discomposed before.

'You recognised somebody here who was in Paris?'

'As you thought, the man they call Mr Brighton.'

My heart jolted, like a salmon trying to leap out of water and flopping back.

'And you saw the portrait?' I said.

'Yes. You're right. There is a very strong resemblance. But you'd expect that, of course.'

'My father saw it. *The dregs of their dull race* – I should have guessed.'

'It wasn't only your father who saw. They were flaunting it. They were a laughing-stock among the Parisians. The very waiters would bow to him in jest, only he took it in deadly earnest.'

'Tell me, please, everything that happened in Paris.'

'There's not so very much to tell. It all happened over just two days and nights.'

'Everything you can remember.'

He took a deep breath.

'It was pure good luck meeting your father in Paris. He inquired at a few hotels where he knew I'd stayed in the past and found me. And, as chance would have it, half a dozen of our mutual friends were there, musicians mostly and . . .'

'And?'

'Lodge brothers. We spent the afternoon in each other's company, talking about all the things you talk about when you haven't seen your friends for months. Your father was in excellent spirits, money in his pocket, looking forward to reaching home and being with you.'

'He said so?'

'He certainly did. We talked a lot about you. We all had dinner together and your father asked if there was anywhere we might have a hand or two of cards, simply for amusement.'

'I know. Money never stayed in his pockets for very long.'

'This time he was determined it should. We went to a place I knew, off the Champs Élysées. He did not intend to play for high stakes, but . . .'

'He won a horse.'

'Indeed he did, from some old marquis who'd won her off somebody else and didn't know what to do with her. But how did you know that?'

'From the same person who told me you were together in Paris. So how does Mr Brighton come into the story?'

'The table next to ours were playing high. There were about half a dozen of them, all English. They were already there when our party arrived and they'd been drinking heavily. Mr Brighton was totally drunk and kept yelling out remarks in that terrible high bray of his. It was a small place and the tables were too close together. At one point, Mr Brighton pushed his chair back suddenly and sent your father's tokens scattering all over the floor.'

'Did my father resent it?'

'No. He had too much good sense to quarrel with a

man in drink. We all picked the tokens up and went on playing. It happened a second time and we did the same thing. By the third time, it was obvious that the fool was doing it deliberately. I said something, fairly mild in the circumstances, about taking more care. Mr Brighton went as red as a turkey cock's wattles. He pulled himself as near upright as he could get and said, "Do you know whom you're speaking to, sir?" Spraying spittle all over me in the process. So, "A clumsy buffoon, so it would appear, sir," I said. I will admit it was not the most politic speech, but I was annoyed by then. A man they called Trumper . . .'

'A fair-haired country squire kind of man?'

'Yes, the very same oaf who tried to carry you off. Anyway, he seemed to realise that his friend was making an ass of himself and took him into a side room, where I assume they continued to play. By then the evening had been spoiled for us, so we finished our hand and left.'

'And nothing was said about a duel?'

'Good heavens, no. It had been an unpleasant few minutes, that's all. Nobody thought of duelling. We went to supper and stayed up late over our pipes and our punch talking of this and that. And there it might have ended if we hadn't been joined by some Frenchmen your father knew. My French is nowhere near as good as his and they were talking away nineteen to the dozen. Something they said seemed to amuse your father mightily so we asked him to translate so that we could all share the joke . . .'

He hesitated. A barn owl flew over the garden, just a few feet higher than the walls. From further off, a fox barked.

'I can remember all of it,' Daniel said. 'All of the words, that is. Only the tune of it will be wrong, if you understand me. It was still a joke to us then, you see.'

'Please, every word.'

'Your father turned to me, pulling a long face. "Daniel," he said, "you are in very serious trouble. In fact, you will be lucky to escape with your head. Have you any notion of the identity of our spluttering young friend whom you so grossly insulted?" Well, by then we were near the bottom of the punch bowl and we all began imitating the young ass's bray, "Do you know who you're speaking to, sir?" Your father sat watching us, grinning over his pipe, until we became tired of it and silence fell. "Well, Daniel," he said, "my Parisian friends here tell me it is an open secret. He goes by the *nom de guerre* of Mr Brighton, but his identity is well known to every pawn shop and gambling hell in this fair city. Young Mr Brighton is none other than . . ." Then he couldn't go on for laughing. I played the farce out, pretending to tremble, knees knocking. "Don't keep me in suspense, old friend," I said. "Who is this gentleman to whom my humble head is forfeit?" And your father, just managing to get the words out between gusts of laughter, replied: "Only the rightful heir to the throne of England, that's all."'

CHAPTER EIGHTEEN

'You'd guessed, hadn't you?' Daniel said. 'Only I've no notion how you did.' His voice was sad at all that laughter gone sour.

'Sir Herbert's desperate to marry him into the family,' I said. 'His daughter's too young, so his stepdaughter has to do, poor thing. She came very near to telling me. Then there was the portrait. As soon as I saw Brighton, he reminded me of somebody. But why should it be poor Princess Charlotte?'

'I've been thinking about that. Do you remember when the princess died?'

'Of course not. I was only two years old.'

He sighed. 'I'd forgotten how young you are, or perhaps how old I am. I do remember. I was in my last year at school.' Another sigh.

'You were sorry?'

'I had no more strong feelings about the deaths of princesses than I have now. But she'd been popular and people mourned her. Then later there were some ugly rumours going round, so ugly that I'm sorry to have to repeat them. You're cold?'

I must have shivered.

'The child Henrietta said she was poisoned.'

He took his jacket off and draped it round my shoulders, in spite of my protests. It smelled comfortingly of violin resin and candlewax.

'Yes, that was part of it. Charlotte was a healthy young woman, you see, with the very best of medical attention. She and the baby should not have died.'

'But women do die in childbirth, even healthy ones,' I said.

'So they do. But some years later rumours started that she and her baby had both been poisoned just after the birth.'

'Why would anybody do such a terrible thing?'

'She was Queen Caroline's daughter. In some people's opinion, Caroline was well nigh a lunatic, certainly an adulteress. Certain distinguished persons at court were said to be determined that neither her daughter nor her grandson should ever come to the throne.'

'But to kill a baby! It's like something from the Middle Ages.'

'Royalty *is* something from the Middle Ages.'

'Did many people believe it?'

'It was a persistent rumour, helped by another unfortunate fact.'

'What?'

'A few months after Charlotte and her baby son died, the gentleman who'd had charge of the birth, her *accoucheur*, shot himself.'

'In remorse for killing her?'

'No, there was no suggestion of that, even in the rumours. But he was an honourable man and, so it's said, blamed himself for not foreseeing the plot and preventing their deaths.'

'Daniel, do you believe this?'

'No. I believe their deaths were sheer misfortune. But it seems some people, including Sir Herbert Mandeville, are determined to revive the rumour – with one essential difference.'

'What's that?'

'Child, you've come so far. Can you not see it for yourself?'

I didn't want to think. I'd thought enough and every time it seemed to have made things worse. We sat for a long while in silence. The day's warmth had faded from the brick wall behind us and Daniel must have been cold in his shirtsleeves and waistcoat, but he gave no sign of it.

'Well, Liberty?'

'The baby didn't die after all. Charlotte died, but her baby didn't.'

'And was spirited away by Charlotte's friends and

brought up safely on the Continent, until the time came to claim what was rightfully his. Yes?'

'No!'

'I agree with you. It's a fairy tale, a horrible, warped fairy tale. And yet it's what Sir Herbert and Trumper and all the other greedy fools think they can get the country to believe. I'm sorry, Liberty. I'm ranting. But their idiocy has killed your father and could do so much other damage.'

He was trembling now, from anger not cold.

'But why are they doing it?' I said.

'Why do men do most things? Money and power. Sir Herbert and his like have been running the country since the Conqueror. Now they're beginning to see some of their power stripped away, and it maddens them. When they knew the poor buffoon William was dying and there'd be a mere child on the throne – a girl child at that – they decided to take their chance. Put in another king, one beholden to them, and no more nonsense about reform.'

'But even if he were Princess Charlotte's son, why should they suppose people would support him rather than little Vicky? He is hardly Bonnie Prince Charlie, is he?'

Daniel laughed bitterly.

'So-called Bonnie Prince Charlie was a fat, red-faced, drink-sodden wreck, yet men died for him fewer than a hundred years ago.'

'And my father died because of Mr Brighton?'

'Yes. I can't see any other explanation. He must have threatened their plans in some way.'

'But how could he? You said it was an open secret in Paris in any case.'

'As a joke, yes.'

'But he thought it was all a joke too. He said so in his letter. And my father wasn't important, not in that way. He couldn't have made any difference.'

'It puzzles me, I admit. But he must have known something, otherwise why should they have tried to kidnap you?'

'It was a woman they wanted to know about. Daniel, do please think. There must have been a woman somewhere, those last days in Paris.'

He shook his head.

'I can't remember him speaking to a woman at all, except the maids at the hotel. And . . .'

He hesitated.

'There's still something you're not telling me, isn't there?' I said.

'No. Nothing that matters.'

'How do you know? Anything might matter.'

'Very well. There was a wine shop on the corner of the street near our hotel. I happened to be walking past and I'm nearly sure he was sitting with a woman.'

'You didn't go in and join him?'

'No. There was no reason. Besides . . .'

'Besides what?'

'The wine shop was used quite a lot by the local

dames de la nuit. Now, don't rush to conclusions. As you know, your father would talk to anybody and . . .'

His voice trailed away.

'It might explain something,' I said. 'Supposing there'd been an English girl there, fallen on hard times. He might have promised to bring her home to her family.'

'Yes, he might.' Daniel sounded embarrassed and unhappy.

'But there's a lot it wouldn't explain, isn't there? Why should Kilkeel be so interested in some poor Englishwoman? Why should anybody kill my father over her?'

'I don't know, Libby. Maybe the woman in the wine shop has nothing to do with it at all. But you asked about women, and I can't remember any other.'

'And he said nothing to you about a woman needing help?'

'No, and that's a puzzle in itself. As you know, your father was the most open man in the world. If he had decided to help some poor dove out of the gutter, I'm sure he'd have discussed it with us that evening when we were all together.'

'The evening that Amos Legge came to make arrangements for Esperance?'

'Who? Oh, the amiable horse-transporter. Yes. Your father said goodbye next morning in the best of health and spirits. That was the last I saw of him. If I'd the slightest idea of all this at the time, I'd never have let him go alone.'

I was crying and sensed he might be near tears too. I felt for his hand on the edge of the water trough.

'Do you think it was Mr Brighton or Trumper who shot him?' I said.

'I simply don't know. It's difficult to think of Brighton even doing up his own shoe-laces. Trumper may be a different matter. You said your father died on Saturday?'

'Yes.'

I could see he was thinking back.

'That's the morning I left for Lyon. I saw both Brighton and Trumper in the street the evening before. In fact, I spoke to Trumper, or rather he spoke to me.'

'What did he say?'

'He came striding up to me like a man wanting a quarrel and said, "Where's your friend gone?" I guessed he meant your father and supposed he might have got wind of how we'd been making fun of them. So I said my friend would be back home in England by now. That didn't seem to please him.'

'Did he say anything else?'

'I didn't give him the chance, just said good-day and walked off.'

'They must have known by then that he'd gone away with the woman.'

'Yes, but Trumper couldn't possibly have got to Calais in time to kill him, however fast he rode.'

He sounded both regretful and relieved. I understood. I wanted more than anything in the world to know who killed my father and yet the prospect of it scared me.

'What about the fat man – Lord Kilkeel?' I said.

'To the best of my knowledge, I never saw him in Paris.'

'So he might have been in Calais on the Saturday. He was certainly there three days later.'

We lapsed into silence again. Bats darted overhead and a hedgehog snuffled. My brain was tired and wanted to curl up and sleep like a hedgehog.

'If you think Charlotte's baby died twenty years ago?' I said.

'I do, yes.'

'Then who is Mr Brighton?'

'Take your pick from twenty or more. You understand what I mean?'

'There is certainly no shortage of Hanoverian bastards,' I said.

That was common knowledge. George III had fifteen children, seven of them sons who grew to manhood, and since he refused to let any of them marry until suitable princesses were available, the natural consequence was many Georgian grandsons on the wrong side of the blanket. The Duke of Clarence, for one, was responsible for at least five such.

'From his looks and his manners, I've no doubt he's one of that stock,' Daniel said.

'And tomorrow, Sir Herbert intends to introduce him to all his friends and supporters as their rightful king.'

'You think that's what will happen?'

'I'm sure of it. Why else all the preparations? Why

else that ridiculous *Welcome Home* piece you're rehearsing?'

'It is indeed an offence in itself. I think you're mostly right, Libby, only it probably won't happen in quite so blatant a way. I don't suppose they'll get straight up from the dinner table and march off to storm Windsor Castle.'

'How, then?'

'These days, the banner would be raised by gossip and hints and whispers. They'll have their dinner party and ball. Mr Brighton is affable, the likeness unmistakeable. Gossip gets back to London, around the salons, the newspapers pick it up . . . So it all starts.'

'I can't imagine how anybody who'd met him could possibly want him for king.'

'If the British public tolerated the Prince Regent, they'll stand for anything. Our standards are not high.'

'Even so . . .'

'And remember, most of the people shouting for him will never set eyes on him. A few nicely placed stories, a flattering engraving or two in the newspapers, and he's England's hope and the people's friend.'

'He's not the people's friend,' I said. 'None of them is.'

'Of course not. But this country's not as safe as some people like to think. There are hungry and desperate people out there, prepared to clutch at anything.'

'But why should anybody just take their word that he's Princess Charlotte's son?'

'A good question. Do you suppose that's what this

whole occasion is about – that they intend to produce something that might be regarded as proof?'

'But how can they, if it's not true?'

'Believable by people who want to believe.'

'Then what should we do?' I said.

'Tell somebody in authority?'

'Do you know anybody in authority?'

'No,' he said. 'If I were to go straight up to London and bang on the door of the Home Secretary, would he believe me? Besides . . .'

I waited.

'Besides what?'

'There is the question of what Blackstone is doing,' he said.

There was a change in his voice, more guarded. It struck me too that he'd said very little during the part of my story where I'd told him about Mr Blackstone.

'You know him well?' I said.

'Quite well, yes.'

I took my hand away from his.

'Is Blackstone another *nom de guerre*?'

'I believe not. We've always known him as Alexander Blackstone.'

'"We"?'

'Your father and the rest of us.' He hesitated, then, 'Liberty, that ring of your father's – did you understand anything by it?'

'Only that it was a favourite of his. He often wore it.'

'He was a freemason, Liberty, that's what it signifies. So am I, and so is Blackstone. I should not be telling you this, but I think you are owed it.'

'But where's the harm in that? Weren't Haydn and Mozart masons?'

'Yes, and you're right, there's no harm in it at all. Mostly we're no more than companionable people with a liking for intelligent company who wish to do good rather than harm. That, I'm sure, is how your father saw it. But some people will tell you otherwise.'

'That you wish to do harm?'

'That we are revolutionaries. They may not be entirely wrong. Some of the leaders of the Revolution in France and the War of Independence in America were masons. We believe in equality among men and have no exaggerated respect for kings or princes.'

'*A man's a man for a' that.*'

'Who taught you that?'

'My father, of course. I am not in the least shocked that you and my father should believe in equality, but I'm at a loss to see what it has to do with Mr Blackstone and Mr Brighton.'

'Because Alexander Blackstone is a revolutionary. As a young man he was put in prison for writing a pamphlet supporting the French Revolution. He came from a good family and had a considerable income, but he's given all his life and fortune to the cause, and I believe now there's precious little of either left. What did you make of him?'

'He's like a black rock with ice on it.'

'You didn't know him in his prime. Neither did I, come to that, but people who did tell me he could have marched ten thousand men on Whitehall by the power of his oratory alone. He was a dangerous man, Libby.'

'I think he still is.'

'Perhaps. But he's a sick man now, and the younger generation don't listen to him like their fathers did. He's never wavered in his belief that there'll be no end to poverty or injustice here until England has a revolution and we become a republic like the Americans. I think whatever he's doing now is his final desperate attempt, before he runs out of money and strength.'

'But why is he so concerned with Mr Brighton? Why did he make me spy for him?'

'I'm angry with him for that, and if I meet him I shall tell him so.'

'But why is he interested?

'I don't know. But, believe me, it certainly isn't for any devotion to the House of Hanover.'

'He knows who killed my father, I'm sure of that. He almost promised to tell me if I did what he wanted.'

'Almost?'

'You think he won't?'

'I don't know. He's a close and secret man,' he said.

'But you admire him?'

'I respect him. He's suffered a lot for what he believes.' He sighed. 'Liberty, I'll ask you again. Please leave this and let me take you away.'

'No. Not before Saturday night.'

'Why?'

I wanted to tell him about Celia's elopement. I knew I could trust him, but I'd implied a promise to her.

'There's the question of the horse,' I said.

'What is this about a horse?'

'The one my father won. Esperance. She's in a livery stables near here with Amos Legge. There's a cat as well. I can't just go and leave them.'

He laughed and his arm came round me.

'Oh child, you haven't changed.'

But I knew I'd changed very much.

'I don't know what to do about them,' I said.

He sighed.

'Then I suppose the horse must come too. Are you able to communicate with this man Legge?'

'Yes.'

'Well, tell him to bring the horse here on Saturday night. I'll stay for the ball and we'll play this execrable *Welcome* for them, and if Sir Herbert wants to raise the banner for the untrue heir, then it's his pantomime. We'll go straight back to London the moment it's over, even if I have to steal somebody's carriage.'

What I'd do in London with a horse, a cat and Amos Legge's expenses to pay, nowhere to live and not a shilling in my purse, was something so far distant that it hardly seemed worth worrying about.

'Very well, I'll tell him,' I said.

Daniel insisted on escorting me all the way back to the kitchen door, although I was afraid one of the other servants might see us together. He had no excuse to be anywhere near the house; because there was no room for the musicians in the Hall, they'd been billeted in a building in the park known as the Greek Pavilion.

At the door, he put a hand on my shoulder and said softly, 'Child, do as little possible tomorrow and Saturday. Stay safe in the schoolroom, if you can. Leave the fools to their folly.'

Something touched my forehead, light as a leaf. It was only after he'd walked away that I realised he'd kissed me.

CHAPTER NINETEEN

Friday, 14th July. *Le Quatorze Juillet*. I woke up thinking about that, of all things. Forty-eight years ago the people of Paris had stormed the Bastille and the world had changed for ever. It had always been a day of celebration in our household, with Tom and I allowed a glass of watered wine to drink to the Revolution and, as it happened, our own names: Liberty, Fraternity. (If my mother had lived longer, I'm sure there would have been a third child called Equality.) But today Revolution had a colder feel to it. I got up at about six o'clock, washed and dressed in the green cotton dress with my muslin tucker freshly laundered and clean white cotton stockings. I'd hoped to go early to the stables to see Amos Legge, but Betty had unknowingly ended that plan when I'd got back to the schoolroom the evening before.

'I'm sorry, Miss Lock, but you'll have to get the children up on your own tomorrow. Two of the lady visitors have come without their maids so Mrs Quivering said would I oblige.'

With the house full of guests and the kitchen preparing for the grand dinner in the evening, all the servants were doing two or three times their normal work. This was in spite of the fact that thirty extra maids, waiters and footmen had been brought in from London and Windsor for the occasion. The maids in the room below me were having to sleep two to a bed to make room for them. I roused the children at half past six as usual, but getting them washed and dressed took much longer than when Betty was there. Henrietta wished passionately to wear her best white silk with the blue sash and sulked when persuaded into more serviceable pink-and-white striped cotton. Charles volunteered to pull out a loose tooth that was bothering James by looping a string round it, tying the other end of the string to the schoolroom door knob and slamming the door. Unfortunately the tooth wasn't as loose as it looked and the resulting howls, blood and recriminations took up the hour when we should have been having our early walk in the garden. There was only time for a truncated prayer session before breakfast was brought up by Tibby the schoolroom maid. Betty arrived as we were finishing it, full of the gossip she'd gathered downstairs.

'You didn't tell me you're to be at the dinner, Miss Lock. Aren't you the lucky one.'

Typically, she was not in the least envious, simply pleased at what she saw as my good fortune.

'It's only to fill up the table,' I said.

'There's going to be real turtle soup. And you'll see all the lovely dresses close to. What shall you wear?'

'My lavender with the silk fichu, I suppose.'

She looked doubtful. 'Will that do?'

'It will have to. Besides, I'll be right at the end of the table and nobody will notice me,' I said, sincerely hoping that would be the case.

We spent most of the morning on Aesop's Fables. The children weren't capable of concentrating on anything more demanding, and neither was I.

When their dinner time came, at half past two, I said I wasn't hungry and would go for a walk outside to clear my head. Betty naturally put it down to excitement and nerves, but I was desperate to find a way of communicating with Amos Legge. In addition to the practical matter of asking him to bring Rancie, there was his mysterious message about the two gentlemen in the travelling carriage. I'd written a note to him during lessons, asking if he could meet me at the bottom of the back road at six o'clock the following morning, hoping I'd be able to manage that even though I couldn't get all the way to the stables. My idea was to find a boy and give him sixpence that I'd discovered in the bottom of my bag to deliver the note. Since the stableyard was usually the best place to find a spare boy, I walked across the courtyard and through the archway. The cobbled yard was quiet and neatly swept, horses dozing in the afternoon calm and the place almost deserted. Not a boy in sight, just a man sitting peacefully on the mounting block, smoking a clay pipe.

'Amos Legge!'

'Good afternoon, miss.' He stood up and put out his pipe with his thumb. 'I asked one of the maids to let you know I was here, but I couldn't tell if she'd heard me right.'

'Just the very man I wanted to see. Mr Legge, could you please have Rancie here in the stableyard tomorrow night, after dark?'

'On the move again, are we?'

'I think so, yes. Only there's so much I don't know, where we're going or even if, or . . .'

'Don't you worry, miss, I'll have her here. Did you get that message I sent you?'

'Yes.'

'That's why I came. I've been turning it over in my mind . . . Maybe it did mean something and maybe it didn't, only it was strange, and seeing as you were staying here, I thought somebody should know.'

'About the two men in the travelling coach?'

'The lardy one and the one that had the accident with his boot. Only I didn't hear about it until after they'd gone, and with the others saying the lad was a bit simple, I didn't quite know what to make of it.'

It was no use trying to hurry him. I suggested we

should sit down on the mounting block and he dusted it off for me with his hat.

'When I left, they were still waiting for the wheelwright,' I said. 'What happened after that?'

'They got the wheelwright in the end. The two gentlemen were waiting in the guvnor's office most of the time. He kept offering them one of his own vehicles to go on up to the Hall, but they wouldn't hear of it. It was go in the travelling coach or nothing. Anyways, there's this lad helps out in the yard sometimes. They make out he's a gawby, but I reckon he's clever enough when he wants to be. He says they had a woman in there.'

'Where?'

'In the travelling coach.'

'Just sitting in it all the time?'

'No, or we'd all've seen her. You know how gentlemen's travelling coaches usually have a place under the floorboards, nice and convenient for anything they might need on a day's journey without having the trunks unstrapped? Quite a tidy space in some of them, big enough to take a woman, if she didn't mind curling up a bit.'

'The boy says he saw a woman under the floorboards in the travelling coach?'

'Not saw, heard. He reckons he heard a moithering voice calling for help and for somebody to bring her a glass of water.'

'Didn't he tell anybody at the time?'

'They was all too busy running around in circles with the coach and the gentlemen to take any notice of him. Afterwards, they thought he was just hearing ghosts again. He's a great lad for ghosts, they say.'

'But you believe him?'

'Can't say whether I believe him or not. But it seemed to me somebody here ought to know about it.'

A groom came into the yard and gave us a curious look.

'I must go,' I said. 'I expect you must, too. Thank you for telling me.'

When I looked back through the archway from the courtyard, I saw him mounting a useful-looking cob, property of the livery stables, presumably. I'd assumed that he'd come on foot and once again marvelled at the resourcefulness of Amos Legge. But how seriously should I take his information? Very seriously, I thought. Gawby or not, the lad had impressed Amos. And if Lord Kilkeel and Brighton had a woman imprisoned in the well of the travelling coach, that explained why they'd refused to leave it at the stables and finish their journey in another vehicle. Could this be the woman from my father's letter? If so, I'd been no more than a few yards away from her in the stableyard without knowing it.

I looked up from the courtyard at the back of Mandeville Hall, a great brick cliff with hundreds of windows. She might well be in there somewhere, among dozens of guests, plus nearly a hundred servants counting the extra ones brought in, so many rooms that a person might spend months there without seeing them all. I might as well try to search an entire town.

As soon as I stepped inside the house, one of the footmen said Mrs Quivering wanted me. I found her in her room.

'There's a note for you from Miss Mandeville.'

She handed me a folded lilac sheet.

Dear Miss Lock,

If you would care to come to my room when you are free, we may plan what you are to wear this evening. There may be some things which I should be happy to lend you.

Signed with her initials in a flourish like the tendrils of sweet peas.

'Miss Mandeville is very kind,' I said.

I didn't think for one moment that Celia wanted to talk about clothes. It was an entirely different plan she had in mind. Still, she'd been clever, even leaving the note unsealed so that Mrs Quivering could read it if she were curious.

I went back to the schoolroom to tell Betty where I was going. She was wide-eyed at my luck.

'Miss Mandeville lending you one of her own dresses! You must be careful not to drop any food on it. Perhaps you should only pretend to eat. I'll try to keep you something back from supper for later.'

'Thank you, Betty, but I'll do well enough.'

'You might even be sitting next to a lord who will fall in love with you. Stranger things have happened.'

'In fairy tales. But no, I'm not. I've looked at the table plan.'

'So who are you sitting next to.'

'Not a lord. Not even a sir or an MP. I have a cathedral canon on my left hand and a Mr Disraeli on my right.'

'Who's he?'

'A writer, I believe. I'm nearly sure I read one of his novels once.'

'Well, I suppose it takes all sorts.'

Betty was clearly disappointed for me. Upstairs in my room, I put on my lavender dress and fichu pelerine and went as confidently as I could manage downstairs and through the door into the family's bedroom corridor. Compared to the last time I'd been there, it was as busy as a beehive on a sunny afternoon. Bells tinkled, maids I'd never seen before ran in and out with armfuls of lace or cans of hot water, voices called from half-open doorways and the sharp smell of frizzled hair mingled with rose-water and lavender. I knocked on Celia's door.

'Come in.'

She was sitting at her dressing table in her petticoats with a silk wrap over her shoulders and her maid brushing her hair. A tailor's dummy covered with a dust sheet stood beside the dressing table. She saw me in the mirror and, without turning, said to the maid 'You can go, Fanny. I'll ring when I want you.' The maid put down the hair-brush and left. Celia spun round in her seat and held out her hands to me.

'Oh, Elizabeth, I'm so glad you've come. I'm so scared. Feel – I'm trembling like an aspen.'

I took her hands. Indeed, they were cold and trembling.

'Then put on something warmer.'

I went to the wardrobe and found a blue velvet pelisse with white fur collar. She let me drape it round her and clutched the fur to her chest as if it were a warm and living animal.

'I wish you'd told me more,' I said.

The conversation with Daniel had hardened me. I was still sorry for her, but angry at what was going on round her.

'More of what?'

'Queen to His Majesty King George the Fifth, was that the idea?'

'The creature's name is Harold, so it would be Harold the Second, wouldn't it? It wasn't my idea, you know that.'

She stared back at me over her fistfuls of fur.

'How long have you known?'

'About the Harold creature being the rightful king? A month or two. My stepfather told me when we all knew King William was going to die soon.'

'Miss Mandeville, he is not the rightful king at all.

It's utter nonsense about Princess Charlotte being poisoned and the baby saved.'

'How do you know? Nobody can.'

'Even if he were – which I don't believe for one minute – what is your stepfather doing? If he tries to put this Harold on the throne, it may mean another civil war.'

'But there'll be one anyway. My stepfather says unless somebody takes a stand there'll be a civil war in England, just like France. It's happening already. People have been stirred up by agitators so that they aren't content any more. They march and burn things down until they're given votes, then when they've got votes they're not satisfied with that and demand other things . . .'

'Like food for their families. Miss Mandeville, your stepfather's talking nonsense. There won't be a revolution here.'

'That's what they said in France. And little Vicky won't be able to stand up to them because she's a girl and even younger than we are, so she'll do whatever the politicians tell her'.

'What about Queen Elizabeth and Queen Anne? In any case, can you see your bonnie prince Harold standing up against a revolution?'

'You know very well he's not my bonnie prince anything. If people like my stepfather help him become king, he'll have to be grateful to them and do what they tell him.'

'Including taking you as his wife?'

'I'm not going to marry him. I find him entirely loathsome whether he's king or not, and that's an end to it. Two days from now I'll be married to Philip, and nobody will be able to do anything about it.'

I realised it was useless to be angry about her political naïvety.

'And that's really the wish of your heart?'

'More than anything in the world. Sit down and I'll show you his letter about meeting me tomorrow.'

'I don't think . . .'

But she was already up and rummaging in a drawer. I settled in a blue armchair and she watched, smiling, as I read. People's love letters should not be inflicted on the public, so I'll say only that it was brave and loving, with a bedrock of commonsense to it as well, and altogether the kind of thing that every woman should receive once in a lifetime. As I handed it back, I was annoyed to hear myself giving a sigh of envy.

'Yes, I think your Philip really loves you.'

'Of course he does. Now, where are you and I to meet tomorrow night? Philip will have the coach on the back road from nine o'clock onwards.'

'Let's meet at nine then, or as soon after as you can slip away. In the stableyard.'

'How do I get there without being seen?'

I was about to say something impatient, then remembered that I knew the geography of parts of her house better than she did.

'You slip out through the kitchens, into the back courtyard and through the archway.'

'Through the kitchens in *that*?'

She laughed and whipped the sheet off the tailor's dummy. Underneath was a shining cloud of white silk and silver embroidery.

'My stepfather chose it in Paris. He insists I wear it.'

'Like a bride.'

'Or a sacrifice,' she said.

'And altogether the worst garment in the world for eloping. You might as well carry a chandelier with you. Are those the shoes?'

Soft white kid, embroidered with silver, that might just stand up to an evening of moderate dancing.

'I must come up and change first, I suppose,' she said. 'We'll meet here instead. Now, what can I find that's drab coloured?'

She walked over to a white-and-gilt-painted wardrobe and opened the door on a muted rainbow of dresses, skirts and bodices in soft blues, pinks, apricots, with shawls of delicate lace or gleaming satin. With some trouble we discovered at the back of it a plain grey dress, a dark gabardine travelling cloak and the stoutest pair of shoes she owned, which were not very stout but would have to do. She ran a hand softly over the rows of dresses.

'I shall hate leaving them.'

'You can always buy more.'

'So I can. Now, let's choose a dress for you to wear tonight. It shall be yours to keep.'

'Won't this one do?'

A quick shake of the head was the only answer. She pulled dress after dress out of the wardrobe, trying each colour against my face, flinging them haphazardly on to the bed when they didn't quite suit, until it looked like a barge fit for Cleopatra. After a while she narrowed the choice to a deep rose damask with silver-grey silk trim or moss-green ribbed silk with enough lace on the bodice to have kept Nottingham employed for weeks.

'Which do you prefer, Elizabeth?'

'Either.'

'You must have an opinion.'

She was as shocked by my unconcern as I'd been at her politics. To please her, I opted for the rose damask, on the grounds that the skirt was less full and the satin pumps that went with it had low heels.

'You must try it on. You're taller than I am and not so . . .' She made a gesture with her hands over her chest. 'But we can always pad out your stays.'

I felt shy of stripping to my stays and petticoats in front of her, so I went behind a gilt leather screen in the corner. Although I'd chosen the rose damask with so little interest, it was sleek and comforting under my hands, like a cat. When I came out from behind the screen, feeling awkward in the grandest dress I'd ever worn, she clapped her hands.

'It suits you so much better than me. It's a great thing I'm not jealous. Come over here to the light.' She looked critically. 'You're too thin for it, though. It hangs awkwardly at the waist. Come here and let me pin it.'

She was as deft as a seamstress. 'Now, pull your stays down and let me lace you tighter. Breathe in.'

'I can hardly breathe at all.'

'It's just a bit short and your ankles will show when you walk. Still, you have good ankles and the shoes might have been made for you.'

She laughed, delighting in it like a child dressing a doll. She made me sit down at her dressing table and did my crinkly hair with her own hands, pinning it up to one side with a mother-of-pearl comb of her own. Then she rummaged in her jewel case, brought out a necklace of opals and garnets on a silver chain and clasped it round my neck.

'There, look at you. You're quite a beauty.'

I'd hardly dared glance in the mirror while all this was going on. When I did, I couldn't help gasping. The nuns and my aunts had all discouraged vanity and although my father had liked to see me well dressed, there were always more important things in life than clothes. The woman who stared back at me had a rather Spanish look with her dark hair and eyes and pale skin, set off by the rich rose of the bodice. Mother of pearl and opals glinted in the light reflected from the mirror.

'You're crying,' Celia said. 'Why?'

And indeed there was a tear trickling down the cheek of the dark beauty. I wiped it away.

'Because my father will never see me and I'll probably be old before my brother comes home.'

She put a hand on my shoulder.

'Oh, my dear.'

We stayed silent for a while, looking at our faces in the mirror. I said I must go and reached up to unclasp the necklace.

'Keep it as your bridesmaid present,' she said.

'Bridesmaid?'

'The nearest I'll have to one.'

She took the pins out of the dress and said I'd have to get Betty to help me alter it. While I was changing behind the screen, trying not to disarrange my hair, I remembered something.

'Miss Mandeville . . .'

'Please, call me Celia. After all, I call you Elizabeth.'

'But my name's . . . Celia, do you know if Mr Brighton and Lord Kilkeel brought a maid with them?'

'Maid? Why would they do that? I know there's a French valet. Here, I've found the rose-tinted silk stockings. You must have them.'

She kissed me on the cheek when I left, my arms weighed down with her finery.

Back in the schoolroom, Betty handled the rose damask with reverence. She took me to her room and made me try it on again so that she could pin and tack the alterations, then left me stitching while she took the children downstairs to make their public appearance. When they came back, the two boys looked stiff and solemn but Henrietta was spinning around like a clockwork toy.

'I curtsied to him. I curtsied to him and he patted me on the head and said I was a pretty dear.'

Betty's eyes caught mine over the child's whirling ringlets. They were worried.

'Miss Lock, what *is* all this about?' she whispered.

I shook my head, from the impossibility of explaining, ran up the rickety stairs to my own room and changed into the damask dress and the pumps. I had to go down to the mirror in the schoolroom to put the mother-of-pearl comb in my hair and fasten the necklace. Betty gasped when she saw me.

'Oh, Miss Lock, you look quite the lady.'

She grabbed a brush and set about my hair.

'That's my brush,' Henrietta wailed. 'And what's she doing in Celia's dress?'

For once Betty ignored her.

'You'll do. And oh, be careful of the dress, my dear Miss Lock.'

She bent suddenly and kissed me on the cheek. I kissed her back then ran along the corridor and down the main stairs. Along the bedroom floor, doors were standing open, giving glimpses of ladies' maids gathering up scattered clothes or just standing there with the numbed look of battle survivors. I went down the next flight, the thin leather soles of the pumps sliding on the carpet, damask skirts making every step feel like wading through water. There was a noise coming from below, a small orchestra playing and a great buzz of talk, like a theatre just before the curtain rises. When I paused at the door

313

to the first-floor landing and put a hand to my chest to steady my breathing, I felt the unfamiliar curve of my own pushed-up breasts, and the smoothness of Celia's opals.

'I'm still who I am,' I told myself. 'I'm still Liberty.'

But I didn't feel it as I pushed open the door and stepped through.

CHAPTER TWENTY

The chandelier blazed with dozens of candles, each flame reflected hundreds of time over in droplets, like a volcano eruption of diamonds. More lights flashed up to meet them from the grand hall below: the jewels in the hair of the women, the decorations on the chests of the men, the champagne glasses. From here, the noise their talk made was something between a purr and a low roar. On a dais by the bottom of the staircase a small group of musicians were playing Mozart, with Daniel directing from the violin, but nobody seemed to be taking any notice. A fire blazed in the enormous gothic fireplace. Alongside, Mr Brighton outblazed the fire, gorgeous in a purple coat, a black-and-gold striped waistcoat, a high white stock, and a whole jeweller's window of gold chains and rings. Beside him, Sir Herbert Mandeville looked stiff and statesmanlike in black and white. Lady

Mandeville stood next to her husband in dark blue silk and a necklace of diamonds and sapphires, her smile as fixed as if it had been cast in plaster of Paris. Celia, in apricot silk with a rope of pearls twined in her hair, was talking to an elderly lady in black velvet, her back firmly turned to her stepfather and Mr Brighton.

I looked at the women especially, wondering if any of them could possibly have arrived curled up in the well of a travelling coach. Surely not the tall copper-haired woman in green, talking with great animation to a knight of the garter? Nor the plump one in purple and pink stripes whose high giggle soared like a hot-air balloon above the rest of the chatter. Nor the buttercup-haired beauty of thirty or so whose white breasts were pushed up so high that it was a wonder she could breathe. Then I saw Kilkeel. My knees went weak and I had to hold on to the curving marble balustrade. He was dressed more plainly than the rest, almost shabbily, and had got his pulpy body reptile-like into a corner, so that he could peer out without being noticed. He was looking straight at Mr Brighton. My nerve almost failed me and I thought I couldn't go down after all.

The scene below me began to change. The noise faded to a quiet buzz. Sir Herbert held out his arm to the woman in purple-and-pink stripes, who gave another of her high giggles and took it. One of the garter knights offered his arm to Lady Mandeville, who stayed exactly where she was, still smiling her fixed smile, until a word and a frown from her husband made her flinch and seize her guest's arm like a wrecked mariner grasping a log. This left Mr Brighton by the fireplace, hands under his coat-tails, a vacant grin on his face. Sir Herbert went up to him and said something. Mr Brighton nodded and moved towards Celia without enthusiasm. She kept her back turned.

'Celia.'

Sir Herbert's sharp command was loud enough to be heard at the top of the staircase. Celia turned reluctantly, but would not take the smallest step towards Mr Brighton. He had to come across the room to her; her father's brows were a black bar. When, finally, she let her white-gloved fingers rest very lightly on his arm, the whole room seemed to relax in a sigh of relief and Sir Herbert and the striped woman led the way into the dining room. Lady Mandeville followed with her partner, like a woman in a sad dream, with her daughter and Mr Brighton behind them and the other guests pairing-up to follow. Celia's eyes were everywhere but on her partner, looking desperately all round the room. I realised with guilt that she was looking for me and must have willed her to look up, because just before they went through the door to the dining room, she did and caught my eye. She smiled, a great beam of relief that I hardly deserved, then mouthed 'Hurry,' and motioned me, with a flick of a fingertip, to come down.

I came as quickly as I could, still unused to the sway of rich fabric and stiff petticoats round my ankles, and tripped on the bottom stair. A hand came on my arm to steady me, a strong and sharp-fingered little hand in a black lace glove. I looked up and there was Mrs Beedle, in black silk as usual. Her only concession to the occasion had been to replace her customary widow's cap with a black velvet turban trimmed with white lace and jet beads. She was frowning. I assumed she was angry with me for being so nearly late and began apologising, but she took no notice and kept her grip on my arm, guiding me to the side of an orange tree in a pot at the bottom of the staircase.

'Miss Lock, something has occurred.' She said it in a low voice, her face close to mine. 'You had better go into dinner as arranged, but as soon as the first couple of courses are over, please make an excuse and meet me in the schoolroom. You must say you're indisposed, or anything you like.'

'But what . . .?'

She shook her head, forbidding questions, and started to move away.

'I hope you won't let me down.'

Then she disappeared through a door behind the orange tree that I hadn't even noticed before.

By now almost everybody had gone through to the dining room. Just one man was waiting, his back to me and his foot tapping impatiently. I hurried towards him, knowing he must be the one obliged to take me into dinner. When he heard my footsteps he turned and I regret to say I stopped and gawped at him like a five-year-old at a fairground. He was beautiful. The dandyism that was an offence to the eye in Mr Brighton had reached a higher level entirely in him. He wore a claret-coloured cut-away coat and black velvet trousers with broad claret stripes down the outside legs. The silver brocade of his waistcoat was almost hidden by enough gold chains to fill a pirate's chest, and the fingers of his white kid gloves sparkled with gold rings. Black ringlets cascaded almost to his collar, his face was as pale as paper, his lips full and as well shaped as a woman's. His dark eyes managed to look at the same time both profoundly bored and very much alive. He stood poised and conscious of his effect on others, like an actor.

'Miss Lock? I understand I am to have the privilege of taking you into dinner.'

His voice was languid, with a tinge of annoyance. I thought of my guest list. He certainly was not a cathedral canon.

'Mr Disraeli?' I said.

He was justifiably annoyed at my lateness. I was prepared for that. What took me by surprise was the look in his eyes when he straightened up from the most perfunctory of bows. There was approval there, the kind a man bestows on a pretty woman. I thought there must be somebody walking behind me until I realised that he was seeing the dark-haired beauty who'd looked back at me from Celia's mirror. It was a strange feeling, as if that made both of us into actors who could stroll across the stage, arm in arm, knowing our lines and our business. I put my gloved hand on the arm he offered me, very lightly so as not to spoil the nap of his coat, and we walked quickly into the dining room.

We'd only just reached our seats at the far end of the table when the bishop was on his feet saying grace. I've sat through sermons shorter than that grace, but at least it gave me a chance to look around, as far as I could with head bowed. The white-clothed table seemed to extend far into the distance. Footmen in black-and-gold jackets with powdered wigs stood along the walls. Silver candelabra blazed all down the middle of the table, although the light of a July evening was still coming in through the windows. Posies of gardenias and tuberoses alternated with the candles, giving off a scent so sweet that it was almost oppressive.

'. . . and guide us, oh Lord, in all our endeavours small and great . . .'

The air quivered from the candle flames so that the group at the top of the table were little more than a blur, though I could make out Celia's apricot dress. Kilkeel must be up there somewhere, but if I couldn't see him, he probably couldn't see me. Trying to keep the seating plan in mind, I managed to put names to some of the faces around the middle of the table. There were ladies whose political salons were so famous I'd read about them in the more frivolous newspapers, gentlemen whose speeches in the Lords and Commons were respectfully noted by *The Times*.

'. . . keeping our minds humbly obedient to Thy

will, Who hath cast down the proud and exalted the meek . . .'

The cathedral canon on my left was echoing every word *sotto voce*. On my right. Mr Disraeli was doing exactly what I was doing, looking round. I sensed an increasing tension in him, at odds with his languid dandy air.

'. . . humble gratitude for Thy bountiful gifts. Amen.'

The footmen pushed forward chairs for the ladies to sit down, mine included. A line of waiters appeared from the kitchens carrying great silver tureens. A buzz of talk started.

'Have you any notion why we are all here?' said Mr Disraeli.

I stared. I'd expected small talk and had prepared myself to make polite dinner-party conversation when my mind and body ached to be elsewhere. Caught off balance by his directness, I was tempted for a moment to be honest with him. I had the strangest feeling of fellowship, as if he and I were both floating free in the world, like limpets that had not found a place to fix themselves. Then I reminded myself that I'd met him only minutes before, that he was presumably a friend of Sir Herbert, and that honesty to strangers was a luxury I could no longer afford. I smiled at him, trying to look cool and quizzical.

'Have you?'

'A lady of my acquaintance was most insistent that I should attend.' He glanced towards one of the political salon hostesses, the copper-haired woman. 'She said it would be useful to my career to meet our new monarch as soon as possible.'

'You were expecting to find the queen here?'

'I believed that was being hinted. I've stolen time from my election campaign. I confess I am wondering why.'

'You do not know Sir Herbert well?'

'Only by reputation.' He did not sound as if he admired him. 'Are you a friend of the family, may I ask?'

I nodded. Any other way of explaining my presence would have been too complicated. I could see he was trying to judge my importance. My place at the far end of the table argued against it; on the other hand a man with an eye for jewellery could hardly have missed the value of Celia's opals.

'What did the old lady want with you so urgently?'

So he was sharp-eyed, as well as impudent.

'That was Mrs Beedle,' I said. 'Our hostess's mother.'

A waiter was ladling turtle soup into our plates, the rich smell of it mingling with hot candlewax and tuberoses.

'What did she mean about your not letting her down? Are you accustomed to letting people down?'

'I hope not.'

I must have put more feeling into that than I intended, because he gave a sharp sideways glance. I took a small spoonful of soup and sipped. I'd never tasted turtle before. It was meaty rather than fishy, almost overpoweringly so. The combination of tastes, smells and his questions was making my head spin.

'So you write novels,' I said, trying to take refuge in the small talk I'd prepared.

'Yes.'

It did not seem to please him. He was looking intently towards the top of the table.

'And you're in the midst of an election campaign?'

His eyes came back to me.

'In a few weeks' time I shall be the Member of Parliament for Maidstone. You haven't forgotten there must be a general election when a new monarch comes to the throne?'

I had forgotten. Too much had happened in the past few weeks for me to care about elections.

'You are sure of being elected?'

'Quite sure.'

A Tory, presumably, since he was on Sir Herbert's guest list. I was sorry about that. The waiters cleared the soup plates away and served turbot. I drank cool white wine. By rights, with the change of courses, I should have turned to converse with my neighbour on the other side, but the canon seemed happily occupied with his fish. I noticed there was an empty place opposite him, and that the woman next to it looked put out at not being provided with a second gentleman. After all the trouble taken with the table plan, this struck me as odd, but I had little time to think about it.

'Are you in Sir Herbert Mandeville's confidence?'

This time there was undisguised urgency in Mr Disraeli's question. Neither of us was eating.

'No.' At least I could answer that truthfully.

'Do you know if he's on particularly friendly terms with Kilkeel?'

A shiver ran up my spine.

'Why do you ask?'

'I know of the man, also by reputation.'

'So what is Lord Kilkeel's reputation?'

He gave me a considering look.

'As one of the greatest rogues who ever graced the Bar.'

'Oh.'

'That surprises you? Offends you perhaps? Are you connected in some way with him?'

'No!' I couldn't help saying it so loudly that the canon glanced up from his fish. Then, more calmly I hoped: 'So he's a lawyer. In what way is he a rogue?'

'He's a constitutional lawyer, probably the best of his generation. Even his enemies have to admit his intellect. He's also the greatest political turncoat of our times. Whatever party is in or out, Kilkeel always has the ear of the men who matter. It's a question of knowing where all the bodies are buried.'

'Bodies?'

'You look alarmed. I speak metaphorically, of course. Any government ever formed has work to do which it can never admit to and, as often as not, Kilkeel is the man called upon to do it.'

'What sort of work?'

He glanced at me over the rim of his wine glass.

'For one thing, he helped fabricate some of the evidence against the late and unlamented Queen Caroline.'

I held his gaze. If he saw confusion in my face he probably thought it was because of the queen's alleged and all too probable adultery. But I was thinking, Charlotte again. Caroline was her mother. He put down his glass and looked me in the eye.

'When Kilkeel is present on any occasion, the prudent man asks himself why. And that is what I am asking myself now, Miss Lock. For some reason, I think you know a lot more about all this than you're telling me.'

By any normal standards, this was intolerably bad manners. After all, I'd claimed to be a friend of the family. When I got to my feet, blushing I dare say, and asked him to excuse me, he must have thought that was the reason. He was, I think, drawling an unflustered apology as I went, but I didn't stop to hear because waiters were coming in with trays of roast beef and it was time to keep my appointment with Mrs Beedle upstairs. I walked past rows of black-and-gold footmen to the door, keeping my face turned away from the top of the table. When I heard a commotion behind me, I glanced round, scared that the inquisitive Mr Disraeli might be coming after me. But it was only one of the waiters. He must have slipped and fallen on his back, overcome by the weight of his tureen of vegetables, because his black-trousered legs were sticking out from a knot of other waiters, and peas and carrots were scattered on the floor all round him.

The hall was deserted. I ducked behind the orange tree and went through the door that Mrs Beedle had used. It led into a servants' corridor that, after a few dozen yards, connected with a back staircase. Mrs Beedle must be familiar with the backstage world of the house. I went up another flight of stairs and into the schoolroom corridor. It felt like home. The schoolroom had come to represent the nearest thing to familiarity and safety I'd known at Mandeville Hall and, with so much bustle and activity downstairs, it was calming to see the glow of a candle lantern coming from Henrietta's half-open door. In spite of her confidence by day, the child suffered from nightmares and feared the dark. Betty slept in the room next door to Henrietta's, usually with her own door half-open, to hear and comfort her if she woke. Tonight the door to her room was closed, so she was presumably still acting as maid elsewhere.

Once past Henrietta's light, the corridor was dim, the door to the schoolroom shut. I tapped on it, softly at first then more loudly, expecting to hear Mrs Beedle's voice telling me to come in. When nothing happened I opened the door. The curtains were drawn across the window, with just enough evening light coming in round the edges to show the shape of the rocking horse, the three desks, the table. I went towards it and started feeling around for the lamp, intending to light it ready for when Mrs Beedle arrived. She'd said she'd be waiting for me, but something must have detained her downstairs. I couldn't find the lamp so I moved round the table. My foot caught on something and I fell to one knee, petticoats tangling round the heel of my shoe. A ruck in the carpet, I thought. But even as I thought it, I knew it wasn't that. It was the smell that warned me. The schoolroom usually smelled of chalk dust, marigolds and custard. Now there was a harsh metallic reek that didn't belong there.

My knee was nudging against something like a cushion or a bolster, but heavier. Scared now, I leaned forward and let my hand rest on it. A silk upholstered curve, slithery under my fingers. My hand moved along and it wasn't silky any more, just bare and loose, yielding horribly to the fingertips. Trying to get away from it, I backed into the rocking horse and set it swaying and creaking. For a while I just crouched there under the rise and dip of the wooden head, but eventually managed to pull myself upright on the cabinet of birds' eggs and stumble to the door. Without knowing it, I'd picked something off the schoolroom floor and had it clenched in my hand. It was quite small and mostly soft. In the dim light coming from Henrietta's room I could make out what it was: a turban of black velvet trimmed with white lace and jet beads.

CHAPTER TWENTY-ONE

'She was an old lady,' Mrs Quivering said. 'Her heart failed, that's all.'

We were in the housekeeper's room, just the two of us. Mrs Quivering was sitting behind her desk, I – at her invitation – in a chintz armchair. She was being kind to me, in that half-fearful way people have when they think you might fly apart from shock, like a glass vase shattering. It was just after one o'clock in the morning. The curtains were drawn over the windows, two candles burning on the mantelpiece. One was almost finished, the flame dropping right down below the candle-holder then rising in a blue splutter.

'Yes.'

'She must have gone upstairs to make sure the children were asleep. She knew Betty couldn't be with them.'

'Yes.'

I had not told her, and had no intention of telling her, that Mrs Beedle had gone to the schoolroom to meet me.

'She was devoted to her grandchildren,' she said.

'Yes.'

'It's possible that she felt herself becoming faint and went to the schoolroom to sit down. Then she must have fallen and hit her head on something – the rocking horse, perhaps.'

The story was improving all the time. We both knew very well that she was talking nonsense. Mrs Quivering had organised the removal of the body from the schoolroom to Mrs Beedle's bedroom. I'd heard her intake of breath when two footmen brought the body into the schoolroom corridor, and the lamp she was holding had swung wildly, sending waves of light all round us. Betty had been summoned and had hustled the children away somewhere, so, apart from the footmen, we were alone. It had looked for a moment as if the infallible Mrs Quivering would collapse like any ordinary woman. Hardly surprising. The grey hair above Mrs Beedle's left ear was clotted with blood, the side of her silk dress soaked with it. Mrs Quivering had to run for towels from the nursery bathroom because blood was seeping on to the carpet. By then, she was in control again. She told the footmen to carry the body down the back stairs, so as not to alarm any guests who might be going to their rooms, and left me to hold the lamp for them. Then she disappeared for a while.

I was sure she'd gone to report to Sir Herbert. What else could she do? I imagined him called away from his port and his guests, some hurried consultation in an ante-room. At any rate, it can't have lasted long because by the time we reached Mrs Beedle's bedroom, Mrs Quivering was there to meet us. She told the footmen to lay the body on the bed then sent them to wait outside, lit candles and dispatched me to the kitchen for hot water, ordering me not to talk to anybody on the way. I came back with it to find that she'd stripped Mrs Beedle of her black silk and replaced it with a long nightdress. Mrs Beedle looked older and smaller in death, false teeth gone and mouth open. I thought of the immense effort of will it must have cost her to keep alive and protect her family, and was close to tears, knowing that I'd failed her after all.

Mrs Quivering told me sharply to come and hold the bowl while she sponged the worst of the blood off the long grey hair and dabbed it dry with a towel. She made me rummage in drawers for a white muslin scarf and a nightcap. We used the scarf to bind up the sagging jaw then put on the nightcap over the damp hair and injured head. When we left, she ordered one of the footmen to stay on guard by the closed door. By that time, the gentlemen guests had joined the ladies in the drawing room and were listening to music. I heard a snatch of a Vivaldi oboe and violin concerto as we came into the kitchen corridor with our bloodstained towels and water bowl, and imagined Daniel with his fiddle to his chin, just a few rooms and a whole world away. I knew that I should never hear that concerto again without smelling blood.

'It must have been most unpleasant for you, finding her,' Mrs Quivering said.

I didn't reply. How could I explain to her that it was doubly bad because it had catapulted me back to the room in Calais, and my father's body? She came out from behind her desk, her face sharp with tiredness, and carefully refilled my teacup from the pot on the table beside me. A footman had brought it in ten minutes or so ago. His stockings were wrinkled, the shoulders of his jacket white from the powder that had fallen out of his wig, but she'd made no comment. He'd been one of the two footmen who'd carried Mrs Beedle's body to her bedroom. If you listened carefully, you could hear the muffled voices and clink of plates as kitchen maids cleared up the remains of the dinner. Wafts of left-over fish and stale claret drifted in and mingled with the smell of the dying candle. Mrs Quivering walked over to it, lit a new one and set it upright in the hot wax.

'It might be best if you didn't talk about this to any of the servants, Miss Lock. These things are very unsettling for them.'

I promised. It would have been easy to assume, because Mrs Quivering was weaving such a hard-wearing lie, that she was responsible in some way for Mrs Beedle's death. I didn't believe that. Mrs Quivering was a very efficient housekeeper, and the centre of a housekeeper's work is to deal with any unpleasantness before it troubles the life of the family. The death was nothing to do with Mrs Quivering and everything to do with me, and that first great lie about my father.

'Does Lady Mandeville know?' I said.

'She went to her room as soon as the ladies left the table. I'm sure she'll be sleeping now. It will wait until she wakes up.'

It was clear from the way she said it that Lady Mandeville had retired to bed worse for drink.

'And Miss Mandeville?' I asked. 'She seemed fond of her grandmother.'

I could see from Mrs Quivering's face that Sir Herbert had given no instructions about that.

'Yes, it would be wrong for her to hear it from one of the servants. I should go to her, I suppose.'

Mrs Quivering began to stand up, so weary that she could hardly force her body out of the chair.

'There's her brother,' I said.

'He's with some of the gentlemen in the billiard room.'

'Does he know his grandmother's dead?'

'I don't think so.'

'I'll go and tell Miss Mandeville, if you'd like me to,' I said.

She sank back in the chair.

'Thank you, Miss Lock. You will do it as kindly as you can, won't you? There is no need for Miss Mandeville to know . . . all the details.'

I promised to do it kindly. I went up the back stairs to the bedroom corridor and tapped on her door.

'Come in.'

Celia was sitting in an armchair in a blue cashmere dressing gown, bare feet drawn up on to the chair. Two candles were burning on the dressing table. Her face was white and she'd been crying.

'Fanny says my grandmother's dead.'

'I'm sorry to say it's true.'

'What happened?'

I thought that there were enough lies, without my telling more. So I told her how I'd found Mrs Beedle. She made a whimpering sound, like a hurt puppy. I went towards her and her cold and trembling hand came out of the dressing-gown sleeve and clasped mine.

'You're saying she was killed?'

'I think she must have been.'

'But who by, and why?'

'I don't know.'

'My stepfather. He never liked her.'

'It can't have been. He was at the table in front of all his guests when it happened.'

'He paid somebody to do it, then.'

'Miss Mandeville . . . Celia, your grandmother spoke to me just as we were going in to dinner. She said something had occurred and I was to leave dinner early and meet her in the schoolroom. Have you any idea what she meant?'

'No.' I didn't know whether she'd even understood my question. She seemed lost in her own thoughts. 'Does my mother know she's dead?'

'Not yet, no.'

Her hand tightened on mine.

'I think I want to see Grandma. Will you take me to her?'

The same footman was on duty outside Mrs Beedle's room, sagging against the wall, half asleep. He woke suddenly and, seeing Celia, opened the door for us. Celia stood for a long time looking down at her grandmother, then, rather to my surprise, knelt on the rug beside the bed and bent her head in prayer. Finally she stood up and kissed her on the forehead, just below the cap. She was crying.

'I was never good enough to her, never grateful enough.'

'I don't suppose anybody ever is.'

'Why would someone do this to a poor old lady?'

'I think she was more than a poor old lady. She didn't like what was happening and was doing her best to stop it.'

'But I don't like it either. Does that mean somebody wants to kill me?'

'I hope not. Just stay quietly in your room today and I'll help you get away tonight, if that's still what you want. They'll have to cancel the ball, I suppose.'

'They won't. My stepfather's been planning this for a long time. He won't let the death of an old lady he hated prevent it.'

'What about the coroner? Won't he have to be told?'

'Sir Herbert is deputy Lord Lieutenant of the county

and chairman of the bench of magistrates. If he says her heart failed, that's what the verdict will be.'

She took a last look at the figure on the bed and turned away.

'I must go to my mother.'

'I think she may be asleep.'

Her look showed she knew exactly what I meant by that. She seemed to have grown up a lot in the last few minutes.

'I'll wait with her till she wakes up. I can't leave him to tell her.'

We went out and I watched her walking heavily away along the corridor. There were several things I must attend to and the first of them was getting out of my ridiculous dinner dress back into proper clothes. The nursery corridor was deserted, Betty presumably else-where with the children. It took some resolution to go past the closed door of the schoolroom with the smell of wet wool in my nostrils where Mrs Beedle's blood had been sponged from the carpet. The staircase up to the maids' dormitory was dark and I hesitated there for some time. For all I knew, the killer might have escaped that way, into the maze of servants' quarters. When I got to the landing by the maids' room, a reassuring sound of snoring came from inside. I hesitated for a while, then continued up the narrower staircase to my room. At the door, I thought I heard a rustling noise above me.

'What do you want?' I said into the darkness.

No answer. Probably a rat or a pigeon in the roof timbers. I opened the door, hoping that if I had to scream at least it would wake the maids below.

'Is anybody in there?'

The sound of my own voice bouncing back told me that the room was empty. It must be dawn in the world outside because a little grey light was coming through the window. I took a deep breath and lit the candle. It took three tries because my hand was shaking, but I felt better when its light flickered round the walls.

The dress, with its array of tiny buttons, had been intended for somebody with a lady's maid and I tore some of them off as I struggled to get out of it. It was a small relief to turn to my own clothes, neatly folded on the bed. Then my heart lurched and I started trembling again because I hadn't left them on the bed. I was quite certain that I'd left them as I always did, folded on the chair. And they'd been turned upside down. I'd left a shawl Betty had loaned me at the bottom, then the dress, petticoats, stockings and garters. Now the shawl had disappeared entirely, the dress was uppermost with the other things underneath it, and one garter was lying on the floor beside the bed.

There was something wrong with the wash bowl, too. I was sure I'd emptied it after washing, but now there were a few inches of dirty water in it and my small cake of soap had been moved. Somebody had come into my room and washed. Somebody who needed to wash blood off his hands? I looked at the water. No blood that I could see or smell, just soap scum. I knelt to pick up the garter and stayed kneeling with my head on the bed, bludgeoned by fear and misery. Not even my room was safe. If somebody had come in and attacked me at that moment, I should hardly have resisted. The long trail that had started in Calais had ended here and I had not the strength or will to do anything about it.

In the end, it was anger that brought me back to my feet. I was sure that the person who'd killed my father was also the murderer of Mrs Beedle. I was under the same roof with him, breathing the same air that he breathed, quite possibly had breathed in this very room. Wasn't that what I'd wanted all along? I put my own clothes on reluctantly, wondering what fingers had pawed them. After a while I went downstairs. It was after five o'clock and the routine of the day had started in the kitchen and scullery but the servants' voices were hushed with the knowledge of the body lying upstairs.

The only idea in my mind was to speak to Daniel. I walked round the outside of the wall of the kitchen garden, on to a pathway that I'd sometimes taken with the children to the Greek Pavilion on its hillock in the park. It was a fine morning, the sky blue and cloudless. The musicians had been playing until late so I hardly expected to find anybody awake at that hour, but when I came up the last spiral of path somebody was sitting on a bench, looking out at the view over the heath. He turned when he heard my steps on the gravel.

'Oh, Daniel.'

'Child?'

He was still wearing his evening clothes. I ran to him and poured out the story as if I really were the child he called me.

'She spoke to me, Daniel. It couldn't have been much more than half an hour before it happened. She must have gone straight upstairs after that and . . . I think whoever did it may have been in my room.'

At some point in the story he must have taken my hand and kept hold of it.

'Have you any idea what it was she wanted to tell you?'

'Something to do with Mr Brighton, I'm sure. Beyond that, no idea at all.'

'And she didn't mention any names?'

'No.'

He said nothing for a long time, holding my hand and looking out at the view.

'Haven't you slept?' I asked.

He shook his head.

'I wish I'd come to find you last night, Liberty. If I'd had the slightest idea what had happened, I should have. God knows I wanted to, but it seemed an intrusion.'

'Why?'

'Yesterday evening, when you came down the stairs, you were so beautiful, I hardly recognised you – no, that's not complimentary, is it? I mean, you were by far the most beautiful of the ladies there. That young fop who took you into dinner was clearly entranced and . . .'

'Daniel, that's nonsense.'

'When I looked for you after dinner, you weren't there. Then rumour began to get round that somebody had died and I couldn't help worrying. You'll say that's nonsense too, I suppose.'

'But you must have soon found out it wasn't me?'

'Yes. The word spread that our host's elderly mother-in-law had died suddenly of a heart seizure. I'm sorry, but I felt like playing a jig when I heard. Not that the bereaved son-in-law would have cared if I had.'

'You talked to Sir Herbert?'

'Yes. I asked him whether, in the circumstances, he wished us to continue to play.'

'What did he say?'

'At risk of offending your ears, I shall quote him verbatim: "Damn your eyes, sir, it's only my mother-in-law. I'm paying you, and if I say so, you'll go on fiddling until hell freezes over."'

'I'm sure he knows something about it. Whoever killed her must have been a member of his household or one of his guests.'

Daniel went quiet again.

'Well, mustn't he?' I said.

'I understand that they brought in additional staff for the occasion.'

'That's true, yes. But why should some jobbing waiter want to kill her?'

'Liberty, there is something it is only fair you should know. I don't think for one moment that it has anything to do with her death, but . . .'

He looked embarrassed and miserable.

'What?'

'My dear, please don't jump to conclusions, but the fact is, Blackstone is here.'

I stared at him.

'What's he doing here?'

'We think he must have contrived to have himself employed among the extra waiters. He collapsed while serving dinner last night.'

I thought of the black legs sprawling among the peas and carrots. If an elderly man had just run up the back stairs and down, he might well collapse. I let go of Daniel's hand.

'Where is he now?'

Daniel gestured to the pavilion behind us.

'Here. Asleep in my bed, as a matter of fact.'

CHAPTER TWENTY-TWO

I felt myself going hard as stone. I pulled my hand away from Daniel.

'What is he doing here?'

'One of my musicians – another friend of his – saw him fall. We couldn't leave him to the tender mercies of the household. All they were concerned about was that he shouldn't get in the way of the other waiters.'

'I mean here at Mandeville Hall.'

Daniel looked surprised at my tone.

'I haven't had a chance to ask him yet.'

'Why not?'

'He's a very sick man, Liberty. He was hardly conscious when we brought him in here last night, certainly not in a state for conversation.'

'Probably not, seeing as he'd just bludgeoned a poor old lady to death.'

'Child, you can't . . .'

'Don't child me. She needed to tell me something, that was why she wanted to meet in the schoolroom. If she'd discovered Blackstone was here disguised as a waiter –'

'Did she even know the man?'

'To the best of my knowledge, no. But what if she'd found out he wasn't a proper waiter, and begun to ask what he was doing here . . .'

'That's mere supposition.'

'You're not claiming that he was here simply as a waiter, I hope?'

'I'm not claiming anything.' Daniel was beginning to be annoyed now. 'And no, I don't suppose he was simply acting as a waiter.'

'Then what was he doing here?'

'I don't know.'

'You should know. He's a friend of yours.'

'Liberty, when he wakes up, of course I'll ask him, provided he's strong enough.'

'He was strong enough to kill Mrs Beedle. He was strong enough to kill my father.'

I stood up. He tried to take my hand again, but I pulled it away.

'Liberty, please. You can't know –'

'I know he was in Calais when my father was killed. Now he's here and she's dead too. What more do you need?'

'Quite a lot more, if I'm to think him guilty of two murders.'

342

'Of course, he's more than a friend, isn't he? What was it you said? A lodge brother.'

'I promise you that if even half of what you suspect is true, that won't protect him. If I find cause to believe he killed your father or that poor old woman, I shall hand him over to the hangman with pleasure.'

'Well, let's go in there now, wake him up and ask him.'

I made for the door of the pavilion. Daniel jumped up and stood in front of me.

'Later, I promise you . . .'

'I'm tired of promises. He made me promises when he wanted me to spy for him, and look what . . .'

It came to me that I might be partly to blame for Mrs Beedle's death, if my reports had brought Blackstone there, and my voice choked with tears. I was too angry with Daniel to let him see that, so I turned away and walked quickly down the spiral path and back across the park.

By the time I reached the house, I'd recovered myself enough to face Betty and the children. The schoolroom was still being cleaned, so they'd been allocated a sitting room at the far end of the nursery corridor that might once have been the territory of a minor relative. Hasty efforts to tidy it had only stirred up the smell of old dust, and the chairs and sofa were sagging and faded. The two boys were at the table, listlessly spooning up bread and milk, with broad black bands round the sleeves of their jackets. Henrietta was sobbing on the sofa in bodice and petticoats, while Betty sat in an armchair, hurriedly stitching away at a small black crepe dress. I supposed it had been saved from some earlier generation's mourning and she was altering it to fit. Betty's eyes were red, her cheeks swollen with crying. I knelt on the floor beside her, threaded a needle and started on the dress hem. My stitches were large and uneven, but it didn't seem to matter. I could see Betty wanted to talk, but we couldn't in front of the children and they needed all our attention.

Once breakfast was over and Henrietta fitted into her dress they had to be taken to pay their last respects to their grandmother.

'You can stay here if you like,' Betty said.

She must have heard from the other servants that I had been the one who found the body.

'Thank you, but we'll both go.'

We filed into the room and stood in a line by the bed, Betty holding Henrietta's hand, I James's, with Charles alone in the middle. For a second time I looked down at that stern, wrinkled face under the nightcap. Somebody had put vases of gardenias and tuberoses from last night's dinner table on either side of the bed. Their sickly smell helped to mask the scent of blood and decay. James's hand tightened in mine. Henrietta started sobbing again, loudly and painfully. It was, I think, their first experience of death. As soon as we decently could, we took them back upstairs.

Strictly speaking, I suppose we should have emphasised the solemnity of the occasion by making them read the Bible or some devotional work, but when I fetched a book of fairy stories and started reading to them, Betty raised no objection. It would have taken more than spells and princesses to keep my mind from dwelling on Mr Blackstone and Daniel. After a gloomy lunch, Betty said I should go up and lie down for a couple of hours. I was reluctant to leave her on her own with them but the effects of a night without sleep were catching up with me and I knew I'd be no use to Celia unless I rested.

I hesitated on the landing outside my room, reluctant to open the door for fear of finding things disturbed again. Now I knew it had been invaded, it wasn't my safe haven any more. There was a wooden ladder fixed to the wall that led upwards from the landing. I'd barely noticed it before, assuming that it was there to give workmen access to the roof. Today, for some reason, it seemed different. Sunlight caught the cobwebs trailing from its rungs and a waft of fresh air came from higher up. My eyes followed the ladder up to a square of blue sky. There shouldn't have been a square of sky. It had never been there before. A trapdoor then, left open to the roof.

The ladder was a rough affair, two uprights nailed to the wall, narrow rungs of raw pine. I put my hands on the uprights, then my foot on the first rung. What I intended to do wasn't wise, but I was too tired and angry for wisdom. I climbed up towards the square of blue until there were no more uprights to hold and my head came out into the warm sun while my hands felt the chill of the lead roof covering, still wet with dew. I pulled myself through somehow, with my skirts and petticoats bunching in the hatchway, and ended crouching in a kind of broad trough that ran behind the parapet of the house. After a while I stood upright and stared out over the battlements to the terrace with its white statues and formal gardens, the meadows and the Jersey cattle looking more golden than ever in the morning light, and beyond them, the heath. I could even pick out a string of horses walking across it in the distance and imagined Rancie in her stall with the black cat watching from the hayrack. The wish to have good, solid Amos Legge beside me was so sharp and sudden that it felt like pain. I put it out of my mind and looked left and right along the ramparts.

The view was similar in both directions, some yards of emptiness and then the solid brick base of a chimneystack, narrowing the walkway. No sign of anybody. But when my eyes adjusted to the light there was a difference between left and right. Something small was lying at the base of the right-hand chimney stack. It looked like a dishcloth at first, until I recognised the green-and-grey stripes of the shawl I'd borrowed from Betty. I took a few steps and bent to pick it up. When it resisted, I tugged harder, thinking it had caught on something. It still wouldn't budge and from behind the chimney stack came a little noise, halfway between a protest and a moan. There was nothing threatening about the sound, so I went round the chimney stack. The rest of the shawl was wrapped round a woman sitting with her back to the brickwork. She was clinging on to the shawl with her right hand and had the other arm raised, guarding her face, as if she expected to be hit. Her hair was a mixture of faded brown and silver grey with a cobweb clinging to it, her dress of thick brown wool. The boots braced against the lead roof were clumsy and dust-covered, with coarse grey stockings showing above them.

'It's all right,' I said. 'I'm not going to hurt you.'

I let go of the shawl. She rocked backwards and let her arm fall, blinking up at me. Her face was yellowish and deeply lined, her grey eyes bewildered. She seemed to be in her late forties. A light came into her eyes as if she thought she knew me, but I was certain I'd never seen her before in my life.

'Are you employed here?' I asked.

In a great household like Mandeville Hall it was possible there might be some servant I hadn't met. She laughed.

'Employed here? On the roof to scare the crows? Oh yes.'

The words were mad, but the voice wasn't. It was hoarse but fairly cultivated, like an upper servant's, though she wasn't dressed as one. She was looking at me as if trying to place me.

'It's my shawl,' I said. 'You can keep it if you like, but did you take it from my room?'

'Your room, was it?'

'What's your name?'

I'd intended to say it quite kindly, as far as I could control my voice when my heart was racing from the shock of finding her. But it must have sounded harsh because she braced her boots more firmly against the roof and pulled the ends of the shawl tightly around her.

'No more questions. I've had enough of questions.'

'Well, you can't stay up here all day.'

'I've been up here all night, so I don't see why I can't stay up here all day.'

'All night? When did you . . .?'

She pulled the shawl up right over her head.

'Aren't you – I mean, you must be hungry and thirsty.'

'Thirsty, yes.' It came muffled through the shawl.

'You'll be like a hotcake on a griddle, up here all day. If you'll come down with me, I'll fetch you some water.'

She seemed to consider it, then: 'Did the old lady send you?'

'Yes.'

It was true, after a fashion. My tongue was twitching with questions I wanted to ask her, but the first thing was to persuade her down from the roof. She poked her head out from the shawl and began to straighten up painfully, pushing against the chimney stack. I helped her along the roof trough and went first through the trapdoor so that I could guide her down the ladder. Her legs smelled sweaty and unwashed, though there was something about her that suggested she had once been a fastidious person.

The moment the door of my room shut behind us she collapsed on the chair and eyed the cold, soapy water in the wash-bowl so thirstily I thought she might lap it like a dog. I told her to wait, ran down the stairs to the nursery kitchen and came back with a jug of water and a glass. She drank two glassfuls of water straight off, closed her eyes and gave a shudder. It seemed to bring her back to herself because she made an attempt at tidying her hair, scooping up the fallen tendrils and re-pinning them with shaking hands.

'I look a sight, don't I? I'm sorry I used your good soap.'

'So it was you in my room yesterday?'

She nodded. At least she'd answered a question.

'What were you doing here.'

'The old lady said I was to stay here until she called me.'

'What old lady?'

'It's no good asking me her name. I don't know.'

'An old lady in black?'

A reluctant nod.

'What were you doing on the roof?'

'It's no use keeping on at me. Where else could I go?'

She gulped more water. I waited.

'So are you going to take me to her?' she said.

'Do you want me to?'

I decided not to tell her at once about Mrs Beedle's

349

death. For all I knew she might have had a hand in it.

'It's not a question of what I want or don't want, is it? I've been passed like a parcel, hand to hand, over the sea and back until I don't know where I am or what I'm doing.'

'Over the sea and back?'

'Over by trickery and back by force. I told the old lady about it. She said she'd look after me, once it was all over. Will she keep her promise, do you think?'

'Why shouldn't she?'

'There was a gentleman promised to look after me too, but he didn't come back.'

My whole body tingled, not with shock yet but the feeling of shock coming, like lightning singing in the air.

'A gentleman where?'

'In France.'

I'd picked up the water jug to refill her glass. I almost dropped it and when I managed to put it down on the wash-stand, my hand was shaking as badly as hers. I tried hard to keep my voice steady.

'You said he didn't come back. What happened to him?'

'They told me he'd been shot. I don't know what to believe from anyone any more.'

'What was his name?'

'He said he was Mr Lane, but I don't know if it was his real name.'

'It was his real name. He was my father.'

Visions of beautiful ladies and angry husbands fell

away. The search for the woman in my father's letter had ended here, in this bleak room, with a dumpy woman in a brown wool dress, water-drops clinging to the little hairs on her upper lip from drinking so thirstily. She was staring at me as if my distress had woken up something in her mind.

'Do you know, I thought you had the look of somebody I recognised when I saw you up there. Only I couldn't call it to mind. There've been so many of them, you see, and I haven't been myself.'

'The old lady, Mrs Beedle, she was killed last night,' I said.

I was past being careful. Her mouth fell open, showing small, gappy teeth.

'Where?'

'Downstairs in the schoolroom.'

'Is that the room with the horse and the big globe?'

'Yes. How did you know?'

'She took me in there, before she brought me up here. She said I was to come back down when she gave me the signal.'

'Signal?'

'She was going to tap on the bottom stair with that stick of hers. I waited. I washed myself and I put on the shawl and I waited a bit more. Then I heard a noise from downstairs.'

'Her stick tapping?'

'It might have been that, or it might have been a door closing, I wasn't sure. I thought I'd better go down, so

I did. The door was closed, but I heard her voice from inside the room, talking to somebody about me.'

'What did she say?'

'It was something like them having no right to bring me there in the first place. Then she said, quite loud, "No, I've no intention of telling you where she is."'

'Who was she talking to?'

'I told you, the door was shut.'

'You didn't hear another voice?'

'I didn't wait to hear anything else. I guessed whoever was in there with her was working for the fat devil, so I was away and back up the stairs. I couldn't stop in this room in case he made her tell him where I was, so I climbed on up the ladder and came out on the roof.'

'Did she sound scared?'

'Not scared, no. Angry.'

I sat down on the bed. We looked at each other, beyond crying, beyond even being suspicious of each other.

'Your name's Liberty?'

'Yes.'

'Your father talked to me about you. He said you were kind hearted and he was going to rent a house in London and I could stay with you until I found somewhere else. He said he was going to write to you and let you know.'

'He did, but he was dead by the time I had the letter. I don't even know your name.'

'Martley. Maudie Martley.'

'Please, Mrs Martley, tell me anything else you can about my father.'

She opened her mouth then closed it again, looking terrified. Somebody was coming up the stairs from the nursery corridor. The steps stopped at the maids' landing and a voice called out.

'Miss Lock, would you come down please.'

Betty, sounding alarmed.

'It's all right, but I must go to her,' I whispered. 'Stay here. Sleep in my bed if you're tired.'

She still looked terrified. I should have liked to tell her that she'd be safe there, but I didn't know what safety was any more. In any case, I'd no idea where else to put her.

'Wait for me,' I said. 'Please wait. I'll be back as soon as I can.'

Betty was on her way back downstairs.

'There's a gentleman insists he must speak to you. He won't go away. I've put him in the boys' bedroom.'

She was hot and miserable at this violation of her sanctuary. I went into the bedroom and there was Daniel, tapping out *Voi Che Sapete* on James's xylophone. He put down the hammer when he saw me.

'Blackstone's woken up. I think you should hear what he has to say.'

CHAPTER TWENTY-THREE

I wanted to run to him with my news, but I didn't trust him over Blackstone. Perhaps I took a few steps towards him and stumbled, because he spread out his arms, as if to catch me.

'Liberty, are you ill? I don't believe you've slept or eaten.'

'I'll do very well.'

I made myself stand up straight and his arms fell to his sides. I took him by the back stairs into the court-yard and round the wall of the kitchen garden. When we came to the spiral path to the pavilion he offered me his arm, but I shook my head and went in front of him. At the door, he asked me to wait while he went inside, then beckoned me to join him. It was a big shadowy room, with camp beds arranged along both sides. Blackstone was lying flat on his back on one of the beds, very tidily, like a man trying not to take up too much space. A blanket covered him from feet to waist. Above it a white shirt slowly rose and fell to his shallow breathing. His complexion was grey, his eyes closed. He seemed even thinner than I remembered, and older.

'Miss Lane is here,' Daniel told him.

He opened his eyes, focused on me and slowly brought his feet to the floor. He was still wearing the black trousers of his waiter's uniform. Daniel knelt by the bed, lending a shoulder to help him stand.

'We can talk here,' I said. 'There's no need to get up.'

'If you'll allow me, I feel a need for the sunlight.'

Blackstone gave a wan smile as he said it, but his voice was as creaky as his joints. He got himself upright, slipped his feet into a battered pair of black shoes and walked to the door, leaning on Daniel's arm. Outside, the two of them waited until I sat down on the stone bench by the wall, then Daniel settled Blackstone next to me and sat on his other side. Blackstone paused for a while with his face to the sun, eyes closed, taking painful-looking breaths.

'I did not kill your father,' he said, eyes still closed. 'I told you that in Dover, but you wouldn't believe me.'

'But you didn't save him either, and you might have,' I said.

His eyes jerked open.

'That is not true. He was dead before I even knew he'd got to Calais. Believe me, if I'd had the slightest idea they would go to such lengths, I'd have found him and warned him. I never wanted him to interfere.'

'But you must have known he'd been killed because of Mr Brighton. You knew he hadn't died in a duel. If you were his friend, why didn't you do something, make people investigate?'

His eyes closed again. A sigh fluttered his white shirt.

'What good would it have done? Only caused a hue and cry that would alert Kilkeel to the fact that I was watching him? Nothing could bring Jacques back. If I failed in my duty to him, it was for a cause that your father would have approved, and you, Suter, approve as well.'

Daniel seemed about to protest.

'What was that?' I said.

'Ridding the world of kings.'

'Not by these methods,' Daniel said.

Blackstone pushed himself away from the wall and sat straight-backed, eyes fierce.

'By what methods, then? By politely asking, Be so good as to go, sir? Please be so kind as to stop fattening yourself and your brood on the wealth of the labouring people. Please be obliging enough to abdicate and let the men you call your subjects grow into free and honest citizens instead of demeaning themselves as your toadies and flatterers. Is that how you'd bring about a republic?'

His voice grew in force as he spoke and some colour came back to his face, like the glow of fire in a grey ember. Daniel looked ill at ease.

'I've never denied my republican opinions, you know that.'

'Oh no, as long as you can sing about them or recite poetry about them or drink toasts over the punchbowl to them, that's well enough. Have you spent time in prison for them?'

'You know very well I haven't.'

'Well, I have.'

'I know that too. You've suffered for a cause we believe in, and I honour you for it. But I still don't understand what you were trying to do this time.'

Blackstone didn't answer Daniel. He sat there, stiff and upright, staring out over the lake. There were a pair of swans scudding across it, wings half-spread to catch the breeze.

'I don't understand either,' I said. 'What was the purpose of dishonouring my father's memory to shield people who are just trying to replace a queen with a king? I don't know anything about little Vicky, but I don't see how she could be much worse than this creature they call Mr Brighton.'

'That is the entire point,' Mr Blackstone said. 'Surely you can see that?'

'I can't.'

'I can't either,' Daniel said.

Blackstone sighed like a schoolmaster with two slow pupils.

'As you have observed, Mr Brighton is – even by Hanoverian standards – more than usually stupid. He is greedy, foppish and entirely at the mercy of the schemers and flatterers who surround him. What's more, he is by nature highly unlikely to beget heirs.'

'How can you know that?' I said.

Blackstone and Daniel looked at each other, then at me, and seemed to consider.

'I think in that respect Blackstone's probably right,' Daniel said.

'Thank you, Suter. In addition, any claim he might have to the throne would be as the grandchild of George IV, one of the unworthiest monarchs ever to infest the throne of England, and of Caroline of Brunswick, who was no better than a whore, and not even an attractive one at that.'

'Blackstone!' Daniel protested, looking at me.

'If I have offended, I apologise. But I believe my point is made. If so-called Mr Brighton had a legitimate claim to the throne, then he would probably be a monarch so spectacularly bad that even the lazy, over-tolerant people of England would rise up in a body and say "Enough."'

Daniel was looking at him in amazement.

'So you'd found out about this plot and you were concealing it, to make sure this country was saddled with a bad king?' he said.

Mr Blackstone nodded his head.

'It was a faint hope, I admit. For one thing, I seriously doubt he could ever prove his claim.'

'And for that faint hope, you were prepared to let

the world believe that my father died betraying his own principles,' I said. 'It seems to me a poor exchange.'

'No, because there was a larger hope. Even if the pretender's claim failed in the end, there were some powerful men like Mandeville and Kilkeel supporting it, so it was quite certain to cause a deal of noise and trouble in the country. The streets of our cities are already teeming with hungry men, our country towns are full of labourers turned from their jobs and out of their cottages. And our politicians expect them to forget their empty bellies and their starving children, throw their hats in the air and cry "God save the queen!" If the people see those same politicians squabbling among themselves whether it's to be Queen Victoria Alexandrina or King Harold on the throne, might not that be the spark that makes them decide to throw off their chains at last?'

Daniel and I looked at each other.

'That wasn't worth my father's life,' I said.

Blackstone closed his eyes and didn't answer. The hectic colour was fading from his cheeks and he gave a shiver.

'Why in the world did you decide to come here yourself?' Daniel asked. 'Why run around playing the waiter when you should have been at home in bed?'

His tone was gentle. I could see that he still respected the man. Blackstone gave another of his thin smiles.

'I needed to see what their next step would be.

Spies have proved to be unreliable and expensive.'

I must have made some sound of protest because he turned to me.

'I exempt you, Miss Lane. I wish everybody had been as honest in the cause as you have been.'

'I don't care about the cause. All I want to know is who killed my father.'

'I believe Kilkeel was deeply involved,' Blackstone said. 'I don't suppose he pulled the trigger himself, but they were all furious about that woman.'

I looked away from him so that he shouldn't see anything in my eyes. In spite of his weakness, I still didn't trust him.

'Who is she and what happened to her?' Daniel asked.

'I still don't know. I believe they intended her as some kind of witness, though witness to what exactly I've no notion. I had a man trying to find out for me, but he became scared and let me down. That was why it was so important that I should be present last night.'

'Nothing happened,' Daniel said. 'Or rather, a lot happened, but there was no mystery woman suddenly produced from behind a cloak. Was that what you were expecting?'

'Something went wrong with their plans yesterday, I'm quite convinced of that,' Blackstone said. 'Mandeville hasn't gone to all this trouble just to give dinner to his friends. He and Kilkeel are still waiting to make their move, and I don't know why. We must find out.'

It infuriated me that, in spite of everything, he was still plotting.

'Did you know Mrs Beedle was murdered here last night?' I said.

Blackstone stared at me.

'I don't even know who Mrs Beedle is.'

'Mandeville's mother-in-law. Did you kill her?'

Daniel started protesting, then stopped when I gave him a look.

'In all my life, I've never killed anybody,' Blackstone said. He looked straight at me, eyes wide open as if he wanted me to see into his thoughts. 'I hope you believe that. I should be sorry to have your bad opinion, Miss Lane.'

His eyes closed. After a while he slid sideways against Daniel. I thought he might have died, but I felt no grief, nothing. Daniel caught my eye and pointed to a couple of young musicians smoking their pipes on the far end of the terrace. I went over to them to ask for their help and the three of them managed to take Blackstone back inside. He tried to walk, but his feet scarcely grazed the gravel. At the doorway he turned and looked at me.

'Do you believe me? About your father, at least?'

I thought of what Daniel had said, that in his prime this man could have marched ten thousand people on Whitehall, and of the thin black legs sticking out among the scattered vegetables.

'Yes, I believe you.'

361

I sat on a bench and after a while Daniel came out to me, head down.

'Thank you for saying that, Liberty.'

'He said something I know is true. That makes me inclined to believe him on the rest.'

'What?'

'My father was killed because of the woman. Don't tell Blackstone or anybody else, but that same woman's hiding in my room. I'd like you to come and speak to her.'

'Your room! For heaven's sake, Liberty! If you're right, two people have died because of this woman, and now you tell me you're hiding her.'

'I don't know what else to do about her. But you must come and speak to her.'

'Please, leave it and come away with me this instant. Mourn your father and let them all play their games and go to hell in their own way. You know now why your father was killed. You know it wasn't poor Blackstone . . .'

'*Poor* Blackstone!'

'Yes. He always told us he'd live to see a republic in England. I don't think he believes it now.'

'I still don't know why my father was killed. I think she does. There's no doubt whatsoever that she's the woman in his letter. In any case, we can't just go and leave her here. We must find a way to take her with us.'

'Did she tell you she knows who killed him?'

'I haven't managed to ask her yet. She's very scared and she doesn't like questions.'

'Liberty, just leave it and –'

'While the man who killed my father is living and breathing, no, I will not leave it.'

He sighed and gave me his hand to help me up from the bench.

'If you won't leave it, then I suppose I must help you, though the gods know there probably isn't a man in the world less fit for this sort of business than I am.'

As we walked back to the house I told him what she'd said, as well as I could remember. I let him take my arm, past caring who saw us. He waited outside the kitchen door while I made sure there was nobody in the chamber pot storeroom, then we went up the back stairs to the maids' landing. He waited there again so that I could go up and warn Mrs Martley. To my relief, she was just where I'd left her, asleep in the hard chair, wrapped in Betty's shawl, her head fallen sideways on to her shoulder. Her eyes jerked open when I stepped into the room.

'You should have slept on the bed,' I said. 'Are you well enough to talk to somebody? He's a friend of my father's and will do you no harm.'

She nodded reluctantly and I went down to fetch Daniel. I'd worried that his presence would make her even more scared than she was already, but I should have trusted more in his natural kindness and gift for putting people at ease. He made a polite bow to her, introduced himself and – after a questioning look to ask my permission – sat down on the edge of the bed.

'Mrs Martley, I am sorry indeed to intrude on you. Jacques Lane was a very good friend of mine, and I'd be obliged to you for anything you could tell me about your acquaintance with him.'

'What do you want to know?'

'How did you come to meet him? Was it in Paris?'

She blinked and pushed back a lock of her lank hair.

'Paris, yes. When I was trying to get away from the fat devil.'

I opened my mouth and shut it again, deciding to leave as much of the questioning as I could to Daniel.

'Fat devil?'

'I don't know his name to this day. He was keeping me shut up in this house in Paris, a servant on watch in the hall day and night. Only, you see, there was one of them liked a drink and one night I looked out and he wasn't there on guard. So I got my few things together and ran down the stairs and out of the door. That was all I could think of, getting away, only I had no more idea of how to get back to England than flying to the moon, and I don't know any French, not a word.'

She stared at Daniel as if her life depended on making him understand.

'And was that when you met him?' he prompted.

'I knew there was a hotel next door with a coach-yard and I'd heard English voices there. So I thought if I went to the coachyard and waited I might come across an English family and beg them for pity's sake to take me back with them.'

'When was this?' Daniel said.

'I don't know. I've lost track. A lot of the time I didn't know whether it was day or night even. So it's no use asking . . .'

She was becoming perturbed again, twisting her fingers in the fringes of the shawl.

'Don't concern yourself about it, then. Did you get to the hotel courtyard?'

'Yes. There was a gentleman there, talking to a horse. I'm sorry, did you want to say something?'

I must have made some movement. My father talked to all animals, from horses to mice. It brought him back to me so vividly that I felt like yelping from hurt. I pressed my lips together and nodded to Mrs Martley to go on.

'He was talking to it in English, saying it was going on a long journey and not to be scared. He sounded a pleasant man so after a while I plucked up courage and went over to him. I said I was a respectable Englishwoman fallen on hard times and I wanted to get home. Well, no sooner were the words out of my mouth than his hand went to his pocket. "Thank you, sir, only it's not just the money," I said to him. "I've no notion how to set about getting back and I've got enemies next door to this very hotel who'll stop me if they find out, then goodness knows what will happen to me." I don't know if he believed me then or not. He took me round a corner to one of those places they have in Paris, like a public house only not so cheerful, and sat me down and looked at me. "You're shaking," he said. "So would you be shaking, sir, if you'd gone through what I've gone through," I said. Then he ordered us a glass of brandy apiece and I started telling him my story. Even while I was telling it, I thought it sounded so fantastical, he wouldn't believe me. He did, though.'

'Yes,' I said. 'My father always trusted people.'

Even the memory of him seemed to have unloosed her tongue.

'It was more than just trusting. He knew the half of it already. While I was telling it, he kept nodding his head as if it chimed in with something else he'd heard. And when I got to the bit about the fat devil asking me questions as if I was in the dock at the Old Bailey he started laughing. "It's nothing to laugh at," I told him. "The fat devil kept on at me until I didn't know right from left or black from white, and all about something that happened twenty years ago. He said I must be sure of everything, very sure, because one day I'd have to stand up in the House of Lords in front of all the judges in their robes and wigs and say the same thing."'

She paused for breath. Daniel poured her a glass of water.

'What did Mr Lane say to that?'

'He said he was sorry for laughing, but it was all a great nonsense and he was sure I shouldn't have to stand up in the House of Lords or anywhere else. Still, he said, it was a very wrong thing that had been done to me and of course he'd take me back to England. He said he was leaving the day after tomorrow and I could travel with him. "But what will I do until then?" I asked him. Well, he jabbered away in French to the man behind the counter and said I could stay there, all meals provided, and he'd come for me early morning, day after tomorrow. "Don't tell anybody," I said to him. I was still mortally terrified the fat devil would find me. So he promised not to tell anybody, not even his friends.'

Daniel looked across at me.

'He kept that promise,' he said.

I think it was in his mind, like mine, that my father might have lived if he'd broken it. She nodded.

'I thought he would. I did as he told me and stayed where I was. The place wasn't much better than a brothel, but he wasn't to know that, and anyway I kept to my room. The morning after next, just as he'd promised, he called for me. He'd taken a couple of seats for us on the stage. There was no sign of the fat devil or his people, though I kept looking around me and I wasn't even half easy in my mind until we were well out of Paris. To be honest with you, I knew I shouldn't be really easy till I was my own side of the Channel again. It took us the best part of three days to get to

Calais. He took two rooms for us at an inn just on the outside of town and went to book tickets on the steam packet. Only it was full up that day so we had to wait until the day after. Couldn't we go on one of the sailing boats instead, I asked him. But he liked the steam packet better, and who was I to argue? Only I wish now that I'd tried to persuade him, because if I had he might have been alive still.'

I got up and walked to the window, trying to keep control of my feelings and not interrupt her story. Of course my father, ever curious for new things, would prefer steam. If he'd been a less modern-minded man, none of it would have happened. He'd have stepped off some sailing boat in Dover, picked up my letter and come running to find me.

'So what happened then?' I said, looking out at two pigeons on the window sill.

'He said he was going for a stroll round the town and that was the last I saw of him. I was feeling ill, from something I'd eaten on the journey, so I went to lie down. He didn't come back that evening and I thought he might have met some friends and was staying out, like gentlemen do. In the morning, I knocked on his door and there was no answer. A serving man at the inn who spoke a bit of English said he hadn't come back at all. So I thought maybe I'd misunderstood and he meant me to meet him by the steam packet. I was still feeling ill, but I dragged myself all the way to the harbour and there were crowds of people, but no sign of him. I was in a fair ferment by then, not knowing whether to go on board or not, but I didn't have a ticket, so I thought better not and went all the way back to the inn. Well, what with the worry and the disappointment, I was running a fever. For the next few days – I don't know how many, so it's no use asking me – I was lying there thinking I'd die and that would be an end to my troubles. Then one morning I woke up, mortally weak but the fever gone, knowing I wasn't going to die this time after all. So I decided I'd better get myself down to the docks and try and find somebody else who'd have the Christian charity to pay for my ticket over. Only when I went downstairs with my bag, the owner of the place took hold of my arm and started jabbering away in French. Your father had gone without paying the bill, you see.'

'I'm sorry,' I said.

Ridiculous, of course, but she was almost crying with the memory of her distress. Counting back, I realised that while Maudie Martley was lying weak with fever in her inn, I was probably no more than a mile away, inquiring for my father around the hotels of Calais. If he hadn't chosen an inn on the outskirts, I might have found her nearly a month ago.

'Then I heard this voice in English asking what was going on. It was a rough sort of voice, but I was glad of it at first, until I turned round. God help me, it was one of the fat devil's servants, grinning like an ape. "Well," he says, "you have given us some trouble. We've

369

been looking all over the bloody place for you." And he says to the Frenchman who had my arm, "You keep hold of her – she's wanted," and goes running off. Half an hour later, a carriage draws up outside and it's the fat devil himself.'

I remembered how the fat man had asked me, *Where's the woman?* He must have been searching Calais for her and, by sheer mischance, he'd found her at last, probably quite soon after they'd tried to kidnap me.

'Did you ask him about my father?' I said.

'I was too terrified to ask him anything. His servants dragged me into his carriage, then we drove off. "Well," he said to me, "you've got yourself in serious trouble now. Trying to defraud an innkeeper, not to mention the money you stole from me when you ran off . . ." I told him, God's truth, I hadn't. I'd never touched a penny of his, but he kept on as if I hadn't spoken, about how he'd offered me a respectable position and I'd deceived and robbed him, and if he told the French police I'd go to prison for a very long time, perhaps even to the guillotine.'

Even the memory of it scared her. Her hand went to her neck.

'They couldn't have done that,' Daniel said.

'He said he was a lawyer, and I heard people calling him milord. Who'd have believed me against him? I was nearly mad with fear and he could see it. In the end he said he wouldn't report me, only I'd have to do exactly what he said. He took me to his hotel and wrote down a long statement that he made me sign. He called in another man to witness it and then he stamped a big seal on it in red wax. He told me that if I ever tried to go back on my word and say I hadn't said it, that would be perjury and I'd be in even worse trouble. I had to promise to go back to England with him and not try to run away again. So I promised. What else could I do?'

She looked at Daniel imploringly.

'I dare say in your place anybody would have done the same,' he said. 'So he never mentioned Mr Lane?'

She looked down at her hands, clenched together in her lap.

'Not as such, not to me. No.'

'To somebody else?'

'I think so, yes. It must have been him they were talking about.'

'They? Who?'

'The fat devil and another gentleman. But I was under the floorboards, you see.'

'Floorboards?'

'Yes, of the coach. The fat devil said I must go back to England with him, but I'd better make sure nobody saw me or I'd be arrested. There were some gaps between the floorboards, just enough to let air in and I could see up into the carriage, but only a very little, mostly his boots and his fat belly.'

'And somebody else was in there with him?'

'Not on the journey over, no. It was when we were

off the boat on the other side at Dover. It sounded as if we were getting ready to drive away, then I felt the carriage tilt the way it does when somebody gets in. This new man's first words were about me. He said to the fat devil, "I still can't find the Martley woman. There's no trace of her this side of the Channel or the other " The fat devil said he could give up troubling himself because they'd found me without his help. The other one said they might have told him, then he asked, "Where is she?" The fat devil gave a thump with his boot, just above my head and I think he must have pointed downwards because the other gentleman said, "You mean she's dead too?" in a quavery sort of voice. And the fat devil said, "No. One's more than enough. What in the world possessed you, shooting poor Lane?"'

Daniel leaned forward.

'He said that? "Shooting poor Lane"?'

'Yes. And the other one said, sounding very hangdog, "It wasn't my fault. When you sent me that message from Paris, you said we had to find him and her at any cost." The fat devil said, quite sharp, "I didn't tell you to kill anybody," and the other one said, "I didn't mean to. I was just threatening him, trying to get him to tell us what he'd done with her. Then he went and made a grab for my pistol and it went off." And the fat man said, "I've heard half a dozen men attempt that defence in court and I attended the hangings of all six of them." The other one made a sort of gulping sound, then the fat devil said it was more than he deserved, but he'd managed to make it look as if Lane had died in a duel, and a lot of money and trouble it had cost him. "So you won't hang this time," he said, "only you'd better get out because I'd rather not be seen with you after what's happened." Then the coach rocked again and soon after that we were on our way.'

CHAPTER TWENTY-FOUR

The world had gone black. I turned my head away, not looking at Maudie Martley any more, hardly even hearing her through the rushing in my ears. I thought anger would blow my head apart. Daniel was asking her a question. He sounded shaken too, but his voice was still gentle.

'This other man, did you see him?'

'Not properly. Only a slice of him, through the gap in the boards.'

'Was he young, old, dark, fair?'

'Not old, from his voice. Dark, I think, quite dark. I was so scared, you see, this talk about people being shot and people hanging – I thought it would be me next.'

'A servant or a gentleman?'

'A gentleman.'

'Would you know him if you saw him again?'

'I think I might.'

'Would you recognise his voice?'

'Yes, his voice more.'

'And the other one, the one you call the fat devil . . .'

'You'll have seen him for yourself, sir. He's in the house here. He's the one who brought me here.'

'Under the floorboards of his coach again,' I said, turning round.

'Yes. How did you know that?' she said.

Daniel looked surprised as well.

'His name's Kilkeel,' I said. 'Lord Kilkeel. Did you never hear him called that?'

She shook her head.

'And he brought you here and kept you shut up in his dressing room?'

'Yes. He told me to stay under the floor down in the coach house till the dead of night, then sent his man down to fetch me. He made me sleep in his dressing room, with his man on a chair by the door. I kept my clothes on, every stitch, except for my shoes.'

'Why did he want you here?' Daniel said.

'I was to talk to some gentlemen. I was to tell them in my own voice what he'd worried out of me in the statement he took in France, not a word different or he'd have me for perjury and I'd be in prison for life.'

'But you didn't?'

'No, because before that the old woman had found me. She just walked into his dressing room yesterday as if she owned the place and told the man watching me to get out. Then she said she knew very well what was happening, but it was dangerous and treasonable and she wouldn't allow it. She took me and hid me here. Only I was scared, you see. I've been scared so much and for so long that I can't remember a time when I wasn't or imagine a time when I won't be.'

There was pity in Daniel's eyes. I couldn't feel it yet. I was still too angry. Even though it wasn't her fault, her story had killed my father.

'There will be a time when you are not scared,' he said to her. 'My friend tried to protect you. For his sake, I'll do all that I can.'

She nodded, her eyes fixed on him as if he were a rock in a rough sea. Knowing how much he disliked conflict and unpleasantness, I was surprised by the firmness of his voice.

'Do you feel strong enough to answer some more questions?' he said.

'What?'

'Like how you came to be in Paris with that man.'

'From trickery, sir. I'm a midwife by profession, to ladies of quality. Some ladies I've helped into the world call me back twenty years on, when they're brought to bed with their own children. Ask anyone in London society, sir, and nobody will have a bad word to say of Maudie Martley.'

'I'm sure of it. But Paris?'

'A message came for me one day, to go to a certain address in Burlington Gardens and meet a gentleman. I

376

went to the address, a very respectable-looking house. The man who spoke to me there wasn't quite a gentleman – more of a gentleman's steward, I should say – but quite polite and agreeable. He said there was an English lady expecting her confinement in Paris who particularly wanted my services. I asked him her name – wondering if it was one of my ladies – and he said it was not in his power to give it. But if I agreed I was to have ten guineas in my hand in advance, all the travelling arranged and paid for, and a further twenty-five guineas when the lady was safely delivered.'

'Were you not suspicious at the secrecy?' Daniel asked.

'It happens sometimes, sir. A lady – for one reason or another – may not wish to have her condition known in London. Usually it will be a matter of going down to some house in the country, but sometimes ladies do go abroad.'

'Had you been to Paris on other occasions?'

'Twice, sir.'

'So the circumstances did not alarm you?'

'No, sir. Only the money offered was higher than usual. Still, that was no reason to refuse.'

'So you accepted?'

'I said there was a lady I must see through her confinement in the next few days, but after that I was at the other lady's service. I was to send word to this steward the moment I was free. So a livery carriage came to collect me and take me all the way to Dover. I was given a ticket for the steam packet and told to look out for a tall coachman with a blue-and-gold cockade in his hat who would be waiting for me on the French side.'

'And you met this coachman?'

'Yes. He was in a terrible hurry, would hardly allow me time to eat and drink when we changed horses at the inns and wouldn't answer any questions, didn't seem to understand English. But I supposed the lady must be near her time and that was the reason for the hurry. So we got to Paris. The house wasn't as grand as I expected, but then if the lady wanted to be secret perhaps it wasn't surprising. A manservant took me to a room upstairs and I said I'd have a wash and be with the lady directly. I took my hat and cloak off and I washed and I waited. And I waited, and I waited. After a while, I started to worry that the lady might need me and there I was, sitting up there on my own. So I tried the door handle and the door wouldn't open. Bolted on the outside. Only of course I didn't know that at first, I thought it had just stuck, so I started knocking on the door and calling out, quite polite at first then more loudly because I was starting to be alarmed. Then there were footsteps, the sound of a bolt being drawn back and the fat devil walked in. "What is this?" I said. "The poor lady might be having her baby at this very moment." The fat devil shook his head. He had a sneering kind of smile on his face and you could smell the brandy reeking off his breath. I can see him now and hear his voice saying what he said, quite quietly: "There really is no hurry, Mrs

Martley. The baby we're interested in was born twenty years ago."'

Maudie Martley looked terrified remembering it, like a woman seeing a ghost. Even though I'd expected it, I felt myself shivering and instinctively moved closer to Daniel.

'Did you know what he meant by that?' he asked her.

'Of course I did. It was the worst night of my life.'

'What did he mean?'

She whispered, 'The princess, of course. Poor Princess Charlotte.'

'Were you midwife to the princess?' I said.

That brought me a warning glance from Daniel, but it seemed to be the cue she needed.

'Not midwife, just midwife's helper. I was only twenty-two at the time, but already married and widowed with a baby of my own. My aunt was a midwife, very well thought of, and she was training me up as her assistant, so that I should have a trade to provide for my baby. Of course, with the princess, it wasn't only a midwife. There were three great doctors there. One of them was Sir Richard Croft, a gentleman that was the best *accoucheur* in London. He trusted my aunt and she often worked with him. Even with great doctors, you see, there are some things that should only be done for a woman by another woman. So my aunt was there and I was there too, just to bring warm water and clean cloths as needed. At the princess's country home it was, in Surrey.'

She paused, eyes on Daniel, as if to make sure he was following her.

'You must have been nervous,' he said.

'Oh, I was at first. Would you believe, the Archbishop of Canterbury and the Lord Chancellor of England and a lot of other gentlemen from the government were waiting in another room. We knew the baby might be king or queen one day, you see, so they all had to be there in the house. We didn't see them, but we knew they were there. I was nearly fainting from nervousness, but my aunt was quite sharp with me, said a birth was a birth no matter who and my business was to do what I was told and not be a silly girl. I was mostly in a closet to the side of her bedroom, with a fire for heating the water. My aunt would call me when they needed anything. Of course, I could hear everything that was going on. She had a hard time, poor lady. She was in labour from the Monday night until late on the Wednesday evening. I knew from the sounds that the baby was coming at last and my aunt called to me to bring warm towels. When I went in, one of the doctors was holding him. He and my aunt wrapped him in the warm towels, but it was no use, no use at all. A fine-looking big boy he was, but blue in the face and dead.'

Even twenty years on, she looked as shocked and grieved as if it had happened yesterday.

'And the poor princess died too,' I said softly.

'Not at once. We thought we were going to save her. She sat up and I was sent down to the kitchen for chicken broth and barley water and she drank some. But then, a few hours later, she died too. Poor Sir Richard was so grieved he shot himself a few months later. But it wasn't his fault, it wasn't anybody's fault. The poor infant suffocated from her being too long in labour. To the highest and lowest it can happen, and it happened to her, poor lady, that's all. And then years later the wicked rumours started. You know what they were, don't you?'

Daniel said sadly, 'That she and the baby were both poisoned by people at court who didn't want to see a child or grandchild of Queen Caroline on the throne.'

'Wicked, wicked rumours. The poor baby was born stone dead and, as for the princess, I carried the broth and the barley water from the kitchen in my own hands and nobody came near them. My aunt and I were angry and scared too, though nobody thought to ask us anything. Anyway, the rumours died down and we thought that was an end of it – until that devil walked into my room in Paris.'

'Did he talk about the poisoning rumour?' Daniel asked.

'Yes, and worse. He said the princess had been poisoned but the baby hadn't. He said it had been taken away secretly by loyal people who knew its life was in danger from the princess's enemies at court and it was all a lie that it had died.'

'What did you say to that?'

'I spoke up and told him that it was nonsense. I'd

seen the poor baby dead. One of the doctors even had to take it downstairs and show it to the Archbishop of Canterbury and the other gentlemen, because that's the law with royalty. "Are you saying that the Archbishop of Canterbury's a liar?" I said to him. And he said, in that nasty sneering voice, "I've no doubt at all that the Archbishop saw a dead male baby, but I'm sure dead babies are easy enough to come by when you're in the midwife's trade." God help me, I wanted to hit him in the fat, greasy chops.'

Under Daniel's influence, some of her spirit was coming back.

'So what did you do?' Daniel asked.

'I said he should take me back to London, that you couldn't lock people up just like that. He laughed and said it was different in France and I'd have to stay until tomorrow because there were some gentlemen he wanted me to see. So he went away and a servant came up with a tray of sandwiches and a pot of tea. Well, I was hungry and thirsty from the journey so I ate and drank it all, but I think there must have been something in the tea because I went straight off to sleep and woke up not knowing where I was or what day it was. The fat devil came back sometime in the day or night with some other gentlemen and a clerk taking notes. He kept asking me the same questions about that night and the baby. Was I sure I remembered right? Might I have been mistaken? Had I been paid by anybody to say the baby died? I think he might have come back several times over, asking me the same questions, and he made me so confused that in the end I didn't know what I remembered and what he'd put into my head. And I had such a thirst on me all the time, they kept bringing me tea and I had to drink it, but I'm sure they were putting things in it. Either I was asleep or it was questions, questions, questions all over again. So I started pouring the tea out of the window and drinking washing water from the pitcher instead, and my head cleared and I knew I had to get away from him.'

I turned away, not wanting her to see my tears. It could so nearly have been otherwise – my father landing safely at Dover and meeting me with rescued Maudie in tow. Only, in his light-hearted way, he never guessed the lengths they'd go to in getting her back. Quite unintentionally, he'd made things worse for her by giving Kilkeel another weapon to use against her.

'So he brought you here to tell anybody who asked that the baby had lived?' Daniel said.

'Yes, sir.'

'And you're quite certain that the baby did not live?'

'As certain as the daylight, sir. And I'll say that to anybody now my mind's clear again. Even if they do put me in prison or kill me for it, I can't go on any longer.'

CHAPTER TWENTY-FIVE

Daniel caught my eye and nodded towards the door.

'You are a woman of spirit, Mrs Martley. Would you excuse us, we must leave you for a while.'

'Will the fat devil come and find me?'

'Miss Lane won't be far away,' Daniel said reassuringly. 'She might even be able to find you a pot of tea and something to eat.'

He and I went down together to the landing outside the maids' dormitory.

'Do you believe her?' I asked him.

'I do, poor woman. I can see why your father decided to help her. I only wish he'd told us about it.'

So did I, but I couldn't afford to think about it now.

'Lord Kilkeel's guilty of a crime, isn't he? He knows who killed my father and he's done nothing about it.'

'I'm no lawyer, Liberty, but I think what she's told

us makes him at least an accomplice to murder.'

'Then what do we do?'

'I don't know. I'm not even sure that conversation she overheard would amount to proof in a court of law.'

'If we were to go to a magistrate . . .' I said.

'In his own county?'

'In London, perhaps.'

'The word of a bereaved daughter, a musician and a woman who would probably be dismissed as mad, against a lord who also happens to be a lawyer? I believe they'd laugh at us.'

'Then what can we do? Isn't there some way of facing him and making him name the man who killed my father?'

'I could challenge him, I suppose.' Even in the half-dark of the landing I could see Daniel's face turning red when he realised the bitterness of his joke.

'Libby, I'm sorry.'

'There has to be a way. Even if they laugh at us, I must at least try telling somebody.'

'Then we must ride this horse as far as it will take us. It occurs to me that there's one gap in the evidence we might fill.'

'What?'

'Getting Mrs Martley to identify Lord Kilkeel as her milord. Is there any way of giving her a sight of him in our presence without his seeing her?'

'But why? It's perfectly obvious. I know he's the

same man who tried to kidnap me in Calais, and I saw him with his travelling coach at the livery stables, at a time when she must have been under the floor-boards.'

'Be patient with me, Libby. I'm trying to think like a lawyer for once. If we could show her Kilkeel and hear her say that he's her man, it might close one loop-hole.'

I was still unconvinced, but Daniel was doing his best, so I tried to think.

'All the house guests will be going in to dinner again tonight. It won't be a grand banquet like last night because of the ball, but Mr Brighton will be there so I suppose Kilkeel will be too.'

'You seem to know all the back ways of this house. Could it be managed?'

'I think so, yes. Possibly while they're all in the hall, before they go in to dinner.'

I thought of Mrs Beedle's door behind the orange tree. Even dead, she was still helping me.

'Can you persuade Mrs Martley, do you think?'

'I'll try,' I said. 'I'm sure she'll be happier if you're there. But what are we going to do with her in the mean-time?'

'Can't she stay in your room?'

'Suppose Sir Herbert or Kilkeel comes looking for her? They know Mrs Beedle was waiting in the school-room, and they might guess she's not far away.'

'Would they even know their way round the servants'

quarters?' Daniel said. 'Leaving her where she is might be safer than trying to move her.'

'Perhaps so. Even if we took her out down the back stairs, where could we hide her? I'll just have to tell her to go up on the roof again if she hears anybody coming.'

'I suppose I must go back to my musicians now, or somebody will be asking questions. When shall we meet and where?'

'Six o'clock by the back door. They're dining early because of the ball.'

Once I had seen Daniel on his way, I brewed tea over the oil lamp in the nursery kitchen and found a piece of stale currant cake and a morsel of cheese that Betty must have missed. It wasn't much, but Mrs Martley seemed grateful when I took it up to her and squeezed my hand.

'That's a good gentleman of yours.'

'He is a good gentleman, but not of mine.'

It was past nine o'clock by then. Betty was giving the children their breakfast and trying not to be annoyed over my long absence. The two boys were sad and listless, Henrietta weeping into her bowl from combined grief at the death of her grandmother and not being allowed to go to the ball. Betty herself had changed into a black dress and made a broad black band for my sleeve. Mourning for Mrs Beedle, both in heart and in the formalities, was observed more on the nursery floor than in the rest of Mandeville Hall.

After breakfast we settled to our studies as best we could in the makeshift schoolroom. Twice I left the children to their books and ran upstairs to see that Mrs Martley was safe. The first time she was sleeping on the bed, snoring gently. The second she was awake, thirsty for the new pot of tea I brought with me, and prepared to listen to the plan for identifying Lord Kilkeel.

'You'll make sure he can't see me?'

'Yes.'

'I'm afraid of being near him. He'll twist my brains again.'

'I'll be there and so will Mr Suter.'

It was the promise of Daniel's presence that won her over in the end, and it was agreed that I should come to fetch her at half past five.

All through the morning I'd been expecting Celia to visit the nursery corridor, guessing her nerves would be on edge too, but by our dinner time at half past two there was no sign of her. After the meal, Betty decided it would be all right to take the children for some air in the garden, and although I was worried at being so far from Mrs Martley, I couldn't think of an excuse. Running about and playing hide and seek were ruled out by their state of mourning and we were all promenading sadly between the clipped box hedges of the knot garden when Celia and her brother came towards us. She was wearing a black-and-grey silk dress and looked as if she hadn't slept, face pale, eyes puffy and even the lustre of her red-gold hair dimmed. Stephen was dressed in black and looked almost as strained as she did. Even in their saddened state, it struck me what a handsome pair they made. He spotted us first and came quickly towards us.

'Hello, Betty. Good afternoon, Miss Lock. I understand you found my grandmother. It must have been painful for you. I'm truly sorry.'

His dark eyes met mine. I looked away and murmured something about sympathy with the family's loss.

'Yes, she'll be much missed,' he said. 'Especially by Celia.'

Celia was standing at a short distance, apparently listening to something Betty was saying, but her eyes were on Stephen and me. I wondered if they'd discussed their grandmother's death and if he knew it hadn't been from heart failure.

'I sense that she'll need your friendship more than ever, Miss Lock. We're both grateful to you.'

I mumbled something, thinking how little gratitude he'd be feeling towards me in a few hours' time, when he found his sister gone. More than ever, I felt guilty about what I was doing. He thanked me again and walked away. Celia was at my side in an instant.

'What were you talking about?'

'Your grandmother.'

'Thank goodness for that. You both looked so serious I was terrified you'd told him about tonight. Feel my heart thumping.' She picked up my right hand and laid it on the pulse in her wrist. It was twitching like something imprisoned. 'Oh, Elizabeth, I am so scared.'

'I'm scared too,' I said. 'By the by, my name isn't Elizabeth. It's Libby, for Liberty.'

I thought I would never see her again after that night and somehow it mattered to say it, although I was not sure that she heard me. She took my hand in hers, hiding it in the folds of her dress, pretending to point out a flower with her other hand.

'I think Stephen guesses something's happening,' she said.

'Yes, I think my brother would have guessed if I were going away.'

'But he mustn't know. He really mustn't know. Don't try to persuade me again because it's no use.'

Her hand was crushing mine.

'Very well.'

'I can feel your heart thumping too. It's good of you to be so scared for my sake.'

I didn't tell her that I had worse things than an elopement to be scared about.

'I shall leave the ball after the first set,' she said. 'Then I'll go upstairs and change into travelling clothes. I've given Fanny the evening off to watch the dancing. Will you wait for me in my room?'

'Yes.'

'I've written a letter to my mother. It's on the dressing table. Please make sure she gets it tomorrow morning when . . . when I'm gone.'

Tomorrow morning seemed a world away, but I promised.

'I shall see you again, one day. If I can ever help you in any way, I shall. I promise, Elizabeth.'

(So she hadn't heard me.) I thanked her, sensing there was still something she wanted to say to me. But her next words were an exclamation.

'Oh, confound the man!'

She was looking at somebody over my shoulder.

'What man?'

'One of the guests. I don't even know his name. He was watching us from the terrace when I began talking to you and now he's coming down the steps. I'm in no mood for talking silly politenesses to people.'

She raised her grey parasol and walked quickly away. I turned to look for Betty and the children and saw the man she meant. He was walking rapidly between the hedges as if determined to catch up with her. Today he was elegant in carefully chosen graduations of grey, his jewellery restricted to a couple of rings and a gold seal on a chain round his neck. His ringlets gleamed and bounced in the sun but his expression was stern. He strode up to me.

'Good afternoon, Mr Disraeli,' I said. 'I'm afraid you've just missed Miss Mandeville.'

'I wasn't looking for Miss Mandeville. I was looking for you, Miss Lock.'

His eyes were cold and challenging. I gave him look for look.

In spite of his sternness, the strange feeling of fellow-ship I'd felt for him at dinner as another adventurer adrift, flared again. Seeing me in close conversation with Celia would have increased the impression I'd given him that I was a friend of the family, but I saw no obligation to correct it.

'And now that you've found me . . .?'

'Now I've found you, I hope we can continue the conversation we were having at dinner, when you fled so precipitately.'

'As you please.'

'Miss Lock, I asked you if you knew why we'd all been invited here. You didn't answer me. I don't take you for a fool, and I assure you that I am not one myself.'

'I'm grateful for your good opinion.'

I tried to speak coolly but sensed an anger in him, reined in by a dandy's concern not to show emotion rather than any concern for me. If I had not been so angry myself, it might have scared me more.

'On the contrary, I'm beginning to have a very bad opinion of all this,' he said. 'On the urgent advice of a friend, I agree to attend a weekend party which seems to consist of out-of-place politicians, several of the most reactionary members of the House of Lords, a senile bishop and one of the biggest rogues ever called to the Bar. And those are only the ones I recognise. I can only guess about the rest. Quite probably you know more than I do.'

'No.'

He moved close to me, so close that an observer might have thought he was speaking intimacies. I smelled oil of jasmine from his curls.

'But as a friend of the family, you almost certainly do know why our host is taking such pains to launch a Hanoverian by-blow on society. Ah, so you did know?'

He must have been watching my expression very closely. I wasn't aware of giving anything away.

'Which of the many twigs of our prolific royal tree does this one hang from, I wonder? The Fitzherberts or one of Clarence's brood? Goodness knows, with so many to choose from, you'd think he might have picked a better specimen.'

'So of no use at all in your political career?' I said, deciding to go on the attack.

'Miss Lock, what is happening here is quite enough to wreck a political career at the outset. I suspect the friend who had me invited of acting from malice, or from very poor judgement, which is even worse. I suppose Mandeville wanted to recruit some of the up-and-coming men to the cause.'

'You being one of the up-and-coming men?'

He nodded.

'Miss Lock, when you and I spoke last night, I sensed something wrong. Now I'm entirely sure of it. What really happened to Mrs Beedle?'

I looked down at a butterfly sunning itself on a clump of mignonette, knowing that in the next few

393

breaths I must make one of the hardest decisions of my life. I needed desperately somebody who might believe my story and be in a position to do something about it. Nobody who mattered would listen to me, nor, I feared, to Daniel. His goodness of heart and honesty might be handicaps in the world of the powerful. Mr Disraeli, on the other hand, seemed to have at least a foothold in that world. Whether he was good-hearted and honest I had no way of telling – I rather feared not – and yet I sensed a kind of honour in him. If the butterfly stays where she is when I move my hand, I thought, I shall tell him some of the truth; if she flies, I'll say nothing. All the time, I was conscious of his eyes on me.

'You spoke to Mrs Beedle just before we went in to dinner. What she had to say to you was urgent. It must have been quite soon after that she suffered her . . . heart seizure?'

He made the last two words into a question. I moved my hand. The butterfly stayed where she was.

'It wasn't a heart seizure,' I said. 'She was struck on the head. My father was killed too, for knowing about Mr Brighton.'

I told him as much of the story as I wanted him to know. It was quite a considerable amount, but there were two people I left out of it: Mr Blackstone and Mrs Martley. I cared very little for Blackstone and yet the memory of him resting his worn-out body on the bench with his face to the sun made me more tender than I might otherwise have been. I said simply that a friend who knew about my circumstances had helped me get employment as a governess with the Mandevilles.

'As a governess?' he repeated.

'Yes, a governess in rose brocade and opals. Borrowed plumes, I fear. Lock's not even my real name. I'm called Liberty Lane.'

I expected some change in his expression, but detected none. I went on with my account, but did not name Mrs Martley or tell him she was actually under Mandeville's roof. When I finished speaking he stood staring down for a while, lower lip thrust out, fingering the gold seal round his neck.

'This woman, this alleged witness you're not naming, you say the old lady took her away from Kilkeel.'

'Yes.'

'Where is she now?'

'Mrs Beedle sent her somewhere safe.'

'And you're not going to tell me where?'

'No.'

'Do you not trust me?'

'I hardly know you, but I think I trust you on my own account. I can't speak for her, though.'

'Do you believe her story?'

He asked the question as if my opinion had some value.

'Yes. Do you believe me?'

He didn't answer at once. Then, 'Yes, Miss Lane. I

think I do. It explains something that has been puzzling me since last night.'

'What's that?'

'Why Kilkeel and Mandeville didn't produce their trump card. I think most of us had an impression that something was intended to happen last night. The stage was set, yet the trumpets never sounded, the clouds never parted and Jupiter never appeared. We were all left looking at each other and the unprepossessing Mr Brighton, wondering why we'd been invited.'

'What will happen now, do you think?'

'I rather suspect that, unless Mandeville manages to produce something tonight, they've missed the tide. Mandeville will lick his wounds and so-called Brighton will be packed back to whatever Continental spa town or lodging house they brought him out of.'

'And Kilkeel?'

'Oh, there's always some new villainy for the likes of Kilkeel.'

'They've killed two people at least. They've committed treason, haven't they?'

He looked down at the mignonette and quoted: '*Treason doth never prosper, what's the reason?*'

'*For if it prosper, none dare call it treason.*' I finished the quote for him and added, 'But it is treason. Surely somebody could do something?'

'Bring them to trial? You need witnesses for that, not hearsay. As for treason, has Mandeville yet said publicly that he believes Brighton to be the rightful King of England?'

'Not as far as I know.'

'I'm quite sure he hasn't. Kilkeel's far too cunning for that.'

'Surely if the government were to ask questions, they'd find evidence,' I said.

'Quite possibly. Then that evidence would have to be tried in court, the whole story would be made public and, however unfounded it proved to be, whatever the verdict was, you may be sure that there'd be the usual assortment of mischief-makers and malcontents who would take to the streets for the rights of poor disinherited King Harold. If you were in government, is that what you'd want?'

'So you can't do anything? Nothing will happen to them?'

He said slowly, 'If I put some of the story around in the right way in the right places, I believe I can get them laughed at.'

'Laughed at!'

'Never under-estimate ridicule, Miss Lane. To an ambitious man, it can be more dangerous than bullets.'

'It won't get justice for my father or Mrs Beedle.'

'Justice is a different matter. Believe me, Miss Lane, if I could supply that for you, I'd do it very willingly.'

'Try, at least. Please try.'

He nodded slowly. 'You have a right to ask. What I can do, I shall.'

Up to that point, he'd spoken like a man very conscious of the effect of his words, but that promise was made simply and quietly. I thanked him and turned to go. There was no sign of Betty and the children, and the garden and terrace were filling up with guests out for an afternoon stroll.

'Where shall I find you in future?' he said.

I hesitated, not wanting to tell him I had neither future nor home.

'I don't suppose you'll be staying as governess to the Mandevilles, will you?'

'No.'

'Where then?'

He sounded impatient.

'You might write to me care of Mr Daniel Suter, addressed to any musical theatre in London. It should find me sooner or later.'

He raised an eyebrow.

'It might be simpler for you to write to me, at the House of Commons.'

I could tell he enjoyed saying it.

I went slowly upstairs, not sorry that I'd taken the decision to trust him, but disappointed it had brought me so little. I checked my room and found Mrs Martley sleeping again, with the shawl wrapped tightly round her. Downstairs, Betty had given the children their slates and pencils to keep them occupied and was making tea.

'There, didn't I tell you,' she said, nudging me with her elbow.

'Tell me what?'

'That you'd make a conquest. I saw you and the young gentleman with your heads together.'

'I assure you, it's not in the least like that.'

She didn't believe me, of course.

I sat with the children for a while then went up to wake Mrs Martley, taking her a glass of water and some bread and butter I'd saved from the children's dinner. She was awake already and nervous.

'I couldn't eat it. Not a crumb. The thought of being in the same room as that fat devil turns my stomach over.'

'You won't have to be in the same room as him. All you need do is look at him through a crack in the door and confirm that he's the same person.'

I managed to calm her and get her down the back stairs. The house was humming with preparations for the ball, all the servants so busy that nobody gave us a second glance. Daniel met us at the back door, in his performance clothes of black breeches, silver-grey stock, black frock coat, blue-and-silver brocade waistcoat. I think his impressive appearance helped calm Mrs Martley's nerves. He offered her his arm and she clung to it on the cobwebby journey along some seldom-used passageways, dimly lit by an occasional narrow window. Now and then our indirect progress took us round the back of the great hall and we heard the buzz of social conversation, the occasional muted laugh, a Haydn string quartet.

Daniel winced, 'They always get the timing wrong without me.'

We turned into the last short passageway leading to the door behind the orange tree. The music and conversation were almost as loud as if we were in the same room. I signed to Daniel to wait with Mrs Martley, then went on ahead and opened the door a few inches. There were more people there than the evening before and it was some time before I saw Kilkeel. I looked first towards the big fireplace. Sir Herbert was there, sipping his wine and frowning, with Mr Brighton beside him, glowing like a comet in stripes of purple and gold. There was no sign of Lady Mandeville – presumably grief, drink or both had confined her to her room – but Celia was standing by her stepfather in her silver-and-white dress, hair glinting with diamonds, face blank. Kilkeel wasn't with them.

I'd begun to think that he had decided not to come down to dinner and our work had been wasted when I caught the smell of him. In a room banked with flowers and delicately scented people, it was a waft of something foul and brought a vivid and unwanted memory of being close to him in his carriage. My eyes followed the smell and found him just on the other side of the orange tree, in profile to me and so close that I could almost have reached out an arm and touched him. Two men were with him, one with his back to me. The other one, facing me, was Celia's brother. From his strained look, Stephen was doing his social duty as best he could, talking to Kilkeel and the other man. Kilkeel was listening with a bored droop of the eyelid and Stephen may have sensed the boredom, because his voice had the loud over-animation of a man trying to hold a reluctant audience.

'. . . so I said to him, fifty guineas he loses by ten lengths at least . . .'

I closed the door quickly. This was far too close for comfort. I'd hoped Mrs Martley would have to do no more than look at Kilkeel across a crowded room. Still, we were too far gone to draw back now and would have to trust to her nerve. I went back to them.

'He's quite near. It will only take one glance.'

She clung to Daniel's arm as we went quietly along the passage. We stopped by the door. Even with it closed, Stephen's voice came faintly through.

'. . . asked me how I knew. Well, it was obvious to anybody who could tell a horse from a jackass, only . . .'

Mrs Martley was trembling like seaweed in a strong current, leaning on Daniel. Now or never. I beckoned them forward, opened the door a few inches. Kilkeel was three-quarter face to us now, unmissable. I hadn't the slightest doubt that she'd identify him. It was no more than a necessary formality. Still, I wasn't prepared for what happened. She hardly even seemed to glance, then she said loudly, 'It's the same man.' It was almost a scream. If it hadn't been for the noise of the party, it might have drawn attention to us. I put a hand on her shoulder to warn her to be quiet, but she was already falling backwards, fainting into Daniel's arms.

CHAPTER TWENTY-SIX

He staggered under the weight of her. I pushed the door shut and ran to help him. Over her head, his anxious eyes met mine. We joined our hands behind her back and half-dragged, half-carried her along the passage, sideways on because there wasn't room for three abreast. After a minute or so she began to recover consciousness.

'It was him.'

'Don't worry about that now,' Daniel said. 'We'll see you safe.'

By the time we reached the stairs she was capable of walking, slowly and shakily. With me leading the way and Daniel murmuring encouragement from behind we managed to get her back to my room. I brought water for her, got her to lie down on the bed and loosened her stays, while Daniel waited on the landing outside.

When she seemed calmer, I covered her over with the blanket and went outside to him.

'I blame myself,' he whispered. 'I didn't know it would be such a shock.'

'Daniel . . .'

'I should have made more allowances for her weakness. The poor woman's been drugged, probably for days on end, and half starved. Simply identifying Kilkeel was too much for her.'

'Daniel, that wasn't her trouble.'

'Of course it was. She simply took one look at the brute and fainted dead away.'

'Just seeing Kilkeel again wouldn't have affected her so strongly. After all, she knew he was here. He was the one who brought her here, remember.'

'Well, what was the trouble then? Libby, why are you looking like that?'

'Because it wasn't Kilkeel she meant,' I said.

'Libby, I simply don't understand you.'

In honesty, I scarcely understood myself. In a few minutes the world had turned upside down again. My mind was moving so fast that I didn't know where it was leading me next.

'I will explain, but later. One of us must stay with her all the time. Could you come back, do you think, after you've played the first set of dances?'

'Why? What will you be doing?'

'Celia Mandeville's eloping. I've promised to help her.'

Until then, I'd kept her secret. Now I needed Daniel's

404

help so much I couldn't hide it from him. He groaned.

'Leave them to their own problems.'

'She's been kind to me. I owe her this at least.'

It was more than that, but I couldn't tell Daniel or he'd try to stop me. I did my best to reassure him, telling him my part in the proceedings would be over as soon as I'd escorted Celia down the back road. He wanted to come with us, but I refused.

'You must stay here with Mrs Martley. Then we have to find some means of getting her away safely.'

'Didn't you mention a horse?'

'I don't think she's capable of riding. We need a vehicle. Perhaps Amos Legge will think of something.'

We settled it that Daniel should rejoin his musicians and play through dinner. After dinner they'd give the first and, he hoped, only performance of *Welcome Home*. He'd direct the orchestra for the first set of dances, then leave them to his deputy again.

'I shall owe that man a year of favours. Still, what must be done must be done. You're terribly pale, child. I wish you'd let me . . .'

'I'll be well enough. Go now.'

Mrs Martley was asleep when I went back inside. Now and then she muttered, 'No, no,' in her sleep and turned her face sideways into the pillow. I sat by the bed looking down at her tired and lined face, with the clamour of the kitchens drifting faintly from below us. Once she opened her eyes and focused on me.

'It was him. His voice.'

'You're sure of it?'

'Yes.'

She slept again. After the stable clock had struck nine and the small rectangle of sky through the window was turning to dusk, Daniel came back. We spoke on the landing.

'I've found a way of moving her,' he said. 'The tenor insists on going back to Windsor tonight. He says another night in the pavilion on a camp bed will ruin his voice. He's a fool, but I said he owed it to the world of music not to take the risk. So he's bribing somebody from the stables to have a vehicle of sorts ready. She'll manage to walk as far as the stableyard, won't she?'

'Yes. By then, I hope Amos Legge will be here with Rancie. We can all go together.'

Daniel put his hands to his head and groaned again.

'I know, but I've got to provide for her somehow. I don't suppose Mr Blackstone will be paying livery bills any more.'

I left Daniel on guard over Mrs Martley, picked up my mantle and ran down the stairs to the bedroom corridor. It was deserted, all the guests gone to the ball. I knocked softly on Celia's door.

'Come in.' Then, as soon as I took a step inside, 'Where have you been? I thought you weren't coming.'

She was half in and half out of her white-and-silver dress, hair coming down and cheeks streaked with tears. There were little white globes scattered on the carpet

406

that I thought were pearls, but they turned out to be silk covered buttons.

'I can't get out of it,' she said. 'It won't let me go.'

She put her arms behind her, wrenching at the long row of buttons at the back of the bodice. More little globes popped to the carpet. She wasn't accustomed to undressing without the help of a maid. I started on what remained of the buttons.

'Do stand still.'

But she was almost past reason, tearing at the waistband. Silk ripped apart with a noise like a knife being sharpened and a cloud of white and silver fell round her feet. She kicked her way out of the stiff muslin petticoat and white kid shoes.

'I think my stepfather suspects something. He kept looking at me.'

The grey dress and a plain petticoat were ready on a chair and I managed to get them on her, having to deal with most of the hooks and buttons myself because her hands were shaking. She slid her silk-stockinged feet into the shoes we'd chosen, took a few steps and stumbled.

'I can't do it, Elizabeth. I can't do it.'

'Liberty. Do you mean walking or eloping?'

'Both.'

I put my hand on her shoulder and turned her round to make her look at me.

'Celia, I promise you that if you don't go now while you have the chance, you'll be unhappy for the rest of your life.'

The near-brutality in my hand and voice surprised even me.

'But you were the cautious one,' she said. 'You wanted me to talk to my mother or Stephen. I've been thinking, perhaps you were right and I should . . .'

I must have gripped her shoulder hard because she cried out.

'It's past all that now,' I said. 'You're lucky that there's somebody who loves you waiting for you out there. You must forget everything else and only think of that.'

She blinked, stared into my eyes and saw something that seemed to convince her.

'I'm sorry. I'm ready now. My cloak and bags are in the wardrobe.'

She'd packed two of them, small but quite heavy. I kept hold of one of them and gave her the other. I had my other hand on the doorknob when she said, 'Wait.' She was looking at her canary in his cage.

'I don't suppose we could take him . . .'

'No. Now hurry.'

I opened the door and looked out. The corridor was still deserted. I led the way at a fast walk to the servants' door and held it open for her. She gave a last glance over her shoulder at the candlelit corridor, the soft green carpet, the cream-and-gold scrolled woodwork and followed me into the near dark.

'Keep close to me,' I said.

I heard the occasional gasp and the bumping of her bag on the stairs as she followed me, but she managed bravely enough. I took my usual route, down the narrow staircase to the chamber pots and out into the back courtyard. There were people there: a boy emptying scraps into the pig barrel, a man and a kitchen maid leaning against the wall talking. She put the hood of her cloak up and they took no notice of us. I led her across the courtyard and out through the archway. By the time we came to where the carriageway divided for the back road, she was breathing heavily.

'Let me rest, just a little.'

'A minute, no more.'

There was still just enough light for anybody to see us. I'd feel happier once we were on the back road with banks and hedges on either side. She put down her bag and drew a long, shuddering breath. The jaunty rhythm of a mazurka came from the house. Lights from the downstairs windows flooded the terrace, so that the marble gods and goddesses seemed to paddle in a sea of gold.

'Ready?'

We walked on, past the old oak where Mrs Beedle had waited for me, its branches black against a darkening sky. At last there were hedges right and left and beaten earth rather than gravel under our feet.

'Another minute, please.'

Before I could answer, a voice sounded a long way behind us.

'Celia? Where are you, Celia?'

Her body turned as stiff as one of the oak branches.

'It's Stephen. My stepfather must have sent him out to look for me.'

'It's some way off,' I said. 'He's probably on the terrace.'

But she was running down the lane, leaving her bag behind. I picked it up and followed at a fast walk.

'Celia?'

Still distant, but a little closer. I could make out her shape, a few dozen yards ahead of me. Then it lurched and disappeared. She gasped.

'Elizabeth.'

'Stay there, I'm coming.'

She was on the ground, hands round her left ankle.

'What's happened?'

'I can't get up.'

I knelt to give her my shoulder and she managed to get herself upright, but gasped when she tried to put her foot to the ground.

'Then you must hop,' I said, drawing her arm round my shoulder.

'What about the bags?'

'We'll have to leave them.'

We managed fifty yards or so. We couldn't hear her brother calling any more but now the hunt was up and when they'd failed to find her in the ballroom or on the terrace it was only a matter of time before somebody came after us. Then, as we stopped for another rest, the ground vibrated and the sound of hooves going at a slow and steady walk came out of the darkness below us.

'Oh thank god,' Celia said. 'It's Philip come for me.'

I was less certain. Philip was supposed to be bringing a coach for her, but I could hear no wheels. It was almost completely dark now, with the hedges dense on either side. We walked on. The black shape of a horse's head and ears came into sight from below us, then became a horse and rider. Celia's fingers dug into my arm.

'It isn't him.'

I was scared too, thinking that some of Sir Herbert's men had come to cut off our escape. A second horse's head came into view. The horse stopped suddenly, aware of us, and blew sharply through its nostrils. A voice reassured it.

'Don't be feared, girl. Nobody's going to hurt you.'

Amos Legge's voice.

'Rancie,' I said. 'Rancie girl.'

'Miss Lane, is that you?'

He was riding the first horse, a big cobby type as far as I could make out.

'Yes. Is anybody behind you?'

'Gentleman with a phaeton, just turning it round in a gateway.'

'Philip,' Celia said. 'That's Philip.'

'How far down?' I said.

'Half a mile or so.'

Celia would never walk that far.

'I've a friend here wanting to get to the phaeton,' I said. 'Can you take her up in front of you?'

I managed to get Celia alongside the cob and he reached down and swung her in front of his saddle as easily as if she'd been a bag of apples.

'Could you take hold of the other one, miss? She'll likely follow in any case.'

He handed me down Rancie's reins and wheeled the cob round. She and I followed them down the lane. Rancie's head was up and she was sniffing the air. We'd only been going for a minute or two when she let out a whinny. I looked past the hindquarters of Amos's cob and saw a circle of light coming up the road. As we drew closer together I could make out a carriage lamp with a man on foot behind it.

'Philip.'

From up above me, Celia's voice sang out as confident and clear as a blackbird. How she knew when he could have been no more than a dark shape to her was a minor miracle.

'Celia.' A deeper-toned bird called back to her.

The light came sliding and dipping towards us at such a rate it was surprising the candle stayed burning. When he reached us and the light fell on him I saw a slim and pale-faced man, probably tolerably good looking but so full of hurry and anxiety it was hard to tell. Celia practically threw herself off the saddle bow at him and without hesitation he dropped the lamp and caught her in his arms. There was a flurry of 'so scareds' and 'darlings' and 'safe now' and 'always'.

'No, you're not safe yet,' I said, bending to pick up the extinguished lamp. 'You're not safe until you're miles away and married.'

The phaeton was visible now, backed into a gateway with its one surviving lamp lit and a groom holding the two horses. Philip carried her into it and sat beside her with his arm round her. The groom jumped on to the box and turned the horses. As the phaeton began to move, Celia turned round.

'Elizabeth –' (So she still hadn't heard me) '– I'll always be so very, very grateful to you. I'll send for you when we have a house, I promise.'

'I doubt it very much,' I said. 'On both counts.'

But I said it to the back of the departing phaeton.

Amos Legge slipped off the cob and stood beside me.

'Where we going now, miss?'

'Up to the house.'

Looking back, it hurts me to think I didn't even thank him.

'Give you a leg up on Rancie, if you like. There's a saddle on her.'

'Better not, thank you.'

Riding astride in skirts and petticoats was not a comfortable prospect. So we both stayed on foot and went slowly up the lane in the dusk, he and the cob leading the way. At a bend, I glanced down to the main road and saw the single light of the phaeton speeding through the dark, probably at a canter. Somewhere, at first light, her conscientious Philip

413

would have a clergyman waiting in a suitably private chapel and whatever happened her name wouldn't be Mandeville any more.

'Mr Legge,' I said into the dusk between us, 'there's something important I want to say to you.'

'Yes, miss.'

The cob plodded on.

'If anything happens to me, please keep Rancie. Or if you can't keep her, find someone who'll treat her well.'

We took another few paces while he considered.

'What are you thinking might happen to you, miss?'

'I don't know. But my mind would be easier if you'd promise.'

Another few paces.

'If it makes your mind easier, yes.'

We went on up the road between clouds of white cow parsley flowers that seemed to glow with their own light against the dark hedges. Rancie walked easily and delicately, occasionally nuzzling my shoulder. We were almost at the point where the back road joined the carriage drive when she stopped suddenly, raised her head and flared her nostrils.

'What's wrong, Rancie?'

The cob stopped too and whinnied. There were lanterns up ahead, two or three of them, and silhouettes behind. Then voices calling out to us, sharp and angry.

'Who are you? Stop where you are.'

And a sharper voice above the rest, 'Celia, is that you?'

I said softly to Amos Legge, 'Do you happen to have a pistol with you?'

'They don't mean us any harm, miss. It's the other lady they're looking for.'

'Do you have a pistol? If you have, please lend it to me.'

It was a real hope. A man who travelled might carry one to keep off highwaymen. In my mood, it seemed downright unreasonable of Amos not to have one. I suppose my voice was sharp, because he tried to soothe me.

'No, miss. In any case, there's no call for one.'

The cob was scared by now and wouldn't budge, so we stayed where we were as the lamps came towards us. There were five men. When one of them turned his lamp sideways, throwing light on the rest of the group, I could see that three of them looked like grooms or coachmen, one was the man who called himself Trumper, and the man leading them was Celia's brother, Stephen. He was hatless, still dressed in the dark cut-away coat, trousers and light pumps he'd worn for the ball. His face was furious.

'Turn the light on them,' he snapped at one of the grooms. Then, seeing Amos Legge, 'Who the hell are you? What are you doing here?'

Amos Legge said nothing.

'Helping the man who's got your sister,' Trumper suggested.

'Is that true?'

415

Stephen Mandeville took a step towards Legge, who didn't move an inch.

'I asked you a question?'

When Legge still didn't reply he raised an arm as if to punch him in the face. Legge simply took hold of the arm and pushed it aside as if it had been no more than a tree branch in the way.

'Take hold of him,' Mandeville said to the grooms.

'Don't touch him,' I said. 'It has nothing to do with him.'

Rancie and I were outside the circle of lamplight and, until then, I think they'd only been conscious of a second horse and person without paying us much attention. Now the light came on us.

'I've seen her . . .' Trumper began.

'Her friend, the governess,' Stephen said.

'She's not a governess, she's –'

'It doesn't matter who she is. She's just come from helping my sister run away.'

Trumper yelled something to a groom about running up to the house and bringing back a couple of horses. Stephen rushed towards me. I couldn't see his face but felt the anger burning off him.

'Are you going to kill me too?' I said.

My hand ached for a pistol, a dagger, for anything. I turned and pulled at the stirrup leather on Rancie's saddle, thinking that at least I might batter the stirrup iron into his eyes and blind him. He flung me against Rancie's side, grabbed the stirrup leather away from me and before I could stop him, vaulted into the saddle and snatched the reins.

'Take the other . . .' he yelled.

I'm sure he was calling to Trumper to take the cob and come with him. He jerked sharply on the reins to turn Rancie facing down the road. She gave him more chance than he deserved. For a moment she simply stood there, surprised by the sudden weight on her back and the pain on the bars of her mouth. He cursed her, jerked at the reins again, dug his heels into her sides. Her head went up, then up and up until her front hooves were in the air and the shape of her was towering against the darkness like some horse in a legend landing from the sky, just touching the earth with the tips of her hind hooves. He was thrown off high into the air over my head, flying then falling like a shot goose, heavy and unwieldy. I felt the impact of the air as he went past and heard the snatched intake of his second last breath. Second last because, I dare say, he might have rattled a last one as he landed on his head on the hard-packed earth of the road and broke his neck more quickly and cleanly than the hangman would have done.

CHAPTER TWENTY-SEVEN

For another heartbeat Rancie reared up against the sky, then her front hooves came down to earth with a thud softer than the one Stephen had made when he landed. After that, total silence for a moment, then Trumper and the grooms ran to the dark figure on the ground and the light of their lamp spread round him. His neck was skewed in a way no living man's could be. One of the grooms started swearing in a scared, meaningless stream. The smell of Rancie's sweat was in my nostrils and Amos Legge's voice in my ear.

'Get up on her, miss. You weren't here. You never saw anything.'

'He's dead,' I said.

His hand rested a moment on my shoulder.

'No great loss, I dare say. Now, up you get.'

Rancie hadn't moved since her feet had touched down.

Her quick, panicky breaths were warm against my hand. I think he must have thrown me up on her, because one moment I was on the ground and the next I was across her back, my fingers in her mane and my face against Amos Legge's chest. He pushed me upright in the saddle and gave me the reins.

'Go on. Wherever she takes you.'

'But you . . .'

'I'll find you. Now go on, girl.'

He slapped a hand on Rancie's hindquarters and she spun round.

'Stop them! The damned horse has killed him.'

Trumper's voice, from only a few steps away. The thought that he wanted to kill Rancie in revenge made me dig my heels into her sides and lean low on her neck. I heard a voice wild as a banshee's yelling at her to go, go, and it was part of the fear to realise that the voice was my own. She hit full gallop in a couple of strides and was off into the darkness towards the main carriage drive. My instinct would have been for the back road, but Stephen's body and the grooms were there.

'Stop! Stop her!'

Trumper's voice, behind us and to the left. No hoof-beats, so he was probably following on foot. He might be trying to cut us off as we turned on to the bridge across the ha-ha, and he wasn't far behind. I urged Rancie on, trying to find the stirrups with my toes. One of my shoes fell off. As we hit the gravel of the main drive her pace slackened a little. A man's scream came from behind us. At first I was afraid it might be Amos Legge, but it was too close for that and the string of curses that followed suggested that Trumper had come to grief. I supposed he'd forgotten the ha-ha and had fallen into it.

As we rounded the curve of the drive a great white shape appeared out of the darkness. I recognised it as marble Europa and her bull at the end of the bridge, so unless Rancie and I were to follow Trumper into the ha-ha, it was time for caution. I drew on the reins to bring her back to a trot, gently I hoped, but she stopped so suddenly that only another handful of mane saved me from going off over her shoulder. Voice shaking, fearing that Trumper would clamber out of the ha-ha and catch up with us, I begged her to go on. Then I saw what was stopping her. There was something blocking the bridge. It looked like a carriage of some description, and my first thought was that it had been put there to bar our way, though how anybody could have acted so quickly I didn't know. Rancie and I froze a few paces from the bridge.

'Oh Lord, he's coming after us.'

A woman's moan of fear came from the carriage. It sounded like Mrs Martley. While I was trying to puzzle it out, another voice from somewhere in the dark behind me.

'Liberty – is that you?'

Daniel's voice.

'I'm here,' I said.

'Thank the gods. Where were you? I've been looking for you everywhere.'

He came up beside us, caught me as I slid down and started hustling me towards the carriage. Rancie's reins were still in my hand.

'They'll blame her. She must come with us,' I said. 'And we must wait for Amos Legge.'

'Legge will look after himself.'

He took the reins from me and tied them to the back of the carriage. I let him guide me, hoping he was right. The sheer relief of finding him took away what was left of my strength. He bundled me into the carriage, next to Mrs Martley, who kept wanting to know what was happening and getting no answer. There was a man sitting opposite her, slumped and silent – presumably the tenor who had been so insistent on getting back to Windsor. The carriage started moving. I looked back at Mandeville Hall, fearful that the doors to the terrace would open and Sir Herbert come rushing out. The doors stayed closed, but all the downstairs windows were blazing with light and incredibly the sounds of a galop drifted out over the park.

'They're still dancing,' I said.

'Last dance in the second set,' said Daniel, part of his mind automatically with the music even now.

So Celia had left home and Stephen had died in less time than it took to skip through half a dozen dances. A scared groom was probably waiting at the back door to find some way of passing the news along a chain of footmen. When we came to the lodge at the bottom of the drive the great gates were open in case of latecomers to the ball, so we drove straight through. For the next few miles I kept looking back towards Mandeville Hall until its brightly lit windows diminished to candle glimmers, then to nothing.

I think Daniel must have told the driver to keep to the back roads in case anybody tried to follow us, because by the time the sky started to grow light we were lurching at walking pace along a rutted lane between hedges. Our carriage was an old and smelly landau drawn by two mis-matched horses, the best the tenor's bribery could procure from the stables. Rancie was pacing along behind like a quiet pony rather than an aristocrat with the blood of Derby winners in her veins. Next to me, Mrs Martley slept with her head against the leather hood and her mouth open. The tenor sitting opposite was a human pyramid of capes and shawls, topped by a pair of eyes filled with misery at what the dawn air might be doing to his voice. Neither was in a condition to care about the story I'd told Daniel as we went along. All the time he'd kept hold of my hand.

'Child, I'd have given anything in the world to have spared you that.'

I think I'd shocked Daniel, describing Stephen Mandeville's end. It would have shocked him far more – Daniel being such a civilised man – if I'd tried to share with him the fierce joy I felt when I knew he was dead. That joy had faded now, leaving only an immense weariness.

'Didn't you guess he'd killed my father?' I said to Daniel. 'You must have known why she fainted.' I nodded across at Mrs Martley, so as not to wake her by saying her name. 'She saw him and heard his voice and knew he was the other man in the carriage.'

Daniel nodded.

'You did guess, then. Why didn't you say so?'

'I was concerned at what you might do, child. I thought if I could only take you away to London, put it in the hands of the proper authorities . . .'

'Who'd have done nothing, you know that. He killed his own grandmother too, and they wouldn't have done anything about that either.'

Even now, although justice had been done in my heart, it would not show in the official records. The version put about by Sir Herbert and Kilkeel would be what the world knew. Mrs Beedle died of heart seizure after all and her grandson in a tragic riding accident while nobly trying to rescue his sister from an abductor. What his sister would feel I should probably never hear. I didn't expect to see Celia again. I'd done all I could at the end to save her from the true story about her brother. Now she'd have to do the best she could with the rest of her life. Like me.

'You're convinced he killed Mrs Beedle too?' Daniel said.

'Sure of it. All his future, even his freedom, depended on pleasing his stepfather and making their plot succeed, and she was trying to stop it. Then there was that empty place opposite me at dinner.'

An empty place near the top of a table must be filled. Therefore, if somebody near the top of the table were called away on other business at the last minute, the place cards would be moved up and the gap left at the bottom instead. The son of the house had been otherwise employed.

'I wish I'd been with you,' he said.

'There was no time.'

I didn't ask the question that was in my mind: 'What would you have done?' We're not allowed revenge any more. It belongs in savage myths and even then usually to men, seldom to women. Yet, remembering Amos Legge's hand resting for a moment on my shoulder, I thought he'd understood. But I'd left him there. He'd given me no choice in the matter.

'We must wait for Amos Legge when we get to Windsor,' I said.

'We're not waiting for anybody,' Daniel said. 'We'll be on the first coach to London. At least the magistrates there can't all be Sir Herbert's friends.'

'I don't think they can do anything against me now. They have too much to hide.'

'Probably, but I'm not taking the risk.'

I said nothing, not wanting to quarrel with him before I must. As the sun came up, a thin mist rose from the meadows on either side. Rancie, who'd been so quiet, suddenly raised her head and whinnied. Mrs Martley's eyes snapped open.

'Who is it? Who's after us?'

There were hoofbeats coming along the lane behind us at a steady canter. Daniel shouted to the driver to go faster, but he was more than half asleep and didn't seem to hear. I turned and saw a heavy bay cob. He needed to be heavy because his rider was built like a young oak tree. I stood up and waved.

'Mr Legge. Amos Legge.'

He came up beside us, bending from the saddle to untie Rancie from the back of the landau.

'Morning miss.'

'What happened?'

'Back there, you mean? Couldn't say. Didn't think I was needed, so I went and left them to it. It's taken me a while to catch up because I couldn't puzzle out what way you'd gone, see.'

He grinned, touched his hat and fell in behind us without another word, leading Rancie beside him. A mile or so on, the lane turned on to a wider road and he came up alongside the landau.

'Everything all right, miss?'

'Yes, thank you. Mr Legge, what shall you do when we get to Windsor?'

My mind was heavy with the thought that we must part there.

'I'll see you and the gentleman on the London coach,

then come on up with Rancie. The post boy can take the cob back to the livery stables.'

'Then home to Hereford?'

'No hurry about it, miss. Hereford's not going to run away. Reckon I might see how London suits me for a week or two.'

I felt warmed by that, until a thought struck me.

'We've forgotten the little cat. What will Rancie do without her?'

He smiled and undid the strap of his saddlebag. Two black paws hooked themselves over the edge of the bag and a pair of golden eyes blinked at the light. I looked from them to Amos Legge's grin, then to Daniel's concerned face, thinking that I was not after all so totally alone. True, I had no roof over my head, only one shoe, nothing in my purse and my only close relative was half a world away. Still, I had a horse, a cat, two friends and the sun was beginning to warm my face. As for the rest of my revenge, maybe Mr Disraeli would at least half-keep his half-promise. I could only hope for that. Amos Legge trotted on ahead, Rancie beside him like a horse treading on air. The walls of Windsor Castle were visible in the distance now, silver against the sun. I supposed little Vicky, if in residence, would be waking soon in her soft bed with all her servants round her. In spite of everything, I did not envy her.

DEATH AT DAWN
EXCLUSIVE BONUS CONTENT

The Lost Princess – a short essay by the author explaining the historical background which inspired the novel

Reading Group Notes

Suggested Further Reading by the author

THE LOST PRINCESS

A few years ago, in one of those spells when writers have to find other means of paying for groceries and cat food, I took a job as a guide at a stately home owned by the National Trust in my home county of Herefordshire. Croft Castle, high on a green hillside near the Welsh border, is remarkable for being on a site inhabited by successive generations of the same family for more than a thousand years. Below it are the water meadows where a fifteenth-century Croft fought in a decisive battle in the Wars of the Roses. Above it, in the woodlands, is the grave of a twentieth century Croft who died in the Commandos in the Second World War. The family could seldom keep out of any battle going.

Inside are several centuries' worth of objects and artefacts, from the halberd that Sir William Croft may have been carrying when he was killed fighting for King

Charles in the Civil War, to some much more peaceable eighteenth- and nineteenth- century furniture, china and portraits. (Later, I borrowed some of those to furnish the Mandeville's London drawing room in chapter nine of *Death at Dawn*.) One object puzzled me for a while, however, because I couldn't see what it had to do with Croft Castle and Herefordshire.

It was an early nineteenth-century porcelain bust of a pleasant-looking young woman, slightly pop-eyed, with a wreath of roses in her dark curly hair. All I knew about her was that she was Princess Charlotte, granddaughter of George III, only legitimate child of his son the Prince Regent, later George IV, so destined one day to be Queen of England. But it never happened and the princess, loved and celebrated in her day, is now only one of the 'ifs' of history. The more I found out about her story, the odder it became.

For a start, it was surprising that she existed at all. Her father had become engaged to Princess Caroline of Brunswick on his father's orders before he even met her. He hated her on sight, was drunk through the marriage ceremony and spent only a few nights in bed with her, but Princess Charlotte was the result. After that came separation, probably well-justified allegations of adultery against Caroline and public rows that reached a climax when she was locked out of her husband's coronation. The other surprise about young Charlotte, given her parentage, was that she turned out to be a lively and generous-hearted girl, even if inclined to bounciness

430

and wearing her skirts too short. The British public thoroughly disliked her father but took to Charlotte. The family married her to a handsome young German prince named Leopold of Saxe-Coburg (the German Chancellor Bismark called the Saxe-Coburgs 'the stud farm of Europe' because they produced such a plentiful supply of princely husbands).

Leopold did his duty and when Charlotte became bloomingly pregnant at the age of twenty-one, everything seemed set fair for the royal succession. On November 3, 1817, she went into labour at her house Claremont, in Surrey. She was in labour for three days and for the final two days the Archbishop of Canterbury, the Bishop of London, the Lord Chancellor, the Home Secretary, and the Secretary for War were all waiting downstairs. According to the law of the time, they had to be present at the birth of heirs to the throne to make sure that no substitutions took place. But the baby, a 'large and beautiful' boy weighing nine pounds, was born dead. Charlotte seemed to be recovering from the birth, but died in the early hours of the following day.

So what was the connection with Croft Castle? Another sad story. One of the medical experts attending the princess was the head of the Croft family of the time, Sir Richard Croft. The Crofts at this point had lost their fortune and Sir Richard lived in London and adopted his father-in-law's profession of *accoucheur*, or gentleman midwife, with many patients among the aristocracy. There is a portrait of him in the dining room at Croft, a sensitive-looking and sad-eyed man, more likeable than the mostly rather self-satisfied males in other family portraits. He blamed himself for not preventing the princess's death, almost certainly unjustly. A few months later – after seeing several of his other patients through their confinements – he shot himself through the head.

His death helped to fuel some vicious rumours that circulated. One of the nastiest was that Charlotte and the baby had been poisoned by her grandmother, George III's wife Queen Charlotte, who was determined that no descendant of the scandalous Caroline should ever come to the throne. No historian takes that one seriously. As for the suggestion that the baby was rescued from the murderous attentions of his great grandmother and lived to claim the throne twenty years later – that's entirely my fiction or, for the purposes of this book, Lord Kilkeel's fiction: 'a horrible, warped fairy tale', as Daniel says.

At the time I worked as a guide, Liberty Lane was already in my mind. I had this picture of her, a young woman totally alone on the Calais sands, refusing to believe that her father had died in a duel. What I hadn't worked out was what had happened to bring her to this situation. Slowly, through two summers, Liberty's fictional story and Princess Charlotte's story came together.

Coming back to history, there was one real and momentous consequence of Charlotte's death. With no direct heir to throne, the Prince Regent ordered his middle-aged royal duke brothers to discard their mistresses, marry princesses and produce legitimate royal children as soon as possible. Edward, Duke of Kent, obeyed efficiently though with no great enthusiasm and baby Alexandrina Victoria, 'plump as a partridge' was born nineteen months later – the Little Vicky whose accession to the throne was eventually to have such a dramatic effect on the life of Liberty Lane.

At the end of *Death at Dawn* Liberty is thinking, without envy, of the distance between her life and the Queen's. And yet there are resemblances between them. They are both young (Liberty at twenty-two is four years older than Victoria) and share the characteristics of being intelligent, self-reliant and stubborn to the point of pig-headedness. In the unlikely event of Liberty and the young Victoria meeting, they might have shared enthusiasms for opera, ballet and riding. Both of them have just lived through momentous changes in their lives and face big questions in the future. We know what lay ahead for Victoria – a long life through one of the fastest-changing centuries in world history. As for Liberty – I want to know and I can only find out by going on writing about her.

READING GROUP NOTES

What do you do when your whole world falls apart? One morning Liberty Lane wakes up as a young woman with a future and a place in life. A few hours later, she is on her own with no friends or family to help her, no roof over her head, just a few sovereigns in her purse and her father's murder to avenge. In the circumstances, the fact that another young woman's world has also changed overnight is of only passing interest to her. It is the summer of 1837. King William has died and eighteen-year-old Queen Victoria has acceded to the throne.

The ways in which people change within the changes of history have always interested me. Almost certainly, very few people woke up on the morning of 20 June 1837 and said, 'Hey, now I'm a Victorian. A new era has begun'. Like Liberty Lane, they had other and more immediate concerns on their minds. But public events have an impact on private lives – gradually in most cases, more dramatically in Liberty's.

Liberty is an independent young woman who travels alone and is reluctant to take anybody's advice. Although her education has been ladylike on the whole, she knows what it's like to go hungry, to have to sell jewellery in a pawn shop or twist stockings round to hide holes in the toes. Is her self-reliance a historical anachronism? I don't think so. We've maybe been too ready to accept a picture of the nineteenth-century young woman as a sheltered flower. Working class women had no choice – they had to earn a living, sometimes in dangerous or unpleasant circumstances – and even those in the higher social classes could find themselves bereaved or deserted, with only their own efforts to rely on.

Also, Liberty is a rebel by background. Her very name comes from her father's enthusiasm for the French revolution. He had little respect for kings and queens and believed, like Robert Burns, 'A man's a man for a' thats'. His daughter is as at home with grooms in a stable yard as she is with ladies and gentlemen in a drawing room. This helps in her quest to find her father's murderer and, in doing so, take the first steps towards making a new life for herself.

Some suggested reading group questions

1) What choices does Liberty have in the first chapters? Why doesn't she make the more conventional ones?
2) In chapter four, a girl in pink satin, a man in black and a hearty squire-type all offer their help. Is she being unreasonable in trying to get away from all of them?
3) Eventually, Liberty makes a bargain with the man in

436

black. It involves lying and deception. Does that make you think less of her?

4) Chapter eleven on: Liberty is now a small cog in a great aristocratic household. How do she and others on the staff keep some of their individuality in a place with fifty-seven indoor servants?

5) The end. Is it a happy ending? Can you imagine her re-making a life from this point?

SUGGESTED FURTHER
READING

These are some non-fiction books that provide valuable and interesting background reading on nineteenth-century women

Coming Out of the Kitchen by Una A. Robertson. (Sutton, 2000)
A very readable study of enterprising women over 350 years, with plenty on the nineteenth century.

The Blessings of a Good Thick Skirt by Mary Russell (Flamingo, 1994)
Women travellers and adventurers, from missionaries to pirates. Covers medieval to present day, again with some fascinating Regency and nineteenth-century characters.

London Labour and the London Poor by Henry Mayhew (Penguin Classics, 1985)
Mostly about men, but also revealing on the women who had no choice but to work, potato sellers, milliners, prostitutes, lodging house keepers, laundresses and laundry thieves etc. A huge work, first published in 1849, available in various hardback and paperback selections. For a good shorter overview, incorporating some of Mayhew's women, there is a chapter, 'Women', in *Victorian London* by Liza Picard (Phoenix, 2006).

Queen Victoria: A Personal History by Christopher Hibbert (HarperCollins, 2001)
Shows that the young queen herself was strong-minded, stubborn and very willing to be amused.

Some nineteenth century women made important contributions to science, including mathematics, astronomy, botany and the study of fossils. A good example is Mary Somerville, largely self-taught, who became a leading mathematician and astronomer. Her autobiographical writings are collected in *Queen of Science* (Ed. McMillan, Canongate Classics, 2001).

Be sure to look out for
the second book in the Liberty Lane series

Death of a Dancer

A public spat between two dancers at a London
theatre comes to a dramatic conclusion that wasn't in
the script: one dead, the other arrested for murder. As
far as the jury's concerned, it's an open-and-shut-case
– but Liberty Lane believes otherwise.

Soon she's leading her own investigation, in a
desperate race against the hangman's noose. And
while the criminal underworld is no place for a lady,
there's no place for a criminal to hide once Liberty's
on the case . . .